A TEXAS
MOON

LAURA CONNER KESTNER

Printed in the United States of America

First Printing, 2020

ISBN 978-1-7327562-4-3

ISBN FOR EBOOK 978-1-7327562-5-0

Sycamore House Publishing

P.O. Box 344

De Leon, Texas 76444

www.lauraconnerkestner.com

ACKNOWLEDGEMENTS

Thank you to Charlotte and Earl Jacks, Ronnie Couch, Earl Baugh, Sue Keith, Tricia Hopkins, Rachel Spencer, Madalene Spencer, Bob and Kathy Tarpley, Karen and Robert Keith, Coby Sauce, Jordan Atkins, Mallie Atkins, Audrey Gibson and Emily Atkins for reading this book and offering feedback.

Thank you also to the following for the support shown me on the release of Remember Texas and A Texas Promise, the first two books in this series: DeLeon Area Historical Museum, Linda Frank, Adina Dunn, Dublin Public Library, Patty Hirst, Dublin Thursday Club, the late Mary Yantis, Karen Wright, Dublin Historical Museum, Dublin Citizen, De Leon Free Press, Rox Ann Myers, Lou Ann Lemons, Anna Horton, Kymbirlee Jeschke, Picketville Chapter of the Daughters of the Republic of Texas, Donna Irby, Kathy and David Prickett, Writing Sisters Mentoring Group, and author Tina Radcliffe. I wish I could name everyone who cheered me on in some way, but there is not enough room here. If you bought my book, wrote a review, told a friend about it, hosted me on your blog, or even liked, shared, or commented on a social media post, I appreciate you more than I can say.

As always, for my husband John Kestner, the nicest guy I know. I appreciate all the encouragement, the new office he built me so I would have a "pretty place" to write, and for the many, many meals he's prepared while I was busy talking and listening to imaginary people.

For Audrey, Ryan, John Ryan, Jordie, Burt, Mallie, Cole, Emily, Coby, Jay, Charlie and Josie—collectively the biggest blessing in a truly blessed life.

For all the Bates and Conner kids—this generation and those who came before.

For Mary Yantis. I miss you.

CHAPTER ONE

Moccasin Rock, Texas
April 1892

NATHANIEL CALHOUN DROPPED down on the side of his bed, yawned and closed his eyes.

He'd spent most of the night sewing up a man who'd picked a fight with a bull, and lost, but thankfully, would live to tell about it. Now all Nathaniel wanted was sleep. He leaned toward the bedside candle just as a sharp knock sounded at the back door.

"Come on, open up," his brother called out. "I got a prisoner at the jail that needs doctoring."

Nathaniel was up, into the kitchen, and throwing the door open while still pulling his clothes on. Buttoning his shirt, he tried to read the expression on Eli's face.

"Saloon fight?"

"Headache."

That was different.

Within minutes Nathaniel was fully dressed and following his brother out onto the street and into the jail, then nearly running him over when Eli stopped just inside the door.

Craning his neck to look past him, Nathaniel caught sight of a woman pushing open a cell door and slipping through. She froze when she saw Eli.

Raising her hands, she gave him a shaky smile. "Sheriff, I didn't expect you back so soon."

"And I didn't expect you to make such a miraculous recovery while I was gone," Eli said. He turned to Nathaniel. "Sorry, looks like I got you out of bed for nothing. The way this woman was carrying on I thought..."

Eli continued talking but Nathaniel was no longer listening. He was looking. And not believing his eyes. The woman wore a resigned expression when addressing his brother, now she was gazing at Nathaniel, wide-eyed and fearful.

And she should be afraid.

Eli glanced back and forth between them. "Everything okay?"

Was it? Nathaniel couldn't answer that question.

"Do you know her?" Eli said.

And he didn't *want* to answer that one.

Eli turned to the woman. "Do you know my brother?"

She nodded, but didn't enlighten Eli further, while Nathaniel continued to study her. Blond hair, green eyes and full lips, he knew that face all right.

She was dressed differently than she had been when he'd last seen her though, a plain brown dress instead of a nightgown, and sturdy boots instead of slippers. Her hair was also different. Although it was pinned up, a few strands were hanging down well past her shoulders. It was longer than before.

"Do you know her?" Eli repeated.

Struggling for control, Nathaniel swallowed several times before he could respond, surprised by how angry he was. *How hurt.* Especially considering he'd never expected to see her again. "We're acquainted. What did you arrest her for?"

"She picked some pockets at the depot last night, including mine. But the reason I locked her up instead of sending her out of town with a warning is because she took a swing at me when I tried to stop her."

Rubbing his jaw, Eli glared at her. "I can't keep a female prisoner here. I brought her in until I could decide what to do. A little while ago she started moaning and carrying on, holding her head. I went to get you. She must've picked the lock while I was gone…" His words trailed off. "What's going on? Who is she?"

Nathaniel reached down and picked up a hair pin from the floor—probably explained the loose strands of hair, and the escape.

"I knew her as Lenore," he told Eli. "I can't tell you if that's her real name, however I can tell you a few other things. In addition to being a thief, she's also a liar and a swindler."

The woman flinched and dropped her gaze, staring at the floor without a word.

Eli gave him a puzzled look. "Okay, let me ask you something else. *How* do you know her?"

"She drugged me and robbed me a few years ago."

Eli's expression didn't clear. In fact, he looked even more bewildered. "How did she manage to drug you?"

Nathaniel bit back a sigh. He should've known that's what Eli would home in on first. "I don't want to talk about it."

Lenore still hadn't said a word. Then again, what was there to say?

Why was she even here? Moccasin Rock was way too small for her preferred method of operation. Especially considering the crowd she ran with.

Speaking of which. Nathaniel turned to Eli. "Was she alone when you caught her?"

"Yep." Eli nodded toward the other cell. "I arrested that fellow, too. But they weren't together. He'd wandered up to the depot from the other direction. Had a little too much to drink. I'll let him go when he sobers up."

Nathaniel hadn't noticed the young man curled up on a cot

in the adjoining cell. Stepping closer to the bars, he studied the short, slender frame, the mop of unruly black hair, and yet another familiar face. "Hello, Gordon."

The man sat up and smiled at him. "Hey, Kid."

Now it was Nathaniel's turn to flinch.

Hoping Eli hadn't picked up on what the man called him, Nathaniel turned his back toward his brother and Lenore, and tossed a whispered question at the prisoner. "How's the extortion business these days?"

Gordon awkwardly pushed to his feet, shaking his head as he limped toward Nathaniel. "Not as lucrative as in the past."

"Other folks not as easy to deceive as I was?"

The man gave him a sheepish grin. "Sorry about that. Hated to take your money, but we couldn't go back empty handed."

"Wasn't referring to the money."

"Oh, you're talking about the other little trick?"

"Don't sell yourself short," Nathaniel said. "That was more of a full-blown production than a trick. Although the judge's performance didn't seem as rehearsed as the rest of them. First time performer, huh? Well, I'm sure he got better in time. Is he here with you and Lenore?"

Gordon's brow furrowed. "Why would he be here?"

"I thought y'all traveled together everywhere. He quit the show?"

"That man wasn't part of the show, Kid."

A prickle of unease shot through Nathaniel, and this time it had nothing to do with what Gordon called him. "If he wasn't one of your little band of thieves, then who was he?"

"Far as I know, he was a judge," Gordon said with a shrug. "If you want to know more, you'll have to ask Lenore. She took care of all the details herself. Never did know why. Sure caused her a lot of grief. The boss was furious."

Stunned, Nathaniel blinked at him. "Are you saying…"

Gordon pushed away from the cell doors and returned to the cot. "Like I said, better ask Lenore."

"You bet I will." But when Nathaniel turned, neither Lenore nor Eli was there. Hurrying outside, he found his brother striding back up the boardwalk, grim-faced...and alone.

Nathaniel's gaze swept the area. In the pre-dawn hours, Moccasin Rock's main street was empty. "Where's Lenore?"

"Gone. While you were talking to the other prisoner, she said she had to use the privy. I was taking her out back when some dog ran up, barking and snarling, grabbing on to my pant leg. Then as quickly as he'd shown up, he was gone. And so was my prisoner."

Nathaniel groaned. "Let me guess. Was the dog a small black terrier type, maybe more mutt than terrier?"

"How did you know?"

"The dog's name is Nickel. *She's* a professional, like the rest of them. Including the drunk you arrested."

Eli's expression darkened. He wasn't known for his patience, or his talkativeness, and both had been taxed tonight. "I think it's time you tell me what's going on," he growled.

Nathaniel sighed. *Might as well get it over with.* "When I met Lenore, she was traveling with a medicine show. They sold various snake oils, patent formulas, and a few concoctions they created right there in their wagons. And they performed—songs, dances, magic acts, card tricks, things like that. But there were a few of the performers who would go into a more populated area and pick pockets, or sit in on card games, while cheating of course. They also ran several other side swindles."

Thankfully, Eli didn't ask about those.

"So, the young man I arrested is one of the medicine show folks?"

"Yes."

Eli pushed his hat back. "Come to think of it, he's made a remarkable recovery, too."

Nathaniel shook his head. "You've been had, Eli. That man, who I know only as Gordon, wasn't drunk. He was trying to distract you—like the dog did—so Lenore could get away."

Glowering in the direction of the jail, Eli asked, "Are there more of them?"

"Yep. Unless they've split up. Used to be four or five painted wagons traveling together. Usually, after they leave a town, they'll get far enough away to where they figure no one's after them, and camp somewhere. Then several of the people will go into a new town and scout it out. If it doesn't look promising, they'll steal what they can, report back to the others, and then they'll all go somewhere with more opportunities."

Unfortunately, he hadn't learned all this until it was a little too late. "My guess is the rest of them are camped close by, waiting for these two to return," Nathaniel said. "Since Moccasin Rock is so small, they'll probably head on into Fair Haven."

His brother nodded. "I'll alert the Claiborne County sheriff. If they're headed that way, he needs to know."

"Good idea. In the meantime, I'm going after Lenore myself."

Eli's eyes narrowed. "Why? She's Claiborne County's problem now."

"That's where you're wrong," Nathaniel said. "She's my problem."

"What makes you say that?"

Nathaniel drew in a deep breath. "She's my wife."

Eli's mouth dropped open. "You mean you married that woman after…"

Even though he didn't finish his question, it was enough to jab a hole in Nathaniel's heart, bringing fresh pain to what had slowly turned to a dull ache.

"Yes, I met Lenore after Tessa, and our child, died," he said flatly.

Eli's disgruntled expression turned to one of compassion. "I'm sorry. I didn't know you'd remarried."

There were a lot of things his older brother didn't know. Even though he and Eli had been left on their own as young boys and had been constant companions until Nathaniel married Tessa, much had happened in the years between then and now.

"You met this woman while you were training to be a doctor?"

"Yes." Nathaniel also trained for some other stuff during that time. He didn't want to talk about those things either. If he'd been back at medical school, doing what he was supposed to be doing, he wouldn't be in this mess right now.

"It was all a mistake," Nathaniel admitted to Eli. And like most mistakes, he would pay for it.

⋘

Heart pounding, Lenore raced through the woods toward the Brazos River. She couldn't let the sheriff catch her. How could she have been so careless? Picking the pocket of a lawman was bad enough—she hadn't seen the badge—but for him to be a relative of the one man she'd counted on never seeing again? Bad didn't even begin to describe it.

Spending a few days in jail would have been terrible, and Ophelia would've punished her for it, but if Nathan caught her, it was all over. Everything she'd fought for—all her hard work—for nothing.

If only he'd smiled. Or seemed happy to see her at all. He still looked the same. Those brown eyes, brown hair, that handsome face, had taken her back to a happier time. But he'd been so cold this time. *Angry.* Not that she could blame him.

Fighting back tears, Lenore raced on toward camp. If only she could run in the opposite direction, turn her back on all of it, all of them, and disappear. But she couldn't. Not yet.

After several more minutes of running, she slowed to catch her breath, then stopped. *Was anyone following?*

Except for the chattering of a squirrel, the woods were quiet. She'd better keep moving, just in case. Giving her heartbeat a moment more to slow, Lenore fingered the money in her pocket. How much did she have? Probably less than five dollars. How much more did she need? Only Ophelia knew the answer to that.

At the sound of rustling in the underbrush, Lenore gasped and darted forward again, then staggered to a stop when Nickel dashed out, dancing circles around her feet.

"Good girl," Lenore whispered, stooping down to pet the dog. "As always, you showed up when I needed you most."

And so had Gordon. Pressing on toward camp, Lenore marveled at the fact Gordon had deliberately gotten himself arrested because of her. Hopefully the sheriff wouldn't be too tough on him.

Considering Gordon's infirmity, most people were apt to cut him a break. If he didn't return to camp soon, Lenore would figure out a way to get him out of jail. She couldn't go back there herself, but maybe one of the others would go.

Lenore's steps slowed as she neared the campsite, dread dragging her down. Nickel didn't seem any too eager either. The dog plopped down at her feet, whining.

"Shh, it'll be okay," Lenore murmured, trying to reassure herself as much as the dog.

The sky was beginning to lighten as she slipped toward the wagons. They were old and faded now, not the brightly painted conveyances Nathan would be looking for. But, still, they would certainly be easy enough to spot if anyone came searching. Two of them were faded red with yellow wheels; one blue with maroon trim, and two, including the supply wagon, in slightly more subdued colors.

Lenore stopped when she realized her fellow travelers were already up and milling about, some tending the horses, and others beginning the morning meal preparations. Thankfully, Ophelia was a late sleeper.

Shipley Bidwell, black trousers pulled on over his red long johns, his long white hair flowing down around his shoulders, tended the fire. He offered up a wave and a quizzical smile, confused about where she'd been.

Pressing a finger to her lips, Lenore shook her head, signaling him to remain quiet. The man was a classically trained actor with a voice that could wake the dead. Lenore wanted a moment to gather her thoughts before she told Ophelia what happened. Shipley nodded and went back to his work.

Quietly making her way toward the wagons, Lenore placed her right foot on the back of the one she called home and hoisted herself up. A hand came down on her shoulder, fingernails digging into her flesh. *Ophelia.*

Dropping down to face the woman, Lenore was startled to realize the boss was not only awake, but fully dressed. She'd probably watched Lenore sneaking in.

Ophelia's hair was pulled back tightly, her gray eyes boring into Lenore from beneath heavy, dark brows. "Where have you been?"

The words were spoken calmly enough but the tone was deceptive.

"I ran into some trouble at Moccasin Rock."

Ophelia's eyes narrowed. "What kind of trouble?"

"I got arrested—" The painful sting of a hand across her face snapped Lenore's head back.

"How stupid can you be?" the older woman hissed.

"I didn't mean for it to happen, and I got away as soon as I could."

"Get busy," Ophelia snapped. "We've got work to do. I'm not waiting around to see if the law shows up."

Lenore drew in a breath. "We can't leave yet. They got Gordon, too."

Fury flashed across the woman's face. "He's an even bigger idiot than you are. I should have sent him packing years ago."

Ophelia didn't say whether she'd help Gordon or not. Lenore rubbed a hand across her face to ease the sting as the woman marched over to tell Shipley what happened.

As usual, he seemed befuddled as Ophelia spoke. The two of them were married now, but Ophelia was still the boss. Thankfully, Ship was a gentle soul, and sometimes had a calming effect on his wife. Hopefully, this would be one of those times.

After talking to him, Ophelia began shouting orders to break camp.

Within minutes everyone was running hither and yon, packing the cooking supplies, dousing the fire, harnessing the horses. Everyone grumbling. There'd be no hot breakfast today.

Lenore helped pack up, then gathering her courage, she approached Ophelia. "What about Gordon?"

"As far as I'm concerned—"

The rumble of a wagon and sound of horse hooves rang out through the morning air, cutting off Ophelia's response.

They both turned in time to see Gordon awkwardly descending from a buckboard driven by an older man.

Lenore bit back a groan when she noticed the badge on the driver's vest. *Another lawman.* Then she spotted three riders approaching on horseback—Nathan and the sheriff, as well as a man dressed all in black.

The black-clad stranger bore a striking resemblance to Nathan and the sheriff. *He had to be a Calhoun.* The man shifted in the saddle and the sight of yet another badge had Lenore's breath catching in her throat.

A five-pointed star inside a circle. She'd been in Texas long enough to recognize it. The man was a Texas Ranger.

Panic gripped Lenore. *What had she done?*

Ophelia was as crooked as they came, and had routine brushes with the law, yet she'd always managed to avoid any serious trouble. Oh, she would be furious about this. *Although you'd never know it to look at her.*

Shoulders straight, head high, Ophelia faced the men with a smile.

Lenore was relieved Gordon seemed no worse for his experiences. Now safely on the ground, he lifted his hat to the wagon's driver, then hobbled away, glancing only briefly in Lenore's direction.

Ophelia shot him an angry glare before addressing the lawmen. "Good morning, gentlemen. What brings you out so early?"

The sheriff answered. "I arrested two members of your traveling party last night at…"

Ophelia raised her hand. "Say no more, Sheriff. We'll be pulling out of here shortly."

The sheriff gave a brisk nod. "That was my next suggestion."

"Land-a-Goshen," Shipley Bidwell declared in his booming, theatrical voice. "If it isn't the Texas Kid." *He'd finally noticed Nathan Calhoun.*

Lenore was surprised to see Nathan wince at the greeting, and then close his eyes. For some reason he didn't like Ship's reference to his past.

Which made sense, she supposed. Nathan had moved on now. He was the doctor in Moccasin Rock, so he must have gone on to finish medical school after she'd known him. Yet Lenore was intrigued by the reactions of those accompanying him. They seemed…stunned. *Odd.*

Ophelia spoke up, "We'll be gone within the hour, Sheriff."

"Good. And I don't ever want to see any of you in Moccasin Rock again."

Even though Ophelia's expression tightened at the sheriff's warning, it was music to Lenore's ears. If she could get out of here, now, she'd still have to deal with Ophelia's wrath, but not Nathan's.

She turned to follow Ophelia back to the wagons when a soft

command brought her up short. "Stay put, Lenore, you're not going anywhere."

Lenore froze, as did Ophelia.

The older woman reacted first. Turning back, smile once again in place, she drew Lenore around with her. "Gentlemen, surely you wouldn't want to separate family."

Lenore choked back a mixture of frustration and fury. Ophelia was no kin of hers. *But these men had no way of knowing that.*

Even though Lenore hadn't said a word, Ophelia must have sensed her outrage. Moving her hand down Lenore's arm, the older woman gathered her close. To their visitors, it must have seemed like a loving embrace. They couldn't see Ophelia pulling Lenore's hand behind her back and twisting her fingers.

A painful warning, and completely unnecessary. Lenore wouldn't say a word.

"Are you her mother?" the sheriff asked.

Ophelia's smile wavered a bit. "No, although she's been in my charge for a good number of years. The poor dear would be lost without me."

Again, rage built inside Lenore, and this time Ophelia pushed her fingers back further. Pain jolted through Lenore's hand and shot up her arm.

As the pressure increased, a buzzing sound filled Lenore's ears and sweat popped up on her brow. The voices of those around her grew fainter, as if everyone had stepped away. Biting her lip until she tasted blood, Lenore still couldn't stop the small moan that escaped her.

Thankfully, the men didn't hear it.

But Nickel did.

Growling, she lunged at Ophelia, tugging on her skirt.

Lenore glanced up to see Nathan staring down at the dog, and then at her, intently.

Ophelia kicked at Nickel, and hot tears sprang to Lenore's eyes.

Everyone looked at the dog now.

Please, please leave. What could she say to get them to go before she or Nickel was seriously hurt?

Suddenly Nathan was off his horse and pulling Lenore free before she could form another thought, let alone a sentence. *He'd figured out what was happening.*

Lenore looked around to see the others—even the old man in the wagon—aiming guns at Ophelia. *They all knew.*

Eyes wide, Ophelia raised her hands as she stepped away.

"She okay?" Sheriff Calhoun asked.

Head still spinning, it took a moment for Lenore to understand he was talking about her. Nathan held her fingers, his own gentle as he examined each one.

"They're not broken," he said, his voice soft but detached.

For a moment at least, he was looking at her through the eyes of a doctor, not a man who'd been wronged. "Probably be sore for a few days."

"Thank you," Lenore murmured, then turned to follow Ophelia.

"Where do you think you're going?" Nathan demanded.

Heart in her throat, Lenore faced him. "To pack so we can move on."

Nathan's brown eyes widened. "After what that woman did? Why would you want anything to do with her?"

Aware of Ophelia's gaze burning a hole in her, Lenore pressed her lips together. There was no way she could explain.

"You seem unwilling to provide answers," Nathan said after a moment, "so I'm going to assume she's got some sort of hold over you. That doesn't change the fact you're not leaving here with her."

Lenore's stomach sank. "Why?"

"I'm surprised you even have to ask. If the man who officiated our wedding was a real judge, then we're legally married. Until I figure out whether we are, or aren't, you're coming home with me. Now go get your things."

Lenore's stomach lurched when Ophelia shot a look of pure venom at her, then stomped away.

The situation was bad before, but at least she'd had a plan. *And hope.* If the show pulled out and retreated far enough to suit the Moccasin Rock sheriff, it might take a lot of time for Lenore to find them. Time she didn't have.

Following Nathan's command, Lenore packed a canvas bag with what clothing and few personal items she owned.

Leaving the wagon, her gaze was drawn to Ophelia and Gordon, engaged now in a whispered discussion. Both looked in her direction more than once. Then Ophelia strode away and began snapping orders to the others in the group.

Gordon continued to stare at Lenore. *He wanted to talk to her.*

She turned to Nathan. "May I please say goodbye."

His eyes narrowed.

Lenore raised her hands. "No tricks, I promise. As you're aware, Gordon is lame. He's not going to whisk me up and go running away."

Nathan gave a brisk nod. "Make it quick."

She hurried toward her friend. Reaching out to hug him, she leaned in and heard the words she needed to know.

"We're going to Cartersville," Gordon whispered. "If that doesn't work out, we'll head toward the next town south of there. You have one week."

Lenore's gaze shifted to the blue wagon, and again tears burned her eyes. "Gordon, please..."

"Don't worry," he told her. "Ship and I know what to do."

Lenore hugged him again and then stepped back. "Thank you. I'll see you as soon as I can."

Shifting, so that his weight rested on his good leg, Gordon admitted to his own concern. "What if you can't get away?"

She patted him on the shoulder. "I'll be there."

"How?"

"I don't know, yet. I'll do whatever it takes." *And she would.*

CHAPTER TWO

LOOKING AT HIS house through Lenore's eyes gave Nathaniel second thoughts on having her stay with him.

The place was small, sparsely furnished, and nearly bleak. The front half was taken up by his waiting area, an office and examining room. The back featured a bedroom and a kitchen.

As he led her inside through the kitchen door, Nathaniel realized it had been a place to sleep, eat, and work for the past year and a half. He'd never really thought of it as living.

When old Dr. Bacchus offered to let him purchase his practice, including the building, medical equipment and supplies, Nathaniel jumped at the chance.

Dr. Bacchus went to live with his daughter in Houston, and Nathaniel had gotten busy cleaning, organizing and refurbishing the office and examining room. All he'd done for the living quarters was clean it.

Where else could she stay? There might be a room available at the hotel, or at the Horton Boarding House. But he couldn't trust Lenore not to take off at the first available opportunity. No, for now, this was the best place.

"Nice," Lenore said, taking in the simple wooden table, chairs, cupboard and bare plank floor.

Was she being sarcastic? Not that Nathaniel would blame her if she was. Even though her living conditions with the medicine show couldn't have been any better than this, she was still here against her will. She wasn't complaining, but she seemed down-right miserable.

He pushed that thought away. Lenore wasn't a victim. The folks she'd robbed and swindled were.

Still, seeing her stand there, gripping the bag that probably held all her worldly possessions, she did seem almost waif-like.

Nathaniel cleared his throat. "If there's anything you need, in the way of personal items, let me know."

"Thank you. There are a few things I could use. I noticed a mercantile near here. Is it all right if I go?"

"Not alone. I'll go with you."

Lenore sighed, and then glanced around again, this time her gaze lingering on the stove.

Could she cook? Nathaniel could prepare a meal well enough to suit his own simple tastes, and sometimes patients would pay him with food, but more often than not he grabbed something from the only eatery in town, Bony Joe's café, or accepted offers to eat with his brothers and their wives. It would be good to have someone else in charge of meals.

Then another thought occurred. Should he let her cook? It wasn't smart to let a woman who didn't like you prepare your food. He'd once treated a man who'd figured that out a little too late.

"Where do I sleep?"

Lenore's softly spoken words pulled Nathaniel back to his cur-rent dilemma and created momentary alarm. He hadn't gotten that far in his planning.

"You can have the bed. I'll sleep in my office."

She followed him into the bedroom, which featured a simple iron bedstead, wooden nightstand, chest of drawers, and small dresser with a pitcher and bowl. At least this room had a rag rug on the floor.

He tracked Lenore's gaze to the window.

"If you try to leave," Nathaniel said, "I promise, I will follow you and bring you back. No matter how long it takes."

She turned a desperate look his way. "I'm begging you, Nathan. Please, let me go."

"I know you don't want to be here, but I'm doing this for both of us. Eli knows a Pinkerton agent that can find out if we're really married. Shouldn't take long."

She looked away again, but not before he'd seen the tears in her eyes.

"We have to get this situation resolved," he added. "Neither of us can have a real life until it does."

Lenore nodded. "What will you do if you discover we are married?"

Another thing he hadn't thought through. "I'm not sure," Nathaniel admitted.

"Just so you know," she said softly, "I really am sorry for everything that happened."

Nathaniel wasn't sure how to acknowledge her apology. He wasn't even sure exactly what all *had* happened. And now wasn't the time to hash it out. But there was one thing he needed to know.

Leaning against the door frame, he tried to keep his voice as casual as possible. "You took something that belonged to me. Did you sell it?"

Before she could reply, a scratching sound filtered in from outside. Nathaniel stepped back into the kitchen and opened the door. The little mutt darted inside, bypassing him without a second glance, making straight for Lenore.

"Nickel," Lenore breathed, smiling as she stooped to pick the dog up. "You found me. Good girl."

Nathaniel started to tell her the dog couldn't stay, and then stopped. If having this rapscallion here could help Lenore adjust to her new surroundings—and maybe keep her from bolting—it would be worth it.

They were both staring at him now, heads tilted, question in their eyes.

Nathaniel nodded, even as it occurred to him that he hadn't thought *any* of this through. He'd have to take Lenore with him when he made medical calls, when he could, and hope that others would help him watch her when he couldn't. And he'd also have to keep an eye on Nickel. He didn't trust the dog any more than he did Lenore.

"I doubt if you got much sleep last night," he said, "why don't you go and rest." Then he said something he should've thought twice about. "Does the dog need a bath?"

Lenore stiffened as her eyes narrowed. "Nickel is cleaner than some humans. I bathe her frequently."

Nathaniel opened his mouth, but Lenore wasn't done yet.

"I suppose I look a little worse for the wear, too. I assure you, I am also clean. Would you like to check us for fleas?"

Heat flooded Nathaniel's face. "Of course not."

She glared at him, started to say something else and then stopped. Somehow the dog managed to look offended, too. After a moment, the two of them disappeared into the bedroom.

Dropping down into one of the kitchen chairs, elbows on the table, Nathaniel pressed a hand against his eyes, weary down to his bones. *Lord, please help me know what to do.*

It didn't surprise him to hear footsteps outside. He'd been expecting his brothers.

But it was Maggie, Eli's wife, standing at the door.

She held up a basket. "Eli told me you have company, and I wasn't sure about the condition of your pantry."

Nathaniel smiled. "I'm not sure about it either."

Maggie returned the smile as she stepped inside. "Well, you

let me worry about that. I brought a couple of meals, and some staples. Flour, lard, salt." She continued calling out items as she unpacked the basket, several times her glance straying toward the other room.

Nathaniel didn't blame her for being curious.

"I'm not sure how much Eli told you," he said. "Lenore, my wi...wife, will be staying, at least for a while. She's resting right now."

Maggie placed the empty basket on the table. "Eli didn't tell me much, but I want you to know I'll help with whatever you need."

"Thanks, Maggie." In the few months since Maggie arrived in Moccasin Rock—scared, desperate and needing medical attention—the two of them had become close friends. Eli had fallen head over heels for her, and Nathaniel was glad to have the sister he'd never had, just as he had been when his younger brother, Caleb, married Abigail Horton.

"Eli wants to talk to you," Maggie said now. "Why don't I stay here and get your kitchen in shape, while you two visit at the jail."

She grabbed a clean dish towel from the cupboard, wrapped some sort of cookies in it from the stash she'd delivered, and handed it to him. "Eli's got fresh coffee over there, but he's always glad to see some baked goods."

Nathaniel took the cookies, mumbling his appreciation.

"I saved some for Lenore," Maggie said, "in case she wakes before you get back. Does she like coffee? Or is she a tea drinker?"

Nathaniel was embarrassed to admit he didn't know.

"Everything will be okay," Maggie said, patting him on the back. "I'm sure of it."

Nathaniel wished he felt the same.

At the jail, Eli waited, although there was no sign of the youngest Calhoun. Nathaniel had expected a full inquisition from both brothers.

He dropped the tea towel full of goodies on the desk, then helped himself to coffee. "Where's Caleb?"

"He went to check on Abby," Eli said.

"Ahh." Caleb's wife was expecting their first baby in about a month, and the proud papa was equally thrilled and terrified. Nathaniel remembered the feelings well.

He settled into the chair in front of the desk. "What did you want to talk about?"

Eli leaned back and pinned him with a hard stare—a look that usually had people spilling their guts, occasionally confessing to crimes they hadn't even committed.

It did *not* work on Nathaniel.

After a full minute, Eli growled, "Why did that man call you the Texas Kid?"

Nathaniel waved his hand. "I can't talk about that right now. I've got to figure out what to do about Lenore."

Eli sighed, then untied the towel and took out a cookie. "Fine, then tell me about Lenore. Where did you meet her?"

"Birmingham, Alabama. I was working there."

"What kind of work?"

Nathaniel again waved the question away. "Let me get through one thing at a time."

Eli bit into an oatmeal cookie and motioned for Nathaniel to continue.

"I knew from the beginning Lenore was part of the medicine show set up outside of town there," Nathaniel said. "And I figured out after a few days that the men who sometimes accompanied her—Gordon and Shipley Bidwell, the man with the long gray hair you saw this morning—were up to no good. Picking pockets was only one of their many talents, as I mentioned earlier."

"What were you doing in Alabama?"

"I'd left medical school. Walked away. My passion for it was running high right after Tessa's death. I'd wanted to save lives, make sure other folks didn't have to go through that kind of loss. Then one day, a couple years in, I couldn't do it anymore. I was still grieving, but for some reason medicine wasn't interesting me. Not much of anything was. Nothing made sense. So, I left."

"Why Alabama?"

"Not really sure," Nathaniel said. "Just where I ended up."

Eli shot another hard look at him, clearly not buying that, but Nathaniel couldn't tell him more.

"So, you met Lenore and y'all courted for a while?"

Nathaniel shook his head. "No. There was no courting involved. Although we did spend time together. She always seemed to show up wherever I was. I guess she followed me around. I was busy, and preoccupied, and didn't really think it odd at the time. I knew she must live a strange life being in a traveling show. She told me at one point that she had no family, and I told her I was also on my own. Even though I was working, we managed to talk, a lot."

Eli's brow furrowed. "Seems odd that a girl could be hanging around while you worked without attracting attention."

Uneasy with the direction the conversation was taking, Nathaniel hurried on. "After about a week of seeing Lenore every day, Shipley cornered me one afternoon, demanding I do the right thing by his daughter."

"I thought she didn't have any family?"

"Exactly. I knew right away it was all some sort of set-up, and not only because she'd already admitted that her parents were dead, but because Bidwell was such a bad actor. He gave this whole long-winded speech about his innocent daughter, and how I'd compromised her. He obviously had the whole thing memorized. Then he said that just because they were poor didn't mean Lenore was trash, something to be used and then discarded. She seemed genuinely humiliated, and I was horrified. Nothing could've been farther from the truth. I didn't think that, and I had never touched her."

Eli got up and grabbed the beat-up coffee pot, refilling his cup and Nathaniel's before returning to his desk. "So exactly how did this swindle work?"

"Apparently they did the same thing in nearly every town they visited. Someone would pick the mark, Lenore would get to know them, and then Bidwell would show up. After an appropriate amount of blustery rage, he would agree to take a settlement of some kind and they would all move on."

"Another way to part people from their money?"

"Yes. Except that Lenore didn't seem as into the swindle as Shipley. She wouldn't even look at me while the man talked. I couldn't tell what she was thinking. I could tell she was miserable. I had no intention of giving them a dime, and I started to tell her so. But Lenore stood there, staring down at her shoes. Bidwell's outrage was faked. Her shame and humiliation weren't."

"What did you do?"

Placing his coffee on the corner of Eli's desk, Nathaniel leaned back and cupped his hands behind his head. "I called their bluff. Bidwell said to come up with a certain amount of money or be prepared to marry his daughter. I said I'd marry her." He smiled at the memory. "The look on his face was priceless. So was hers."

Eli blinked at him. "Why would you do that?"

Nathaniel sighed. "I honestly don't know. I guess because I liked her, and I hated she was being used like that. I didn't love her, but it occurred to me I could help her get away from those people. I'd been alone for several years and liked the idea of having a home again. Trying to build a life. And it wouldn't exactly be a hardship for me. After all, she is attr...attractive."

Eli arched one eyebrow and battled a grin as Nathaniel stumbled over the word again.

"All right," Nathaniel said, "she's beautiful. That really wasn't why I agreed to marry her. I was determined to be a good husband. Successful marriages have been built on less. I had good intentions."

"I believe you," Eli said.

The quiet statement meant a great deal to Nathaniel.

"At first Lenore seemed panic-stricken, then this odd look came over her face. She pulled Shipley off a little ways, whispering something to him. Then she came back and said she knew someone who would marry us that very night. After a brief ceremony, we checked into a hotel there. I don't remember everything." *He did remember some things about that night, but he wasn't sharing those memories with anyone.*

Nathaniel stood and began to pace. "I planned to head back to Texas the next day and start my new life with Lenore. The bride and her friends had another set of plans entirely. I woke up the next morning, alone and broke. I didn't need a medical degree to know I'd been drugged some time during the night. I went looking for Lenore. There was only one wagon at the edge of town where they'd been set up, and one fellow heading to the blacksmith shop to repair a wagon wheel. Everyone else had gone on ahead. With a little persuasion, the man told me that what had happened to me was one of their usual routines."

"I'm surprised they hadn't all been arrested," Eli said.

"Yes, but even you admitted you were willing to run Lenore out of town instead of locking her up. I think that's the way it was everywhere. Individually, most people didn't lose enough to make it worth locking them up or tracking them down. As thieves, collectively, they were bringing in a substantial amount of money. Most people let it go, I guess."

"It got personal for you."

Very. "The man who'd stayed behind admitted that the men they targeted were usually rich, always married, always innocent; someone who wouldn't want any trouble, someone who would quietly pay out. Then Lenore and Bidwell would disappear. That woman, Ophelia, was the mastermind, but there were others."

"That's some scheme," Eli admitted.

"I've never been so angry in my life," Nathaniel said. "And I've never felt more stupid. Apparently, I was the first one who chose to marry her. After talking to the fellow who was still there, I decided they'd only pretended to do a wedding. I still don't know why they picked me. I wasn't rich. After the life you and I lived, surviving on the streets. I should've known better."

Eli agreed with him, then added, "You said she robbed you?"

"Yeah, they took my money, and the one thing I truly valued, the pocket watch with Tessa's picture in it. I wanted it back."

"You went after them?"

"I started to. Then a man I knew was severely injured that day, and I was the only one available to help. By the time I was free to travel again, I'd decided to go back to school. Being able to help someone, even with my limited training, meant a lot to me. I renewed my commitment to medicine and forced Lenore and our sham of a marriage out of my mind."

Nathaniel straightened, reluctantly admitting something to Eli. "To be honest, after my initial anger, I was almost relieved. My guilt was already eating me alive."

"Guilt? About what?"

"About abandoning my feelings for Tessa so fast."

"She'd been gone several years by that point. Wouldn't exactly call it fast."

Nathaniel shrugged. "Maybe not. But in my heart, I felt married to Tessa, not Lenore, so her being gone wasn't altogether a bad thing. Then lo and behold, she shows up here."

"Speaking of that, how are you going to introduce her to folks? If Myrtle Dunlop gets wind that there's any doubt you two are legally married, and Lenore's living in the house with you, Myrtle's going to pitch a hissy fit."

Nathaniel groaned. Myrtle Dunlop was a bitter busybody who knew exactly how everything should go. Her way. She was always stirring things up in town over some perceived slight or sin. Her husband, George, had recently been appointed Moccasin Rock postmaster, which made her feel even more important.

"If anyone asks," Nathaniel said. "I'll mention we said our vows in front of a judge before I came here. And that Lenore's been staying with friends. Both are true. That's all Myrtle needs to know."

"What are you going to tell Mama?"

"For now, nothing. I want to figure this all out myself before I talk to her about it."

Eli nodded. "I still don't understand why Lenore would marry you, for real, I mean, and then leave you?"

"Doesn't make sense," Nathaniel agreed. "Gordon said Ophelia made things real bad for Lenore afterwards, that she paid for what she'd done. Gordon didn't know why she did it either. But I'll get the truth out of her. One way or the other."

CHAPTER THREE

STIFLING A YAWN, Lenore leaned against the door of the livery stable and listened to Nathan and a man named Eagan Smith discuss horses.

Apparently, Nathan was going to check on a woman "up in the hills" and Lenore was being dragged along.

Lenore wasn't sure why they were leaving at the crack of dawn, or where "the hills" were, but she understood why she had to go. Nathan expected her to run the first chance she got. And he wasn't wrong. *She had to get away.* So far there'd been no chance to do so.

She was lucky he left her alone long enough to bathe or go to the privy.

For the past four days, Nathan had rarely let her out of his sight—she'd even accompanied him on medical calls.

On the few occasions when it wasn't possible for him to take her, his sisters-in-law had shown up to keep her company. Abby and Maggie were nice, even friendly. Lenore didn't want friends. She wanted out of here so she could get to Cartersville.

"You want the buggy?" Eagan asked.

"No, going up to Sister's house. Rough terrain, better take one of the wagons."

Lenore moved over to the stalls and stroked the animal's noses as she waited for the men to hitch a team to the wagon. She loved animals, but she was also making note of the layout in case she needed a horse to make her getaway.

"Who is this we're going to see?" Lenore asked once she and Nathan were on the road.

"I don't know her real name," he said. "I was told when I got here that her name was Sister. But nobody could tell me whose sister she was. Nobody seems to know."

"Why are we going to see her so early?"

"Because I want to be back here in time for church."

A knot formed in Lenore's stomach. *Oh.* She didn't ask anything else.

It didn't take her long to understand why Nathan had asked for the sturdier conveyance. They left the road after a while, the clop of horse hooves and the cawing of crows the only sounds as they headed up a barely discernible trail. Compared to the hills she was used to, this wasn't much, but they were definitely going up. The path was rocky and uneven, the cedar and oak trees growing thicker the further they went.

The first sight of the house reminded Lenore of scenes from her childhood. A weathered, tumbledown log cabin clinging to the side of the hill, the yard overgrown with brush and vine. Smoke curling from the chimney. The medicine show wagons passed many such places through the years.

Nathan stopped before they got close. "We'll go in on foot from here," he said, grabbing his black bag from beneath the seat.

Lenore hopped down before he could offer a hand.

"This place was built years ago," he told her as they drew closer. "Probably one of the first homesteads in this area, long before there was a town. There's another one like it over on Eli's land. He's built a new house, but he left the cabin. Fixed it up some. Sister's place needs repairs badly. Every time anyone comes to talk to her about it, she gets fighting mad."

"Why does she get mad?"

"She doesn't like company, of any kind, and she especially doesn't like anyone telling her what she needs to do."

"Will she let us in?"

"She'll not invite us in, but she probably won't shoot."

That was comforting.

They'd reached the porch, cluttered with a rickety old chair, a couple of buckets, an empty crock, and a hoe.

Nathan tapped on the door. "Sister, it's me, Dr. Calhoun."

When there was no reply, he eased the door open and stepped inside. Lenore waited a moment, then followed.

There were only four small windows, with shutters, yet the place was decent sized. Looked like it might've been two rooms at one time. A cupboard anchored one wall, with a huge fireplace on the opposite side. A table and two chairs stood in the center, and an old iron bedstead against the far wall.

A scrap of a woman was sitting in a rocking chair by the fireplace. She was as pale as if someone had hung her in the sun for days. Even her lips were colorless. Long gray hair hung in strands around her shoulders, and beady little eyes peered out at them from a wrinkled face. She wore a threadbare dress and a pair of old socks that sagged around her ankles.

The only spot of color on her was what appeared to be a burn on her left leg, visible between the hiked-up dress hem and the top of the socks.

Even though the cabin was clean, there was a stench in the air. At first Lenore was afraid it was coming from the woman, then she noticed a cast iron cauldron on a hook in the fireplace. Something— probably opossum, judging by the odor—was boiling away inside.

Nathan wrinkled his nose, then rolled up his sleeves. "Nice and toasty in here."

Lenore had been sure the woman was near death, but the moment Nathan spoke, a spark entered her eyes. She glared at him, then tugged a blanket—more holes than cloth—from the basket near her feet and pulled it across her lap. "I was thinking it a mite drafty."

She'd clearly demonstrated her rebuttal to Nathan's opinion. She was also trying to cover up the wound.

Nathan moved closer to her. "I came to check on you, Sister. Nobody in town remembered seeing you in a while. Thought you might be sick. Glad to see you're looking like your same old self."

Lenore's startled gaze flew to his. *The woman always looked like this?*

"Course I look like myself," Sister snapped. "Who else would I be looking like?"

Nathan laughed. "It's just an expression."

"Well it don't make a lick a sense," she said. "And you needn't have come up here. I'm fine."

"I can see that." Nathan continued talking, even as he casually reached out with his left hand and encircled her wrist. "You're probably doing so well because you gave up snuff like I suggested."

The cackle emanating from the woman sounded surprisingly strong. "That's where you're wrong. I ain't give it up."

"No? Why not?"

As Sister went into a long list of reasons—including the fact that doctors have less sense than turnips—Nathan managed to look interested and even offended, and at the same time, move the blanket aside, ease the hem of her dress higher, and examine the wound.

Lenore was impressed. It was similar to the sleight of hand and diversion she used when picking pockets.

When the woman finally quieted, Nathan pointed to her leg. "How did this happen?"

Sister waved a hand. "Got a little too close to the fireplace and scorched my dress."

"More than a scorch, and more than your dress," Nathan said. "That's a bad burn on your leg."

"It ain't nothing that time and some raw potato scrapins won't heal."

Nathan opened the black bag. "Well, just to make me happy, why don't you let me use this salve on it instead."

Sister's mouth dropped open so far she almost lost her snuff. "Why would I want to make you happy?"

"I thought you cared about me." Even as he spoke, Nathan was applying the salve to the wound.

After another round of cackling laughter, Sister seemed surprised to see what he'd done.

Nathan stood up. "Is there anything else you need?"

"Nary a thing."

"I'll leave this salve," Nathan said. "Apply a thin layer again in the morning."

Ignoring him, Sister turned in her chair, reaching for a long, wooden spoon laying atop a crate. She leaned toward the pot in the fireplace. It was obviously paining her to move that way.

Before she had a chance to object, Lenore took the spoon from her, and stirred the pot, releasing fresh aromas into the room. *Yep, opossum for sure, plus some turnips and onions.*

The woman glared at Lenore a moment, before shifting her attention back to Nathan. "Who is she?"

"That's Lenore. My wife."

Sister's brows rose. "Didn't know you was hitched."

"Yep. But I want to talk about you, not me. Have you thought any more about moving to town? I could find someplace for you to live."

"I'm fine up here."

"It's too isolated, Sister. You need to be closer to other people."

The old woman was shaking her head before he could finish. "Just because I'm all by my lonesome, don't mean that I'm lonesome. I ain't seen a soul in weeks and I'm doing fine. I cook what I want, eat when I want, and sleep whenever I please. I talk to God of an evening and listen to the birds singing of a morning. I lived most of my life in this cabin. I aim to die here."

"All right, have it your way," Nathan said. "But unless you figure on dying real soon, you'd better use the medicine I'm leaving."

That put some starch in her. "What's wrong with my medicines? Everything I need can be found growing in a field, in those woods, or along the crick."

"I don't disagree with you," Nathan said. "God gave us some wonderful natural remedies. But unless you can go foraging for them, how're they going to help you?"

The old woman seemed to wilt at that. "I got to admit, it was easier when I was young. Most times my folks gathered what they needed when it was abundant, and then saved it up for later. I've got a few things put by, but not as much as I once had."

Nathan's concern was obvious. "You have plenty to eat? I should've thought to bring you food."

"More than plenty. Cupboard's full. Even if it weren't, there's poke salat growing right up nearly to the door. And I trapped me a big opossum." She gestured toward the fireplace. "That'll be good eating for days."

Nathan suddenly looked a little green around the gills. Lenore knew her words to be true.

"Come to think of it," Sister said, "there is something I need from you."

"What's that?" Nathan asked.

"I need you to grab my dishrag yonder and take it around the room and into the four corners."

He stared at her blankly. "Why?"

"I want you to gather the sickness and get it out of here."

Now it was Nathan's mouth that dropped open. "You think the dishrag will do that?"

Sister gripped the arms of the rocker. "Anybody with any sense knows it will."

Nathan sighed. "All right." With barely concealed disdain, he took the rag from the side of the basin and went to the southwest corner and waved it around. "Like this?"

Sister eyed him with suspicion. "Ain't you ever done this before?"

"No, can't say that I have."

She snorted. "And you call yourself a doctor."

Nathan muttered something under his breath, but he didn't say anything to the old woman as he moved on to the next corner.

When he finished, he crossed back to the basin. Sister stopped him.

"Now that you've gathered the sickness, I need you to take the rag outside and bury it."

Lenore knew before he opened his mouth that Nathan was going to refuse. She hurried over. "I'll do it."

His brows shot up, but he handed her the rag without comment.

"Do you have a shovel?" Lenore asked Sister.

"Probably one in the barn. It'd be easier to use the hoe by the porch. Scrape out a trench. It don't have to be deep, as long as the rag is covered over by the dirt."

By the time Lenore was done, Nathan was packing up his bag and Sister was dozing in her rocker. He'd left the salve in the basket by her feet. Hopefully she would use it.

They left, easing the door shut behind them.

"You mentioned that no one had seen her in town," Lenore said, glancing around to make sure she hadn't missed a wagon, horse or mule. "How does she get there?"

"Believe it or not, she walks."

At the wagon, Nathan took soap from the black bag, and a canteen of water, and then lathered up his hands. When he was done, Lenore poured water from the canteen over them. Then he did the same for her before reaching for a piece of toweling.

He was studying her with a curious expression. "You don't believe that nonsense with the rag will heal her leg, do you?"

Lenore shook her head. "I imagine the medicine you brought will do it."

"So why did you bury the rag?"

"Because it won't hurt anything. If it brings her comfort, what harm will it do?"

Nathan's expression tightened. "You'd be surprised how much of this foolishness I deal with. I have to fight to get folks to try the medicine I suggest, then when they get better they claim it was because of some crazy thing like sleeping with an axe under the bed or rubbing a spiderweb over a wound."

He sounded more frustrated than upset, but Lenore still didn't want to argue with him. She couldn't risk making him any angrier with her.

Yet she couldn't resist asking one question. "Do you really think Sister will live long enough to prove you're right about all of it?"

Nathan looked away. "She's in surprisingly good health, for her age."

"How old is she?"

"I don't know," he admitted grudgingly. "If I ever find out whose sister she is, I'll ask them."

Lenore hid a smile as she dried her hands. "She's not telling you the truth about everything. Sister said she's been all alone up here, but that's not true."

His gaze sharpened. "Why do you say that?"

"The woman can barely get around right now, yet she had plenty of firewood."

Nathan shrugged. "Most people keep the wood box full. Probably been there a long time."

"Some of it was still damp. And there were two bowls on the table. Not one dirty, and one clean, like she'd used one and was fixing to use the other. They were both clean and placed across from one another. With two spoons."

"I didn't notice that." He sounded annoyed. "I guess I was

too busy checking out her wound to be looking around for what I could steal."

Lenore jerked back as if he'd struck her. "That's not what I was doing. I just notice things. I thought it might make you fret less if you knew that she's not always alone."

It was almost as if he purposefully hurt her. She understood, though. She'd hurt him.

And he didn't even know the worst of it yet.

After Nathan packed everything back up, he helped her into the wagon. His hand on hers was bittersweet for Lenore. She loved the feel of it, but she wished he didn't seem like a stranger. And that she didn't have to leave. *But she did.*

Reins in hand, he cleared his throat, started to say something, then stopped. He seemed almost embarrassed about the way he'd lashed out. "You ever eat opossum," he finally asked as the horses headed back down the hill.

"Yes. It weren't...wasn't my favorite, but it wasn't the worst."

He shuddered. "I won't ask what was worse. For the record, I've eaten my share of things that others would be appalled by, including crumbs and crusts from trash cans when I was a kid. But as far as I know, I have never eaten opossum. And if it always smells like that, I hope I can keep on saying that."

"It surprises me that you're so squeamish. You're a doctor, you see blood...and worse."

He grumbled something she couldn't quite make out.

Even though Lenore was still aggravated with him, she had to bite her lip to keep from laughing.

The rest of the trip was made in companionable silence, but the closer they got to town, the more Lenore's anxiety increased.

She did *not* want to go to church.

CHAPTER FOUR

THEY SWUNG BY the livery stable to drop off the wagon, and then walked to the house. The minute Nathan opened the door, Nickel shot out and down the road.

Nathan smiled, but he seemed distracted as he went to the bedroom. "I need to get my church clothes from the wardrobe." A few minutes later he came through the kitchen. "The bedroom's all yours."

"I'll finish my ablutions and be right with you."

He looked at her blankly. "Ablutions?"

"You know, grooming oneself. Washing up. What do you call it?"

"Washing up."

"Oh." Sometimes she wished she hadn't wasted so much time memorizing that blasted book.

As Lenore brushed her hair and then pinned it up, taking extra care to make it look nice, she tried to think of an excuse not to go to church. With any other man, she could pretend to be sick, or stumble and hurt her ankle. This particular man would see right through both of those excuses. Just her luck.

After pouring water from the pitcher to the bowl, Lenore washed up, then changed into the only dress she owned that might be suitable for church, a plain brown one. She paired it with a beige shawl. She'd been wearing the same dress the night she'd been arrested. Only Nathan and his brother Eli, would know that.

Lenore wet the cloth again and sponged at the dust along the hem of her dress. Straightening, she pressed a hand to her stomach and stared into the mirror. Is this what her mother had looked like? Did she have green eyes? The same nose or mouth? Lenore had wondered so many times.

She shrugged the thoughts off and headed for the kitchen. Opening the door, she whistled for Nickel and then put out a bit of food and some fresh water.

Nathan came in from the hall. Lenore stared at him, too spellbound to even blink. Crisp white shirt, black vest and suit coat, gray trousers, shiny black boots. He was holding a black Stetson hat, his long fingers curled around the brim. He'd shaved, and the scent of soap and some sort of cologne wafted toward her.

During the week, he'd worn black trousers with a beige or tan shirt and black suspenders and had looked fine. More than fine. But this reminded her of when they'd first met.

They stared at each other, gazes lingering. Did he like the way she looked too? Or did he like the way she was looking at him? Either way, his reaction bolstered her confidence, giving her a little courage as they left the house.

At the church, all courage left her.

"Go on," he said, holding the door open and motioning her forward.

Shaking her head, Lenore dug in her heels.

Nathan pulled her forward and into the church. "It's only a simple Sunday morning service," he whispered. "What are you so worried about?"

How could she explain? It probably wouldn't make a bit of sense to him. The long and short of it was that God and preachers scared her to death—even more than lawmen. Churchgoers unnerved her, too. Throw them all together in one stuffy room and it was a nightmare.

Standing inside the church door Lenore busied herself straightening her shawl, anything to keep from making eye contact with anyone. She wanted to get this over with.

With an exasperated sigh, Nathan placed the Stetson on a hat rack near the back wall and motioned for her to precede him down the aisle. Again, she hung back. With a shake of his head, he took the lead, and—knees threatening to buckle—Lenore followed him.

Thankfully, he didn't go all the way to the front, stopping at about the halfway point. She slid into the pew and kept her head down, looking up long enough to see Eli and Caleb walk toward them, along with their wives. Both women were beautifully dressed.

Lenore was surprised when they each stopped and said hello to her. They'd been polite and even kind at Nathan's home. She hadn't expected them to acknowledge her in public.

After returning the greetings, Lenore sat in silence as the church filled and a woman took a seat at the piano and began playing. When the service began, the others sang along. Lenore only listened. She loved music, but she'd never heard this song before.

Then the preacher stepped up. He was tall, red-haired, young, and soft-spoken, and maybe a nice man. But Lenore closed her mind and her heart to his message. No matter what he said about Jesus forgiving sinners, he wasn't talking about people like her.

She didn't draw a full breath until the service was over. More than ready to make her exit, Lenore led the way down the aisle as the congregation spilled out of the church.

Then she froze. The preacher was standing near the doorway, shaking hands with each person as they left.

Was there another door? Lenore didn't have time to find out. Nathan stepped around her and propelled her forward with him.

Then he was grasping the preacher's hand and telling him how much he'd enjoyed the sermon.

Nathan didn't introduce her, not that she'd expected him to. Lenore was surprised when the preacher smiled and offered his hand. "I'm Wilkie Brown. Nice to see you here this morning. I didn't get your name."

"I'm sorry," Nathan said, then stammered out the introductions, stumbling over the word "wife" and acting as unnerved as Lenore felt. *Good.* It served him right for forcing her to be here.

Lenore suspected that the preacher knew exactly who she was—Moccasin Rock was a small town and news of her presence had surely been discussed. In some strange way, Pastor Brown had made her feel welcome. She still didn't want to talk to him.

After one final nod to the man, Lenore made her way down the porch steps and headed in the direction of Nathan's house.

But if everything went as she hoped, she wouldn't be there long.

Lenore made it as far as the road before Nathan caught up with her.

"Eli and Maggie invited us to dinner," he said. "We'll ride with them. There's room in the back of the wagon for us."

He didn't ask if she wanted to go, just informed her they were going. Swallowing her disappointment and irritation as they retraced their steps, Lenore was horrified to overhear Eli inviting the preacher to join them.

"Thank you," Pastor Brown said, "but I've already accepted an invitation from the Miller family."

"Maybe next time," Eli said.

Breathing a sigh of relief, Lenore let Nathan help her into the back of the wagon.

Before he could join her, Eli's wife suggested Nathan sit up front.

"That way I can sit in the back with Lenore," Maggie said. "She and I can have a good visit."

Lenore was soon sitting across from the young mother, who was holding her infant daughter, Lucinda.

Maggie Calhoun was a friendly, brown-haired woman, and the baby was rosy cheeked, plump and adorable. Maggie had mentioned previously that the baby was six-months old, and their son, Brody, was fourteen.

Lenore looked away now as Maggie adjusted a sunbonnet over the baby's fair hair, an old familiar longing hitting her like a blow.

"We'll be two short for dinner today," Maggie said. "My father is visiting an old friend in Mineral Wells. His health is poor, and the friend suggested that he partake of the mineral waters there. Some people drink the water, others bathe in it. Figure it can't hurt."

"I'm sorry to hear that he's feeling poorly."

"Thank you," Maggie said. "And Brody won't be here, he's eating with the Wilson family."

Lenore knew that both Brody and Lucinda were adopted, after being orphaned, and that the kids were not blood kin to each other.

So far, Maggie hadn't gone into any detail, and neither had Nathaniel. No matter, Lenore told herself, it was really none of her concern. But she was glad, for the children's sake, that someone wanted them.

Even though she wouldn't talk much about her own family, Maggie began telling Lenore about some of the people who'd been at church, and which business they owned, or where they worked, as if Lenore would be staying in Moccasin Rock and needed to know those things. The names and details began to run together, but the picture Maggie was painting was a town full of friendly, helpful people. Lenore was glad for Nathan's sake that he'd found such a place. It wouldn't matter for her.

Lenore clutched at the wagon's sideboard as it began turning from the road onto a long, dirt drive leading to a house sitting back in a grove of live oak trees.

"Is that your home?"

Maggie smiled. "Yes, Eli built it."

"It's wonderful," Lenore said. *And everything she'd ever dreamed of.*

Though simple in design, it was generous in size and featured a tin roof, tall windows and a couple of fireplaces. But it was the porch that most enchanted Lenore. With cedar post railings, and two rocking chairs side-by-side, it stretched across the whole front of the house.

Lenore was only half-way listening as Maggie began rattling off information about how Eli used a lot of available materials, including cedar and limestone, and that other building supplies were brought in from Fort Worth, Fair Haven and Cartersville.

The mention of Cartersville captured Lenore's full attention. "I know where Fort Worth and Fair Haven are. Where is that last town you mentioned?"

If Maggie thought the inquiry a curious one, she didn't let on. She also wasn't particularly helpful. "Not far, if you're going by train."

"Which direction?"

Maggie pointed toward the south, then became distracted when the baby managed to pull her bonnet off again.

"It's a good thing we're home," Maggie laughed, running her hand over Lucinda's hair. "I have a feeling she and I would've gone through that routine over and over again if it had been a longer trip."

Caleb Calhoun and his wife, Abby, arrived in their own buggy as the others trooped inside.

The house was as lovely inside as out. Although several pieces of furniture were a bit grander than the rest, the feel of the place was comfortable. Wood floors were polished, white lace curtains draped the windows, and a wide doorway provided easy access to the kitchen, making it seem almost like one large space.

The kitchen featured some modern conveniences, including a pump at the sink and a cookstove almost as decorative as artwork, but it too was homey. There was a white pitcher filled with blue and yellow wildflowers sitting in the middle of the huge table.

After donning aprons, both Maggie and Abby began preparing the afternoon meal, while the men folk gathered in the front room. Eli had taken charge of the baby and seemed perfectly at ease balancing her on one arm while conversing with his brothers.

Standing between the two rooms, feeling awkward and out of place, Lenore silently observed it all.

Maggie and Abby both appeared to be comfortable in the kitchen, something she'd never experienced. They were hurrying around, yet there was a confidence to their busyness. Lenore wanted to offer to help, but if she did, and they took her up on it, there was always the possibility she wouldn't know how to do what they asked. Not that she was completely without skills. If they needed someone to steal the silver, without anyone being the wiser, she was the woman for the job.

"Is there anything I can do?" Lenore finally asked.

She'd barely gotten the words out when Abby, a brown-haired, blue-eyed woman in an advanced state of pregnancy, appeared in front of her with a bowl of potatoes. "Sure," she said with a smile. "You can peel these."

Grateful for something to do, Lenore sat down at the end of the table and got right to work. This was something she was well-acquainted with. And from her vantage point, she could see and hear all that was going on in both rooms.

Lenore's gaze was drawn to the front room. She was fascinated by the change in Nathan, eyes crinkling at the corners, head tilted back as he laughed, almost boyish. He was like a different person with his family.

With his patients he was kind, compassionate, steady as a rock. With her he'd never been unkind, just...distant. She knew he was capable of being warmer with her, because he had been before. Heat filled her face, and Lenore looked away from him. Even if their acquaintance had been heartbreakingly brief, and ended in disaster, she cherished the memories of their time together in Alabama.

He laughed again, at something Caleb said, and it tugged at Lenore's heart. *Should she tell him the truth? Did she dare risk it?*

A knock at the front door had Eli pushing to his feet and welcoming the old deputy. "Hey, Bliss. What brings you by? Did you smell Maggie's cooking clear back to town? I'll go tell her to put another plate on the table."

"No, I didn't come to eat," the old man said. "Although I gotta admit it smells downright tantalizing."

"So, what's going on?"

The deputy grinned at the baby and tickled her under the chin before answering Eli. "I wanted to tell you about a place that sprung up over on the other side of the river, just shy of Boone Springs."

"Heard about that," Eli said, waving the man toward a chair. "Don't like the sound of it. Sort of a no-man's land out there. No telling what's going on. I'd already planned on checking it out."

Lenore's eyes remained on the potatoes, but her ears were trained toward the men's discussion.

"What place are you talking about?" Nathan asked.

When all three of the others started to answer him, Lenore had trouble following along. They seemed to be talking about a saloon of some sort, and there was gambling involved. Several times their voices dropped too low for her to make out what was being said.

All of a sudden Eli headed for the kitchen, passing Lenore with a nod, and held the baby out to Maggie. "Sorry. Bliss and I need to talk outside."

Wiping her hands on her apron, Maggie took the baby. "Outside?"

"Yes, might not be a fit discussion for feminine ears."

To Lenore's surprise, Maggie rolled her eyes. "But dinner's almost ready."

Eli's answering grin was just as unexpected. "I won't be long, darlin'."

As he left the house, followed by the other men, Lenore considered their exchange. Obviously, there was a warmer side to Elijah Calhoun. Although most likely his family members were the only ones to ever see it.

Lenore finished peeling the potatoes, quartered them at Maggie's request, and was again wishing for something to do.

She noticed Abby, stirring gravy at the cookstove, turned sideways to better accommodate her pregnancy, one hand pressed to her lower back. Lenore wasn't the only one who noticed.

"Oh, goodness. Let me do that," Maggie said, shooing Abby away from the stove. "Get off your feet."

Abby sank down into one of the kitchen chairs, pulled up the hem of her apron and fanned her face with it. "Thank you. I'll sure be glad when this little one gets here, and life returns to normal."

"You will be glad, but don't count on normal for a while," Maggie said as she adjusted her hold on Lucinda and turned toward the stove. "A baby sure changes things." She smiled. "Most of it for the better."

Lenore stepped toward Maggie, tentatively stretching out her hands. "Can I hold her?" Unsure of who's rejection would come first, mother or baby's, Lenore braced herself.

Maggie simply transferred the child to Lenore's waiting arms, and Lucinda blinked at her.

"Thank you," Maggie said, as she grabbed the whisk and gave the gravy a good stirring. "I made her a bottle a few minutes ago. If you don't mind feeding her, there's a rocker in the front room."

As Lenore fed the baby, rocking gently back and forth, she listened to the murmur of voices from the front yard, and from the kitchen, and realized she liked these people. All of them.

She didn't want to like them. It was going to make what she had to do much more difficult. She only had a couple of days to make it to Cartersville, and Nathan had made sure she was rarely alone.

Which meant she'd soon have to resort to deception, trickery…or worse.

Holding a stack of plates, Maggie stepped to the doorway and whispered, "How's it going? Is she almost asleep?"

Lenore nodded.

"Good," Maggie said. "I'll set the table and then I'll put her to bed."

The front door opened as she withdrew, and the Calhoun brothers stepped inside. Nathan was the last one through, stopping short when he saw her sitting there with the baby.

There was such a look of pain on his face that it took her breath away. But there was something else there, almost a yearning.

Without a word, he turned and stepped back outside.

Eli followed him, while Caleb moved into the kitchen and hovered over Abby, asking how she felt.

The baby was asleep now. Lenore kept on rocking, pondering the look on Nathaniel's face. *What had it meant?*

Maggie appeared in the doorway again, a platter full of chicken in her hands. "I'll be back in a minute for Lucinda."

"I can put her to bed," Lenore offered.

Maggie smiled. "Thanks. First door on the left down the hall."

The bedroom Maggie directed her to wasn't small, although the furnishings made it seem so. A huge four poster bed sat against the far wall, with a matching dresser and chest nearby. About the fanciest furniture Lenore had ever seen. There were combs, mirrors and jewelry scattered across the dresser top, and she could tell at a glance that most of it was silver or gold. What was Maggie thinking, leaving all this finery laying around.

The crib, on the opposite side of the room, was simpler in design than the other furniture, though still lovely.

After gently placing the baby inside, Lenore cupped her hand around those soft curls one last time.

Turning away, she stilled at the sound of voices. The window was open, and Nathan and Eli were talking on the front porch. She couldn't hear everything they were saying, but it was enough to know they were discussing her—and then she heard Nathan's voice loud and clear. "I don't trust Lenore yet, not sure I ever will."

Gripping the side of the crib until her knuckles turned white, Lenore fought back tears. *No, she couldn't confide in him. There was too much at stake.* Better to cut her losses and leave.

Seated at the dinner table, Lenore managed to keep her voice steady and a smile on her face, even as her unease and discomfort increased ten-fold. Everything from the prayer Eli said over the food, to trying to remember the social niceties that her grandfather taught her from the book, had Lenore ready to jump out of her skin.

The meal was a feast compared to the usual fare available to her, yet she found it difficult to swallow more than a few bites. No matter how friendly these people were, and how much she liked them, the fact was they had the power to ruin her life, even jail her. *She couldn't let that happen.*

Once during the meal Lenore forgot her problems when it dawned on her that Nathan might be keeping his own secrets. She distinctly remembered him telling her his parents were dead, and yet he'd just referred to his mother as if she were alive. *Which was it?* Again, she reminded herself, it wouldn't matter to her.

Someone remarked on the unseasonably warm weather. Lenore thought it was hotter than blue blazes. Course, women didn't talk that way, so she kept her opinion to herself.

Thankfully, the meal was finally over, and once they'd finished eating, the men returned to the front room and cleanup began in the kitchen. That was something Lenore knew how to do, and with all three women working, in no time at all everything was spick-and-span.

Afterwards, Nathan announced they would walk home. "It's not far as the crow flies."

"If you go through the woods," Eli agreed. "Otherwise you're welcome to take the wagon."

"Thanks, we'll walk," Nathan said. "It's a beautiful day. Do us good to get some air."

Abby and Caleb had already gone home, so it was only Maggie and Eli who stood on the porch and saw them off.

Knowing it was probably the last time she would see Maggie weighed heavy on Lenore. In other circumstances she would've loved to have her for a friend.

When Maggie hugged her, talking about how she'd enjoyed the company and looked forward to seeing her again, it was all Lenore could do not to burst into tears.

Nathan didn't seem to notice, in fact he was completely preoccupied, even after they'd started for home. They'd been walking for a while when he stopped, nodded toward a fallen log and invited her to have a seat. "Let's talk," he said.

Lenore sat down, smoothing her palms over her skirt and then clasping her hands together in her lap to keep them from shaking.

Nathan seemed so serious. What did he want to talk about?

CHAPTER FIVE

NATHAN LEANED AGAINST a tree, facing her, his dark eyes troubled. "I noticed you studying my brothers several times today. I suspect you were deciding their strengths and weaknesses, areas of vulnerability."

Astonished, Lenore gaped at him. He was right, and she hadn't even known she was doing it.

"Does that come naturally to you," he asked, "or were you taught it by others in the show? Is it because they're lawmen?"

Heat filled her face. "A bit of all that."

"So, what did you decide about them?"

Lenore hesitated for a moment, and then decided to tell him the truth. *What difference did it make at this point?*

"I believe Caleb is more trusting of the two, more easy-going," she said. "He has the hardened lawman look, but he has to work for it. A smile comes easier for him."

Nathan didn't contradict her, only gave a little half nod, so she continued. "On the other hand, I suspect Eli had the lawman look even before he was one. That he's lived a hard life, and at times he still teeters on the line of respectability."

Lenore also suspected that even though the ranger was probably authorized to track her anywhere in Texas, the sheriff would do the same, authority or no, and make it a personal mission all the while.

"You're very perceptive," Nathan said. "You're absolutely right about Eli. However, I'd caution you not to underestimate Caleb. He is the more easy-going of the two, but he'll do what needs doing."

A shiver ran down Lenore's spine. Ignoring it, hoping to learn something that would aid in her escape, she pressed on. "The two of them seem close, yet at times it's as if they're just getting to know each other. All three of you do."

His gaze sharpened. "Did Maggie tell you about our past?"

"No, she wouldn't tell me much." *Not for lack of trying.*

"We didn't even know about Caleb until last summer," Nathan said. "Eli and I had the same father as Caleb, but different mothers. Through a series of tragic events, Daddy thought we were dead. He started another family. Eli and I grew up without him."

"I'm so sorry. I didn't know."

"So, what did you and Maggie talk about when you were together this past week?"

"The weather, and the garden Maggie wants to have, and… children." Lenore's voice broke on the last word. Again, he didn't notice. "Both Maggie and Abby have been nice," she added, "but they didn't talk much about their husbands, or you."

Nathan shrugged. "Understandable. They don't really know you, and they're protective of me. I've become like a brother to them. They don't want to see me hurt again."

Lenore winced. "I understand, and I appreciate their kindness. And envy them a little. They seem to be as close as true sisters."

"Yes, they're very close," Nathan agreed. "And like their husbands, they've lived completely different lives. Both have seen rather sudden reversals of fortune. Maggie grew up rich, and recently lost everything except for some furniture and her personal possessions."

Nathan pushed away from the tree, tugged off his suit coat, and then folded it over his arm.

"And Abby has lived a simple life helping her folks running a boarding house," he continued. "Since marrying Caleb she's adjusting to a life of wealth. Did you have all that figured out? Would you have known the right one to steal from?"

That stung, but Lenore supposed she had it coming. "I have no intention of stealing from any of them." *And she wouldn't.* She still had almost five dollars, that would have to be enough.

He gave her a skeptical look, then offered a hand and pulled her to her feet. They started walking again.

"You have no siblings?" he asked.

Usually, Lenore had to think twice before she answered something like that. Trying to remember what lies you'd told could trip a person up. This was one thing she'd been completely honest about, at least with Nathan. "No, no siblings. As I told you, I have no family. I never knew my parents, my grandfather raised me."

"He was part of the medicine show?"

"Yes. He died not long before I met you."

They didn't talk now, each lost in their own thoughts.

Once they reached his house, Nathan held the door for her to enter the kitchen first, then stepped aside as Nickel shot out. They both smiled.

He placed his coat on a hook, then Lenore did the same thing with her shawl. The sight of their garments hanging there, side-by-side, tugged at her heart strings. *If only.*

Lenore leaned against the counter, watching silently as Nathan pumped water for the coffee pot. After it was on the stove, he began to pace around the kitchen, rubbing his hand along the back of his neck, glancing at her more than once.

Clearly there was something else he wanted to say. Just as Lenore was on the verge of asking, he stopped abruptly in front of her.

"Is that what you did when you picked me for your scheme in Birmingham?" he asked. "Study me, decide how vulnerable I was?"

Lenore stared at him, unable to say a word.

"I really want to know. Why me?"

The words were softly spoken, yet they created an earthquake of emotion in Lenore. She swallowed hard before saying, "You were young, nice, polite, clean. The list is endless."

Clearly taken aback by her answer, Nathaniel blinked a few times before saying, "Then why did you leave me, Len?"

He'd shortened her name like that several times in Alabama, and once had even called her Lenny. It made her smile, then. Now it made her want to cry—just as his question did.

Dropping down into one of the kitchen chairs, she waited until he was seated across from her before answering. She owed him this much.

"Leaving wasn't my idea. I wanted to be your wife. I planned to confess everything to you the next morning. Tell you all about the schemes and swindles we operated, and hoped you'd still take me with you. I wanted us to start out with no secrets. Then, while you were sleeping, Ophelia showed up and..."

"And what?"

"She threatened to ki...kill you."

His eyes widened. "Kill me? Why?"

"So I would leave with her, so there'd be no reason for me to stay. I made a lot of money. If I left the show, she would definitely feel the pinch. I wanted to get away from her more than you can imagine."

Lenore pressed a hand to her eyes, the sorrow sweeping over her again. "I told Ophelia I was going away with you to start a new life; that I was your wife. She was furious. Within minutes she had one of her hired bruisers standing there in the hall, a knife in hand. She said that if I didn't get to the wagons, I would be a widow, not a bride."

Nathan's brows drew together. "Why didn't you go for help? There had to have been someone you could approach."

"I considered that. What exactly would I have told them? Ophelia warned me on other occasions when I threatened to leave, that she would tell the authorities I was a thief. She said she'd have witnesses to back up her claim. That I'd be jailed."

Lenore looked down at her hands. "And she did have witnesses. I was a thief."

Nathaniel's jaw tightened. "Even though I'm appalled to learn there was a discussion going on about whether I lived or died, I'm angrier about you drugging me. Was that necessary?"

"You woke up while I was gathering my things. You seemed confused about what was going on, and even where you were. I knew you wouldn't take kindly to any of what was happening. I didn't know you well, but I'd seen enough to suspect that you'd try to keep Ophelia from taking me. And I didn't want you to get hurt, or worse. I always carried a bottle of sleeping elixir Gordon created, in case I was ever in trouble, so I gave you some of that."

"Gordon? You gave me something *Gordon* created?"

Lenore nodded. "I stirred a little of it into a cup of water and offered you a drink."

Nathaniel shook his head. "I can't believe you're so blithe about drugging me."

"I was desperate." Lenore leaned forward. "I knew you'd be furious, but I figured it was more important for you to be alive and mad, than...you know."

Should she tell him the rest of it? The other reason she'd married him? No. He wouldn't understand that kind of cruelty. Nathan was a good, decent man. Which made what she was about to do even more difficult.

Scooting her chair back, Lenore stood. "Coffee?"

"Sure." He handed her his cup as she passed by.

Pouring with her right hand, Lenore slipped her left hand into the pocket of her dress. *It was now or never.*

Easing the stopper from the small glass vial, she tipped the contents into his cup. There were only a few drops left. Hopefully it was enough.

Throat tight from suppressed tears, and soul weary from past mistakes and new regrets, Lenore returned to the table and waited.

⌘

Nathaniel took the cup of hot brew from Lenore, noting how her hands trembled. Clearing the air wasn't easy for her, but it needed doing. And there was more he wanted to know. Before he could ask anything, Lenore surprised him by voicing the same question he'd put to her.

"So why did you agree to marry me? Why didn't you tell Shipley and me to get lost?" Her voice was husky and unsteady. The answer was important to her.

After a moment's hesitation, Nathaniel told her the same thing he'd told Eli. Then he added something he hadn't mentioned to his brother. "And because I was so lonesome I thought I'd go insane."

Lenore's eyes rounded. "You never let on. You were always surrounded by others."

Nathaniel shrugged. "I didn't know any of them well. It's not the same as having someone to share a home with, a life with."

"You'd had that once?"

Nathaniel nodded, wordlessly.

"The woman in the watch? She was your wife?"

"Yes. Her name was Tessa."

"Tell me about her."

Nathaniel was surprised by the request, and for some strange reason he did as she asked. "We were married young. Eli and I were staying with her parents at the time. After we were married, Eli left to find his own way, and Tessa and I set up housekeeping and dreamed of starting our own family. In time we had a child. Then sickness swept through the area. Tessa got it first, then the baby. I've never felt so helpless in my life."

Nathaniel was covering multiple years in single sentences and hurrying through it all. If he tried to detail too much, he'd be sucked back down into a dark hole of grief that could swallow him alive.

"Was your baby a girl or boy?"

"A girl. Her name was Becky." Nathaniel's voice cracked. *She was perfect.* "She and Tessa are buried together in Galveston."

"I'm so sorry," Lenore whispered.

He acknowledged her condolences with a nod.

"Is that when you decided to go to medical school?"

"Not right away. I stayed on with Tessa's folks for a while. Tessa was born to them late in life, a miracle they'd never thought to experience. They were overcome with grief. And I shared in that. I also felt angry and guilty."

"Guilty?"

Nathaniel sipped his coffee. "For being alive. For not being able to keep Tessa and Becky from dying. I started talking about going to medical school, hoping to help keep others from going through something like that. Tessa's father thought it was a fine idea. Said he'd pay for it. How could I refuse? Later, I began to wonder if anger and guilt were the best motivation for studying medicine. That's why I left school. Wasn't sure I had any right to be there."

To his surprise, Lenore disagreed. "From what I've seen, you're a wonderful doctor. You are kind, and I can tell when you're talking to folks how much you want to fix what ails them."

As she talked on about his medical skills, Nathaniel noted with curiosity that her vocabulary was a blend of streetwise waif and educated young lady. He'd noticed it before. Sometimes she'd say a few words, then pause and rephrase her response. She also seemed bent on displaying mannerly behavior, yet it wasn't her first inclination.

And she had an accent that was different. Definitely Southern, a mix of several different areas if he had his guess. The way she pronounced some words made him want to smile. One syllable words often became two, two syllable words became three, and so on.

"Thank you for that," he said when she paused. "You seem to know more about me, than I know about you. For instance, where were you born?"

"Tennessee. But I spent more time in Alabama than anywhere."

"How old are you?"

She bit her lip. "I don't know."

Nathaniel shook his head, fighting off confusion and a sudden drowsiness. "You don't know when you were born?"

"No. Grandpa said he'd written it down in his Bible, but he'd misplaced it somewhere. Really bothered him. He was forgetful in his later years. By the time I was old enough to ask questions, he was too old to answer them. There were more important things I needed to learn. My age wasn't at the top of the list."

He let that soak in a minute. Then he tugged on her hand, wanting to lighten the mood a bit. "Come on, let's go to the livery stable."

Lenore's eyes widened. "Why?"

"We can get Eagan Smith to check your teeth. That's how he tells the age of a horse." Nathaniel laughed at her expression, and then yawned.

Lenore smiled, but for some reason there were tears in her eyes now. He hadn't meant to upset her.

"I'm sorry. I should have asked how old you were before the wedding."

"Don't fret. I'm plenty old enough."

Good.

"How old are you?" Lenore asked.

"Thirty for another month," he said. "I noticed the wagons were a little run down. The show not as prosperous as it once was?"

"I'm not sure," Lenore admitted. "But I know things are different now. In the show's heyday, there was so much excitement. People clamoring for the elixirs and tonics. Shipley was part carnival barker, part professor, and all actor. There were fortune tellers and magic acts. Not that I got to see much of it when I was young. Grandpa kept a tight rein on me at night. Wouldn't let me out of his sight. It aggravated me back then. Now I'm grateful."

"How did you end up here in Texas?"

"I'm not sure. Ophelia never tells me where we're headed. Lately, she hasn't lingered anywhere. She takes whatever money we bring in, and then presses on. We don't know where we're headed. Some medicine shows have a regular route that loops around on a schedule. Ophelia never doubles back because people are usually angry with us when we leave."

Nathaniel had no trouble believing that.

"How did Gordon end up with y'all?"

"Much like my situation I'm told. Some of his family traveled with the show, but now there's only him."

Nathaniel stifled another yawn. "How much schooling did you have?"

She shook her head. "Not much. My grandfather taught me to read and write, and most everything else I've learned from Shipley Bidwell, Gordon and the others. I know a lot about some things, and not nearly enough about others."

"Who taught you to pick pockets?"

"Ophelia."

"Who taught you to gamble."

"Ophelia."

There were other things Nathaniel wanted to know. What happened to her parents? How long had she been with Ophelia and the medicine show? How had she and her grandfather gotten mixed up with them in the first place? And why was she willing to stay after what Ophelia did to her? But all of a sudden Nathaniel was exhausted.

He was fighting to stay awake when Lenore spoke again. "I know you were willing to remarry, since you did. Were you wanting to have children again?"

Nathaniel shook his head, the room spinning about him. "I can't let myself think about it." *Hurts too much.*

Had he said the last part out loud? Folding his arms on the table, Nathaniel lowered his head and closed his eyes. *Only for a moment.*

He sighed when a soft hand touched his brow. For a time, Tessa visited him in his dreams. Now she was back. Yet even as he thought it, Nathaniel realized something was different.

This presence was more than a dream or a memory, and the hand on his hair wasn't Tessa. Yet there was a sadness to the moment that seemed familiar.

This was goodbye.

CHAPTER SIX

THE POUNDING ON the door matched the one in Nathaniel's head. Struggling to open his eyes, he tried to figure out what was happening. The last thing he remembered was sitting in the kitchen with Lenore.

Looking around, he groaned. He was still in the kitchen, but he was alone. Head heavy, heart heavier, he pushed to his feet, not bothering to search the rest of the place. She wouldn't be here. Lenore had drugged him and taken off. *Again.*

He opened the door to find Bliss standing there, eyeing him with a look that was difficult to decipher. "You okay?" the deputy finally asked.

Nathaniel started to nod, then thought better of it. "I'm fine," he said, pressing a hand to his temple to still the throbbing. "What brings you by?"

"Thought I'd let you know that woman of yours caught the ferry to Boone Springs a little while ago."

"Boone Springs?" *How much time had passed?* It was nearly dark outside. Nathaniel motioned Bliss in, then moved to the sink, pumped a glass of water, took a swig, and then pumped more to splash over his face. All while trying to make sense of everything the old deputy was telling him.

Bliss was known for his slow talking and long, drawn-out stories. Nathaniel wasn't catching all of it, but he understood enough. Lenore was gone.

"Thanks, Bliss. If you hadn't come by, there's no telling how long I would've slept. Guess I'd better get to looking for her."

"You want me to tag along?"

Nathaniel considered it for a moment. Bliss was a former Texas Ranger, a crack shot and, despite his age, a surprisingly good fighter. Still, the whole situation was too embarrassing. To have been drugged by Lenore once was bad enough. But twice?

"I'll handle it," he told the old man. "Thanks for the offer, and thanks for letting me know."

With a slow nod, Bliss turned to leave, then stopped. "There was one thing struck me as odd."

"What?"

"Lenore was dressed kinda fancy. All dolled up in a red dress."

Anger flashed through Nathaniel. "Hold on a minute," he told the man. A quick check of his office revealed that none of his money was missing. *She hadn't robbed him this time.* She would still need money.

"At least now I know where to start searching," he told Bliss when he returned to the kitchen.

"Why's that?"

"Lenore would dress in a more subdued manner to pick pockets, but she has other ways of earning money. One of which she's exceptionally good at."

The old man's mouth dropped open.

"Not what you're thinking," Nathaniel said. "I'm talking about gambling. I only saw her play one time, but I've never seen anybody better. And Eli and I spent a good chunk of our younger days in saloons and gambling houses, so I've seen plenty."

"She cheat?"

"Most assuredly. She's good at that, too. She's as fast with cards as Eli is with a gun."

Bliss let out a low whistle.

"That saloon you and Eli were talking about earlier today, did you mention it's near Boone Springs?" *Lenore had probably heard every word.*

"Yep. And there's gambling. From what I hear, you can find at least a few folks there any day of the week."

"Thanks," he said. As Bliss stepped outside, Nathaniel added, "Don't tell Eli and Caleb about this."

Not acknowledging his last remark, Bliss continued on, whistling a tune as he left. *Had he heard? Hopefully so.*

By the time Nathaniel made his way to the ferry—thankfully back on the Moccasin Rock side—his headache was better, and his mood was worse. And it wasn't only anger he was feeling. He was also worried.

Was Lenore trying to get back to the medicine show? What if something happened to her before she caught up with them? What if something even worse happened after she did? Ophelia had already proven herself capable of hurting Lenore. No telling what she would do when no one was looking.

After the ferry docked on the other side of the Brazos, Nathaniel set out on foot. The man who operated the ferry could only tell him that he'd carried a young woman matching Lenore's description to the other side. He had no idea where she was going.

Nathaniel had heard enough from Eli and Bliss earlier in the day to figure out where the new saloon was located. He'd about decided he'd heard wrong, when he caught sight of a little dog near a bend in the road.

Nickel. She didn't wag her tail, or run to him, just sat there as if she'd been waiting.

Glad to see her, Nathaniel bent down and rubbed her head. "Thanks, girl. You know where we're headed?"

The dog's tail wagged a half-beat, then she darted away, stopping once to make sure he was following.

Nathaniel's first glimpse of his destination did little to relieve his worry over Lenore. The place appeared to have been constructed in a hurry—without a measuring stick or plumb bob—and in danger of collapsing in the first strong wind. The door wasn't a typical saloon door, and there was no signage, but there was no mistaking what the place was.

Sounds, including a tone-deaf singer, raucous laughter and raised voices, spilled out from the gaps and cracks around the windows and doors, along with the smell of cheap alcohol. It all conjured up unpleasant memories from his childhood, and as always, Nathaniel shook them off like the dust from his feet.

Mounting the rickety steps, he pushed his way inside. He was so relieved to see Lenore, alive and well, that the icy knot in his stomach started to thaw even as he took in his surroundings.

Several patrons—including a young man lighting candles and lanterns—stopped what they were doing to stare at him. After a cursory glance around the room, Nathaniel returned his attention to Lenore.

She was sitting at the largest of four tables, wearing a fancy red dress, cards in hand, surrounded by some of the dirtiest, roughest looking men he'd seen in a long time. These weren't the much-lauded gentleman gamblers of dime novels, or the local fellows who gathered for a game at the Moccasin Rock saloon.

These men were trouble, and probably not good sports about losing. And with Lenore playing, they would lose.

On the table, money was piled up, and Lenore was looking at him over her cards. Her hands were steady. She appeared to be calm and cool, totally in control—except for the slight tremble to her lower lip and the desperation in her eyes. *Why was she desperate?*

This sure wasn't the time or place to find out. Without considering the consequences, Nathaniel strode forward, grabbed her arm and pulled her up. "Come on."

He'd expected Lenore's protest, but was surprised when everyone at the table objected. "You're not taking her anywhere, Mister," said one man as he pushed to his feet. "She's got too much of my money."

With a sinking feeling in his stomach, and, he hoped, an unconcerned expression on his face, Nathaniel studied the man who'd voiced the objection.

He was tall, even taller than Nathaniel's own six-foot-one, with a bushy black beard and eyebrows to match. His voice was low and raspy, and he seemed unsteady on his feet for a moment, yet his eyes were clear. The man's right hand was now hovering near the gun strapped to his hip. Nathaniel didn't take his eyes off that hand, even as Lenore struggled to get away from him.

Pulling her close, Nathaniel whispered in her ear, "You should think twice about fighting me. I don't think these men will take kindly to that ace up your sleeve."

Lenore's gaze flew to his, then all the fight went out of her. With one last longing look at the money, she stepped away from the table.

Now the two other men were on their feet. They weren't quite as big as the first one, but they were spoiling for a fight. And not only with him. Now they were arguing with each other over who was going to shoot him, and who was going to take Lenore. Nathaniel wasn't completely unarmed, but he doubted that the knife in his boot would be sufficient against several men with guns. *Lord, please help me make the right decisions here.*

Nathaniel's back was to the door when the noise around him ceased. He knew without turning around that Eli and Caleb were standing there—badges flashing, guns in hand. A glance over his shoulder confirmed it.

The relief and gratitude he felt was replaced by a surge of annoyance. Didn't they think he could handle himself?

Nathaniel turned away from the gamblers, noting they seemed more interested in the money on the table than they did him and his wife. The big fellow bolted for the back door. Dragging Lenore with him, he strode toward his brothers. "What are y'all doing here?"

Eli shrugged. "Thought you might need some help."

"I could've handled things."

"Of course," Caleb said. "But it never hurts to have someone with a gun on your side."

"If I'd needed a gun, I would've brought one."

"It doesn't hurt to have someone who knows how to *use* a gun either," Eli said in his matter-of-fact way.

Frustration boiled up inside of Nathaniel. About everything. He pointed to Eli's Colt .45. "May I see that?"

Shrugging, confusion apparent, Eli handed it to him.

Before the lecture on how to use it could commence, Nathaniel gripped the gun, spun on his heel, fanned the hammer, and shot at the candles in each corner of the room—extinguishing the flames and leaving the candles intact.

It was a small structure, so there was no real talent required, at least not much. Plus, he knew how to make it look more impressive than it was. With two bullets left, he spun again and shattered two bottles behind the bar.

Twirling the smoking pistol once, Nathaniel offered it to Eli. "Might want to reload that before you head home."

Ignoring Eli and Caleb's stunned expressions, he tugged Lenore through the door. She was the only one who didn't seem at all surprised by what he'd done. Then again, she'd seen him shoot before.

They'd made it only a few steps before a hand came down on Nathaniel's shoulder.

"Just when did you learn to shoot like that?" Eli demanded as Nathaniel whirled around to face him.

"And where?" Caleb added.

"I don't have time to talk about it now. I've never said I couldn't shoot. I may not be as fast as you," he said to Eli. "Or as accurate as you," he added to Caleb. "But I can shoot."

Both Eli and Caleb opened their mouths to respond. It was Eli who spoke first. "I'm glad to know that. However, being *able* to shoot, and being *willing* to shoot, is something entirely different. And with the attention you're drawing these days"—he glanced at Lenore and then back at the saloon—"that could be an important distinction. Something tells me you'd hesitate to pull the trigger if it was a person and not a bottle. And hesitation could get you killed."

"I can take care of myself," Nathaniel said.

After studying him for a moment, Eli shrugged. "Fine. Guess you don't need us."

"Well…actually I do need help with something."

"What," Caleb asked.

"I left home without much money and…"

Both brothers grinned, irritating him all over again.

Eli crossed his arms. "You want us to go back in and settle up for the damages?"

"Please," Nathaniel ground out.

They were laughing at him now. But Nathaniel had more important things to deal with.

After they'd gone, he expected Lenore to start in with a line of excuses and lies about what she'd done, and why. She surprised him.

"They don't know?" she whispered.

Nathaniel shook his head. "I've never told them about that time in my life."

"Why? It's nothing to be ashamed of. It's not like you were breaking the law."

"No, but it was complete idiocy." He stopped. This was a discussion for another time. Right now, they needed to get something else settled.

Nathaniel gripped both her shoulders and fought off the urge to shake her. "Lenore, if you ever, and I mean ever, put anything in my coffee again, I will…" He didn't finish his threat. He was so furious and frustrated he couldn't even think straight. "What if someone had needed me? What if there'd been an accident?"

Lenore's mouth dropped open. "I'm so sorry. I didn't even think about that."

He let her go, and then rubbed his hands over his face. "I told you that if you took off, I would follow you. If you try to leave again, I'm going to have Eli place you in custody."

Tears sprang to her eyes. "Nathan, please. I can't stay here. I'm not trying to hurt you. It's not personal. I *have* to go."

That's when it hit him. Lenore wasn't running to get *away* from him. She was trying to get *to* someone else.

Who? She had no family left. A sudden spark of jealousy shocked him. "Who is he? One of the traveling show men?"

That brought a gasp from Lenore, not a denial.

"You might as well tell me," Nathaniel said. "If I have to, I'll get the Pinkerton agent to look into it."

Lenore's shoulders slumped. Lowering her head, she mumbled something he couldn't understand.

Hand under her chin, Nathaniel tilted it up so that she was looking him in the eyes. "Who is it you're so all-fired eager to get back to? There is someone. Admit it. Who is he?"

"Yes, there is someone," she finally cried. "It's not a man. It's my baby."

"Your baby!"

Lenore nodded. "My son."

A dozen thoughts came hurtling at Nathaniel all at once. Two shot to the top. *Lenore had gotten herself into even more serious trouble than she had with him. Had she married that man, too?* What a mess.

"Where is your baby?" he asked more gently.

"I'm not sure exactly, somewhere in Cartersville."

"His father took him?"

That seemed to startle her. "No. Ophelia has him."

The thought of that abusive woman anywhere near a child was enough to give Nathaniel chills. No wonder Lenore was desperate to get to him.

"Okay, start over. Why does Ophelia have your baby?"

"She's keeping him until I can pay her a debt I owe."

Stunned, Nathaniel stared at her. "That's monstrous."

"Yes, it is. And typical of Ophelia. Now that you know, will you let me go?"

Nathaniel shook his head. "No. But I will get your baby back for you. Tonight."

Instead of bringing the relief such a statement should have, it elicited a state of panic in Lenore. "Oh no, no," she cried, grasping at his sleeve. "Just let me go. I can deal with Ophelia. Please, stay out of this."

She was so near hysterics that Nathaniel wrapped his arms around her. Drawing her close, he guided her head to his shoulder, patted her back and murmured soothing words.

Lenore was more of a victim than he'd wanted to admit. She wasn't blameless, but Nathaniel doubted if she'd ever had any real control over how things played out. He couldn't change her past, but he could help her with this.

Her tears had tapered off now. "Nathan, please don't go to Cartersville tonight. Promise me. It'd be the worst possible thing you could do."

Nathaniel tightened his arms around her again. "Shh, I promise. We're heading straight back to Moccasin Rock. You'll feel better after you've gotten some rest."

At the sound of footsteps, he looked behind him, relieved to see Eli and Caleb. No matter how much he'd objected earlier, Nathaniel was going to need their help again. He'd promised Lenore he wouldn't go to Cartersville to get her baby tonight.

He hadn't said anything about tomorrow.

CHAPTER SEVEN

SINCE HE AND Lenore slept in separate rooms it wasn't difficult for Nathaniel to slip away the next morning and catch the early train to Cartersville without her knowing. He'd brought his black bag along in case the baby needed medical attention.

Nathaniel knew Lenore would be upset when she found out he went without her. He also knew that it was in her best interests to keep her as far from Ophelia as possible. No telling what the older woman would do when she realized she was losing control over the younger one.

Yes, leaving Lenore behind in Moccasin Rock was best, but he was glad to have Eli and Caleb along.

"So, what's the plan?" Caleb asked, and not for the first time. *On second thought, maybe he should have left his brothers in Moccasin Rock, as well.*

Leaning back in the train seat, Nathaniel admitted the truth. "I don't have a plan. And I don't know how old the baby is, and I don't know how many people are with Ophelia. And before you say it, yes, I should have done more investigating. I was afraid if I asked too many questions, Lenore would know something was up and take off on her own. For some reason, she thought she'd fare better without me interfering."

"I wasn't going to say any of that," Caleb said. "I'm sure you did what you could. I'm just eager to get this done. The fewer surprises there are, the faster we can find her baby and get back home."

Nathaniel knew why Caleb wanted to rush through this. He was worried about his own baby and scared to let Abby out of his sight. No matter how many times Nathaniel told him that babies being born was a routine thing, it hadn't sunk in.

And Nathaniel didn't blame Caleb. It was different when it was your own child making their way into the world. But Abby was healthy, and according to Peg Harmon, the midwife, the pregnancy was progressing fine. Still, Caleb worried.

"You could've stayed home," Nathaniel said. "I really do understand."

Caleb dismissed the idea. "Not a chance. I want to help with this."

Across from them, Eli leaned back in his seat, elbows on the armrest, hands together and resting on his stomach, looking almost bored.

It was a deceptive expression and posture. Nathaniel knew from experience that Eli was following their conversation, and he was equally aware of each fellow passenger in the car. Not that there was any danger. It was just what Eli did. Had always done.

"Even if it's not a plan, you must have some idea how you want to proceed once we hit Cartersville," Eli said a moment later. "Tell us what's on your mind."

Nathaniel hesitated only for a moment. "I think Ophelia will be expecting us to look for the wagons. I believe they'll keep the baby somewhere else. If we concentrate on things they'll need, maybe we can follow them back to their hiding place."

"Things they'll need?"

"Yeah. Such as food. Lenore's mentioned that for the most part they ate a lot of squirrels, rabbits, fish, wild greens, even opossums. Whatever they could find in the woods or the rivers."

"Pretty much the same thing we ate," Eli said.

"We ate *most* of that at one time or another," Nathaniel agreed. "Lenore also said anytime they were near a town, they'd lay in some supplies, and also have some meals from restaurants. I'm not sure whether they bought the stuff or stole it, but they availed themselves of food. I think we should check with all the mercantile and eating establishments in Cartersville and see if anyone remembers meeting any of them. When they want to, most of the medicine show folks can blend in anywhere. Yet Shipley, Gordon and Ophelia stand out. And having a baby along will also make them memorable."

"Sounds reasonable," Eli said. He looked at Caleb. "You have a better idea?"

"Nope. Let's do it."

Nathaniel let out a sigh, thankful they'd agreed to his plan. He wanted to get Lenore's child back to her, and then figure out where in the world they needed to go from there. Not that he expected it to be easy.

Something had happened to him the day before when he'd walked into Eli's house and seen Lenore holding the baby. It hit him hard. And he wasn't even sure why. Through the years, he'd braced himself not to react to every infant he saw.

He'd distanced himself each time he'd treated Lucinda, and he'd do the same thing with Caleb's little one. He would treat them, and love them, but he couldn't let it hurt him.

And yet yesterday, with Lenore, it had. Nathaniel stopped puzzling over it. The sight caught him by surprise, that's all. *He needed to toughen up.*

Now he understood that Lenore was missing her own baby. She must've been in pain, too. Nathaniel had questioned her before she'd gone to sleep the night before to learn everything she knew regarding the baby's whereabouts. Which wasn't much. He'd tried to find out more about the baby's father, but Lenore became physically ill. Once she had her child again, maybe she'd be more willing to discuss things.

He was glad to figure out Lenore's secret, or at least part of it. He still didn't know why she owed Ophelia money, or how much.

Lenore told him Ophelia had given her one week to get back to the show. Or what? Was the older woman planning on taking the child away forever? Would she harm him? A renewed sense of urgency filled Nathaniel.

Once they arrived in Cartersville, they spotted two eateries near the depot. Doubtless there were others further on into town. This might take longer than he'd hoped.

As they headed down the street, Nathaniel shook his head when several people glanced briefly in his direction before their gaze settled in on one of his brothers for a longer look. Some folks didn't seem to notice him at all.

That's what happened when you went anywhere with a Texas Ranger and a sheriff. It was about as close to invisible as a man could get. Nathaniel was used to it, and at times it suited him fine.

Their first stop was the café nearest the depot. The young woman running the place said she'd seen a man matching Shipley Bidwell's description the day before. She didn't know where he went, or which direction he'd come from.

Caleb thanked her, then asked, "Did he have a baby with him?"

"No. He was alone. Sorry I couldn't be more help." The woman fluttered her eyelashes so fast Nathaniel marveled that it didn't extinguish the candle on the counter.

Caleb smiled and tipped his hat as they left. "Much obliged."

It didn't take them long to settle into a routine. If they needed charm to get information, Caleb took the lead. If they needed intimidation, Eli did what came natural to him. Nathaniel stayed back, studying and searching every face, hoping to recognize someone from the show. So far, no luck.

At the general store across town, they finally hit pay dirt.

When asked about anyone new to town, the clerk shrugged and shook his head.

When Nathaniel, on a hunch, asked if there'd been any unusual purchases lately, the man scowled. "Not unless you count a squirrely old man buying a lady's handkerchief and a box of candy." Nathaniel had been thinking more along the lines of baby clothes or blankets, or bottles.

The clerk reached out to straighten a display of shoe polish. "Or a crazy bachelor fella buying a whole bill of groceries, including beans, flour, lard, coffee, and six apples, when he usually only buys cigars and whiskey. And then telling me to deliver it all to a widder woman's house instead of his own."

Another customer hailed the clerk, and he hurried over.

"Sounds like he knew both of those men," Caleb said. "Do you think there's anything to any of that?"

"Don't really see how the man who bought the candy and handkerchief would be relevant," Eli said, "but the other fellow sounds interesting. Could be buying up supplies for folks who were too skittish to be seen themselves."

"That's what I'm thinking, too," Nathaniel agreed.

When the clerk returned, Nathaniel asked if he knew where the man who bought the bill of groceries lived.

"He lives over on Center Street, but he wanted the food delivered to a house over by the grist mill. You won't find him in either place yet. Said he had to run several other errands after he left here."

Caleb and Eli exchanged a look at that last bit of news. The Calhouns would be waiting on him at the "widder" woman's house.

After getting the address, they left, nearly stumbling over an old man who was standing on the boardwalk with a box of candy and a ladies' kerchief in one hand and a bunch of halfway wilted wildflowers in the other, mumbling to himself, "These are for you, Mary Ann."

Smiling, they moved on.

Thinking they were looking for some sort of fortified hide-away, Nathaniel was surprised to find that their destination was a small, ordinary house, surrounded by other ordinary houses. No sign of guards or lookouts. If Ophelia was hiding the baby here, it shouldn't take long to locate him.

With Caleb posted near the back of the house, and Eli near the corner by the front, Nathaniel walked up the front steps and knocked. He was already thinking about where they'd search next, when the door swung open.

The Mexican woman motioning for him to step inside wasn't Ophelia, yet she did act as if she'd expected him.

"You are here for the child?"

Nathaniel blinked. "Yes. How did you know?"

"I heard them talking. They say his mama will come. Or, his papa, the Texas Kid."

Nathaniel was aware that both of his brothers had joined him on the porch, and were now staring at him, aggravated all over again about the reference to the Texas Kid.

For a moment he enjoyed it.

Then it dawned on him what the woman said. Ophelia had expected Lenore or the child's father to come for the baby, that made sense. Why did she think Nathaniel would come?

Had Ophelia been so sure he'd help Lenore?

And how did this woman know about The Texas Kid? There'd been some posters with his image, but not anywhere around here.

Before he could ask those questions, Eli thought of a more pertinent one. Stepping up beside Nathaniel, he whispered to the woman, "Are they inside?"

She took a step back when she noticed the gun Eli held, then relaxed after looking him over. "No, only me and the boy." When Caleb stepped up to join them, her eyes widened.

"These are my brothers, Eli and Caleb."

She looked all three of them over again, then nodded.

"What's your name?" Nathaniel asked.

"Call me Esme."

"Esme, I'm Dr. Nathaniel Calhoun, I'm here on the mother's behalf. May I come in and talk to you?"

The woman didn't hesitate, waving them all three inside. "She said you would come. I'm not supposed to let you take him. Not the mama either."

"Ophelia said that?"

"Si. That is her name. She said the Texas Kid, Dr. Calhoun, his papa, could not take him. Nor the mama."

Was this some sort of set-up? "How did you know I was the Texas Kid?"

"Because you look like him."

Nathaniel glanced in the direction the woman pointed, and all the air left his lungs in a rush.

A small child was sitting at a table. He was fair-haired like his mother, but that's where the similarities ended. Otherwise he was all Calhoun. Right down to the big brown eyes and the solemn look. It was like looking at a smaller version of himself.

Heart thudding against his ribs, he walked over to the table, dropped down and balanced on his boot heels in front of the boy.

Rubbing a shaky hand across his mouth, Nathaniel glanced at his brothers. They were also staring, wide-eyed.

"That boy's the spittin' image of you when you were younger," Eli said quietly.

"I know." Nathaniel stood and turned to the woman. "How old is he?"

"Three."

Even without knowing an exact date, it didn't take a genius to do the math. He had a son, and Lenore kept it a secret from him.

The woman interrupted his thoughts. "You are the boy's papa, The Texas Kid, the doctor." It wasn't a question. She'd been saying that all along, but Nathaniel had just now caught on. He'd been assuming there was an "or" in between those words.

"Yes. I'm his father."

Esme launched into an explanation then. Her broken English was better than Nathaniel's broken Spanish, yet he was still having trouble understanding her. After a few minutes she lapsed into Spanish, speaking so rapidly that even if Nathaniel were fluent in the language, he would've had a hard time keeping up with her.

Thankfully, Caleb was having no such problem. After listening for a moment, he turned to Nathaniel.

"She took the boy in because of the money they offered, then she realized that they're up to no good," Caleb said. "She'd decided to take him to her brother's house and then try to figure out what to do from there. She'd tricked the guard into going to the store and then on several other errands. Told him she wouldn't cook anymore meals until he got her everything on her list. She was actually planning to leave in a few minutes."

The woman pointed to a small bag sitting near the back door.

The boy was still staring at Nathaniel. Hadn't said a word. Didn't seem frightened. Just no emotion at all. Nathaniel crouched down again. "What's your name?"

When there was no reply, he turned to the woman again. "Do you know his name?"

She looked up at the ceiling, as if trying to remember, then said the name Jedidiah. "They said to call him Jed."

He turned to the boy and smiled. "Hi, Jed."

The boy didn't respond, but he was following the conversation. His brown eyes weren't dull. He was alert and curious. All good signs. As was the lack of fear.

Nathaniel stood, trying to draw a full breath. There was food on the table, the room was clean, and this woman was treating the boy with kindness. All things that Nathaniel hadn't known much of as a kid. And yet he was angry enough to spit nails.

The anger was directed at Lenore, but he still didn't understand this woman's part in it all. "Why didn't you go to the authorities?"

Again, she launched into rapid fire Spanish, and again his younger brother translated.

"She hasn't had a chance. There's been a man with a gun here. She also has rheumatism. There was no way she could fight or run." The woman's swollen fingers and stilted gait gave truth to her explanation.

"Plus, she wasn't sure how to explain why she had the boy," Caleb said. "She was going to ask her brother for advice. She was planning to go to him today. She's glad we're here."

Esme began speaking in English again. "Ophelia was here yesterday and—" Esme reached down and hugged Jed to her, making sure his ears were covered. "She said if I do anything she did not like, she would kill us." The woman more or less mouthed the last few words.

The fact that she cared enough to protect his son from hearing the threat, endeared her to Nathaniel as nothing else would have.

"Esme, this boy is my son. I mean to take him outta here, now. Are you going to give me any trouble?"

"No trouble. He goes with you."

Even though she was saying all the right things, the woman kept casting fearful glances toward the front of the house. Was it more than the guard she was expecting to return?

"Where is Ophelia?" he asked. "Why didn't she keep the boy with her?"

"She said you would find the wagons and find her. You wouldn't find him."

"Where are the others?"

Esme made a circling motion with her hand. "I hear them talking, they are around the town. Waiting for the mama to show up."

They were waiting. Why hadn't they made a move? Maybe because they'd been expecting Nathaniel or Lenore, not Eli and

Caleb. The others wouldn't do anything right now, but what would happen to this woman once he took Jed?

Nathaniel didn't want to leave her to face Ophelia's wrath alone. "Do you want to leave with us? We'll make sure you're safe."

"My brother lives near Bitter Creek. I will go to him."

Esme was probably pushing seventy-five. Nathaniel couldn't imagine her having a brother young enough to help. "Will he be able to protect you?"

"Si. He has four sons. Big ones. I will come back here when the woman is gone."

A noise from the front of the house drew her attention. "That is him," she whispered, "the man with the gun."

Nathaniel put a finger to his lips, then motioned her and Jed into the next room. Hopefully if things got ugly, she'd protect the boy from seeing the worst of it.

Eli and Caleb took up positions on either side of the doorway, while Nathaniel stood in the middle of the room, facing the door, and waited.

A man walked in with a gun on his hip, and some sort of package in his arms. "Well, Esme, you can stop your griping. They'll be delivering the food you wanted. You can start cooking again soon."

He dropped the package when he spotted Nathaniel, then whirled around at the sound of guns being cocked behind him. He raised his hands at the sight of Eli and Caleb, guns drawn—a Colt .45 aimed at his head, a Remington 44-40 at his chest.

The man started babbling that he was innocent, even though no one mentioned him being guilty of anything, while Nathaniel studied him.

The store clerk seemed to know the man, or at least his buying habits, and Nathaniel didn't remember him being part of the medicine show Lenore traveled with. But then he hadn't met all of them, and there were probably some new ones anyway.

Nathaniel questioned the man, wanting to find out about Ophelia. He swore he didn't know anything.

"I only got hired to do one thing," he said. "To watch this woman and that kid, and make sure no one took the boy away. I don't know anything about the lady who paid me, or her plans."

Esme stepped in from the other room. "He is telling the truth, at least about some of it. He did live in town before Ophelia and the others come. They pay him to guard."

After agreeing that they probably wouldn't get more information from the man, Caleb approached him. "You have two choices. You can high-tail it out of here, leaving Esme alone, or I can arrest you."

"I'll go," the man sputtered.

Eli stepped closer to him. "And I'm going to ask you, nicely, not to say a word to the folks who hired you. You need to head on somewhere else, with your mouth shut…"

The man left so fast Eli didn't get to finish his request.

After he was gone, Eli looked at Nathaniel. "We don't really have a guarantee that he won't alert Ophelia and her bunch to what's happened. Just in case, we should get Esme to her family as soon as possible, and get on back to Moccasin Rock."

"I'll go to the livery stable and see about a wagon," Caleb said.

While he was gone, Eli kept watch, and Nathaniel helped gather Esme's bags as she finished packing. He tried talking to Jed a few times, but the boy didn't respond.

When Caleb returned, together they escorted Esme to her brother's house.

Nathaniel had never heard of Bitter Creek and didn't recognize any of the landmarks Esme mentioned, but it didn't take long to reach their destination.

Even after they arrived, Nathaniel was still hesitant to leave the woman. The old man sitting in the front yard beside a sleeping dog, didn't look like he could fend off any harm to his sister.

Then the dog woke and started barking, and several younger men walked out of the house.

Esme hadn't exaggerated when she said her nephews were big. She hadn't mentioned that they were also armed, and more than a little curious about why three men were accompanying their aunt.

Nathaniel didn't know exactly what they asked, but there was obvious concern for their Tía Esme. The woman answered them in Spanish, and Nathaniel could only hope that the Calhouns would come out okay in the telling. Apparently, they did, because all the men relaxed.

While Eli and Caleb unloaded her bags and handed them off to the nephews, Nathaniel pressed the money he had with him into Esme's hand.

She shook her head. "Ophelia paid me."

"Please take it," he said. "I want you to have it. Thank you for taking care of my son."

She solemnly nodded, tucked the money away in a pocket of her dress, and hugged Jed goodbye.

Back in town, they returned the wagon to the livery stable, and then made their way to the train station. Nathaniel was carrying Jed. When the train pulled into view, whistle screaming, steel wheels screeching, the boy threw his arms around Nathaniel's neck, shaking.

Turning, so that he put himself between the child and the train, Nathaniel hugged him close. "It's okay. It won't hurt you. I won't ever let anything hurt you."

Despite his reassurances, Jed kept his head pressed against him until they'd boarded and were seated inside. Only then did the boy pull back and look at him.

With a tightness in his chest, Nathaniel stared into the solemn little face. *God, please help me know what to do here.*

Nathaniel was a stranger, and this kid hadn't blinked an eye when told they were leaving. How many places had he stayed? What all had he seen? Would the boy remember Lenore?

She'd told Nathaniel the night before that she only got to keep her *baby* infrequently. Ophelia always kept him close, but most of the time, just out of Lenore's reach. Sometimes, the woman would disappear with him for days.

He felt pity for Lenore, missing anything of this child's life. Then again, Nathaniel had missed everything.

He smiled at the boy. "You can call me Daddy."

The boy didn't return the smile, or say a word, but once again his eyes were taking in all that was going on around him.

Nathaniel wasn't sure what to do going forward. The only thing he knew for sure, was that he planned on raising his son.

And no one was going to stop him.

CHAPTER EIGHT

LENORE SMILED AND nodded as Abby rolled out a pie crust, talking the whole time about how there'd been a record crop of peaches last summer.

"Are you sure I can't help with anything else," Lenore asked. She'd chopped vegetables for the pot of stew Abby had simmering.

"Can you give the stew a good stirring?"

"Of course."

It was quiet in the Horton Boarding House kitchen, between breakfast and the noon meal. Abby was preparing several desserts for later that evening.

Fortunately, Abby seemed content to carry on most of the conversation, because no matter how much she talked about cooking, Lenore's mind kept circling around and around on the same thought.

Where was Nathan?

He'd probably gone to see a patient, which should've provided the perfect opportunity for her to slip away. Unfortunately, his family and friends were watching her even more closely than he did.

Time was running out. She had to get to Cartersville.

Her thought, early in the day, was to distract the old deputy stationed outside Nathan's door and make a run for it. Then Abby arrived and asked Lenore to keep her company at the boarding house.

"My mother and grandmother have gone to Fair Haven to purchase a new rug for the parlor," Abby said, "and my father and brother are also off running errands. Sure would appreciate the company."

Lenore knew there was more to the invitation than Abby was letting on, but she was so genuinely sweet that it was difficult to think ill of her.

Still, the later it got, the more uneasy Lenore became. Here it was mid-morning, and she was no closer to Cartersville than when she woke. Although she appreciated Nathan's offer of help, she couldn't let him do that. There was too much at stake.

She was more afraid of Ophelia than she was of him, but they both had the power to take away the one thing in her life that made it worth living. She needed to get to Cartersville alone.

"A good pie crust can make all the difference," Abby said as she laid aside the rolling pin. "And I believe in using lots of butter. Makes the crust light and flaky."

As she pressed the dough into a pie pan, Abby talked about the filling. "My mother, grandmother and I canned some of the peaches last year. Lots of them. You get sick of doing that at the time, but it sure is good later. We made cobblers and pies all winter."

"Sounds good," Lenore murmured. *She hated to do it, but she was going to have to sneak away.*

As she began to push to her feet, wondering how to create a distraction, Abby provided a possible answer. "It looks like we're out of ginger for the filling. Do you mind if we walk over to the mercantile? Might be nice to get out of the house for a bit."

"I'd like that," Lenore said. *Instead of outwitting Abby, she would outrun her.* In the woman's current condition, it shouldn't be difficult.

Abby moved the stew pot to the side of the stove, then retrieved her bonnet from a hook, removed her apron and placed it on the same hook.

They left through the back door. Even though Nickel had been waiting in the front, Lenore wasn't surprised to see her trot around the corner of the house and follow along.

Anxious to avoid the jail in case Eli Calhoun should take a notion to join them, Lenore was relieved when Abby turned in the other direction. "We'll cut through here," she said.

The boarding house shared an alley with the main street. It didn't take long to reach the center of town.

Moccasin Rock was small enough that you could almost see from one end of town to the other, no matter where you were standing, but there were streets Lenore hadn't explored yet. She should be able to dart off and lose Abby without any problem.

It was busier than Lenore had expected it to be. Since it was a weekday—Saturday was usually the day when most country folks made their excursions into town—Lenore could only assume that these were mostly town folk.

They passed businessmen in suitcoats talking in front of the post office, a thin man who resembled a scarecrow sweeping the sidewalk in front of Bony Joe's Café, a brawny fellow sporting a white apron over his clothes, washing the large windows of Finley's Saloon.

There were buggies, wagons, horses and mules in front of every business.

As if she'd heard Lenore's thoughts, Abby began talking about the town's recent growth, including several new businesses. "We also have a brand-new bridge across the Brazos, connecting us to Boone Springs—but it's not open, yet—and we're getting a new courthouse."

Lenore took a quick step back as a mule and a goat walk by. Abby laughed. "Those belong to Adger Wilson. He has nine children, and more animals than he can count, or keep up with. Usually, there's a pig running with them."

Lenore listened, contributing a few words here and there as Abby talked on, but now she was checking out the side streets and alleys. She would wait until Abby was busy in the store before making her move.

Her hopes were dashed when the sound of boots rang out on the boardwalk behind them.

Which of the Calhouns was it? She turned to see the deputy smiling at her.

The old man tipped his battered hat. "Mornin', ma'am."

Lenore gave him a shaky smile. "Good morning."

Bliss waited outside when they stepped into the mercantile. While Abby chatted with Mr. Silas Martin, a bald man with a droopy mustache, Lenore looked for another way out.

In the background, she heard Abby asking about ginger, coffee, vinegar, and white thread. Her list grew longer as she spotted several other things she needed. *Good.* That bought Lenore more time.

Her gaze was drawn to a set of stairs, but she didn't figure jumping from a second-floor window was her best bet for escape. She was eyeing a curtained doorway, hoping that even if it was a storeroom it would lead to the alley, when she realized Abby had called her name.

"Yes?"

It was the storekeeper who answered Lenore. "I was wondering if you needed anything, ma'am."

Nothing except a way out. "No, thank you, Mr. Martin."

They left a few minutes later. "Do you feel up to walking for a bit longer?" Lenore asked.

"Sure. The pies will keep."

"Let me carry your packages," Lenore said. They weren't heavy, but they were unwieldy and bulky. Lenore would leave them somewhere that Abby would be sure to find them easily.

Bliss had been following along, but now he stepped up beside Abby. "Let me carry those for you."

Lenore's face filled with heat. Did the man think she was going to steal them? Or was he just being a gentleman?

"Thank you, Bliss," Abby said with a smile. "Did my husband ask you to keep an eye on us?"

The man returned Abby's smile, while his gaze drifted to Lenore. He didn't say so, but they both knew that Lenore's husband was the one who'd requested his help.

"It's an honor to be carrying the packages for such lovely ladies as you two," was all he said.

While he and Abby talked, Lenore dropped back, stopping in front of the window of the newspaper office as a man leaned over a printing press. Lenore had read newspapers when she got the chance, one of her favorite pastimes, but she'd never seen one being put together. She was so caught up that she almost forgot what she was doing. Then she remembered.

When it seemed as if Abby and Bliss were both sufficiently distracted, Lenore took a couple of steps in the opposite direction. She paused when Bliss turned and started following. He didn't try to stop her, just walked along beside her.

"Was there somewhere else we need to stop?"

Lenore battled against the panic welling up inside of her.

"Hey, where are you two going?" Abby called out, oblivious to the tension. Yet Bliss was eyeing Lenore in a way that concerned her. They returned to the boarding house a short time later.

Once in the kitchen, Abby moved the stew back to the stove, and began working on the pies again. "Since peach pie is one of Nathaniel's favorites, I'm making an extra to send home with you."

Lenore suffered a stab of jealousy that some other woman knew more about her husband than she did. Then she remembered that Abby was a member of his family. Of course, she'd know that sort of thing.

"It's kind of you to make his favorite," Lenore said.

"Oh, I'm glad to do it. He does so much for everyone here. He's one of the nicest men I've ever met." Abby smiled. "Look who I'm telling. You already know that."

Lenore's answering smile felt so shaky that she ducked her head. *Yes.* She did know that.

Should she tell Nathan everything as soon as he got home? *The whole truth.* And ask for his help?

While the pies cooked and then cooled, Lenore helped Abby clean the kitchen. "Do you and Caleb live here," she asked.

"No, we rent a house here in town. We're planning to build one out near Eli and Maggie. I come here often and help out though. If I'm away too long, I start to miss it."

Once they'd finished cleaning, Abby seemed ready to drop.

"You should rest," Lenore told her, truthfully concerned.

"I think I will," Abby said. "I appreciate you passing the time with me, I enjoyed our visit."

Outside, Bliss was waiting, and with no more than a nod, escorted Lenore to Nathan's house. He then settled down on the bench right outside the back door. There was no longer any pretense that he wasn't keeping her from leaving.

Was the office entrance being watched?

Lenore tiptoed from the kitchen to the office and peeked through the window there. Sure enough, there was some man she'd never seen before sitting outside the door. Any attempt to leave would probably end with her in jail. Then what would happen to her son? Talking to Nathan when he returned was her only hope.

With time on her hands, Lenore spent several minutes looking around. She'd seen Nathan's office and the rest of the house, but she'd never looked at the examining room, or the waiting area. The rooms were clean, neat, organized. Filled with medical books, medications, all sorts of contraptions, and even a microscope. The kind of place that would fill a patient with confidence.

She studied his diploma from the University of Virginia Medical School, proud of him and for him. In his office, she saw the bedroll he'd been using, the pitcher and bowl. His razor and strop. The strop shared a place on the hook next to his stethoscope. He had another scope that he kept in his bag. *She didn't see the bag anywhere.* So, he had gone to see a patient. Had they taken a turn for the worse?

Maybe Sister was in a bad way. *If that was the case, why hadn't he asked her to go with him?*

Returning to the kitchen, Lenore pumped water to fill the tea kettle, then placed it on the stove. She also made a pot of coffee. While waiting, she paced back and forth.

When the tea kettle whistled, she found the tea leaves in the cupboard. It was a new tin. Did Nathaniel buy it for her? No. He probably didn't know any more about her likes and dislikes, than she did about him. More than likely, Maggie or Abby thought of it.

She poured a cup of coffee and took it to the deputy. He seemed bewildered, then suspicious, looking first at the cup, then at her.

He knew what she'd done to Nathan. Heat crept up her neck. "It's only coffee," she assured him. "I promise."

Bliss studied her face a moment, and then took a sip. "Much obliged, ma'am."

Lenore then took a cup to the front. It was Eli and Maggie's son, Brody, on the bench now. He probably came here as soon as school was over. She felt bad that he was spending his afternoon this way.

His eyes widened when she handed him the coffee. "For me?"

"Yes. I didn't put any sugar or cream in it. Wasn't sure how you drank it."

"This is fine."

He hesitantly took a sip, then smiled. Was this his first cup of coffee? When Lenore left, Brody was grinning big. It normally would've made her smile, too. But worriment and fear were working their way deep inside her.

She returned to the table. Nickel curled up at her feet. The sound of the clock on the wall was driving her crazy. Knowing that each tick was counting down the moments to her son's disappearance.

Wrapping her shaky fingers around the teacup, Lenore welcomed the warmth even though it wasn't cold in the room. The chill she felt went clear to her heart.

If she'd managed to escape earlier, she might've had time to get to Cartersville, search, and then move on to the next town south of there. If Nathan had come home, they might have made it there together. Now, she could never get there in time. *What if Ophelia moved on without leaving any word? What if they disappeared completely?*

Just as Lenore imagined the worst, nausea hitting her so hard that she leaned over the table, the door opened.

She looked up to see Nathan staring at her. Unsmiling. Jaw rigid. Mouth compressed into a tight line. It unsettled her, but she had to ask for his help anyway. *Beg him if necessary.*

Lenore was so focused on Nathan's face that it took her a moment to see the child at his side. The boy saw her at the same moment and lunged for her.

"Jed," she breathed, stumbling as she tried to stand. Falling to her knees, she reached for him.

Nathan held the boy back for a moment—a moment that shook Lenore to her soul—before releasing him.

As Lenore wrapped her arms around her son's little body and held him close, Nathan continued to stare at them wordlessly. Lenore dreaded the confrontation that was coming. But Jed was safe. *That's all that mattered for now.* Tears streamed down her face. Nickel seemed torn between comforting Lenore and greeting Jed.

The next few minutes were a blur of excited reunion—with

both Jed and Nickel ending up in Lenore's lap—and breathless anxiety as Lenore waited for Nathan to say something. Anything.

When he finally spoke, it was to Jed. "You hungry?"

Jed nodded and Lenore hopped up, placed him in the chair, and then filled a bowl with some of the stew Abby sent with her. After giving Jed his portion, she offered a bowl to Nathan. He refused with a small shake of his head.

It was obvious that Nathan didn't want to upset Jed any more than she did.

While the boy ate his supper, his father leaned against the counter with a strange look in his eyes. Nathan was watching Jed with a blend of awe and fascination, a stark contrast to the looks he sent her way.

He glanced up and caught her watching him. "Jed seems to have a hearty appetite."

"Yes, he does," Lenore said. "He's also a very sound sleeper, and he's rarely sick."

She felt awkward telling this man things about his son—information he would already know if things had gone differently. Glad that Jed was distracted by Nickel, Lenore lowered her voice. "Did Ophelia put up a fight about you taking him?"

"She wasn't there. Some other woman was watching him."

"Who?"

"A woman named Esme."

Lenore glanced at Jed, worried. "I don't know who that could be."

"Someone Ophelia hired in Cartersville. An older Mexican woman. She didn't seem to know anything about what was going on."

Lenore didn't like the thought of her son being cared for by a stranger.

"She was kind to him," Nathan added. "He wasn't afraid of her."

Her anxiety eased.

"Jed didn't have much in the way of clothing," he said.

"I can look for him something at the mercantile tomorrow. I was there with Abby earlier. I noticed that Mr. Martin had some things for children."

His expression hardened again. "I'll find him something. Don't leave this house."

Nathan resembled his brother, Eli, at that moment. She'd known he'd be angry, but this still left her feeling unsteady.

While Lenore cleared the table and tidied up the kitchen, Nathan disappeared into his office. *What was he doing? What was he thinking?*

After finishing with the cleaning, she grabbed the lantern and took Jed outside to the privy. As soon as they stepped out the door, Nathan was right behind them. When they were back inside, Nathan disappeared into his office again, and she poured water from the pitcher into the basin to wash Jed up for bed.

Jed was tired, but while they were alone, he told her about the train, and about the woman named Esme, who made oatmeal that he liked. His stories were told quietly, punctuated by yawns, and several spontaneous hugs for Lenore. With a full heart, she lay beside him until he drifted off.

She then went looking for Nathan, ready to fight it out. Until she saw him. Sitting at his desk, head in his hands, a defeated slump to his shoulders.

"I'm sorry," she whispered.

He straightened to face her. "You seem to say that a lot. I'm not sure you even know what it means."

Oh, she knew the meaning of that word more than most people.

"Why didn't you tell me, Lenore?"

"By the time I knew Jed was on the way, we were miles from where I'd last seen you."

"You could've told me any time this past week."

"I was frightened," Lenore admitted. "You were so angry that night at the jail, about how I'd left. I couldn't gather the gumption to tell you. I was afraid you'd take Jed, make me leave, and raise him on your own. I asked you if you wanted children and you said you couldn't let yourself think about it. I couldn't risk it. I was working on getting him back from Ophelia. I can't lose him again." *I won't lose him.*

"So, when I was asking you about the baby's father last night, you must've had a lot of fun at my expense. Although I will say that I'm glad there's not another husband out there somewhere."

Lenore's calm words belied the frustration building inside her. "You are the only man I married."

He scowled. "When was Jed born? And where? What's his full name?"

Lenore told him the boy's birthdate. *Her son would always know when he was born, and where.* "We were in Mississippi by the time he was born. His name is Jedidiah Nathaniel Calhoun. Named for my grandfather and you."

The look he gave her was skeptical. "I don't know whether to believe that or not. It could be something you're making up as you go. Is there a record of his birth? Who was the doctor?"

"No records, no doctor. Do you doubt that you're his father?"

Shaking his head, Nathan said, "No doubts about that at all. What I doubt is that he's really named after me. You lie when it would be every bit as easy to tell the truth."

Lenore wanted to pick up one of the big medical books on his desk and hit him over the head with it. But she swallowed every bit of her frustration and fury.

As always, she was up against someone with more power. Nathan Calhoun was a fine, upstanding citizen. A doctor, with two lawmen for brothers. The whole town seemed to know and love him. If ever there was a question of who should raise the boy, the decision would not go in her favor.

Even if it galled her to do it, she would say whatever Nathan wanted her to say, or do whatever he wanted her to do, in order to stay near her son.

"He was glad to see you," Nathan said. "Does he know who you are?"

"Yes, he knows I'm Mama. Just not sure what that means to him." *Not as much as it would mean someday.* She would spend the rest of her life making up for the time they'd lost together.

And no one was going to stop her.

CHAPTER NINE

LENORE WATCHED NATHAN and Jed as they walked along the banks of the Brazos River searching for rocks, smiling at her son every time he glanced in her direction.

For all outward appearances she probably seemed serene. But inwardly, she was shaky and scared. *What was Nathan planning to do?*

She'd spent the past two days in an emotional turmoil, pondering that question. One minute, Nathan would be deep in thought, then next he'd be talking to Jed, gently teasing, trying to coax a smile from the boy, and all but ignoring her. It was nerve-wracking wondering when he'd ask her to leave.

Nathan no longer took her with him when he tended patients. Instead, he took Jed.

Was it because he knew she wasn't going anywhere without her son? Or because he didn't want her around? *Or maybe he hoped she'd leave while they were gone.*

If the latter was what Nathan was hoping for, he was in for a disappointment. She wasn't going anywhere without her child.

Nathan hadn't been openly angry with her or said anything hurtful since the night he'd returned. That was part of the problem. He hadn't *said* much of anything. Not after he'd asked her the questions. And hadn't believed her answers.

What had she expected? That he would suddenly announce they could be a family. That he loved her. Standing, Lenore brushed dirt from her dress, and walked along the bank with Nickel for a while.

Nathan had announced at breakfast that they were going to the river. He wanted Jed to spend some time outdoors. He didn't realize they both spent a great deal of time outside. Lenore often walked beside the wagons instead of riding, and once they'd set up camp, she'd been off and exploring as a child. Until it was time for her to go to work. Jed hadn't spent as much time outside as she had, but he enjoyed it, too.

Nathan and Jed took their boots and socks off now and waded into the water. He was showing the boy how to skip rocks.

Lenore looked around. They weren't far from where the medicine show set up camp. If she hadn't been arrested, Nathan might never have known about his son. Lenore couldn't regret that.

What had happened to the show? She missed Gordon and even Ship. But not the others. Ophelia was sure to be furious that her plans were thwarted. Hopefully, she hadn't taken her anger out on them.

Noise from the woods behind her drew Lenore's attention.

As if her thoughts had conjured them up, Shipley and Gordon emerged, followed closely by Sheriff Eli Calhoun and Deputy Bliss.

"Found these two prowling around your place," Eli told Nathan.

Nathan scooped Jed up and held him close, then walked over to stand by Lenore.

Even though Lenore knew Gordon and Shipley wouldn't hurt her son, she was glad Nathan was willing to protect him.

The men greeted both Jed and Nickel, fondly, while the dog danced around their feet, and Jed smiled at them. All of it seemed to irritate Nathan.

Gordon and Ship looked a little worse for the wear. Gordon's unruly black hair needed a combing, and the few scraggly whiskers on his chin meant he hadn't shaved in days. His clothes were ragged, his shoes worn and scuffed.

Ship's clothing was clean, his long gray hair was combed, yet even he looked less than his usual polished self.

"What are y'all doing here?" she asked.

Shipley gave a despondent shrug. "Looking for you."

"The others took off," Gordon said. "They stole some of the wagons. And Ophelia's gone. She and the main wagon disappeared."

Gordon didn't seem terribly upset about the fact. Then again, the boss was harder on him than the others. Lenore never understood why he'd taken it. Even though Gordon was crippled, there had to have been a better life out there. She guessed he'd find out now.

"Ophelia just left y'all?"

Ship nodded. "She was upset about..." He tilted his head toward Jed but didn't finish the sentence. "We didn't realize what she'd done until it all started falling apart. I thought she'd sent the boy back to you. She didn't tell me or Gordon what was going on. Sorry, lass."

"The thieves took my laboratory," Gordon added before Lenore could respond.

Poor Gordon. "I'm so sorry." The young man fancied himself a chemist, mixing and blending various medicines and elixirs, adding his own secret ingredients. He'd called his collection of tubes, funnels and bottles his laboratory. When they had a show, his concoctions were always well received by the public. Gordon gave out free samples and people always came back for more. He usually sold out. People would swear they felt better afterwards.

Lenore wasn't sure how much of it was the young man's talent, and how much was the proven popularity of anything with a high alcohol content. But Gordon believed it helped people, and that truly made him happy.

"We came to see what you're doing," he said now.

With a resentful look over his shoulder at Bliss, Shipley added, "Didn't know it was a crime to visit an old friend."

Nathan spoke up. "Were they actually in the house?"

"No, by the backdoor," Eli said. "Thought maybe you should know."

Eli's expression was hard to read, but the old deputy glared at the pair—letting his dislike for them show, loud and clear.

"Are they under arrest?" Lenore asked.

Eli answered. "No."

"But we've been asked to leave," Gordon said.

"Oh."

"They said we could say goodbye to you," he added.

"I'm glad you did. What are you two going to do now?"

"Thinking I might head to California," Gordon said. "Wanted to see if you were interested in coming with me."

Lenore didn't need to think about her answer. "No. But I hope you're happy there. I wish you all the best."

Even if that destination appealed to her, Lenore wasn't leaving Moccasin Rock without her son, no matter what Nathan decided about their marriage. She turned her attention to the older man. "What about you, Ship?"

He heaved a dramatic sigh; head back, eyes closed. "There is nothing either good or bad, but thinking makes it so."

Lenore recognized the quote from Shakespeare. As usual, it didn't answer her question. The deputy's expression of disgust was almost comical.

"Are you going to California with Gordon?" Lenore asked.

"No, I'll keep searching for Ophelia," Shipley said. He swept his arm out in a theatrical flourish. "But for two-bits I'd throw myself into that there Brazos River."

Bliss started digging around in his pockets. "I know I've got that much somewhere," he muttered.

Eli, lips twitching, shot him a warning look.

"The man thinks the sun comes up in the morning just to hear him crow," Bliss whispered loudly. "Ain't nothing he says makes a lick of sense."

Eli pulled him away, "Let them say their goodbyes."

Lenore was probably the only one who noticed Ship's expression. He wasn't insulted by the deputy's comments. He was pleased. To Shipley Bidwell, attention of any kind was preferable to being ignored.

When Gordon waved goodbye to Jed, Ship did too. Jed smiled, then tried to get down from his father's arms.

"I think he wants to hug them bye," Lenore whispered. She could tell it bothered Nathan, yet he handed Jed to her without comment.

He watched Ship and Gordon closely while they talked to the boy, ready to pounce if they made a wrong move. She understood his concern, but he should be grateful. These two had made Jed's life better than it might have been. Hers too.

"Will you write me a letter?" Gordon asked Lenore. Nathan had Jed back and it was time to go.

Lenore smiled. "If you'll send me one first so I'll know where to send it." She hugged them both, feeling tears well up. These two were the only friends she'd had except for her grandfather, and the only ones after he'd died. "Now y'all take care of yourselves."

After they'd gone, under the watchful eye of the law, Lenore returned to her previous spot and stared out over the water, not even attempting conversation with Nathan.

He came and sat beside her, still keeping watch on Jed and Nickel.

"I need you to help me understand all this," he said softly. "I know you were with the show because your grandfather was. And

I know you left on our wedding night because Ophelia threatened to kill me."

He turned and looked her in the eye. "But there's more. Why did you really marry me?"

When faced with such a direct question, and obvious need for the truth, what could she do?

Drawing in a shaky breath, Lenore said, "I married you because I'd found out Ophelia arranged for me to be married to someone else. And a payment had been arranged."

He looked at her, eyes wide. "Payment? She was paying someone to take you?"

"No, someone was paying her."

His jaw tightened. "They should've both gone to jail for that."

Probably so. "Since Grandpa died, I'd been planning on leaving the show. But I was scared. Not only that Ophelia would find me, but that I would be on my own. I'd never been alone before. I was trying to figure it all out in my head. One morning while we were working in Birmingham I went into town with the others, and then back to the wagon to get the potion Gordon gave me in case I got in trouble."

Nathan seemed to bristle at the reminder of that, so she hurried on.

"I overheard Ophelia talking to someone. It was an older man. He'd been out to the campsite once before. Ophelia made me talk to him that first time. He was wearing fine clothes, but he stunk to high heaven. He wasn't overly fond of bathing. I didn't like the way he looked at me. Made my skin crawl."

Lenore rubbed her arms against the chill seeping into her, but it went deeper than her skin.

"On this particular day, I'd spotted his fancy carriage. That's why I snuck in. Didn't want to talk to him. When I was leaving camp again, I heard Ophelia say I'd be packed and ready to go the next morning. Then she asked when she'd be paid. He told her she'd have her money when he had the girl. Then he asked...some personal questions about me. I couldn't quite make sense of what they were talking about. Then I finally understood."

Nathan closed his eyes. *He understood, too.*

"My stomach hurt so bad I couldn't breathe," Lenore said. "I knew then that I should've run away when I had the chance, the day after grandpa died."

Lenore resisted the urge to close her own eyes, to block it all out. She needed to tell him everything. "I made it back to town that day where the others were working the crowd, but I was so shook...shaken, I couldn't get my bearings. I was supposed to send a signal to Ship, so he would know who the mark was when it was time for him to start his carrying on. I forgot all about that. Instead, I went looking for you. I never intended for you to get caught up in everything. I knew you didn't have any money. We'd talked enough. But I hadn't even thought to find anyone else."

He turned a puzzled glance her way. "Why were you looking for me?"

"I don't know. I was hurt and scared, and for some reason the first person I wanted to talk to, was you."

He turned to stare out at the water again.

"Then, just when I found you, Ship marched up and started in with the whole routine before I could stop him. I was so embarrassed, imagining what you were thinking. When you said you'd marry me, I about fell over. I knew it was wrong. You were being threatened. But I saw my chance to get away, for good. And I liked you so much. As I said before, you were clean, young and nice. My freedom, a chance at happiness, was standing right in front of me, and I grabbed for it. I'm so sorry."

Nathan closed his eyes again. "What happened after you left me...after Ophelia came and got you that night? Why didn't you run when you got to the next town?"

"I wasn't in any condition. I couldn't work because of the beating she gave me."

"Ophelia beat you?" There was an edge to his voice now.

"Yes." *And it would've been worse if Shipley and Gordon hadn't intervened.* "Ship stopped her. Told her he would leave if she ever touched me again. Gordon did, too."

"Good! I'm glad you had someone standing up for you."

"But I wanted her to send me into town. I was going to find someone and beg for help. I figured in that condition, maybe someone would believe me. But she'd realized that, too. She kept me under close watch. Still, I was determined to find my way back to you."

He nodded but didn't say anything.

"When I was healed enough, Ophelia decided since I'd ruined her plans and gotten married behind her back, that I owed her the money the man was willing to hand over."

"How much was it?"

"That's just it, she would never tell me an exact amount. I agreed to continue with what I'd always done, but I was buying time. I planned on making a run for it the first chance I got. Then the sickness came. I didn't realize Jed was coming. I think Ophelia knew before I did. She was furious. I was so sick that I lost weight, couldn't even crawl out of bed some days."

Lenore realized she was twisting her hands together and forced herself to stop. "After a few months, when the swelling came, I didn't work as much. It wasn't like I could slip on a fancy dress and into a gambling house. And I couldn't get close enough to pick pockets. In some ways, those were the happiest few months of my life, and in other ways I understood I'd always had it easy."

His brow wrinkled. "Easy?"

"In some ways. Ophelia always made sure I was kept fed and clean and had pretty dresses to wear so it would be easier for me to get close to people. Since I couldn't do that anymore, she put me to work doing the laundry, gathering wood for the fires, fetching water, even trapping animals for our supper. But I was so sick I didn't even do most of that well enough to suit her."

"She didn't have you examined by a doctor or midwife?"

"No. And I didn't know enough about birthing to even be scared or worried. I didn't know what was in store."

"Was it a difficult labor and delivery?"

Lenore shrugged. "I don't know. Not sure what it's like for other women. I missed my grandpa during that time. Knowing I'd soon have a little one kept me going."

"Who delivered Jed?"

"There was a girl who traveled with the show for a while, telling fortunes. A skinny, pale girl with the deadest eyes I'd ever seen. I felt sorry for her and wasn't even sure why. She'd given birth, somewhere at some time, and she came and told me what I needed to know. She was there for a while when Jed came. I was grateful. I didn't know anything about babies. I even asked her when Jed's eyes would open. I'd only ever been around baby animals. I didn't know that human babies were different."

Nathan was shaking his head, eyes closed again. Lenore couldn't tell what he was thinking.

She started to tell him about the other thing that had gotten her through those long days and nights, but she was afraid he wouldn't believe her. She wasn't sure he was believing anything she was saying. *It was all the truth.*

"When Jed was born, I once again made my plans to leave. I didn't tell a soul, not even Gordon or Ship. As soon as I was on my feet again, I made a sling out of one of the fortune teller's scarfs to tie Jed to me so I could walk faster. The weather was bad, and I was waiting for it to get better because I wasn't sure where or how I'd find food or shelter. During those months, I walked with Jed strapped to me so I could get used to it."

Lenore didn't really want to talk about the days that followed.

The most wretched days of her life. But he needed to know how she'd ended up in the predicament she was in. "One morning, right before I planned to leave, Ophelia came and took Jed from me. He was eating some soft foods by then, but he wasn't fully weaned. I fought her, but she had her henchman holding me back. She'd waited until Shipley and Gordon were gone to do it. She said I could have my baby, and my freedom, when I made enough to repay her. That Jed would be staying with her, and if I tried anything at all, she'd disappear with him and I'd never see my baby again."

Nathan's hands curled into fists as he muttered something under his breath. The muscle in the side of his jaw ticked.

"At first I was so miserable I thought I would die," Lenore said. "A few days later Ophelia brought him back to me because he was fussy, then took him again the next day. Sometimes she'd bring him to me when he was getting on her nerves. Whenever it was inconvenient. I cherished those moments. But she always, always, had someone waiting, watching. Guarding me. And she delighted in telling me how pathetic Jed's life would be if I was ever arrested. And that she could make it happen."

He turned a disbelieving gaze her way. "This went on for a couple of years? Why didn't you knock her in the head and run?"

Lenore struggled to explain. "She kept me off-guard, unbalanced, especially with those big men she'd hired standing right beside her. Sometimes, while she and I argued, she'd hand Jed to one of them, knowing that the sight of my innocent baby in their hands would shut me up, shut me completely down." Lenore curled her own hands into fists. "I plotted and planned my getaway over and over again. I could've escaped numerous times, but not with Jed. And I wasn't about to leave him."

"Of course not. I'm glad you didn't."

"When your brother Eli caught me the other day, and I saw that badge, I nearly fainted. Then I started fighting. And not only

because Ophelia would be furious. I kept thinking about Jed growing up without me. I couldn't let that happen. By the way, I think
the only reason Eli caught me was because I was distracted. He
looked familiar."

She couldn't keep the tremor from her voice. "I figured surely
I'd made enough to pay Ophelia back by now, and she'd let me
take Jed and go soon. Then you made me stay here in Moccasin
Rock, leaving Jed with Ophelia. Gordon said he and Shipley would
watch over him, they've done it before. I thought I could get away
and get back to Jed…" She let her words trail off. He knew what
happened from that point.

Nathan was silent and perfectly still for several minutes.
Finally, he said, "I'm sorry, Lenore."

*Sorry for what? For what she'd gone through? Sorry he'd married
her? Sorry he wanted her to leave?*

Nathan suddenly pushed to his feet, but all he said was, "I
think we should get on home."

All that day Lenore waited for him to ask her more questions.
She was ready to tell him anything he wanted to know. But he'd
gone quiet again. She couldn't sleep that night, holding Jed and
scared to let him go.

The next morning, Nathan seemed fine at breakfast, eating
the fried eggs and biscuits she made for him. She wasn't sure they
were prepared the way he liked, and she'd almost burned the biscuits, but he didn't complain. Yet two things bothered her. He still
wasn't talking much, and he was wearing his church clothes again.
Where was he going?

With one last drink of his coffee, he pushed his chair back and
stood. "I've got something I need to do. I'll be gone a couple of
days. If you or Jed need anything, anything at all, tell Eli or Caleb.
They'll take good care of you."

He was leaving town?

Nathan walked down the hall to his office with Lenore on his heels. Picking up a satchel, he withdrew a few items and placed them on his desk, then returned to the kitchen and on into the bedroom. Again, Lenore followed, watching as he took clothing from the dresser and placed them in the bag.

"Where are you going?"

He ran a hand through his hair, avoiding her gaze. "I don't know how to explain, but there's something I need to do."

What did that mean?

Nathan wasn't being unkind, he was…distant. Again. It was driving her crazy. Lenore almost preferred the anger he'd shown before. At least she understood that emotion. Was he going to see a lawyer? That shouldn't take days unless he was seeing one in another town. She thought back on the businesses she'd seen while walking with Abby. *No lawyer here.* Unease filled her heart and mind again.

Back in the kitchen, Nathan stared at Jed with such tenderness that it hurt Lenore to watch. Then he shifted his attention to her. "Lenore, don't leave Moccasin Rock." He didn't seem angry anymore. Just resigned.

Lenore did what she'd always done, choked back any protest or whisper of defiance. And disappointment. He still didn't trust her. Had she traded one keeper for another?

Nathan crouched down in front of Jed. "I've got to be gone for a little while. I'll be back as soon as I can. Do you understand?" Jed didn't speak, but he nodded as Nathan hugged him.

Lenore was glad her son understood. But she didn't.

CHAPTER TEN

NATHANIEL WALKED DOWN the street, amazed he was managing to put one foot in front of the other.

He was still reeling, not only from finding out about Jed, but from everything Lenore told him.

It felt kinda like the first time he'd been thrown from a horse. It hadn't been a straight fall like he'd expected. The animal had jerked and bucked around so much Nathaniel hadn't known up from down until he hit the ground.

And that's the way it was now. Disoriented didn't even begin to describe it.

As much as he hated hearing what he had from Lenore, Nathaniel knew in his heart, in his gut, that she was telling the truth. About everything. He believed every horrific, nauseating detail.

And she'd been on her own. He hadn't known whether to laugh or cry when she'd admitted not knowing when a baby's eyes would open. He wished he could've been there for the birth. To help her, to help *them.* His son had been born in a medicine show wagon and Nathaniel hadn't even known. Now that he did, what should he do? What could he do?

Things were spinning out of control. He needed to get his life in order. But there were things he had to tend to first.

His first stop was Peg Harmon's house. After practicing midwifery in the area for years, the woman had picked up an impressive list of other medical skills. If she was willing, and had the time, she was more than capable of looking after his patients for a couple of days.

Since his mother was staying with Peg, he would talk to her at the same time. After growing up without her, and believing she'd been killed when Indians raided their cabin, he and Eli had been reunited with their mother last fall. She'd moved in with Peg, temporarily, then stayed on to help her with a record number of births in the area. Mama had gone through so much, and he hadn't wanted to add to her burdens by telling her the mess he'd made of his life. He'd been avoiding her in hopes that she hadn't heard about Lenore yet. But it was time.

Peg Harmon's house was the last one on the eastern-most street in town. She was sitting on the front porch.

She greeted him with a smile. "Hey, Nathaniel, what brings you by? Your mother's still with the Holcombs, helping with the new twins. It's hard to believe two tiny babies can keep four adults so busy. It's taken all of us to care for them."

Peg was one of the first people Nathan had met in Moccasin Rock and was still one of his favorites. Tall, willowy, with gray hair she wore in a braid wrapped around her head, she had a quick smile and a soft voice.

He lowered himself into the other chair. "How are the babies doing? I told Timothy Holcomb to send for me if y'all needed anything."

"They're doing fine. Small, but strong. You want some coffee?"

"Just had a cup. I do need a favor, though. I'll be gone for a few days. Is there any way you could keep an eye on a few of my patients?"

"Sure. Anyone in particular?"

"Old Ezra had a run-in with a bull. I sewed him up, but I'm worried about infection." As they discussed that case and a few others, Peg nodded along, asking a question here and there. "I'll handle it," she said when he was done.

"Thanks, I sure appreciate it. When will Mama be back? I... have something I need to talk to her about."

Peg's eyes filled with concern. "She should be back tomorrow. Is everything okay?"

"Have you heard about my wife being here?" He didn't stumble over the words this time, but it still felt strange.

"Yes. I figured you'd bring her by when you got the chance. I missed seeing her at church, we were already at Holcombs." Peg leaned back in her chair. "Your mother doesn't know about your wife?"

Nathaniel shook his head. "It's a long story. I wasn't sure what was going to happen between me and Lenore. And then I found out I have a son."

Peg's eyes lit up. "That's wonderful news. Isn't it?"

"Most definitely. But Mama's going to fall in love with Jed the second she lays eyes on him. Maybe Lenore, too."

"I see. You didn't want her to be hurt if things didn't work out."

"Yes. I wasn't sure Lenore wouldn't try to take off."

"I think it's normal to feel protective of your mother, but she's tougher than you know. Especially after everything she's been through."

He hadn't considered it that way. "I guess she'd have to be. I'll tell her everything as soon as I get back."

Nathaniel stood to leave. Peg stopped him with a question. "How old is your son?"

"He's three. His name is Jed." Nathaniel heard the pride in his own voice and marveled at the feeling. *He was a father again.*

She rose to her feet and hugged him. "Congratulations."

"Thanks, Peg. And thanks for helping me out."

After leaving her house, Nathaniel walked to the school, on the western most edge of town.

The teacher, Miss Wilhelmina Kirk, had come down with a severe case of laryngitis more than a week ago. A real problem for someone in her profession. Nathaniel had recommended a course of treatment for her, but with the unexpected turn his own life had taken, he hadn't thought to follow up on it.

Before leaving town, he wanted to know if the treatment was successful or not.

Nathaniel eased open the door of the school, not wanting to interrupt. He remained in the cloakroom, peering in at the class. He could see Mina, a pretty, dark-haired woman, writing spelling words on the blackboard—words for the younger students on the left side, words for the older students on the right.

The children were dutifully bent over their slates, chalk in hand, some flying through the assignment, others laboring along.

Turning, Mina spotted Nathaniel. He pointed to his own throat in question. She smiled and nodded, assuring him she was better, and then turned to the board again, writing across the bottom, "Test on Friday. Study," and underlining it.

Nathaniel heard a couple of audible groans from the class. If Mina heard them, she didn't react. She really was a sweet woman. He'd accompanied her to a church social once, at the urging of several other church members, but nothing about the outing seemed right.

Not wrong, exactly, just not right. *Now he knew why.*

Eli's son Brody turned and waved at him, as did Jamie Wilson, and Abby's brother, Robby. They were all sitting together. He got the feeling they'd rather be somewhere else—either fishing or exploring. Jamie also did deliveries for Silas and other merchants, to earn extra money for his family. Class time really cut into his entrepreneurial endeavors.

There were lots of other Wilson kids scattered around the room, and still others at home. There were nine of them all together.

Jillie Wilson was back in class. He'd removed her appendix a few weeks ago and she'd declared them friends forever. She smiled and waved now—one of the cutest kids he'd ever seen—reddish blond pig tails, a sprinkling of freckles across her nose, and a couple of missing teeth. Nathaniel winked at her. She giggled, then placed a hand over her mouth. The child had been fascinated by her own surgery, asking him all sorts of questions before and after. Wouldn't surprise him if she grew up to become a nurse someday. Or perhaps even a doctor.

Jillie turned back to her work, but Nathaniel didn't leave right away. He tried to imagine Jed here in a few years, with his books and lunch pail. Would his son be a good student? He and Eli owed their early education to a few kind-hearted people they'd met along the way. Learning a lot about some things—things they may have been better off not knowing—and little about others. He and Lenore had that in common.

Then later, Tessa's father insisted they get a real education. Eli had been ready to bolt when the man had taken them to school, so Judge Stewart hired tutors. Eli still hated it, and hadn't lasted long, but he'd learned enough to get by. Nathaniel had thrived on it. Loving the challenge. It would be interesting to see how it went with Jed.

With one last look at the kids, Nathaniel headed on to his next stop, the new drug store in town.

He smiled at the new gold lettering on the large plate glass window. *Moccasin Rock Drug Store. Carmichael Cook, Druggist. Established 1892.*

Right after the first of the year, Carmichael—a young man with short curly hair and a ready smile—had shown up in Moccasin Rock, bringing along a wagon load of goods and a dream for the future. He'd purchased an empty building downtown and set up shop.

At first Silas Martin considered him competition—they sold some of the same merchandise—but the young druggist's sunny disposition and work ethic quickly endeared him to everyone. Nathaniel could see the man now through the window, working behind the counter.

Carmichael sat aside the mortar and pestle he was using and wiped his hands when Nathaniel pushed open the door. "Come on in."

"How's business?"

"Splendid," Carmichael said. "I've had people in and out all morning. A few of them actually made purchases."

Nathaniel laughed. "Don't get discouraged. It takes time to build up a business."

"Don't worry. I'm in this for the long haul. I've heard that Fair Haven is the future, but there's something about Moccasin Rock I like. I plan on living the rest of my life here."

"Glad to hear it."

Being the only physician in town, Nathaniel missed having someone to talk to about medicine. He was grateful for Peg, and now Carmichael. The first time they'd met, after a Sunday church service, he and the young druggist discussed everything from leeches and bloodletting to advancements in the treatment of childbed fever. Even in a few short years, medicine had come a long way.

What would Carmichael say if he knew Nathaniel had recently used a dishrag to "gather" sickness? He'd tell him about it next time they had a chance for a long conversation.

"I came to ask for a favor," he told Carmichael now.

"Sure, Doc. Anything you need."

Nathaniel explained about being gone for a couple of days. "If

Peg Harmon needs anything, especially in the way of medications, will you help her out?"

"Of course. I appreciate all the help you've given me getting started."

More at ease now that he'd arranged for help, Nathaniel mentioned a few of the cases he'd discussed with Peg, and then headed on to his next stop. The bank.

The bank president, D.L. Jackson, greeted him as he walked through the door. The man had thinning gray hair, and a thick mustache he constantly smoothed. "Morning, Dr. Calhoun. What can I do for you?"

"Making a payment. The last one, if I've been keeping up with it correctly."

"I believe you're correct," Jackson said as he led him into his office. "Congratulations! Seems like such an auspicious occasion deserves some sort of celebration. Can I buy you a cup of coffee and a piece of pie at Bony Joe's?"

"I'm on my way out of town," Nathaniel said. "I'll be glad to take you up on that offer when I get back."

Nathaniel tucked the receipt into his pocket. "Wasn't sure you'd be here. Thought you might be at the planning committee meeting today."

"I was," Jackson said. "Left early. Couldn't take any more."

"That bad, huh?"

"Worse. You'll read all about it when the paper comes out."

After signing various documents and one ledger, and shaking the banker's hand, Nathaniel found himself back on the street.

Now he needed to find Eli. The jail was empty, but he knew where to find his brother. He was probably trapped in the same meeting Jackson had fled.

Nathaniel headed to the far end of the street. When he was done with Eli, he'd track down Caleb, and then be on his way.

Just before he reached the courthouse, the door opened, and

both his brothers stepped out, followed closely by several bickering town council members.

Falling into step beside his brothers, Nathaniel asked Eli, "They get anything settled?"

"Nope. Still about evenly divided."

"On what?"

"Everything," Eli said. "Especially where the new courthouse should be built, and who should build it."

"And how it should be built," Caleb added. "Some want limestone, others sandstone, and so on."

The old log cabin courthouse was too small. Everyone agreed on the need for a new one. But that's all they agreed on. Originally, Yates County was comprised of several tiny towns, but the others had dried up and blown away. Only Moccasin Rock was thriving, with a newly rebuilt hotel—after it burned the previous year—several new businesses, and a new bridge across the Brazos connecting them to Boone Springs.

There'd been talk that Claiborne County, of which Fair Haven was the county seat, would annex what was left of Yates County. Moccasin Rock citizens fought tooth and nail to protect and keep what they had. Now, they were fighting each other.

The problem, or one of them anyway, was that Moccasin Rock had not been laid out with a courthouse square. Now that they'd agreed on the need for a new courthouse, some people wanted to destroy main street and design a proper square, while others liked the idea of the current location at the end of the main street.

Nathaniel stepped out of the way as the postmaster, telegraph operator, and newspaper publisher passed by, all arguing.

"It's about to get even more contentious," Eli said. "They're running telephone line from Fair Haven within the month. Everybody's arguing over who will have the first phone and the switchboard."

"I hadn't heard that. What'd they want with you?"

"To take sides. The new courthouse will hold the jail, so they're each promising all sorts of things if I'll throw my support behind their particular idea."

He glanced at the satchel Nathaniel carried. "Were you coming to the meeting?"

"No. Glad I'm not involved."

Caleb grinned. "Oh, but you are."

"How's that?"

"You are part of the official opening ceremony of the Boone Springs bridge. Big doings." Caleb cast a grin in Eli's direction. "County and city officials and dignitaries of every sort will cross the bridge first, including the local sheriff. I can't remember exactly who, or in what order, but as the town physician you are expected to participate. Then the common town folk will cross."

"Good grief."

"Yep."

"If you weren't coming to the meeting, where you headed?" Eli asked.

"I'm going to be gone a couple of days. I was wondering if you two would keep an eye on Lenore and Jed."

Eli's brows shot up. "You're leaving? I figured you wouldn't let that boy out of your sight for a while."

"I don't want to," Nathaniel admitted. "Considered taking him with me. But I didn't want to do that to him or Lenore."

"Where you headed?"

"I'm going to see Tessa's folks."

Eli's expression softened. "Tell them hello for me. I've thought about them so many times through the years."

"Have you heard anything of them lately?"

"No," Eli said. "We sent letters back and forth for a while. I didn't hear anything after the last one."

Caleb had been quiet while they talked, now he cleared his

throat. "I'm glad you're both here. I've been meaning to ask y'all something. As you know, Abby is going to have a baby soon."

Nathaniel couldn't resist the urge to tease a little. "Do tell."

Caleb's exasperated look would've been comical if it wasn't so heartfelt.

"I know you're worried," Nathaniel reassured him, "But Peg has everything under control. And I'll be here to help if she needs me."

"Thank you. This is about something else. I was wondering how you two would feel about me naming the baby after Daddy. Just his middle name, Joseph. Not Amos. I will save that for one of y'all."

"I appreciate you asking," Eli said, "but you didn't need to. He was your father as much as he was ours."

"He's right," Nathaniel said.

Caleb glanced at the ground. "Yes. But I was blessed to have Daddy for most of my life. Y'all were robbed of that. I'm not taking his name too."

Nathaniel was touched by Caleb's statement, as was Eli, he figured. Most times, you couldn't tell what Eli was thinking, unless he wanted you to.

"What if it's a girl?" Nathaniel asked.

Caleb blinked at him. "We will call her Julia Irene, after my mother and Abby's. But that will be for our second child. This one's a boy."

Nathaniel and Eli exchanged glances. Caleb was so serious that it didn't seem right to laugh at him.

They were still talking when Al Jenkins, the man from the telegraph office, walked back up the boardwalk.

"Glad you're still here," he told Caleb as he handed him a message.

"Thanks, Al."

Caleb read it immediately. "It's from Captain Parnell. He

wants me searching for a man named Vincent Shields. Horse thief
and murderer. Rumored to be in this vicinity now. Captain wants
the fellow captured and confined by the time he gets here." He
glanced up. "Don't suppose either of you know where I can find
this Vincent."

"Never heard of him," Eli said. "It'll help if we have a
description."

Caleb nodded. "I'll get a telegram off to Captain, see if we
can't get one."

"I don't know anything about him either," Nathaniel said.
"But I don't like the idea that he's anywhere around here."

Folding the telegram, Caleb put it in his pocket. "Me either.
This changes things. I'm not sure how much help I'll be watching
over Lenore and Jed. I'll do what I can, though."

"Everyone will help take care of them," Eli said. "Go on and
do what you need to do, both of you."

After Caleb left, Eli walked with Nathaniel to the depot. The
place was busy, people milling all around talking to each other,
which provided a bit of privacy for the conversation he wanted
to have. He opened his mouth a couple of times, unsure where
to start.

Eli noticed. "Something on your mind?"

"Yeah, but I'm not sure how to say it."

"Just spit it out."

"Do you think it's possible to love two women equally, I mean
really love them both? And if not, is that fair to the other one?"

Eli pushed his hat back. "Love them? At the same time?"

"No, I mean during a lifetime."

"Sounds like you're doubting it."

Nathaniel shrugged. "I loved Tessa with all my heart, but I also
feel something for Lenore. I get aggravated with myself, and even
with her, because of it. Which doesn't make sense."

"Feel something? Like what?"

"I don't know. I was mad as all get-out when she first got here, over what happened in Alabama, but I think maybe I was angrier than the situation warranted. Plus, I can't help feeling sorry for her."

"Why's that?"

"In addition to taking her child, Lenore said Ophelia also beat her and kept her confined. I believe it. You and I know what that kind of life will do to you."

"Yep."

He and Eli had met with misfortune and cruelty at every turn for a while.

"But you're feeling more than pity for her?" Eli asked.

"Yes. Like I said, mostly anger, for a while. I was furious she hadn't told me about Jed. Imagining what could've happened to him if we hadn't gotten there when we did."

"Yes, that whole thing was a strange set-up."

"I was ready to strangle Lenore, or at least threaten her with that possibility. Then, when Jed and I walked in the door, she was hunched over the table like she was in physical pain." *He'd felt that pain.* "Until she saw Jed."

"Was the boy glad to see her, too?"

"Oh, yes. Without a doubt." Nathaniel hesitated again. "I know she's a criminal. Guilty of everything from petty theft to extortion. I also know she loves her son. My son. I'm never going to let her leave here with him. Ever. I don't want to take him away from her, either. For his sake, and for hers."

"I never figured for one second you'd take him away from her," Eli said. "You'd better figure out a way to make a family together. Soon."

The old feelings of guilt swamped him again. "That's what I'm worried about. What if I never feel about Lenore like I did Tessa?"

"Maybe you won't. But that has less to do with Lenore, than it does with you."

"What do you mean?"

"You're a different person now. You were young when you married Tessa, and after the life we'd led, you needed someone like her. I've thought about that before. Tessa was one of the first genuinely good people we were ever around. It was only natural to be drawn to her."

"Do you think Tessa and I would've outgrown that love?"

"No, I think you both would've grown, together."

Made sense. "I feel something for Lenore, I'm not going to deny it. But it's different than what I felt for Tessa."

Eli shrugged. "They're two different women. If you're expecting a girl who was raised like Lenore was to be the same as Tessa, that's unfair. My advice is to learn to appreciate Lenore for who she is, who she's capable of being. Tessa helped make you who you are. Lenore will do the same. Don't forget, though, that works both ways. You will influence her, too. Make what you say and do count for something."

That made even more sense. "How did you get to be an expert all of a sudden?"

Eli raised his hands. "Hey, you asked."

"I'm not sure how to move forward," Nathaniel admitted. "If I suddenly declare my love for Lenore, she'll know it's not true." *Was it?* "And anything else would be an insult."

"Yeah, you got to be careful about upsetting her," Eli said, rubbing his jaw. "She's a fighter."

Nathaniel cringed. "Sorry about that. I've never seen her react violently. I've seen her use charm and trickery, but not violence. She was terrified."

Eli nodded. "Even when it happened, I knew it was instinct. You and I have both been there."

"Yes." Lenore was no innocent, yet there was something both fierce and fragile about her that pulled at Nathaniel's heart in a way no other female had.

He told Eli about going to see Sister. "Lenore helped her in ways I didn't think were important at the time. In hindsight they meant a lot to Sister. And that mattered to Lenore. You can pretend to be a lot of things—at least for a while—including smart and sophisticated. Kindness is harder to fake. It's the little things. She's not a bad person."

"I noticed you let her call you Nathan," Eli said, in a slightly disgruntled tone.

"What?"

"You wouldn't let me call you that."

"Oh, come on. I haven't minded being called Nathan in years." As a youngster, he wanted to be called Nathaniel because he thought that made him sound older. Growing up in Eli's shadow, asserting his independence had been important to him.

"I have such mixed-up feelings about Lenore," he told Eli now, struggling to explain something he didn't even understand himself.

"Like I said before, you'd better get it all sorted out. Soon. There's a kid involved now."

CHAPTER ELEVEN

In Galveston, Nathaniel felt as if he'd stepped back in time.

The sun, the salt air, the screech of the seagulls overhead all evoked memories of another life, another *him*. He walked along the beach, but stayed away from the crowds, memories assaulting him with every soft laugh that floated his way.

Remembering times when he and Tessa had left footprints in the sand, her torn between showing her ankles, or having the hem of her skirt wet. Him hoping for a look at her ankles. Pockets full of seashells they'd gathered. A bonfire on the beach sponsored and chaperoned by the church.

After Tessa and the baby died, even thinking about those times had made him feel like he was drowning on dry land.

This time, something was different. It took him a moment to realize what it was.

He was remembering, but he could still breathe. And he was smiling at the memories. For so long he couldn't.

Leaving the beach and heading toward the Stewart home, Nathaniel thought back to the day he and Eli first met the judge.

Their father had disappeared one day and never returned. Then their mother was gone in the blink of an eye. He and Eli were on their own at an age when most kids couldn't even tie their shoes. The ensuing years were spent trying to survive. At one point they'd been taken in by a snake of a neighbor, another time by a charming psychopath in San Angelo. Escaping by the skin of their teeth both times.

There had been nice people along the way, but none with the means or motivation to help them long term. Until they'd crossed paths with Judge Stewart.

They were older by then, but still too young to be on their own. After yet another series of narrow escapes, he and Eli had decided to seek their fortunes in New Orleans. Then they'd fallen asleep on the docks and were arrested for vagrancy. They were too old for an orphanage, but they could still be sent to the poorhouse, or worse. Some young boys were sent to jail. No telling what would've happened to them there. Same thing if they'd made it to New Orleans.

They hadn't known that back then, of course, all they'd known was they were in trouble. After surviving the tragedies of their childhood, a lack of sleep was their downfall. At least that's what they'd thought at the time.

One man and woman made all the difference in the world. Edward and Frances Stewart saw something in the Calhoun boys that was worth rescuing.

They'd provided shelter and food. They'd taught them respect, for others and for themselves. The couple also insisted the boys attend church. At the time it hadn't meant much to them. Nathaniel had been more interested in the opportunity to sit next to Tessa for an hour. But the Stewarts had not given up on the Calhoun boys.

Eventually, they'd given their blessing to Nathaniel marrying their daughter. If they'd hoped for someone else, someone with more promise or potential, they'd never let on.

How old were they now? Had they ever adjusted to life after Tessa and Becky's death? After graduation, Nathaniel had sent a letter letting them know he'd completed his studies. He hadn't heard back from them.

Turning onto the street where they lived, Nathaniel was struck by how ordinary the house appeared. There were grander structures, mansions, nearby, and there were also cottages a short distance away. This house fell somewhere in between. To the casual passerby, it would seem unremarkable in every way.

It would always be special to Nathaniel. This is where he'd known comfort and security, and, if only for a time, true happiness.

He climbed the steps, mind grappling with what he'd say. Then he noticed the welcome mat was missing, and the planters were empty. The swing, where he and Tessa whiled away hours talking about their future, was gone. There was an air of neglect to the place.

Concerned, Nathaniel tugged on the bell pull, relieved at the sound of footsteps. But it was an unfamiliar face that greeted him. A young boy. Perhaps thirteen or fourteen.

"Yes, sir?"

"I'm here to see Judge and Mrs. Stewart."

The boy's brows drew together. Clearly, it wasn't what he'd expected Nathaniel to say. "But they've passed away."

Nathaniel's stomach sank. "They're dead? Both of them?"

"Yes, sir."

"I didn't know."

"Were you a friend of the family?"

"Son-in-law."

"Oh. I'm sorry." He invited Nathaniel to step inside. As the boy spoke, explaining that his family recently purchased the home, Nathaniel glanced around.

"We have only begun to refurbish," the boy said. "Papa wants to paint the parlor white, but Mama is fond of a seafoam color." He lowered his voice. "I suspect Mama will prevail."

Several young girls entered the room. Each with big eyes, merry smiles, and matching white ribbons in their long brown hair.

"These are my sisters, sir."

Nathaniel nodded to the girls as the boy rattled off their names, while his mind was taking in the changes to the place. The furniture was different, the old grandfather clock was missing, even the photographs adorning the mantle were of strangers. The Stewarts were truly gone.

"Sir, would you care to sit and rest awhile." The boy made the offer tentatively, and Nathaniel could tell he was relieved to have it refused.

"I appreciate your kindness, but I must be going."

Back on the street, Nathaniel wandered around aimlessly for a while. He wasn't sure exactly why he'd wanted to see the Stewarts. Or what he'd have said had they been there. But to miss the opportunity to speak with them one last time—to thank them again—was a blow he hadn't expected.

There was comfort that the old house would know the ring of laughter and the sound of children's feet for years to come, but how he wished he'd gone to see them as soon as he returned to Texas. Why hadn't he?

Partly because he'd been caught up with his new medical practice, and partly because he was afraid it would bring up painful memories of their loss.

Without being aware he was headed there, Nathaniel looked up to find himself at the cemetery. The iron fence had a fresh coat of black paint, and there were more graves since the last time he'd been there, but it didn't take long to find the Stewart family plot.

It looked different than it had when he'd seen it last. There was a new headstone.

One of the good things to come from his time as the Texas Kid were regular wages. The first thing he'd done was send money to Judge Stewart and ask him to purchase a marker.

But Nathaniel's contribution alone couldn't have paid for this—a large angel, wings unfurled and face to the sky—standing atop a marble base. *In Loving Memory. Tessa Jane Calhoun. Rebecca*

Jane Calhoun. "I shall dwell in the house of the Lord forever." Psalm 23:6

It was beautiful.

Edward and Frances were buried next to their daughter and granddaughter, simpler stones marking their graves. They'd died six months apart, with Frances going first. What happened to them? Nathaniel wished he'd asked the boy at the house more questions.

He sat down on a nearby bench, realizing suddenly that he'd wanted to tell the Stewarts about Lenore and Jed.

For some reason he'd wanted their advice. Their blessing.

He'd wanted their forgiveness for moving on.

Eyes closed, Nathaniel lowered his head. He straightened at the sound of someone clearing their throat.

An older man dressed in work clothes and leaning on a hoe, was staring at him. "You all right?"

"I'm fine," Nathaniel said.

The man inclined his head toward the tombstones. "Those your folks?"

"Yes. My wife. My child. My in-laws."

The caretaker's expression softened. "You're a mighty young fellow to have gone through that much loss."

Nathaniel didn't feel young.

"My own wife died not long ago," the man said, as he settled down on the bench beside Nathaniel. "We were together more'n fifty years. Kinda lost on my own at times, but at least I had her with me for a good long while."

"I'm sorry for your loss," Nathaniel said. It didn't matter how long you'd had someone, or how old they were when they left you. It was going to hurt.

"Thank you," the man said. "Have you remarried?"

"In a manner of speaking."

"Don't rightly know what you mean by that."

"It's complicated," Nathaniel said. "There are some problems."

His expression cleared. "Oh. She's mean, huh?"

"No."

"Ugly?"

Nathaniel choked back the sudden urge to laugh. "No, she's not ugly." *Far from it.*

The man pushed his tweed cap back and scratched his head. "If she's halfway passable to look at, and ain't mean, then I don't see that you have a problem. Instead of mourning over what's gone, I'd grab on to what you got."

As the caretaker talked on, Nathaniel realized he was right. And Eli was right. After the man was gone, Nathaniel didn't linger.

With one last look at the angel marker, he traced their names with his fingertips and whispered a goodbye.

Letting go didn't mean forgetting. They would always live in his heart; but his life belonged to Lenore and Jed now.

He'd spoken vows to love, honor and cherish Tessa, "Til death do us part." And he had.

But he'd spoken those same vows again in Alabama. It was time he lived up to them.

No matter what Lenore's reasons were for marrying him, Nathaniel went into the marriage with his eyes wide open.

He hadn't known the extent to which he was being manipulated, but he'd known Shipley and Lenore were up to something.

Nathaniel wasn't waiting to hear from the Pinkerton agent before deciding what to do. He and Lenore would get married again. She and Jed were his family. He needed to get on home.

He'd planned on staying in Galveston overnight, but decided to return to the ferry instead. In no time at all he was on a train rolling north.

After eating the sandwich he'd picked up at a café, he tried to get some sleep. But he couldn't stop thinking about what he would say to Lenore.

How would he explain where he'd been, or why he'd felt it necessary to go?

Thankfully, Jed was too young to need explanations, but there were so many other things he needed. The one uppermost in Nathaniel's mind, was a father.

Nathaniel had missed out on having one, he wasn't going to miss out on being one. Lenore loved the kid, without a doubt, but had anyone else treated him kindly? Shipley and Gordon, he supposed.

Jed hadn't even smiled at him yet. *Not once.* Was it from fear? Or was it the same defensive measure he and Eli developed? He hoped not. Because that stoicism developed as a barrier, a guard. Protection. It was more difficult for someone to hurt you, or humiliate you, if they couldn't be sure it was working.

Nathaniel didn't want that for his son. He wanted a life of love and laughter. Lenore deserved that, too. But where did he start?

CHAPTER TWELVE

LENORE PEEKED OUT from the mouth of the cave at the rain coming down in sheets, trees bending nearly double, some breaking, from the fiercest winds she'd ever seen.

Stepping back, she called Nickel to follow as she returned to Abby's side further on into the cave.

"Still raining?" Abby's voice was showing the strain of the past few hours.

"Yes, coming down in buckets."

Abby had paced for a while. Now she was sitting down against the wall, with her hands behind her back. *She was hurting again.*

"That wind is unbelievable," Abby said. "If I didn't know there were no tracks out here, I would've sworn a train passed by."

Lenore shivered. "I heard it, too."

When they'd ducked into the cave to escape the downpour, neither knew it would be such a lengthy wait. *What a strange interruption to what started off as a day of fun.*

With Nathan gone, his family had once again been pressed into service to spend time with her. Did he think she'd still try to run? Or was he concerned for her and Jed's welfare?

Since the men folk were concentrating on finding some outlaw, Lenore hadn't seen much of them, but Maggie and Abby both acted like they were glad to see her, and they'd both accepted Jed into their homes without question, and without hesitation.

Lenore would be forever grateful for that.

They spent the previous day with Maggie, most of it outdoors. Despite Lenore's worry over Nathan, it had been one of the most carefree days she and Jed ever spent together.

Maggie had taken them to the creek that ran behind their house, and Jed had played with tadpoles and a grass snake. On the way back, Lenore had pointed out some poke weeds, or poke salat as some folks called it, explaining how good it was.

"You mean to eat?" Maggie's tone was skeptical, but she'd been willing to try it.

So, they'd gathered the weeds, and Lenore prepared them— the way she'd always done it. Boiled twice, drained, then added to scrambled eggs. It had made a simple, but satisfying, dinner.

Maggie had grown up in a big house in Fair Haven and hadn't foraged for much in the way of edibles. But she'd enjoyed the experience. *Or so she said*, Lenore recalled with a grin.

Today, Abby suggested the picnic. Jed had enjoyed the previous day's outing so much that Lenore jumped at the chance for another day in the sunshine and fresh air. Again, they'd had a great time, but the weather seemed odd from early on.

The sun had been beating down on them, hotter than Lenore was used to for sure, and even Abby noted it was strange for this time in April. Then the sky darkened.

About the time Lenore said, "I think it's blowin' up a storm," it was almost on them. The heat gave way to a wonderful coolness as she and Abby threw everything back into the picnic basket. Then the rains came, along with thunder, and jagged lightning crisscrossing the sky.

Fortunately, Abby had known about this cave near the Brazos River. They'd ducked inside right before the hail hit, still carrying the picnic basket and blankets. The cave was dark and damp, but at least they were safe from the howling winds and the downpour.

Once inside, Lenore was pleased and surprised to find there were a few candles, a match tin, and some other things in a burlap bag. She'd been even more surprised when Abby said they'd been left behind by her father the previous summer when he'd hidden in the cave after escaping from Caleb.

"Oh, everything worked out fine," Abby had said with a wave of her hand.

That was over an hour ago. And still the rain came.

Lenore returned to Abby, relieved to see her eyes closed.

Picking up a candle, hand around it to guard the flame from any wayward gusts, Lenore knelt to check on Jed. Still asleep. She was grateful he was such a sound sleeper, and that he was good and truly worn out.

Where had his father gone? Nathaniel acted so mysterious when he left. Was he trying to figure out how to legally remove her from his son's life?

Why hadn't she run with Jed when she had the chance instead of going on a picnic?

"Lenore?"

She hurried to Abby. "You okay?"

"I'm fine. Thought for a minute I'd dreamed all this."

"You're not dreaming, unless I am, too." Taking the remaining blanket from the basket, Lenore bunched it up and pushed it behind Abby, giving her at least a little something to lean into. Abby murmured thank you and then drifted off to sleep again.

Lenore couldn't nap, but her thoughts drifted, thinking about how she'd gotten to this place, to this point. She had regrets aplenty about her life. But she wouldn't undo it all or she wouldn't have Jed.

Of course, she hadn't known that when she'd first laid eyes on Nathan. She'd fallen in love with him pretty much at first sight.

But then a lot of girls, and even grown women, were awe-struck by the Texas Kid.

Lenore smiled at the memory. He'd seemed like something from one of the old yarns that Shipley told around the campfire. Those fairy tales. There was always a handsome prince, or a knight. But instead of a crown, or a coat of armor, Nathan had been decked out in white—from his hat to his boots—and had ridden in on a white horse.

It was an awe-inspiring sight. Still, if he'd been full of himself, Lenore probably would've lost interest in him pretty quick.

But she could tell that Nathan thought the whole thing was a lot of tomfoolery. He'd seemed almost embarrassed by the attention.

And that fascinated her.

Lenore had stopped picking pockets and pressed as close to the barricade as she could. Afterwards, instead of meeting Ship and Gordon, she'd slipped away and gone in search of the Texas Kid.

She often dressed as a boy, to better work the crowds. That day it had been an advantage. No one gave her a second glance when she followed Nathan after he left the arena. He'd dropped his hat when someone bumped into him. Lenore scooped it up and handed it back.

Nathan's eyes widened when he realized she was a girl, then he'd winked at her.

She'd been a goner from that moment on.

Ophelia had been making a windfall on the crowd the Turner Wild West Extravaganza drew—big crowds, big money for pickpockets—so they'd stayed in Birmingham until the larger show was scheduled to pull out.

While the others worked their usual games and tricks, Lenore had done just enough to keep Ophelia from guessing anything was different. Meanwhile, she'd followed Nathan everywhere, helping him with his horses and his scheduled practice of shooting and roping. And he'd let her tag along. Hadn't seemed to mind at all.

Ship and Gordon assumed she was carrying on with business as usual.

Lenore was supposed to pick the man in the crowd who looked like he'd have money, then talk to him enough to make sure he did.

Instead, she picked the one whose most treasured possession was a watch she'd had to pry from his hand.

Returning to Abby's side, Lenore studied the other girl's face in the flickering candlelight. Tensed up and troubled, even in sleep. Though Abby had remained outwardly calm, the experience was starting to wear on her. But it was more than that. Lenore had a sinking feeling there was about to be a baby born.

Abby's eyes opened. She seemed confused for a moment.

"How are you feeling?" Lenore asked.

"I'm okay. My back's hurting, but I'm sure it will pass. I've never been prone to backaches, but the last few days have been bad. This time is the worst yet."

When Jed was ready to be born, that's exactly how laboring started for Lenore.

Should she tell her? Abby's eyes drifted closed again before she could decide. Lenore went to the burlap bag and started going through it again. She removed the two remaining candles. She didn't want to waste them, but it was better than letting the one go out.

There'd been only one match in the tin. Being here, trying to deliver a baby without any light, was a terrifying thought. Hopefully, the rain would let up soon and she could go for help.

CHAPTER THIRTEEN

NATHANIEL SIGHED WHEN the train stopped at Donevy Gap. It was an unscheduled stop, and he wanted to press on. He hadn't slept during the night. He couldn't shake the feeling something was wrong. Nothing specific, nothing he could name. Just a feeling that had grown in the past few hours. He wanted to be home.

Several of the passengers stepped out on the platform, stretching their legs. He followed along. It had been hot earlier in the day, now there was a cool breeze blowing, and clouds dotted the midday sky.

There was a water barrel beside the door of the depot. Nathaniel used the dipper to take a drink and then approached the man behind the ticket window.

"Excuse me. Can you tell me why we stopped?"

"Checking the track."

"Thanks." Nathaniel was already turning away when the man's next words struck him like a blow.

"A tornado hit Moccasin Rock. We're making sure there wasn't any damage to the track between here and there."

Nathaniel shook his head. *He hadn't heard right.* "A tornado?

The man nodded so vigorously that his glasses slid down. "Yes, sir. The way I hear it, a fellow there rode a horse to Fair Haven, which is north of Moccasin Rock, to tell them what happened and to ask for help. Fair Haven relayed the news to several other towns. Said it hit right before the noon meal today. Nearly wiped the place clean off the map."

Nathaniel's stomach lurched. *No.*

The man talked on, "Fair Haven is sending a train with food and supplies. Supposed to be some nurses and doctors, too. But the track has to be examined first. We can't go on until we check this stretch from the south."

Spinning on his heel, Nathaniel bolted for the door.

"Hey mister, where you going?"

"Home. I've got to get home." *Please, God, let there be a home to get to.*

"But the train's not leaving yet."

Nathaniel heard him but didn't take time to respond. He wasn't waiting. Grabbing his satchel from the seat he'd occupied on the train, Nathaniel dashed off in search of the livery stable.

He finally located it, on the other end of town. He told the man where he was headed and was instructed to leave the horse with a Mr. Eagan Smith.

"Moccasin Rock got hit by a tornado," Nathaniel told him. "Not sure how Eagan's livery fared. But I still need to get home."

"I understand. Leave her in Boone Springs."

"Will do."

Grateful to be on his way, with a spirited animal that seemed ready to run, Nathaniel tore down the road in the direction of Moccasin Rock. He was praying it wouldn't be as bad as he'd heard, but he was also going over things he'd said and done before he left, and things he wished he'd said or done.

It was raining before he reached Boone Springs. Turning his collar up, Nathaniel pressed on, speaking words of encouragement to the horse, and praying.

Coming into Boone Springs from the other side, it took him

a minute to get his bearings, but he finally found the livery stable and left the horse—glad the man pulled the saddle off and began drying the mare down immediately.

Leaving the stable at a run, Nathaniel raced through town and toward the Brazos. Coming around a curve in the road, he stumbled to a stop when he encountered a huge pile of rubble before he got to the river.

It took him a minute to recognize it as the saloon where he'd found Lenore.

Nathaniel searched through the debris but didn't see anyone. He raced on again, telling himself that this wasn't a sign of how bad things might be in Moccasin Rock. This saloon was poorly constructed—he'd noticed it right away. It wouldn't have stood a chance against any high winds. *It wouldn't be this bad at home.*

He'd planned to take the ferry once he reached the river, but it was on the other side. Nathaniel thought about jumping in and swimming for the other bank, but the rain swollen river was high and raging. He stood there, trying to draw a full breath, panic clawing at his chest.

Then he remembered. *The bridge.*

Nathaniel took off up-river. Then another thought occurred. What if the bridge had been destroyed? Relieved to see it still standing, Nathaniel hurdled the barricade without slowing down.

The first Brazos River crossing at the new bridge hadn't been the celebratory occasion the local dignitaries imagined. But considering the circumstances, Nathaniel didn't think anyone would mind.

Hopefully, the clerk at Donevy Gap had heard wrong. *It couldn't be as bad as he'd said.*

⋧

The rain was still falling, but at least the wind had let up. Lenore returned to Abby's side.

"How are you feeling?"

"I'm all right," she whispered.

Lenore doubted it. But this woman was too polite, too nice, to say much else. Hopefully, there was a core of strength that ran through her. Maggie Calhoun had it. She was every bit as nice as Abby, but there was something about her that told you she could withstand any trial.

There was an innocence to Abby that Lenore couldn't have put into words if she tried.

But she could pick people like this out in a crowd. *Had picked them out.* Lenore envied such people in the past. Even resented them for how naïve they were.

Now she found herself hoping with all her heart Abby would always have that innocence. For now, though, she would also need a strong streak of fortitude and strength.

Gumption, Grandpa would've called it.

Lenore thought of Nathan's wife, Tessa. *First wife,* she reminded herself. Even though she and Tessa never met, Lenore knew the woman was one of those innocent people.

How did Nathan feel about being married to someone who wasn't so innocent? Is that why he'd been so quiet? Lenore couldn't change her past. She'd stolen, cheated and lied more by the time she'd reached adolescence than any ten people probably did their whole lives. But she could try harder to act like a lady now. More like Abby and Maggie. *Maybe then Nathan would want to keep her.*

"Is Jed still asleep?" Abby whispered.

"Yes."

"I'm glad, because I think I'm in trouble," Abby said.

"Is the pain getting worse?"

Abby nodded, then bit her lip. "And my water…" She gestured to the ground beneath her.

Oh, no. "Abby, do you know what to expect?"

"Yes. I've talked to Peg Harmon."

Lenore knew who the midwife was, but she hadn't met her yet. Hopefully, the woman had told Abby everything she needed to know. And hopefully the young mother-to-be listened.

"I hate to sound like a child," Abby said, "but I sure would be happy to see my mother and my grandmother right about now."

Lenore seized the opportunity to distract Abby, asking about her family. As Abby talked, Lenore listened, but she was also trying to figure out what to do.

This baby was coming soon. She should have gone for help, even in the storm. But she hadn't wanted to take Jed out in it and hadn't wanted to leave him behind. Now it was too late.

"I don't think I can make it back to town before the baby comes," Abby said.

Patting Abby's arm, Lenore stood. "It'll be okay. We'll do this together."

"Have you ever delivered a baby before?"

"No. But I did have a baby. And I was alone for a lot of it."

Abby's eyes widened. "Really?"

Nodding, Lenore told her a little about her experience as she searched through the bag that had been left behind. *When would Nathan be back?*

Lenore hadn't noticed the rain had stopped until Nickel shot out of the cave, clearly unable to take confinement for one minute more.

"I don't blame you," Lenore whispered.

CHAPTER FOURTEEN

NATHANIEL'S FIRST SIGHT of the devastation and destruction at Moccasin Rock staggered him. The further he got from the river, the worse it became.

Trees were stripped of leaves, trunks twisted or broken off at odd, jagged angles, or completely uprooted. Branches were strewn with clothing, paper, shingles, even a whole prickly pear cactus plant, roots and all.

The closer he got to town, the thicker debris became. Splintered wood, twisted metal, broken glass, bricks, and things he couldn't even identify clogged the roads. On the main street people were hurrying by, in some cases flat-out running, all over the place.

Sidestepping the rubble, slogging through the mud, he raced straight to his home…or where his home had been.

Nathaniel's heart stopped beating for a moment as he stared at the wreckage.

Hands shaking, he plunged in and began digging, heedless of the splintered boards and broken glass. *Please, God. Don't let me find their bodies.*

He was pulling on the wall that once separated the office space from the kitchen, praying there was no one underneath, when someone shouted his name.

He looked up to see Caleb hurrying toward him, shirt torn, blood on his neck, covered in mud.

Nathaniel climbed out of the debris. "Where are Jed and Lenore?"

Caleb shook his head, fear and disbelief etched on his face. "I don't know."

Stomach pitching, Nathaniel turned to the wreckage again.

"I searched there," Caleb said. "No sign of them."

Before Nathaniel could fully appreciate the relief those words brought, Caleb added, "I can't find Abby. I got back to town right before the storm hit. Mrs. Horton said Abby had been feeling restless. She, Lenore and Jed were out for a walk. They took some food for a picnic."

Nathaniel grabbed Caleb's arm. "They were out in the open?"

Caleb rubbed a shaky hand across his eyes. "Yes. I was searching for them when the tornado hit. I saw it coming down out of the clouds, then pulling back up. It did that several times, right over the center of town. I've heard descriptions before, but I'd never seen one. Unbelievable. I jumped into a ravine, trying to get as low as I could. It still threw me around."

"You okay?"

"I'm fine, physically, only a few cuts and scrapes," Caleb said. "But I'm about to go crazy. Our place was destroyed, too. Thankfully, they weren't there either. I've searched all over town. Abby's folks are looking too."

Nathaniel stepped back into the street, turning in circles, unsure where to look first, where to look next.

His gaze searched each face, hoping to see Lenore, Jed, his mother...any of his family. But all he saw was desperation and disbelief.

Then he noticed the buildings that had been damaged or destroyed. Martin's Mercantile was the biggest building on a corner lot, and most of the upper floor, and one outer wall was gone.

The post office and newspaper office were in shambles, the drug store had only a broken window. The bank, the café, the barbershop, the telegraph office, and the jail were damaged, but still standing. He bolted toward the jail. "Nobody there," Caleb called out. "I checked."

Nathaniel stopped and turned back. "Any sign of Eli or Bliss elsewhere?"

Caleb shook his head.

"Carmichael Cook or Peg Harmon?"

"Haven't seen Carmichael but Peg's here somewhere."

"Doc!" someone called out. "Man am I glad to see you. Heard you were out of town."

Nathaniel turned to see the telegraph operator, Al Jenkins, and the newspaper publisher, Luther Tilman, struggling to carry a door with George Dunlop, postmaster, stretched out on it. There was no arguing among the three men now.

Nathaniel started running alongside them. "Where are you taking him?"

"The saloon," Tilman said. "We've cleaned it out and are taking all the wounded there. Peg Harmon has been tending folks inside."

"What about the hotel? Can we use it? It's bigger."

"It's still standing, but the storm hit it hard. Knocked it off the foundation. Saloon's the largest space that wasn't damaged. Several men are setting up sawhorses to make tables. Using whatever else we can find."

Face ashen, Jenkins shook his head. "It's bad, Nathaniel. Homes destroyed, people hurt. Silas was killed. He was in the store when the wall fell. I've heard there are others who didn't make it, but I don't know who yet."

Silas was dead. Others. Nathaniel and Caleb exchanged a glance, scared to put their fear into words.

George Dunlop groaned, and Nathaniel waved the men on.

"Tell Peg I'll grab what medical supplies I've got and be right there. Have you seen any of my family?"

Both men shook their heads before disappearing through the saloon doors.

More people rushed by, some of them bleeding. That jolted Nathaniel into motion again. Turning to the other side of the street, he started compiling a mental list. Sutures, needles, rolls and rolls of bandage...no way did he have everything he needed in his office.

That's when he remembered. His office was gone.

Someone stepped out on the boardwalk and yelled at Nathaniel from the saloon.

"Go," Caleb said. "I'll keep looking for Abby, Lenore and Jed."

"Send word to me immediately when you find them." Nathaniel swallowed hard. "No matter what." Then he shook his head. His family was fine. Wherever they were, they were fine. *They had to be.*

"Someone told me there's a train heading this way from Fair Haven," he told Caleb. "Bringing help. Doctors, nurses."

Nickel darted up, barking and dancing around Nathaniel's boots. *One of the more beautiful sights he'd ever witnessed.*

"Follow her," Nathaniel told his brother. "She'll take you to Lenore."

Caleb didn't waste time asking questions. He whistled for the dog. She looked once at Nathaniel, head tilted, then at his brother, and took off like a jack rabbit, Caleb right behind her.

Turning back to what was left of his office and home, Nathaniel proceeded with more caution this time. He found the glass fronted cabinet that once stood in the corner. It had been tossed all the way to the kitchen. The glass was broken, and so were the bottles. But he found several salves, tinctures, and ointments in tins.

He couldn't find a lantern or lamp that wasn't broken, but he did find some candles. He also unearthed his medical bag, still closed. Nathaniel opened it and breathed a prayer of thanks when he found scalpels, several containers of catgut sutures, horsehair ligatures, needles, thread, a stethoscope, rolls of gauze, a thermometer, a bottle of carbolic acid, and laudanum, all undamaged, and his anesthetic vaporizer, tucked securely away in its own leather carrying case.

Nathaniel wasn't sure what he would need, but he was grateful to have found this much.

His second stethoscope was still hanging from a hook on the examination room wall…but the wall was now in the alley.

The more he surveyed the damage around him, the more unbelievable it was, and the more grateful Nathaniel was that Lenore and Jed hadn't been here.

But where were they?

⸙

Lenore made Abby as comfortable as possible, which considering where they were, wasn't comfortable at all.

Still, Abby wasn't complaining. Hadn't said a cross or unkind word.

"Are you scared?" Lenore asked. "I want you to know it's okay if you are. I understand."

"I'm not scared, exactly," Abby said, "but I am ready for this to be over. I want to hold my baby. I want to see Caleb."

Abby's voice wobbled when she said her husband's name, but she didn't cry.

"Well, you're braver than I was," Lenore admitted. "I'm sorry this experience won't be like you wanted. That your mother and grandmother aren't here. But I will do everything I can to help you."

"Would you pray with me?" Abby asked.

Pray? Lenore gave a reluctant nod.

Abby held out her hand. After a moment, Lenore took it in

her own. She intended to shut her mind, as she had at the church, but for some reason she couldn't.

As Abby spoke to God, Lenore closed her eyes, blocking the sight of Abby's earnest face, and wishing she could free her hand to cover her ears. Abby was asking God to be there with them. Not only her and the baby, but Lenore, too. Then Abby asked God for his help, for his guidance, for his mercy.

Not long after Abby whispered "Amen," a noise near the front of the cave had both women glancing eagerly in that direction.

Lenore never imagined a time she'd be grateful to see a lawman, but when Caleb Calhoun stepped into the cave, yelling his wife's name, it was all Lenore could do not to run and hug him.

"We're back here," she said, hurrying forward.

"Where's Abby?"

"She's resting. We took shelter in here when the storm came. It was raining so hard we could barely see."

"The rain's gone now," he said. "Let's get y'all out of here."

Caleb had reached his wife by this point. Abby took one look at him and immediately burst into tears.

He dropped down on his knees beside her. "Darlin' don't cry. I'm going to get you outta here right now."

Abby was trying to explain but her explanation was punctuated by sobs.

"It's her time," Lenore said.

Caleb peered up at her blankly. "Time? Time for what?"

"To have her baby."

His mouth dropped open. "That's not supposed to happen for several weeks."

"I don't guess the baby knows," Lenore said, trying to suppress a smile.

"Then we need to hurry and get her out of here."

"She shouldn't leave," Lenore added. "She's in no condition to be moved. Hopefully, we can get the midwife to come here. I wish Nathan was back."

Abby cried out, causing Caleb to turn back around. "Everything's going to be okay," he told her. "This is a Calhoun wanting to be born. We're not known for our patience."

His wife had finally noticed his disheveled appearance. "What happened to you?"

"Caught out in the storm," he said, "I'm fine." He kissed Abby's brow, then stood and gestured for Lenore to follow him to the mouth of the cave.

"Can you help her?"

"*We* have no choice," Lenore said.

Caleb gulped, and after another wide-eyed look toward Abby, nodded his head in agreement.

"How did you know where to find us?" Lenore asked.

He pointed to Nickel. "Nathaniel told me to follow her."

"Good girl," she said to the dog, grateful once again for her canine companion.

Lenore's relief at seeing Caleb, and knowing Nathan was near, was replaced with a sense of foreboding at the worry on his face.

"I don't want Abby to know yet," Caleb whispered, "but it was more than a storm that passed through. A tornado hit Moccasin Rock."

No. "Was anyone hurt?"

"Yes, and there are people missing. At least one death, and rumors of more. Homes were destroyed, including mine and Abby's...and Nathaniel's home and office." He hurried on before Lenore could even react. "Thank God, you two have been accounted for. Where's your son?"

"Jed's here. He's asleep, a little further back. I moved him away from Abby when I realized what was happening."

"Nathaniel said there's a train heading this way soon from Fair Haven," Caleb said. "Doctors, nurses and supplies. But they're not here yet. Nathaniel's already working on the wounded. Peg, too. We're on our own here."

Abby cried out, louder this time, and they hurried to her side.

Once again, Caleb knelt and attempted to calm his wife.

"I've dreamed many times of having a baby," Abby said, "but I never dreamed it would happen in a cave."

"Everything's going to be okay," Caleb said. "Imagine the stories he'll be able to tell someday."

Abby's brow wrinkled.

Caleb had managed to distract her, but probably not in the way he'd intended.

"What makes you think it's a boy?" Abby said.

"I just do."

"Do you have names picked out?" Lenore asked, as she placed her hands upon Abby's shoulders and gently guided her down on the blanket.

"Since Abby's brother is already named for her father, we agreed on Joseph Hamilton," Caleb said. "My father's middle name, and the name of a dear preacher friend of ours."

"And if it's a girl," Abby said, "which I firmly believe this one is, we will name her Julia Irene. After Caleb's mother and mine."

"I like both those choices," Lenore said.

Caleb smiled at Abby. "Those are wonderful names, Darlin'. We will save them for our next baby. I want a girl as much as you do. But this one is a boy."

While they talked, Lenore unbuttoned the cuffs of her own dress and rolled the sleeves up.

Caleb did the same just as Abby moaned again, grabbing at her stomach with both hands.

"We'll have to pick this up again later," Caleb said, his voice a little shaky. "Joseph will be here soon. He'll have his mother and father waiting here for him." He looked up. "And his Aunt Lenore."

Lenore's throat tightened. She was surprised by how much she liked the sound of that. But still, she couldn't keep the fear from creeping in.

With Caleb calming his wife, and the candles flickering, the place was cozier than it had been earlier, but it was still a cave, and there was no midwife or doctor. Things could go wrong, probably things she'd never even considered.

Lenore wished—not for the first time in her life—that she could call on God for help, and for a calming of her mind and heart, the way Abby had.

CHAPTER FIFTEEN

NATHANIEL STARED DOWN into the face of Jillie Wilson, willing her to open her eyes, to smile at him. She was breathing, but otherwise lifeless. Her father was standing there, waiting for answers, looking as sick as Nathaniel felt.

"When will she wake up, Doc?"

"I…I don't know, Adger. Let me finish my exam, and get her cleaned up and stitched up, and then I may know more." The odor of carbolic acid solution stung his nostrils as Nathaniel shook it out over his hands to sterilize them. He hadn't been able to find the atomizer he normally would've used to mist it, but this method would have to do.

As he worked on the various cuts, scrapes and abrasions covering Jillie's body, Nathaniel's gaze drifted to her face and head more than once. No cuts there, no lumps, bumps, or bruises. So why was she unconscious? There was dirt and mud on her, like the others he'd seen, but no serious wounds.

What exactly happened to her? Were there any of the other school kids hurt? He'd asked Adger, but the man kept shaking his head and mumbling. And with this bedlam, this clamor and confusion as everyone rushed around, it was difficult to hear anything anyway.

Peg Harmon, working on the other side of the room, had sewn up the jagged hole in George Dunlop's leg, and had moved on to the next patient—a man with a sliver of wood the size of a pencil imbedded in his neck. Nathaniel had checked her work, finding it well done, and was more grateful than ever for her being here, and willing to help.

Once he finished with Jillie, who remained lifeless, he tried to convince Adger to go home, or at least go outside. "It's crowded in here," Nathaniel said, "and there's nothing you can do. I will monitor her closely, I give you my word. There's a lot you could do out there. A lot of people who need help. Try to keep busy, it'll be good for you, and help others at the same time."

Adger nodded, his Adam's apple bobbing up and down as he worked to control his emotions. "Okay, Doc. I'll see what I can do. You'll send for me?"

Nathaniel patted him on the back. "As soon as I know anything."

Adger had no sooner cleared the back door, when his wife entered through the front and planted herself in the same spot her husband had stood. Susana Wilson refused to be dissuaded. In truth, Nathaniel couldn't blame her. He'd do the same thing if it was his kid. But everyone needed room to work.

Calling on two other men to help him, he picked Jillie up, cradling her with care, while the others grabbed the board she was laying on, sawhorses and all, and moved her to the back room. There, they set up a place for her, tucked away in an area under the stairs. There were a couple of chairs stored nearby. Nathaniel placed one near Jillie's bed.

"This is a better spot," he told Mrs. Wilson. "I have to go see to the others but if she wakes up or starts talking, or seems to be in distress of any kind, come for me immediately."

Susana sank into the chair, nodding and wiping tears from her face. "Is there anything I can do?"

Nathaniel gave her shoulder a squeeze. "Pray," he told her.

Back inside the main room, people were still bringing in wounded. Just as Nathaniel wondered what the saloon owner thought of his business being turned into a hospital, he realized the patient on the table in front of him was Big John Finley himself, suffering from multiple contusions, abrasions, lacerations—and sporting hoof marks.

"My back hurts bad," John mumbled.

"What happened?"

"I was at the livery stable talking to Eagan when it hit. Animals scared to death. Trampled me."

"How's Eagan?"

"Up and moving."

"Don't worry, we'll get you fixed up, and on your feet again."

Even as he worked, Nathaniel was thinking about Jed, Lenore, and his mother. *Where were they?*

For that matter, where were Eli and Bliss?

Had Caleb found anyone? Was everyone okay?

His attention was drawn to the activity around him. Someone had brought in cots they'd tracked down, and a couple of mattresses from upstairs. Everything appeared to be clean. Others had fired up the woodstove and were boiling water. He'd been able to sterilize the tools he needed.

Nathaniel lifted his head at the sound of footsteps to see Al Jenkins and Luther Tilman carrying an injured woman between them. "This lady needs help," Tilman called out. "Found her in her yard a couple of streets over."

More lacerations and abrasions, at the very least.

Turning to leave after seeing the woman safely into Peg's care, Jenkins stopped. "Doc, you got a telegram right before all this hit. The last one that came through." He patted at his vest, fished out a piece of crumpled paper, thrust it in Nathaniel's hand, and left.

Nathaniel shoved the telegram into his pocket without reading it. He didn't have time now. Besides, he was still of the same mind he had been when he left Galveston. He and Lenore were getting married again, no matter what the Pinkerton agent discovered.

After making Big John as comfortable as he could, Nathaniel checked on Jillie again. No change. He crossed the room to help Peg sew up a man who'd been thrown into a barbed wire fence. While they worked, he finally had a moment to talk to her.

"You've done a great job, Peg. I'm so sorry I wasn't here."

"Thank you. And no need to be sorry, how could you know something like this was going to happen."

Nathaniel asked Peg the same question he'd asked everyone else, hoping he hadn't already asked her. "Do you know where Lenore and Jed are? Or Mama?"

"I don't know about your wife and son, but your mother was back up at the Holcomb's. From what I'm told, the path of the tornado was nowhere near there."

Thank God.

Someone entered the room again. He turned hoping to see Lenore and Jed, Caleb or Eli, or anybody who could tell him where everyone else was.

But it was young Jamie Wilson. Nathaniel motioned him closer so they could talk, as Peg hurried across the room to help someone else.

"You hurt, Jamie?"

"No, sir. Not a scratch. How's Jillie?"

"She's sleeping right now. Your mother is with her. How was Jillie hurt?"

"At the school," Jamie said. "Miss Kirk made us all get down on the floor when she saw the storm was coming. Then the door blew open. Jillie ran to try to close it. Miss Kirk grabbed her and tried to pull her back. The wind tore Jillie right out of Miss Kirk's hands. They both ended up out in the schoolyard."

There was something about the way the kid was talking—slow and stilted—that filled Nathaniel with dread. "Is Miss Kirk okay?"

Jamie shook his head. "They found her a little bit ago. She was kilt. Somebody said her neck was broke. They hauled her to the undertaker."

Nathaniel stood there, unable to speak, unable to think. Then he pulled himself together. "I...I'm so sorry, Jamie. How are all the kids?"

"They're okay, some cuts and stuff, but nobody hurt bad. The roof came off some, peeled right up. Glass busted. I don't know where my schoolbook is."

Throat working, Nathaniel turned back to the task at hand. There was nothing he could do for Mina Kirk now. But Jamie needed something to keep him busy, and Nathaniel could use the help.

"Can you give me a hand with something?"

Jamie's eyes rounded as he looked at the needle Nathaniel held, and the bloody rags at his feet. "What do you want me to do?"

"I need you to round up supplies. There's supposed to be help on the way from Fair Haven, but I'm not sure when it will get here. I can't wait."

"What kinda supplies?"

"Anything I can use for bandages or slings. Sheets, tablecloths, clothing. If it's clean and dry, and people are willing to part with it, bring it to me."

Jamie snapped into his usual efficient manner. "Yes, sir." And was gone in a flash.

Nathaniel murmured a prayer as he worked, for his family and friends, all of them, and for a way to help those who were hurting.

Jamie returned within the hour. In addition to the items requested, he'd also brought lanterns and lamps. Nathaniel would rather work with him than many adults he knew. "Great job, Jamie. Thank you."

Nathaniel hadn't heard the train whistle, but he asked anyway. "Any sign of the folks from Fair Haven?"

"No, sir. Saw some strangers, but they didn't come in on the train."

"Where were they?"

"They were in a wagon. Leading several horses behind it."

Strangers bringing horses? Nathaniel had seen people swooping into an area after a disaster, charging an exorbitant amount for horses, wagons, any mode of transportation at all.

Thankfully, Eli, Caleb and Bliss would soon put a stop to any unlawful activity.

"Did you see either of my brothers? Or the deputy?"

"No." Jamie mentioned the people he'd seen who appeared to be unhurt.

Nathaniel felt a surge of relief as he mentioned a long list of town folk.

"Some of them had blood on them, but they were walking around, like Mr. Eagan Smith."

"What was he doing?" Nathaniel asked.

"He was chasing his horses. They got out when his building fell down."

Things were becoming clearer.

"And all the Horton family is fine except for Abby," Jamie added.

Nathaniel held his breath. "Is Abby hurt?" He tried to keep his voice calm. No sense scaring the kid.

"Don't rightly know. Nobody's seen her since this morning."

"Any sign of the new pharmacist?"

"Nope."

Nathaniel swallowed. "Have you seen my wife?"

"I saw her at church with you Sunday."

"Have you seen her today?"

"No."

Finished stitching up the man with the barbed wire injuries, Nathaniel straightened, stretched, and moved on to the next patient.

Bony Joe had a deep laceration to his scalp, and although he'd had a full head of hair the day before, he now had a receding hairline. Nathaniel cleaned him up, then dosed him with laudanum before attempting to suture the wound.

He looked up to see Jamie standing there, out of the way, but clearly interested in what was going on, no longer squeamish looking. *Jamie might make a doctor someday, too.*

"I saw some of the damage to this area," Nathaniel said, "how bad is it for the other businesses?"

The boy rattled off a list of the buildings he'd taken note of, the ones destroyed, like the livery stable and Nathaniel's office, as well as those with minimal damage, and those that seemed untouched, like the depot and the courthouse. "The hotel is still standing, but it's kinda crooked."

Nathaniel tried to imagine that for a moment. It was probably an accurate description from a kid's viewpoint.

The sound of a whistle in the distance brought a shot of hope for Nathaniel. "Jamie can you go see if that's the train from Fair Haven? If it is, will you send them here?"

"Be right back."

When he was working, time was harder to measure, but Nathaniel was still surprised by how quickly the folks from Fair Haven stepped into the saloon.

Three men and four women, doctors and nurses. After a brief introduction, they explained to Nathaniel that several other people from Fair Haven were setting up tents near the depot and preparing food.

"That's wonderful. I can't tell you how much we appreciate it."

"You've accomplished a lot," one man said as he looked around the room.

Nathaniel pointed to Peg, introducing her. "She got started even before I got here."

"Why don't you rest?" an older doctor said after a sweeping glance of both him and Peg.

"I'm all right," Nathaniel said, "don't need to rest, but I would like to take a minute to see how bad the damage is." *Try to find my family.*

"Go," the man said, stepping up to take over Nathaniel's work on Bony Joe. The others were already examining patients.

Nathaniel stepped outside, and then walked to the edge of town.

Somebody had started to gather rubble in a pile so folks could pass safely through the streets. Getting rid of debris was necessary to decrease the risk of injury or illness, but Nathaniel hoped they wouldn't start burning his place. He needed to figure out who was in charge of this and let them know he still hoped to salvage some of his equipment and personal belongings.

Walking on a little further, he discovered that the tabernacle had been reduced to a pile of kindling. The church had taken a hit, roof missing, one wall nearly gone. *This would be devastating to so many people.* Including him.

Pastor Wilkie Brown lived in a small house on the other side of the church. It appeared to be undamaged. Nathaniel knocked on the door, to be sure Wilkie was okay, but there was no response. *He was probably off helping folks.*

Near the depot, three tents had been erected by the people from Fair Haven. They explained that one would offer a place for men and boys to sleep, another for women and girls. The third would be for meals. Nathaniel marveled at how quickly and efficiently the Fair Haven team worked.

He turned around in time to see Lenore walking in from the direction of the river. Skirt sodden, dirt and mud-covered, carrying Jed, weariness in her every step. *And such a beautiful sight.*

Nathaniel bolted forward. He meant to embrace them both, but when he reached out, Lenore misunderstood. Fear flared in her eyes as she tightened her grasp on Jed.

That was Nathaniel's own fault. He hadn't given her any reason to think he'd be glad to see her. She was braced, as if ready to fight him for their son.

"It's okay," he soothed. "I wanted to make sure y'all weren't hurt."

Her shoulders relaxed. "We're fine. We took shelter in a cave by the river, soon as the rain started."

Nathaniel didn't try to take Jed from her, but he placed his hand on the boy's head. "May I?"

Her hesitation was brief. "Sure. He walked part of the way, but I admit he's getting to be a load to tote."

Nathaniel looked at Jed. The boy seemed wide-awake and well rested compared to his mother. But as usual, no sign of emotion. He was so glad to see him that Nathaniel couldn't help giving him a hug. *Thank you, God.*

"Where's Abby?" Nathaniel said. "Did Caleb find y'all?"

She adjusted Jed's sock, which drooped around the boy's mud-caked boots. "Yes, he did. He got there in time to help deliver his son."

Nathaniel blinked. "His son? Are Abby and the baby okay?"

"They're doing great." Lenore smiled. "I'm not sure about Caleb, though. He said it was the hardest thing he's ever been through."

Nathaniel couldn't stop the grin that spread across his face. In the midst of the death and destruction, there was new life, a new beginning. "You said 'help' deliver his son. Who was he helping?"

"Me. It was only me and Caleb. He's with Abby right now. She didn't want him to leave, and I was ready to get out of there. He asked me to go get her parents. He's going to need help getting Abby and the baby home."

Home. "Lenore, things are bad. There are people hurt. Some dead. Some folks are still missing."

Her eyes filled with concern as she took in her surroundings. "I'm so sorry. I'll go tell the Hortons about Abby, then I'll change clothes, clean up and help where I can. There was some soap at the cave, I cleaned up a little in the river, but not enough."

"I don't know if there's anything to change into, or exactly where you can clean up yet. The house and office are gone. Whatever you had is gone, or damaged." Nathaniel started speaking in a rush. "Just stay with our son. Keep him safe. I know things haven't been good between us, and I'm sorry. We need to talk later. Until then, I'm begging you, don't leave with Jed. Please, give me your word that you'll stay in Moccasin Rock."

The oddest expression came over her face and Nathaniel wanted to kick himself. *He should've said he didn't want her to leave either.* The way he'd phrased it made it sound as if he was only concerned with whether Jed stayed.

Before he could clarify, she said, "You have my word. I'll stay."

Then Nathaniel realized he didn't know *where* they could stay. From the corner of his eye, he saw a woman standing in front of the rubble where his office had been, head down. Crying.

Mama.

With Jed in his arms, Nathaniel headed toward her, motioning for Lenore to follow.

At the first glimpse of him, Cordelia Calhoun grabbed Nathaniel's face with both hands, and cried even harder. He shifted Jed to one arm and wrapped the other one around his mother.

"Mama, everything's going to be okay."

"Thank God you're safe. Where's Eli?"

"I haven't seen him yet, but I'm sure he's fine. I've got to get back to the saloon, that's where they've set up the injured."

Her gaze shifted to Jed, eyes widening.

"Mama, this is Jed. Your grandson."

"Well, I could tell that much. Where did he come from? What's happening?" Even as she asked, she was touching Jed's hair, his face. Her eyes wide with wonder.

For once, Nathaniel was glad Jed wasn't scared of strangers. Or maybe the child understood that this was someone who loved him already. Nathaniel and Eli had been lost to her when they weren't much older than Jed.

"I don't have time to go into it all right now," Nathaniel said. "And you're going to have more questions. I'll talk to you about it as soon as I can."

Nathaniel glanced over at Lenore. There was worry on her face, that lower lip trembling. *Did she think he was going to let his mother take Jed away from her?*

He had so much to make up for. But that would take time. Again, time he didn't have right now. He tugged her forward. "Mama, this is my wife. Lenore."

Both women seemed shocked at the introduction.

"I'll explain everything later," he told his mother. He looked at Jed. "This little fellow's been through a lot. So has Lenore. They need you."

Lenore's eyes got wider, but his mother's curiosity was immediately replaced by concern. "Oh, dear. What can I do?"

"I need a safe place for them to stay. Is Peg's house still standing?" In all the confusion he hadn't even thought to ask.

"Yes. There's some damage to the back porch and part of the roof. But it's standing."

"Do you mind if Lenore and Jed stay there with you?" He became aware of the dog at their feet, patiently waiting to follow Lenore wherever she went next. "And this is Nickel. She needs a place, too."

His mother glanced down. "Of course. I'm sure it will be fine with Peg."

"Thank you. I'll talk to her to make sure. I'll dig through

what's left of the house here and see if we can find something for them to change into. Although most everything is wet."

"I've got some things," his mother said. "I'm sure there are others who'll be needing...everything. I'll start gathering what I can find."

He kissed his mother on the cheek and handed the boy to Lenore.

"You'll be safe and comfortable, and so will Jed," he told her. "If I have my guess, he'll be pampered and spoiled a bit. I'll see you back here when you can. If you still want to help."

She nodded, confusion apparent in the green-eyed gaze she fixed on him.

"Be careful when you come out," he said. "Things like this bring out the best in some folks, people who genuinely want to help. But there'll also be those aiming to profit from a tragedy. Plus, there's an outlaw supposed to be somewhere in the area. I didn't think to ask Caleb if they found him."

"He didn't say."

Robby Horton ran by. Nathaniel stopped him. "Robby, I've got a message for you to deliver."

"Yes, sir?"

"Go tell your parents that Abby took shelter in the cave when the storm hit, and she had her baby there. Caleb's with her, but he'll need help getting them back to town."

Robby's mouth dropped open.

"Tell them that everyone is okay," Lenore added. "And tell them to bring lots of blankets or quilts. It won't be an easy ride home."

"Abby had her baby?"

Nathaniel patted him on the back. "Yep. Helped along by Caleb and Lenore. Congratulations, Uncle Robby."

As Robby ran to find his parents, and Lenore followed his

mother, Nathaniel drew in the first full breath he'd taken since leaving Donevy Gap.

Somebody yelled for him. "Doc, come quick." There were three men headed his way, and still it was a struggle for them to move with the door they were carrying. An arm was dangling over the side, sleeve torn and soaked in blood. "He was near the river bottom, under a plow," one of the men said. "I'm not sure he or the plow started off where we found them. There were all sorts of things blown around. Craziest thing I've ever seen."

Nathaniel's attention went first to the damaged arm, then his gaze drifted up to the face.

His breath caught in his throat. *Eli.*

CHAPTER SIXTEEN

LENORE HURRIEDLY BRUSHED her hair, pinned it up, and then slipped into a blue calico dress that Cordelia Calhoun loaned her. It was good to be clean and dry.

She laid the brush on the doily-covered dresser top and took a deep breath.

Although Cordelia had been hospitable and gracious, she'd looked at Lenore with a strange expression. Lenore wished she could hide for a while. But there were people who needed help out there.

"Best go on and get this over with," she whispered to herself.

She followed the sound of clattering cookware to the kitchen. Nathan's mother was standing at the stove stirring something in a cast iron skillet, and Jed was sitting at a table nibbling on cornbread.

"Glad that fit," the woman said when Lenore entered the room. "I cleaned your shoes, and Jed's and left them by the door."

"Thank you…Mrs. Calhoun."

"Call me Cordelia." She picked up a bowl and began stirring whatever was inside. "Peg has some things in an old trunk in the front room. She said to use them however I needed, so take what you want."

Cordelia Calhoun was a slight woman, with light gray hair and piercing brown eyes. She gave the food another quick stir. "How long have you been here? Nathaniel hasn't mentioned you before."

"I've been here about a week and a half," Lenore said.

The woman glanced from her to Jed, brow wrinkled.

"I've been in Moccasin Rock for that long," Lenore said. "But Nathan and I met almost four years ago." When Cordelia's eyes widened, Lenore added, "We've been married almost four years."

Lenore suspected this woman was going to dislike her anyway, when she learned of her past, but in case she was the type of person who would dislike a child based on the sins of the mother, she didn't want to make it even worse than it was.

"I can't imagine why Nathaniel hasn't said anything to me," Cordelia murmured. "Not a word."

Lenore wasn't going to answer for Nathan, but she did try to smooth things over as much as possible. "I'm sure he'll explain everything soon."

Cordelia nodded absently. Her attention shifted to Jed. There was such tenderness in her expression that Lenore knew she'd not have to worry about her son with this woman.

"It doesn't matter how y'all got here, or when," Cordelia said softly. "I'm just glad you're here."

"Thank you," Lenore said. "That means a lot." *More than she could express.*

"Now, you go on and do what you need to help Nathaniel. I'll take good care of this child."

After putting on fresh stockings, again provided by Cordelia, Lenore pulled her boots on, hugged Jed and told him she'd return soon, then left the house and hurried toward the saloon.

She'd been stunned when Nathan asked for her word that she wouldn't leave with Jed. Nobody had ever thought enough of her to take her at her word.

He hadn't said he wanted her to stay forever, but he wanted

her to stay. If that was all she could get, for now, she would take it. But she mustn't ever forget that it was Jed who made the difference. Nathaniel hadn't been glad to see her that night at the jail.

Peg Harmon's house wasn't far from the main street, but Lenore was distracted by the storm's path, her gaze sweeping back and forth, trying to remember exactly what the town looked like when she'd walked through with Abby. *Unbelievable.*

At the saloon, she stepped inside, her gaze drawn straight to Nathan. He was facing away from her, head bent, working on a patient. There were several other people in similar positions around the room. So many injured. Lenore stepped aside as two men carried in another one.

Nathan never glanced up.

A stranger approached her. Lenore wasn't sure if it was someone from Moccasin Rock or one of the people who came in from Fair Haven.

"Can I help you?" he asked. "Are you looking for a patient?"

Before she could answer, Nathan glanced up and beckoned to her. He appeared tired already. But there was more than worry and fatigue in his eyes. *There was fear.*

She stepped closer. "I came to see if you needed anything. I'm glad you have so much help…" Her words trailed off as she got a glimpse of the person laying on the table. *Eli Calhoun.*

"Is he…" She couldn't bring herself to say the words.

"He's alive," Nathan said. "He fainted when I started to cut his shirt off and hasn't come to yet. I'm going to operate. Try to save his arm." His voice was flat. "Did Mama get y'all settled at Peg's house?"

"Yes. Everything is fine." Lenore wanted to ease his mind on at least one of his worries. "We're not going anywhere."

His shoulders lost some of their stiffness. "Thank you, Lenore. Please don't say anything to Mama about Eli being injured. I'll tell her after I know more."

"I won't. If you don't need me here, I thought I'd go help around town."

"I think we're set. Please, be careful though. Watch where you step. We're getting some people in here who weren't injured during the tornado but got hurt trying to deal with the aftermath."

"I'll take care."

He was bent over Eli again before she left the room.

❧

"How's Maggie…the kids…Mama?" Every other word from Eli was punctuated with shallow little breaths and small groans.

As glad as he was to hear Eli talking, Nathaniel needed him to conserve his strength. "Just be quiet and still. I'm sure they're fine. Let's concentrate on you."

"You've…seen them? I was trying to get home. Storm threw me."

To keep him quiet, Nathaniel told him what he knew. "Mama's fine. Jamie Wilson and Robby Horton are making the rounds and checking on everyone. They said the path of the tornado was nowhere near your place."

"See that they're okay. And whatever you do, don't tell Maggie I'm hurt."

Nathaniel wasn't about to agree to that. He stared at Eli's arm. Radius broken in two places, ulna in one.

"It's busted?"

That was one way to put it. "Yes."

"Can you fix it?"

Nathaniel had been discussing that issue with the other doctors. One doctor had taken a quick glance and recommended amputation above the elbow, mentioning he had bone saws, and experience. Nathaniel had threatened to shoot him if he came near Eli with a saw, then thanked the man for his opinion.

The doctor had shrugged and moved on to another patient, without discussing any other options. Not that Nathaniel blamed him. The need for medical care was great, and this would take hours.

"I'm going to operate," he told his brother now. He'd do everything in his power to make sure Eli kept his arm. He might never regain full use of it, but he would have it.

It was only a moment before doubt set in. *What if Eli bled to death during the lengthy procedure, what if infection set in?*

Nathaniel had done surgery plenty of times, but mostly—except for routine, simple procedures—it had been in a controlled environment.

Eli closed his eyes, sweat dotting his forehead. "I need Bliss and Caleb. Need help."

"I haven't seen Bliss yet, but I did see Caleb. He's out at the river. Abby had her baby a little while ago. Don't worry. Everything's fine. Fair Haven's sent help. There are doctors and nurses working on people right now. Tents set up for housing and food. Everything will be okay."

Nathaniel hesitated a moment before telling Eli the next part. "I can't just give you laudanum for this. I'm going to need you to be asleep before I begin the operation."

Some people resisted the idea of sedation. Others actively fought it. *Eli would probably be the worst.*

His brother surprised him. "Do what you need...to do. But I need things...too. Can't wait."

"This surgery can't wait!" Nathaniel's worry made the words sharper than he'd intended.

It didn't bother Eli. He asked Nathaniel to send Silas Martin and Big John Finley to him.

"I can't," Nathaniel said. He'd explain later.

Eli, glassy eyed and shaking now, asked for several other people.

"For one reason or another, most of them are gone," Nathaniel told him. "Some are looking for survivors in the outlying areas."

Eli's jaw clenched. "Then get me Henry Barnett and Walter Miller."

"Why?"

"I need to…deputize someone."

Nathaniel knew then what Eli was worried about. He should've known earlier. The vultures could be circling soon, and not the winged variety.

"I'll send someone to hunt for them. But if we can't find them, fast, it will have to wait. I've stopped the bleeding, but time is critical, Eli." His brother's eyes were closed, and he didn't respond. *Had he passed out again?* "What else do you need?"

"Why…did they call you Texas Kid," Eli whispered.

Nathaniel smiled, giving a disbelieving shake of his head. "I was part of a Wild West show. I'll explain later. Anything else?"

"Yeah, tell me again how hard you studied."

Nathaniel's smile faded as he swallowed around a lump in his throat. "I'm good at what I do, Eli. I've trusted you with my life many times. Let me handle this."

Going to the door, Nathaniel stuck his head out and flagged down Jamie Wilson.

The boy scurried over. "Hey, Doc. Did you need something?"

"Yes. Do you know where Henry Barnett is? Walter Miller?"

"Henry stopped by the house a little while ago to check on us, but I haven't seen Mr. Miller."

"Will you track them both down for me?"

"Sure, what should I tell them?"

"That Sheriff Calhoun wants to speak to them." The boy was gone in the blink of an eye, and back within minutes, running in just ahead of both men.

Henry was a farmer who grew a variety of crops, and raised horses and mules. He was Abby's childhood friend, and had recently married Caleb's childhood friend. He was one of the nicest fellows Nathaniel had ever met.

Walter Miller, also a good man, was a teacher turned carpenter who Eli had arrested a few months ago after a momentary lapse of judgement. He and Eli had since become good friends.

Henry paled as he looked around at the makeshift tables, the doctors at work, and the bloody rags. "What do you need, Doc?"

Pointing to the table, Nathaniel said, "He wanted to talk to y'all."

Walter's eyes widened when he realized it was Eli stretched out on the table.

Gritting his teeth, Eli drew in a labored breath. "If you two have no objections, I want to deputize you."

Henry was the first to react. "Me? You want me to be a deputy?"

"Yes. But..." Eli stopped talking. Just as Nathaniel started to tell Walter and Henry to leave, Eli rallied. "You'll be answering to...Caleb and Bliss. After what happened, there'll be people coming in from all over. Some will be here to help, but others looking to take advantage. Seen it before. Innocent people could be hurt."

"Okay, what do you need us to do if someone's in danger?" Henry said.

"Stop whoever's trying to hurt them. Don't...get yourselves hurt."

Brody pushed through the doors.

Eli tried to sit up. "How's Maggie...the baby?"

Nathaniel pressed Eli back down. "Be still! You're bleeding again."

Brody rushed toward Eli, pale and shaken. "They're both fine. They're still at the house. We were worried about you."

Eli closed his eyes, a look of peace settling on his face. "I'm fine, son. Take care of them. Henry, you ready? Walter?"

"Yes." The word was spoken softly, but Henry drew himself up and stepped closer. Walter gave a brisk nod, his expression grim but determined.

Eli deputized them in short order. After the new deputies were gone, with Brody following along to help, Nathaniel enlisted the aid of several men to move Eli away from the stove—ether was flammable—and closer to the plate glass window to make use of the light.

As he prepared Eli for surgery, Nathaniel prayed, something he'd been doing nearly non-stop since he'd stepped off the train at Donevy Gap. Disjointed, frantic, fragmented thoughts and pleas, hoping that God could make sense of it. He didn't realize he'd started praying aloud until Eli whispered, "Amen."

Nathaniel attached the gauze to the metal anesthetic vaporizer, placed it over Eli's mouth and nose, and began dripping ether into the device, turning his own head away to avoid the fumes as he measured out the dose.

It wouldn't do him or Eli any good for them both to be sedated. Eli was a big man, getting an accurate dose was tricky.

What would Eli do if he couldn't use his gun hand? His job would be in jeopardy.

Eli's eyes fluttered open over the ether mask. He was proving difficult to sedate. Not that he was fighting it, at least not consciously.

As Nathaniel carefully dripped more ether onto the gauze, and waited, he recalled a moment in his young life when he and Eli were on a barge that capsized. After years of being beaten on and knocked around by whatever ill-tempered adult was handy, he'd been thrown into the water, thrashing around, frantically trying to find his way to the top, then surrendering, realizing how much easier it was to just let go.

The next thing he knew his big brother was grabbing onto his shirt and yanking him out of the water. Once they were on dry land, Eli shook him until his teeth rattled, all while delivering a blistering lecture.

When Nathaniel whispered that it had seemed easier to give

up, Eli grabbed him by the shirt front again. "Of course, it's easier. Don't you ever give up," he'd yelled. "You fight. Always."

It was something Nathaniel never forgot. Even though Eli had already moved on by the time Tessa and Becky died, Nathaniel heard those words echoing in his mind many times. It was one of the things that got him through.

Now it was his turn to return the favor. "I'm going to do my part, Eli. You do yours. You hear me?"

But Eli had finally gone under.

CHAPTER SEVENTEEN

AFTER LEAVING THE saloon, it occurred to Lenore that one of the biggest needs would be someone to do laundry. That's something she could handle. She made a mental list of things she'd need—wash tub, soap, washboard, a place to start a fire to boil water. Maybe Cordelia Calhoun could point her in the right direction.

She stopped to let a wagon pass through. She didn't recognize the driver, but the man on the seat beside him was Caleb Calhoun.

"Lenore," Caleb called out at the same moment, hopping off the seat and waving her toward the wagon.

She hurried forward, happy to see Abby, laying in the back, gazing down at little Joseph with a look of awe. There was an older woman sitting beside her, also with a loving gaze directed toward the baby.

"Lenore this is Abby's mother, Irene Horton," Caleb said, then tilted his head toward the driver. "And her father, Bob. This is Nathaniel's wife, Lenore. She's the one who delivered the baby."

The Hortons both expressed their gratitude, as did Abby.

"How bad are things?" Irene Horton asked, looking around with tears in her eyes. Since Abby was laying down, she couldn't see the full destruction of the tornado. Better that she didn't yet.

"I really don't know," Lenore admitted. "Nathan is tending the wounded in the saloon, and there are a good many of them. But there are doctors and nurses who came from Fair Haven to help." She hated to tell Caleb about his brother, but he needed to know. "He was operating on Eli when I left."

Caleb's expression grew grim. "How bad is he hurt?"

"Nathan didn't really say."

Standing at the side of the wagon, Caleb glanced down at his wife, obviously torn about what to do. "Go," Abby said, "I've got help."

He grabbed Abby's hand, squeezed it. "I'll be back as quick as I can."

"We'll take care of her," Bob Horton said. "Do what you need to do."

After he'd gone, Lenore explained that she was still figuring out where she was needed the most. "For now, it appears one of the biggest needs might be the laundry. I'm on the hunt for soap and wash pots."

Irene Horton gave a brisk nod. "Come to the boarding house first thing in the morning. We've got everything you need. We'll help."

"Thank you." After the Hortons headed home with Abby and their new grandbaby, Lenore made herself useful in whatever way she could, shadowed everywhere by Nickel.

On one street, she was stopped by a stick-thin woman with her lips pressed into a tight line.

"Who are you?" the woman demanded.

"I'm Lenore Cal...Calhoun." Stumbling over her own last name didn't lend credence to her statement. "I'm the doctor's wife." That sounded even stranger, but it certainly got the other woman's attention.

"Oh, yes," the woman snapped. "I meant to talk to you at church, but I didn't get the chance. When did you two get married? Where are you from? Does your family live around here?"

Even if Lenore had been inclined to answer the woman's questions, she wouldn't have been able to keep up with the rapid pace with which they were hurled at her. She was still trying to decide how to respond when the woman was distracted by someone on the other side of the street.

"You, there. Who are you?"

Lenore made her getaway while she had the chance. Thankfully, she knew how to disappear in a hurry.

She was surprised and a little suspicious to stumble across Gordon and Shipley around the next corner. "I thought y'all were leaving town."

"We are," Shipley said. "We weren't far away when we heard that a cyclone hit Moccasin Rock. Wanted to make sure you and Jed were okay."

They both seemed genuinely concerned.

"We're fine, thank you for checking. Nathan's office and home were destroyed, so we're without lodging. But we're not hurt, and Nathan's mother has taken us in. Grateful for both of those things."

"Since we're here, we thought we'd see if we could be of any use," Shipley said.

"Is Ophelia with you?"

"No, it's just us."

"All we want to do is help," Gordon added.

Lenore didn't know whether to believe them or not, but it was unfair to assume the worst. Nathan wouldn't appreciate them showing up, of that she was certain, nor would his brothers. For all their sakes, it would be better to keep these two busy away from the main area of town.

At that moment, Eagan Smith, the man from the livery stable walked by. His clothing was torn and bloody.

"Are you all right?" Lenore asked. "There are doctors tending to folks in the saloon. We'll be glad to help you get there."

Smith shook his head, a dazed expression crossing his face as he glanced around. "I'm not badly hurt, and I need to keep searching." He told them then that his stable had been destroyed, as well as the wagons, and other conveyances he'd usually rented, and his horses were missing. "I'm hunting those now," he said.

"I'll help you," Shipley volunteered, as did Gordon. Lenore vouched for her friends, hoping she wouldn't regret it, and Eagan accepted the offer of help. It occurred to her after the fact that Gordon's foot might start paining him, and was pleased when Eagan suggested that he stay near the stable, or what was left of it, and wait for any animals that might return. "Be good," Lenore whispered to him before they left.

As she continued through town, she noticed the church. The roof was missing over a big portion of it, and one wall nearly gone. *This would be a blow to so many people.* A movement inside drew her attention. Someone was crawling through the wreckage. *The preacher.*

Lenore rushed in, careful to watch her step, and hurried to his side, her aversion to preachers momentarily forgotten.

"How bad are you hurt?"

"Not bad."

One leg of his trousers was blood-soaked and torn. "You sure?"

Wilkie Brown gave her a crooked smile. "I'm fine, but my leg seems to feel otherwise. I was caught under the wall that fell. Several people came by to check on me, but they were checking the house. I tried to call out to them, but no one heard, and I kept going in and out."

Remembering how she helped her grandfather get around enabled Lenore to get the preacher up and, at his direction, into the church yard, where he sat down, leaning against the side of the building. Outside, he didn't seem as scary as he had behind the pulpit.

"I'm so sorry about the church," Lenore said.

Wilkie grimaced as he tried to straighten his leg. "Thank you.

In times like this, it's difficult to know why some things happen. We may not understand until we get to heaven."

Lenore was more worried about him bleeding to death and getting there sooner than he intended. "I'm going for help, Preacher. Save your strength. I'll never be good enough to get to heaven, so I don't need to hear this."

His eyes widened. "It's not about being good. If it was, no one would get in. Everyone sins."

"Not as many times as me. I don't have enough money to give, either."

A look of sadness flickered over his face. *Had he thought she was going to make a contribution to his church?*

"Is that what you think," he whispered. "That you have to be good, and give money, and not have many sins to get to heaven."

Lenore stared at him in confusion. *Shouldn't he know how it was done?*

She backed away. "I'm going to see about getting you some help."

"Wait. I want to talk to you."

But Lenore had reached the edge of the church yard, nearly running, and didn't look back. At the saloon, she saw that Nathaniel was still working. An older man was standing next to him. *Good.* She was glad he wasn't facing Eli's surgery alone.

Finding one of the other doctors from Fair Haven, she told him about the preacher, and where to find him, then left. She'd now fled from two of Moccasin Rock's citizens. Nathan's friends. Even if he wanted her to stay, how would she fit in?

Lenore was still fussing at herself when she spotted one of Eagan Smith's horses later. Following the frightened animal, Lenore tried to catch up to it, but despite her coaxing, it ran faster. Thankfully, it was running toward the direction of the stable.

Lenore came to a tree across the trail—with legs and boots visible in amongst the branches. She darted forward, then remembered Nathan's warning about using caution. *This could be the missing fugitive.* Glancing around, it occurred to her that she'd gotten further from town than she'd realized. There was not a soul in sight.

Nickel darted toward the tree, sniffing, but not barking or growling. If there was danger nearby, the dog wasn't aware of it.

Lenore began easing forward herself, then hurried when someone called out, "Don't just stand there, help me." The voice was weak, but familiar.

Deputy Bliss.

⤴

Nathaniel straightened, flexed his shoulders and took a deep breath. Dr. Montgomery Helms had gone, called to help somewhere else, but he'd stayed long enough to help him set the bones in place. A two-person endeavor, at best.

Eli was breathing well, his color was good, and his pulse was strong, but they weren't done yet. Nathaniel looked up, glad to see the doctor returning. Helms was an older man with a stocky build, intelligent eyes and gray hair.

He glanced down at the patient, then back at Nathaniel. "I'm glad you didn't let anyone talk you in to amputating."

"Not a chance." Nathaniel bent to his work again.

"Sounds personal."

"It is. He's a lawman, right-handed…and my brother."

"Then you made the right decision, personally." Dr. Helms stepped near, examining the arm more closely. "And you made the right decision from a medical standpoint, too. For what my opinion's worth."

"Are you a surgeon?"

The man nodded but didn't elaborate.

Nathaniel was grateful for the validation that he hadn't put his brother through a lengthy procedure for nothing. "Thank you. Probably shocking for you to see this type of surgery performed in these conditions, but I had to try."

"I've operated in worse."

Nathaniel glanced up at him. "Where?"

"Battlefield. There, many of the operations ended in amputations, even when that wasn't my original intent."

"I can't imagine," Nathaniel admitted.

"After a while, you grow numb. As numb as you wish your patients could be. Or at least I did. Everyone is different."

"Bet you were grateful to put all that behind you."

"I'm not sure that's possible. But you learn to live with the memories."

Nathaniel couldn't disagree with that quiet statement. After another quick glance at the man, he resumed the operation. Thankfully, the muscles, tendons, and ligaments weren't damaged as badly as he'd feared.

As Nathaniel worked, Dr. Helms began speaking about surgical advancements, techniques, and instruments. His voice was calm and steady, reminding Nathaniel of the lectures at medical school. Drawing his attention away from the clamor around him, enabling him to focus on the task at hand. He didn't realize it was even happening until he heard Dr. Helms say something about a train engine.

Helms smiled when Nathaniel looked up. "Sorry, ran out of things to talk about."

When Nathaniel needed an extra set of hands, the man stepped up, but he didn't try to take over.

"Capillary function?" Helms asked at one point. Nathaniel nodded, glad there was no problem there, and thankful that if he missed anything, Helms would spot it.

When Nathaniel finished—back tight, eyes burning with

fatigue—it was hard to express his gratitude without emotion. But he'd never forget this man's help. "Thank you, Dr. Helms."

"You did all the work," Helms said. "When it's time to cast, we have plenty of plaster and gauze strips with us." He looked Nathaniel up and down. "You should probably move around for a while, get your bearings."

Nathaniel cleaned up, took the coffee someone handed him, and stepped outside for a moment—wrung-out and overwhelmed. He walked to the end of the block, still not quite believing his own eyes when he looked around.

In the moonlight, the destruction seemed so complete it was difficult to even imagine the town whole again. Doubts, concerns, questions crowded his mind, tumbling over one another, with no real answers.

Then he looked up. The moon was full and bright, and one of the most spectacular he'd ever seen against the Texas sky.

The God that hung it there was still in control. That's all he needed to know for now.

Taking a deep breath, Nathaniel headed back. At the saloon, he checked on Jillie Wilson, listening to her breathe. Adger had joined his wife at the girl's bedside, and Nathaniel comforted them both as best he could.

He then stepped into the main area of the saloon. Maggie, one of the strongest, and most strong-willed women he'd ever known, was standing by Eli's bed with tears streaming down her face. He wanted to hug her, but he was covered in blood. Some of it her husband's.

Nathaniel figured he'd have a hard time getting her to leave— as he had with Caleb earlier on. But she needed to go, for all their sakes.

She looked up as he drew near, "How is he?"

Nathaniel started to tell her about the surgery, but she didn't need to hear all that. She did need to hear the truth. "I believe he'll get to keep the arm, but I can't promise it will ever be the same."

Maggie scrubbed at the tears on her face. "As long as he lives, I don't care. When can I talk to him?"

"He'll be out of it for a while. He's going to be in a lot of pain when he wakes. I don't think he'd want you to see that."

Her jaw tightened, but she didn't argue with him. "Have you seen Brody?"

"Yes. Before I put Eli under, he deputized Henry and Walter, and sent them off with instructions. Brody went with them to help. There's a lot to do out there."

Maggie drew herself up. "I'll go help where I can. It will probably aggravate Eli more to know I sat here staring at him. When he wakes will you tell him I was here, and I'll be back."

"I will. Have you talked to my mother?"

Maggie nodded. "I stopped by there to check on her and see if Eli was there. She and Jed are doing okay. She kept Lucinda with her. She said it wouldn't be any trouble to watch them both."

"Does Mama know about Eli?"

She glanced at her husband again, struggling to keep her composure. "No. I'll go and stay with the kids and let her come and see Eli for herself. No matter what she hears, she'll want to see him."

"You're right. But make sure she knows it's better for her to keep busy somewhere else for now. Too crowded in here, and not much she can do."

"Do you know where they need help the most?"

"From what I've seen, help is needed everywhere. There are homes destroyed, people injured, missing and dead." He swallowed hard. "Silas Martin and Mina Kirk died."

The tears sprang to Maggie's eyes again. "I'm so sorry to hear that. Silas was the first person I met in Moccasin Rock. And Brody thought the world of Miss Kirk. This doesn't seem real."

No, it didn't. After Maggie had gone, Nathaniel checked on the other patients, then Eli again. He took his pulse, then shook the thermometer and placed it under Eli's good arm. No fever. Nathaniel used the stethoscope to listen to his heart, strong and steady, and then listened to his breathing. Everything looked good so far.

Sitting on the floor nearby, Nathaniel leaned against the wall. He remembered the telegram, digging through his pocket until he found it.

His eyes were heavy, the paper was crumpled and stained. But he could still read it. *Nathaniel Calhoun and Lenore Adams legally wed in Birmingham, Alabama.*

A mixture of elation and fear flashed through him. He had a wife. And a child.

But no real relationship with either, no place for them to live, and no way to provide for them.

CHAPTER EIGHTEEN

In a blind panic, Lenore pulled at the tree for several moments, unable to budge it, before the deputy's words reached her. "You're going to need help," he wheezed.

The tree had landed across Deputy Bliss Walker's middle. He was trying to tell her what happened, his speech punctuated by groans and half-finished swear words.

"I'd been hunting the fugitive before the storm hit. I was waiting out the rain in an old corncrib when things got real still. I stepped out to see what was happening. Then all hel…" Bliss paused. "Then things got bad, fast."

Parts of the tree were splintered and charred. "Did lightning strike the tree?"

"Lightning got the tree," he said, "then the tree got me. I fired off a couple of shots for help, then thought better of giving away my position, in case it was the fugitive who heard me. Also wanted to keep a few bullets in case I was still out here when night fell."

Lenore glanced around at the lowering shadows, the moon rising. "I don't want to leave you," she said.

"Go. I'll be okay."

Taking off at a run, Lenore didn't get far before once again crossing paths with Shipley and Gordon—this time riding in a wagon harnessed to a mule. And once again, suspicion crossed her mind.

"Where did y'all get this rig?"

Gordon answered. "Some fellow named Henry started helping the livery stable man. Then after a while, he took us to this wagon, hooked a mule up to it, and told us to start clearing the roads and trails."

"He had a badge on his shirt," Ship said, "didn't figure on arguing with him."

Lenore leveled a look at them. "I don't know who that is, but do not run off with the man's wagon, mule, or anything else."

Ship clutched at his chest. "Lenore, you wound me. How could you even suspect such a thing?"

Since there was an obvious answer to that question, Lenore didn't bother to voice it. Regardless of their intent, she was glad to see them. *Bliss needed help now, and these two were closer than anyone in town.* "Y'all can come back for the debris later," she said. "Bring that wagon and come with me."

She explained what had happened. "The tree isn't that big, but it injured him," she added, "and he wasn't able to push it off. And I couldn't do it on my own. But with the three of us we should be able to get him out from under there and get him to the saloon."

She began to second guess her choice of help when they reached the deputy. His pain seemed to worsen when he spotted Ship.

"Can't you find someone else? Caleb, Eli, Nathaniel? I'll wait right here."

Lenore shook her head without explanation. He'd be upset when he heard about the sheriff being injured. "We're all you got, but don't fret, we'll get you to Nathan. He's doctoring folks. There are other doctors and nurses who came from Fair Haven to help."

Bliss's eyes widened. "How bad is it?"

If Lenore told him the truth, it might upset him more. She saw Shipley opening his mouth and gave a slight shake of her head.

"I don't really know how bad it is," Lenore said, honestly. "If you let us get you into this wagon, you'll be able to see it for yourself."

All three of them worked to remove the tree. Suddenly, Ship began speaking with a Scottish brogue. That was Ship. Sometimes he talked with an English accent for days. Drama was such a part of who he was. Lenore wasn't a bit surprised, but Bliss's eyes grew huge.

Once they'd budged the tree enough to reach the deputy, Ship pulled him clear.

Lenore wasn't sure how old either of the men were, but Deputy Bliss Walker was not happy when Ship picked him up. Eyes narrowed, jaw clenched, Bliss said not a word.

Lenore suspected that his reaction wasn't all due to his injury. This whole experience was humiliating for him. She kept an eye on his gun hand.

Once they had him in the wagon, Shipley sat with him, trying to hold him steady. "We don't know what's wrong yet, jostling around might make it worse."

The deputy's eyes were closed now, and he didn't rouse when she said his name. Had he fainted?

When they got to the saloon, Ship stood, ready to carry the deputy into the makeshift hospital.

Lenore stopped him. "I'll get someone from inside to help."

"But why?" Ship asked. "I'm perfectly capable of carrying him. The man's light as a feather."

She could sense Bliss bristling, see the tension in his face. For all Ship's education he could be so clueless at times.

"I know you are capable," she said softly, "and I sincerely appreciate your help. I know the deputy does, too. But there are others to do this, and someone with your strength is probably needed elsewhere."

As Ship hurried off with a purposeful glint in his eye, Lenore was grateful for the man's willingness to help, and for his ego. She went inside.

Several men hurried out to assist Bliss, while Lenore looked for Nathan. She finally spotted him, leaned against a wall near his brother's bed. Despite the noise and activity around him, he was asleep.

A sound sleeper, like his son. And in this unguarded state he seemed almost as young and innocent.

Where had he gone in his church clothes? He said they needed to talk. She knew it was true. Still, she couldn't help but worry.

Nathaniel woke to find that someone had covered him. He wasn't sure how he knew it, but either his mother or Lenore had been involved.

Dr. Helms approached him with a cup of coffee.

"How long was I asleep?"

"Just a few hours."

Hours? Angry with himself, and terrified for Eli, Nathaniel struggled to his feet.

"Your brother's doing fine," Helms assured him.

A minute later Nathaniel was seeing the truth of that for himself. No fever, and the bandage had been changed.

He thanked Helms, then added, "I can stay up for hours, days, and still work, but once I fall asleep, I can sleep through anything. Embarrassing."

"Think nothing of it," Helms said. "Not unusual. By the way, your mother was here," he added, confirming Nathaniel's hunch. "Not to worry, I didn't leave her on her own. I found her a chair, and a cup of coffee, and then addressed any concerns about her son—both sons, in fact. I answered honestly, but without undue detail."

"Thank you."

Dr. Helms smiled. "No problem, I assure you. Your mother is an extraordinary woman."

"How so?"

"Her time with the Indians, and then afterward. Fascinating."

The man had Nathaniel's full attention now. Had his mother told Montgomery Helms more than she had her sons? She hadn't told them much at all. In a way, that made sense. It was easier to talk to a stranger at times. Especially if you didn't want to worry your family.

"Your wife was also here," Dr. Helms said. "She didn't linger."

So both had been here. "How's everyone else doing? Jillie Wilson?"

"Most are stable. Little miss is the same. There are a few new patients still being examined, but only one we're having trouble with."

Nathaniel was about to ask for a name or description when he heard a familiar voice. *Bliss.* Hurrying to the other side of the room, he saw the old deputy—battered, bruised, and to use one of Bliss's own favorite phrases, looking like he'd been drug through the brush backward.

Bliss reached out to him. "Nathaniel! Just the man I wanted to see. Tell them to let me outta here. I got work to do."

Nathaniel stared at him. "You're in no condition to work, Bliss. I'm not even sure what's wrong with you and I can tell you that much. What happened? Where are you hurting?"

"A tree fell. Only grazed me. I was trapped for a spell. Dang near everything hurts, but it's nothing I can't walk off."

"Where were you?" Nathaniel tried to remove the old man's shirt. Bliss slapped his hand away.

"I was out tracking that fugitive when the storm hit. I couldn't get out from under a tree. Lenore found me."

Nathaniel glanced around. "Did she bring you in?"

His mouth tightened. "Yep. With the help of those friends of hers." He put such emphasis on the word friends that Nathaniel knew he'd shown remarkable restraint in his description.

He was glad the men had helped Bliss, but he wasn't crazy about the thought of them still being in town. "Was Ophelia with them?"

"Didn't see her," Bliss said. "Now, tell these folks to let me go. I got work to do."

"Everything's under control. You need to concentrate on recovering."

"Eli will need some help keeping the law."

"No, he won't. Eli can't do anything right now, either."

Bliss stilled. "What do you mean?"

"He's injured, too. Right arm."

"Busted up?"

"Yes. I've done surgery. Managed to save the arm, but not sure how it will work yet."

The old man's voice dropped. "Who's doing the law-keeping?"

"Eli deputized two people before I put him under."

"Who?"

Nathaniel hesitated. "Henry and Walter. Brody is helping them."

Bliss renewed his efforts to rise. "Let me up from here."

"That was the only two people he could find at the time," Nathaniel soothed. "Caleb's in charge now."

The old man was silent for a minute, white around the mouth. Was it from pain? Or because he was angry and aggravated?

"I'd just as soon mend at home," he finally whispered.

Bliss had been renting a room from Eagan Smith. A room over

the livery stable. Again, Nathaniel hated to be the one to tell him. "Your place is gone. The livery stable was destroyed. I'm sorry."

The man closed his eyes. "Ever wonder what the point is? If your life amounted to a hill of beans?"

"Yes. Everybody probably has from time to time."

Being nice was the worst thing Nathaniel could do. He needed to be tough with the old man. Get him riled up. "You've had worse wounds and lived to tell about it."

"Maybe so," Bliss snapped, "but I wasn't a hundred and ten years old back then."

"You're not anywhere near a hundred and ten now. And the fact that you're slender and wiry played in your favor. The tree might have injured you and left you trapped, but at least the full weight of the trunk didn't hit you. I guess God wasn't through with you yet."

That got a spark of temper from Bliss. "Well, I hope he ain't expecting a whole lot outta me considering the condition I'm in!"

"I've got other folks to see to, Bliss. Let me examine you."

"Don't waste your time on me," he mumbled. "Go tend to somebody else."

One of the nurses from Fair Haven stepped over. "Looks like you could use some assistance."

"I'm trying to examine this patient and he's not cooperating. I doubt any amount of help will make a difference."

Bliss was so startled when the woman placed her hands on his shoulders that he lay quietly while they removed his shirt.

With the shirt off, there was a web of scars visible across the man's chest and abdomen. Old bullet wounds. There were also fresh bruises.

The nurse's gaze flew to Bliss's face.

"Enough to turn your stomach, ain't it?" he drawled.

"I've seen men with worse."

"Were they still alive?"

The nurse nodded. "I didn't mean to stare. Such scarring can tell me a lot about a person."

"That so." Bliss's tone of voice said what his words didn't. He wasn't interested in hearing more.

Nathaniel stifled a sigh, but Bliss's indifference didn't discourage the nurse.

"Yes. For instance, I know that at some point you've made somebody angry enough to shoot you, more than once. I'm figuring you're either a bandit, a lawman, or an 'ornery old cuss.'"

The ghost of a smile flashed across Bliss's face. "You were right the second time, and maybe the third time. The bullets were courtesy of some bandits that ambushed me and another ranger."

The nurse took a rag from a basin nearby, wet it from the bucket of hot water, and began washing Bliss, starting with his face. He was resisting until she said, "A Texas Ranger, huh? Believe it or not, I have a ranger story of my own."

The woman had finally captured the old man's interest. And Nathaniel's.

"When I was a baby I was kidnapped by some Indians," she said. "Actually, I was exchanged with an Indian baby. Never did know for sure why. My parents didn't know either. They were some of the first white settlers in the area. One day while my father was plowing in the field, my mother went to the spring to fetch some water. When she got back to the house I was gone. There was an Indian baby in the basket where I'd been sleeping. My parents were hysterical of course, but two rangers came after me."

She stilled. "One of the rangers died, but not at the hands of the Indians. They were friendly from what I've been told. It was outlaws who killed him. Have you ever heard that story?"

"A time or two."

Wasn't Bliss going to tell her? Nathaniel had only learned the story last fall, but he sure thought it was important enough to share. Especially if a person had just been wondering if his life, or life's work, had amounted to anything.

Well, if the old man wouldn't do it, he would. "This is Rueben Walker, also known as Bliss," Nathaniel told her. "He's the ranger who got you safely home. He's now the deputy for Moccasin Rock."

The woman's eyes rounded before they filled with tears. "Oh, my."

Bliss shot an angry glance at Nathaniel, but when he spoke, it was to the nurse. "The ranger who died was named Joel James Harmon. Everybody called him Blue. One of the finest individuals to ever walk this earth."

The nurse grabbed a handkerchief from her pocket and dabbed at her eyes. "My parents probably knew his name, and yours, but somewhere through the years it was forgotten. I will never forget it again. I'm deeply grateful to both of you. I cannot wait to tell my family I met you."

She was still talking when Nathaniel left after examining Bliss and wrapping his ribs. The old man had contributed an occasional word here or there, but for the most part, he was silent. Which was totally against his nature.

Was he seriously injured, or put out at being injured and unable to help? Old people sure could be contrary. But he suspected Bliss had been that way since birth.

That train of thought brought him to Sister.

Had anybody checked on her?

CHAPTER NINETEEN

"I've got another line strung up," Bob Horton called out from the side yard of the boarding house.

Lenore grabbed a tub of wet laundry and headed in his direction, glad Abby's father was willing to string clothesline. It hadn't taken long to use all the available places on the block. There were clean sheets, towels, rags, on every fence, wire, bush, or tree that could be found.

The Hortons had some damage to their home and property—including to the roof—but it was nothing compared to some others. Since Abby and Caleb's house was among those destroyed, they'd moved into the boarding house with her folks. Abby was upstairs now with baby Joseph.

Mr. Horton and Robby were still rounding up chickens and helping neighbors find and corral their animals. There were reports of some found more than two miles from Moccasin Rock. Most had not survived the experience.

Mr. Horton and several other men had also worked on getting outhouses repaired and back in place throughout town.

"Here's more soap," Agatha Culpepper said. Lenore had just learned that this sturdy woman with the cheerful disposition was Abby's grandmother. The woman had been going back and forth between the kitchen and the back porch, helping Irene Horton with cooking for the boarding house guests, as well as helping Lenore and several neighbors work on the laundry.

Agatha sliced the soap into little slivers before adding it to the boiling water, while another woman used a stick to stir the linens.

While they worked on that, Lenore hung another basketful on the line. Between the sun and the breeze, it shouldn't take long to have them back at the saloon and ready to use again.

Her thoughts turned to Nathan. How had he fared overnight? Had he gotten enough sleep? She and Jed spent a comfortable night with Peg and Cordelia. Peg had also hosted an older couple, who slept in the front room. Irene Horton said there were a half dozen people who slept in the boarding house hall, and in the parlor. All of them had lost their houses.

They'd all gone out again at first light, determined to start rebuilding their homes, their lives, right away. Lenore assumed there were also people staying in whatever other buildings were available, as well as the tents from Fair Haven.

She switched duties with Agatha Culpepper and rubbed sheets on the washboard while the older woman took a turn at the lines.

They'd finished up and made arrangements to meet again the next day, when Maggie arrived to see the baby. "I'm sorry I didn't get here sooner. I'll be glad to help with this."

"We've had plenty of help, but we'll be doing the same thing again in the morning."

"I'll be here."

"How's your husband?"

"I still haven't spoken to him," Maggie said, her voice a little shaky. "Well, I've spoken to him, but I'm not sure he heard me. Nathaniel said he's doing well. All the signs look good. Whatever that means."

"I don't think Nathan would say it if he didn't believe it was true."

"You're right." Maggie smiled. "Want to go see Abby and the baby with me?"

"Sure," Lenore said, following Maggie inside and up the stairs.

Before they could even ask about the baby, Abby wanted an update on the storm damage. Her concern would be understandable in any case, but Abby had grown up in Moccasin Rock and had known most of these people her whole life. After Lenore shared what she knew, and Maggie did the same, Abby grabbed a handkerchief from the bedside and wiped her eyes.

The other two fussed over the baby to give Abby time to gather her thoughts. "I sure wish I could help."

"I know," Lenore said, "but there are people from Fair Haven who came here just for that purpose. And everyone that's unhurt is out there helping somehow."

Then she mentioned the woman she'd happened across who'd demanded to know her identity.

"Who was it?" Abby asked.

"She didn't introduce herself, but she was skinny, kinda pinched-looking, and almost hostile."

"Myrtle Dunlop," both women said in unison.

"In most ways, she's harmless," Abby added. "Although it doesn't feel that way when she's attacking you or your family. Believe me, I know."

Handing the baby back to Abby, reluctantly, Maggie said, "If you encounter that woman again, don't pay any attention to her."

Abby nodded her head in agreement. "Myrtle knows there's a God in heaven, but for some reason she seems to think that he's put her in charge here on Earth."

"Like everywhere, there are a few bad apples in Moccasin Rock," Maggie said. "They're far outnumbered by good people. When I got here, all I had was a baby in my arms, and the clothes on my back. I didn't even have any shoes."

"Oh my."

"So many people stepped up to help me and Lucinda." Maggie looked at Abby. "And this sweet girl brought me clothing and other things I needed."

"Speaking of that," Abby said. "I may need to borrow something to wear in a few days. Most everything at the house was destroyed or blown away. I've ordered a few things from a catalog, but I'm not sure when they'll get here."

"Of course," Maggie said. "I should've offered sooner. I'm sorry you lost everything."

Abby gazed down at the baby. "Thank you, but I have what's important. So grateful we weren't at the house, and that Lenore was with me."

Maggie nodded, then turned to Lenore. "It only now occurred to me that you lost everything, too. I have clothes that should fit you."

"Thank you," Lenore said, appreciative and embarrassed at the same time. She hadn't really had much in the way of clothing to lose. Or much of anything. She wasn't like these ladies. Maybe never would be. But she got the feeling they really did like her. And not only for Nathan's sake. That gave her hope he would let her stay.

After leaving the two friends to visit, Lenore joined the other women downstairs. "I know there's a tent set up to feed people," Irene told her, "but I've made plenty, and I was thinking it might be a good idea to take it to those who can't get to the tent."

Everyone agreed, and most had an idea of where to take the food. Lenore's first thought was Pastor Wilkie Brown, and then Sister. Both had been on her mind. She should probably check with Nathan before heading up to Sister's place, but she could take food to Wilkie Brown now.

When she arrived at the church, carrying a small box with a plate of scrambled eggs, diced potatoes, ham, and biscuits, along with a jar of coffee, a cup, fork, and a napkin, she found the pastor in the yard between the church and a small house. He was sitting in a chair under a shade tree staring at the cemetery with tears in his eyes.

He smiled when she walked up, the smile widening when he saw the food. "Thank you for thinking of me, and I'm especially grateful that you sent a doctor yesterday."

"Glad to do it. I'm only toting the food, though. Mrs. Horton at the boarding house did the cooking. What did the doctor say about your leg?"

"It'll be awhile before I can get around easily. Adger Wilson fashioned me a crutch and brought it to me. I can get to the outhou…"

The man turned about ten shades of red. "I am so sorry, Mrs. Calhoun. I honestly do not know what possessed me to babble on in such an unseemly manner in front of a lady."

Lenore was fascinated. She'd been called Mrs. Calhoun a few times now, but this was the first time she'd ever been referred to as a lady. She could get used to both.

After stuttering to a stop with his apology, Pastor Wilkie asked about the conditions around town. Lenore provided what information she could, then told him she'd come back later for the plate.

"Please don't go," he said.

"Is there something else you need?"

"I wanted to talk to you."

"About what?

"Some of the things you said yesterday have been bothering me."

Lenore blinked at him. "I'm sorry."

"There's no reason to be sorry, but I'd like to talk to you about it."

She should've let someone else bring the food. "I'll come back later."

"If you have the time," Wilkie said, "I'd rather get this off my mind now, it'll help me rest easier. Please."

When he put it like that, she couldn't very well refuse him the chance to talk, but that didn't mean she had to really listen. "I'll stay while you eat, then I need to get on back."

"Of course." Taking a bite of eggs, he chewed, swallowed, wiped his mouth, and then began talking in a rush. "You were worried about sins. It says in the Bible that when we repent and ask God for forgiveness, that's exactly what he does. Forgives us, removes our sin as far as the east is from the west. That gives you a new start."

This man didn't understand. "I've sinned too many times to count." She couldn't even remember how old she was the first time she'd picked someone's pocket.

To Lenore's amazement, Pastor Wilkie didn't ask her to tell him everything, or even anything, about her past.

"That's between you and God," he said. "But I can assure you, nothing's too big for him to forgive."

"Do you really believe that?"

Wilkie looked her straight in the eye. "With all my heart. Sin is sin. It says so in the Bible. God can, and does, forgive it all if we repent."

He paused to spear some potatoes with his fork. "Now, the earthly consequences for sin are different. You pay more dearly for some sins here on earth, than you might for others."

"Believe me, that I understand," Lenore said. Her words were resigned. "Even if God forgave all my sins, I'm not sure I'll ever be good enough to be a Christian."

Pastor Wilkie's brow furrowed. Once again, she'd said something that upset him.

"It's not about being good," he insisted. "None of us are good enough. It says in the Bible that all have sinned and fallen short of the Glory of God. And it says, '*For by grace are ye saved* through faith; and that not of yourselves: it is the gift of God: Not of works, lest any man should boast.' You don't work for a gift, Mrs. Calhoun."

He shooed a fly away from his plate without ever breaking eye contact with her. "I, too, have a past I'm not exactly proud of. God can use anyone, can do amazing things to the heart and soul."

Lenore didn't know whether to believe him or not, but to her own surprise, she was interested in what he was saying. Especially it coming right on the heels of Abby's prayers. Yet there were still things that bothered her.

"I've met some preachers," Lenore told him. She tried to think of a way to say it—what she'd seen, what she'd heard—that wouldn't shock him. "They weren't nice people," she settled for saying. "They would say one thing and do another."

He nodded. "Charlatans. I understand. But there are folks in all walks of life who aren't what they seem."

"Yes, but not all folks are standing between me and heaven, like preachers are."

Wilkie Brown dropped his fork, eyes widening. "There's no one standing between you and heaven except for Jesus. And he's not blocking the way, he *is* the way."

"But I heard a preacher say that if people gave money to him during the service, that they'd have good fortune, and a place in heaven. Sounded to me like he was the way in."

The pastor's expression tightened. "What he said was a lie. Straight from Satan's lips. Money does help keep the church doors open. It helps spread the word of God. But you don't have to give one red cent to get to heaven. Not one. I'll say it again, 'For by grace are you saved by faith.' Jesus died on the cross—shed his blood—for your sins. My sins. All the sins of mankind. Repenting and accepting him as our Savior is how we get to heaven."

Could it really work that way? "So I'd need to go to the front of the church to be able to accept?"

Wilkie shook his head. "You can if you want, but it's not necessary. Being saved is truly between you and God. Can happen any time, any place."

Lenore poured some coffee from the jar to the cup. "It's still sorta hot," she told him.

He accepted the cup, then gave a satisfied sigh after taking a sip, but it didn't distract him from his talking. "Don't get me wrong, I hope you come to church, I urge you to. I think it's important. To everyone. If a person doesn't know Jesus, it's the best place to learn. And if you do know him, it's a way to learn more, to grow. Plus, there are people here to encourage you."

"People might be a problem," Lenore admitted. "There'll be some who look down on me. I don't want that to hurt my son. Or Nathan."

To her surprise, Wilkie didn't disagree. "You may be right. There are people in this world who have opinions about everything, strong ones, even when they know little to nothing about the subject at hand. And there are those who believe their opinions are the only ones that matter. It happens to me too. Some people think my sermons are too long, some think they're too short. Others think I talk about hell too much, others that I talk about heaven too much. I could go on and on. My advice is to quit worrying about them. Find the ones who care about you, and want the best for you, and cling to them. Starting with Jesus."

Lenore was silent as she gathered the dishes, jar, and napkin, deep in thought as she headed back to the boarding house. *Was he right?*

As she reached the main street, someone called her name. *Nathan.* He was leaving the saloon. He'd cleaned up and changed, but the shirt seemed a little big. She wasn't the only one wearing borrowed clothing. His hair looked as if he'd run his hand through it instead of a comb, and he was clearly exhausted. He was still the best-looking man she'd ever seen.

Falling into step beside her, he offered to carry the box. "Where you headed?"

"To take this back to the boarding house. Mrs. Horton is

cooking for those who can't get to the tent. I took Pastor Wilkie something."

"Good. I heard about his leg. I plan on checking on him myself. Then I'm going to see Sister. I borrowed a wagon from Henry Barnett. Eagan is still trying to put things back together. Do you want to go with me?"

"Sure. I was hoping we could take her food. I need to get Jed first. I'm sure your mother's getting tired."

Nathan smiled. "She's not. I checked on them. They were planting some seeds for Peg. She had a garden spot plowed behind her house a month ago, but hasn't had a chance to work it, so Mama is doing it. And Jed is helping. Believe me when I say she's enjoying spending time with him."

That warmed Lenore's heart. "I'm so glad. It's good for Jed, too. How's the deputy doing?"

"Cracked ribs, and most likely a bruised spleen. I think he'll be fine. Thanks for making sure he got back here."

"Shipley and Gordon really made it possible."

"I'll thank them when I get a chance," Nathan said.

'How's Eli?"

"So far, so good. The folks from Fair Haven are watching and ready if he needs anything before we get back."

He handed her the crate when they reached the alley leading to the Horton place. "I'll go check on Wilkie while you pack the food for Sister. I'll feel better once I make sure she's all right."

"Me too. For some reason she's been on my mind a lot."

CHAPTER TWENTY

AT FIRST, NATHANIEL slowed every time they passed a storm damaged area on the way to Sister's, but they found only debris, no people. By now, most everyone needing help had ended up in Moccasin Rock proper, even if they hadn't gotten there under their own steam.

Lenore was holding Nickle, who hadn't enjoyed gardening as much as Jed did.

"You sure you don't mind her coming along?" Lenore asked.

"I'm sure." Nathaniel was growing fonder of the dog with each passing day. "What did you bring for Sister?"

"A big jar full of chicken and dumplings, some cornbread, and some pie, and some stuff that'll keep for later."

"Sounds good."

In time, Nathaniel left the signs of destruction behind and they began the ascent to Sister's house.

From the looks of it, the tornado had bypassed this area entirely. At first glance, the cabin appeared undamaged.

Yet something seemed off.

There was no smoke curling from the chimney.

"I don't remember ever coming here when there wasn't a fire,"

Nathaniel said. "Sister's always either cold, or cooking. And that fireplace is her only answer for both."

"That is worrisome," Lenore agreed.

Once again, Nathaniel left the wagon when the going got steeper, and they headed in on foot. Nickel followed along with occasional side-trips into the woods. "It doesn't look like she got much more than a heavy rain up here," he said. "No storm damage."

But the moment Nathaniel knocked on the cabin door, then pushed it open, he knew Sister was facing trouble of another kind.

She was laying on the bed, on her side, eyes closed, facing the door. He thought at first that she was dead. Her skin appeared paper thin, stretching across her prominent cheekbones. She'd always been pale, but now she'd developed bruises.

When he reached for her wrist, her eyes fluttered open. "What are you doing here?"

"Checking on you," Nathaniel said. "We're taking you into town. Don't bother arguing with me." He checked her leg. Better. He wasn't sure what was wrong, but it wasn't related to the burn.

"No, I'm not going anywhere." Her objection was as fast as always, though it wasn't the vehement one she'd put up in the past. "I'm dying. I'd as soon do it here. I'll be gone before the day is done. I'm old. It's my time to go."

Nathaniel withheld further comment while he checked her blood pressure. *Low.* Then her pulse. *Weak.* He put the stethoscope to her chest and listened to her heart. Sister was right, she didn't have long. But he didn't think it was from old age.

He removed the stethoscope from his ears. "Are you hurting?"

"My belly hurts. And my mouth's burning." She listed a few more symptoms. Some of them, like tremors, could be a sign of old age, but she'd never exhibited evidence of them before. And some of the other symptoms sounded more like she'd ingested something toxic. There were plants and herbs in the area that fit that description.

"Have you been out gathering any remedies lately?"

Her head moved back and forth on the pillow, then she moaned again and grabbed at his arm. "Please bury me here. Don't take me off no place else."

He patted the gnarled old hand. "I don't know if the undertaker would agree to come up here. He's overwhelmed right now. There was a tornado."

"Then you dig the grave and put me in it."

Nathaniel glanced at Lenore. She was staring at the woman with tears in her eyes but offered no advice.

"Don't worry, Sister," he said after some thought. "We'll take care of everything. I'm sorry I didn't get up here quicker."

The old woman closed her eyes. "Don't matter. When it's a body's time, it's a body's time. You kinda know it in your heart before you know it in your head."

She fell asleep, and Nathaniel covered her with a blanket and checked her vitals again, aware that Lenore had slipped outside. There were several chairs at the table. He moved one closer to Sister's bedside and settled in, checking her frequently, hoping she'd rally.

She woke several times over the next hour. Sometimes talking, other times staring at the ceiling of the cabin. "Did you bring your wife with you?"

"Yes, she's here."

"That girl's a good 'un," Sister whispered.

"Yes." *She is.*

Then later she roused again. "I spent most my life here, you know. I was a young girl when they brought me here from Kentucky."

"Yes, ma'am."

"My family's all gone." Sister turned her gaze to Nathaniel. "I never allowed that young preacher feller to visit. He tried. But I...discouraged him. Now, there won't be no one to pray over me, lesten you do it."

"I'll do it," Nathaniel said, then added, "I should at least know your real name if I'm going to pray for you."

She sighed. "Jesus knows who I am, and when to expect me. He'll recognize me when I get there."

Nathaniel couldn't argue with that.

A bit later she told him to give her possessions to anyone who could use them. Then her eyes snapped open, her voice gaining strength. "But don't give a blamed thing to *him*. I tried to get shed of the man. Don't trust him."

"Who? Do you have family around here?"

"I done told you, I don't have no family. They all gone on to heaven."

Nathaniel chalked the odd comments up as delirium and concentrated on making her as comfortable as possible.

Once she woke and seemed startled to see him. "When I was young, I would fall asleep on the floor in front of the fire," she said. "Daddy or Mama would pick me up and take me to the bed. I've dreamed several times lately that one of them was near, waiting for me to fall asleep."

Nathaniel took her hand in his. *How sad it must be to be the very last of your family.*

"My name's Bessie Davis," she whispered, closing her eyes.

He gently squeezed her hand and prayed, reassuring her she wasn't alone.

One of the last things Sister said didn't make any sense at all. "He's not my nephew. He wanted me to say that, but I wouldn't. No use for the man. No good. He'll bring trouble."

True to her word, Sister breathed her last by midafternoon.

Nathaniel went outside to locate a spot for the grave. Lenore had beaten him to it. While he'd been tending to Sister, Lenore had searched out a shovel and a spade and gotten started.

"There's an old barn further back," she explained. "Not much in it, and everything that is there is covered in rust, but I reckon they'll dig as good as they always did."

"As long as the handles hold out," Nathaniel agreed.

"Is this spot okay?" Lenore seemed to be second-guessing her decision.

"Yes, I think Sister would approve." It was far enough from the cabin, in case anyone ever lived there again, and the ground was soft due to the recent rains.

In addition to finding the tools they'd need Lenore had gathered rocks to place atop the grave. Nickel lay nearby, dozing in the shade.

Nathaniel grabbed the spade and started digging. "This is not the first time you've done this, is it?"

Lenore shook her head. "No. I buried my grandfather. Like I said, he passed away right before I met you."

"I hope you didn't have to do this alone?"

"No. Ship, Gordon and the others helped, however they could."

Nathaniel was curious if the man died from illness or accident. Lenore supplied the answer without him asking.

"Grandpa was sick for a long time. When I didn't do what Ophelia wanted me to, she'd threaten to leave him on the side of the road somewhere."

Just when Nathaniel thought the woman couldn't be any more despicable.

"Of course, that meant I tried even harder to toe the line, doing whatever she wanted. But every free minute I had I spent with Grandpa. I cooked for him, kept him clean, read to him. He'd done all those things for me through the years."

Nathaniel didn't know whether to get her mind off the loss by speaking of something else, or to keep her talking. He decided that talking was better. "What did your grandfather read to you?"

Lenore shrugged. "Lots of things. Even the dictionary. He made me learn a new word every week. Somehow, he'd also managed to get his hands on a book called, 'The Young Lady's Guide to Gracious Living,' and he was bound and determined that I would learn all of it. Everything that I needed to know. He dreamed of a better life for me. When I was younger, I hung on every word. Believing that it would happen."

"That changed as you got older?"

She looked away. "I guess. Shipley filled my head with stories, too. He had a few old books he lugged around. Including the works of William Shakespeare."

"Ship read you Shakespeare? What did you think?"

Lenore wrinkled her nose. "Didn't care for it much. Course I don't know how much of it was real. It was so strange that sometimes I thought Ship was making it up as he went along."

Nathaniel turned away to hide a grin.

"My favorite stories from Ship were the ones he called fairy tales," Lenore said. "The ones that began with once upon a time and ended with happy ever after. That's what I dreamed of. None of that panned out, any more than the gracious living. But I'm happy and grateful. I've got Jed and…"

She clamped her mouth shut.

What had she started to say? *Jed and you?* The idea that she'd be grateful for him, after everything that happened, humbled Nathaniel.

His chest tightened at the thought of Lenore reading the book about manners, and hearing the stories that Shipley told, and imagining a better world, hoping for a better life.

Nathaniel was certainly no prince, but he was going to do his best to provide a wonderful life for her. But he couldn't tell her exactly how or when, because he didn't have a clue. "I heard from the Pinkerton agent," he settled for saying.

Lenore stopped digging and looked at him. There was no question in her eyes. She wasn't curious about what he'd discovered because she'd known all along.

"We are legally married."

She didn't say, "I told you so," but her expression did.

Nathaniel was more curious than ever. "How did you manage that? You've explained to me why you did it, but now I'm curious how."

She hesitated, then said, "The judge had caught me picking pockets the day before. He'd started to hand me over to the law, then discovered that I was young, and a girl. He gave me a lecture instead. He wanted me to promise him that I'd quit stealing and make something of my life. Then the next day I heard Ophelia talking about marrying me off to that old man. Like I said before, I went looking for you, and then Ship thought you were the mark."

Lenore paused, rubbing at the palm of one hand with the index finger of another.

"Blister?"

"Not yet." She adjusted her grip on the shovel and resumed digging. "I was floored when you said you'd marry me, then I remembered what that judge said. I knew where to find him. I went and explained that I found someone who was willing to marry me. That I was leaving town and starting over. He was happy to hear it. Of course, that's not how it all turned out. But I had good intentions."

Another thing he and Lenore had in common.

After they'd finished digging, Nathaniel prepared Sister for burial—wrapping her in the covers—and then took her to her grave as he'd promised.

Once they'd replaced the dirt, and added the rocks, Nathaniel drew water from the well, took soap from the bag, and washed up, then drew a fresh pail for Lenore. After she was done, they returned to the gravesite.

Nathaniel had been to plenty of funerals, but for the life of him he couldn't remember a single word that was normally said.

So he prayed. Then he recalled the verse from Tessa's tombstone and recited Psalm 23.

Lenore picked some wildflowers growing near the edge of the yard and placed them on the mound of dirt. All-in-all, it wasn't much in the way of funeral services, but they'd done the best they could.

Nathaniel gathered the tools they'd used and headed for the barn. He stopped. No sense in putting things back when he'd have to remove them again when he returned.

"Sister wanted me to give her belongings to anyone who could use them," he told Lenore. "There are plenty of people who lost everything. I don't have time to gather it all now. We can come back for everything later."

He needed to get back to town and check on his patients. Worry over Eli had circled through his mind all day.

Nickel had been laying nearby this whole time, head on her paws, watching. With a little yelp, she jumped up and ran into the woods, growling and barking.

"Probably a squirrel," Lenore said, as she followed the dog. "Here, girl. We need to get on back."

Nathaniel waited for Lenore, growing concerned after a few minutes. He was about to go after her when she emerged, hair in disarray and a worried look on her face.

"What happened?"

"I don't know what Nickel was chasing, but I discovered something in the brush."

The fact that the pocket of her dress was full should have been his first clue that she'd brought it back with her. "What was it?"

When Lenore pulled her hand from her pocket, it was wrapped around a clump of matted black fur. It took a minute for Nathaniel to realize the clump was alive—barely.

"Do you think we can save it?" she asked.

"That depends," he said.

"On what?"

"On what it is."

She smiled. "It's a kitten. I wanted to make sure we can keep him before Jed sees."

"Ahh. Here, let me have a look." Not only was the animal malnourished, but there was a place on his front leg that was scraped raw.

"I looked for his mother, but there was no sign of her," Lenore said. "I couldn't leave him."

"No. Let's take him inside and see what we can do." The kitten couldn't have weighed more than a few ounces, even soaking wet, and yet it took Lenore and Nathaniel to bathe him. Then Lenore poured a bit of juice from the chicken and dumplings onto a plate and let the kitten lap it up, while Nathaniel found some salve for his wounds.

"We'll need to bandage him," he said, "so he won't lick the medicine off."

Lenore found a rag, tore a strip from it, and cradled the kitten while Nathaniel wrapped the leg.

"Tiniest patient I've had in a while," he said, grateful for a reason to smile.

"Thank you. I think this little fellow will be good for Jed. Nickel made such a difference in my life."

"You've had her since she was a pup?"

"Yes. She wasn't very old when you first met her. But she's a fast learner. The main thing she's good at, is following me, protecting me."

"Why did you name her Nickel?"

"Because that's what I paid for her."

The dog under discussion suddenly went into a barking frenzy behind the cabin. It was Nickel's, "I'll protect you" bark. Tucking the kitten in her pocket again, Lenore followed Nathaniel outside to investigate.

Fully expecting to see something that Nickel would consider dangerous—a rabid animal, a snake, another person—they were surprised to find the area deserted.

Lenore whistled, her brow furrowed when it took a while for the dog to return from the woods. Even then, Nickel kept looking toward the area and growling.

"You ever get the feeling someone's watching you?" Lenore asked after the dog had quieted.

"Yes." *That's exactly what he'd felt.*

With no real reason for doing it, other than the odd feeling, Nathaniel waited until Lenore wasn't looking, then removed the knife from his boot.

"Expecting trouble?"

Not easy getting anything past this girl. "Not expecting it. But trouble has a way of finding you sometimes, whether you're expecting it or not."

They stepped back into the cabin to get the food they'd brought and the black bag.

It was strange how a house could feel so empty just from someone taking a last breath.

The cabin had been quiet and dark when they got there, but now it seemed to have given up.

After one last look around, Nathaniel admitted something. "I should've made Sister move into town. I hate that she was sick and alone."

"I think it would've killed her even sooner to leave here," Lenore said.

"Maybe so. I'm grateful that we got here when we did." *At least she hadn't died alone.*

CHAPTER TWENTY-ONE

Lenore balanced a stack of freshly laundered sheets and toweling on one arm and pushed open the door to the saloon with the other.

In the past two days, real beds had been brought in for the people who weren't able to go home to get better…recuperate, the doctors called it. Makeshift screens had been set up between the beds, and the windows had been covered, giving everyone a sense of some privacy. Medicines and medical equipment had been lined up behind the bar. The bar top was covered with trays, pitchers and glasses, all making it easier to dispense medication.

Lenore was impressed with Nathan's ingenuity. She'd never been inside a hospital, or even a doctor's office until she moved into Nathan's house, but she figured they'd be hard pressed to come up with any better design.

Some of the Fair Haven folks had gone home. The older doctor, and two nurses were staying on for another week, sleeping upstairs.

Lenore hadn't seen much of Nathan since they'd returned from Sister's cabin two days ago. He'd been thrown into work as soon as they got back to town. And then he'd learned that his friend, Carmichael Cook, had died. Since the drug store had appeared undamaged except for the broken window, no one had looked for him there. But the brick that had flown through the glass, struck the owner in the temple, killing him on the spot. And some man named Ezra also died in the storm.

After one stricken look at hearing the news, Nathan had gone on about his work, with seemingly little reaction.

Then, later that night, Lenore had walked into the front room at Peg's and found him sitting there in the dark. Tears on his face. The losses were adding up. And he hadn't had time to grieve for any of them. Lenore hadn't known what to say, so she'd sat down beside him, slipping her hand into his, and he'd wrapped his fingers around hers. In a way, it seemed odd for a husband and wife to sit there holding hands and not saying a word, and at the same time, there'd been something special in the moment.

The next morning, he left the house before she woke, and the same thing had happened today. There'd been funerals yesterday—with more to come—so he'd been busy. Hopefully he was holding up okay.

Nearing the corner of the room where Eli was recovering, Lenore slowed, then began to creep along. She'd heard that the sheriff was awake now. And refusing laudanum for the pain. So far, she had managed to avoid direct interaction with the man, but she'd have to face him someday. *Hopefully not today.*

Reaching his bedside, Lenore moved the pitcher of water on a table to make room for a clean towel, glad that someone else was charged with tending to him. She nearly knocked the water over when a deep voice—unsteady and pained—spoke out. "I sure could use a drink of that right now."

She looked up to see Eli propped up in the bed. The beard stubble made him appear even more frightening.

"Of course." She grabbed a glass, filled it, and handed it to him. He seemed to have trouble using his left hand, so she waited to see if he needed help.

When he had a good grip on the glass, Lenore stepped away, removed a rag from her pocket, then ran it along the table gathering non-existent dust, before finally shifting her gaze to Eli. He was watching her every move. She backed up a little more.

"You know, I think we're alike in some ways," he said.

That stopped her in her tracks. "How?"

"We're both good at figuring people out, fast, and we've both done what we had to do to survive."

What?

Eli cleared his throat. "But the reason we need to be friends, is because we both love Nathaniel."

Lenore stood there, speechless.

First, Maggie had trusted her enough to let her wander through her house and hold her baby, Abby had prayed with her, Caleb referred to her as the baby's aunt, Nathaniel asked for her word as if it meant something, and Mama Calhoun hugged her and was watching her child.

Now this from Eli. The Calhoun she'd been most afraid of.

Lenore felt like she'd been knighted, like one of the folks from Ship's old stories.

She burst into tears.

Eli's eyes widened. "Don't do that."

"Okay," Lenore gulped, but she couldn't stop the tears. It wasn't only from Eli's gesture of friendship. It was sort of a culmination of everything. She couldn't explain that.

Since Eli looked like he was ready to climb out of bed and run if she didn't stop, Lenore pulled herself together. She took the glass from him and finished her chores.

She left a few minutes later, smiling when she heard him grumbling that he was, "Never, ever talking to another blamed female as long as he lived."

Lenore stepped out on the street in time to see Nathan leave the barbershop. Freshly shaved, hair trimmed.

He was again wearing garments she'd not seen before. Black

denim, black shirt with shiny buttons, and a gray kerchief tied around his neck. His boots had been polished.

Nathan looked up to see her staring at him and hurried across the street. "Everything okay?"

"Yes."

"Good. For a minute there you had a strange expression."

Heat filled her face. "I was noticing that you've shaved and gotten a haircut."

"Oh," he self-consciously ran a hand over his head. "I got a real good look at myself in the mirror this morning. Looked like a cross between a grizzly bear and a sheep dog."

She grinned. *Hardly.*

"I've been meaning to get you and Jed some clothes," he said, "but so far I haven't had a chance. I will soon. Caleb was in Fair Haven and he picked this"—he grimaced—"out for me. My younger brother has very unusual, almost gaudy, taste in clothing."

"I've seen you dressed gaudier."

"That's true." He grinned, then sobered. "Have you been crying?"

"Not really."

"What happened? Did someone hurt you? Or say something to hurt you?"

Lenore hastened to reassure him that everything was okay, even as she thrilled at having a champion. He sure sounded like he cared about her.

What would he say if she told him that the only person who had the power to hurt her, really hurt her, was him?

When he'd told her about the telegram from the Pinkerton agent, Nathan immediately asked how she'd managed to get a judge to cooperate.

He hadn't said anything about what he planned to do now that he knew the truth.

⁓

After Lenore left, Nathaniel checked in on his patients, and then headed for the cemetery, bracing himself for another goodbye.

Caleb and Captain Joshua Parnell were coming out of the jail as he passed. Parnell was a square-jawed man with gray hair and a scar that ran from the bottom of his left ear across his cheek and all the way up into his hair line. Nathaniel didn't know how he was injured, but he knew it wasn't a doctor who stitched him up. At least not one with proper training. The man had a no-nonsense look to him that told you he didn't suffer fools gladly, especially fools of the criminal variety.

Parnell greeted Nathaniel but didn't linger, while Caleb stopped to ask about Eli and Bliss.

"Glad they're okay," Caleb said after Nathaniel filled him in. "Will be even more glad when they're back on their feet."

"Needing help?"

"No. It feels strange without the two of them, that's all." He nodded toward the jail. "Booked a prisoner. Henry Barnett caught him loading up a wagon at a house on the Boone Springs road."

"Let me guess, it wasn't the man's wagon?"

"Right. And not his house."

Criminals were getting bolder. If Henry hadn't known the folks involved, it might've been possible for the thief to get away with it.

"All some people have left are farm implements and other tools," Caleb said. "They need those to rebuild, to survive."

Even as Nathaniel agreed with every word his brother said, and meant it, he was uncomfortable. He was married to a thief. Although he believed that Lenore never wanted to do the things she'd done, it didn't change the fact that there were people she'd wronged.

Then he realized what a hypocrite he was being. He and Eli had done things they hadn't wanted to do. Things that their benefactor insisted on. In the end, they'd run, and their lives had changed. *What if no one had ever given them another chance?*

That brought his thoughts to Lenore's former traveling companions. He still wasn't sure what to think of them. "It wasn't Shipley or Gordon was it?"

"No. Henry put them to work the first day, and as far as I know they've been at it pretty steady."

"Where are they staying?"

"In one of the tents."

Since Ophelia left with the last wagon, they were as homeless as anyone else, including Nathaniel.

"I didn't recognize the man I arrested," Caleb said. "No one else did either. We think he came here to profit from the tornado."

That wasn't unexpected, but it was infuriating. There would always be people who took advantage of others. Some were lazy or opportunists, while others were plain rotten.

As Caleb left, Nathaniel was glad that things hadn't been any worse. With Eli and Bliss injured, and Caleb and Captain Parnell looking for the fugitive, there wasn't much in the way of law enforcement in the town, and there were still people spilling in from everywhere.

Folks from Fair Haven said their telegraph office and telephone switchboard had been inundated by reporters from across the country. The Moccasin Rock tornado had made the front page of newspapers as far away as New York City and San Francisco. *Unbelievable.* Some folks, closer by, had even traveled to see the destruction first-hand. Families loaded into wagons, single men with wagon loads of goods to sell. Most were honestly curious, or trying to make an honest buck, but there were always those meaning to do more.

Nathaniel was headed to the cemetery when he noticed Myrtle Dunlop standing behind the mercantile. He started to turn around.

Her husband was a nice enough fellow, but Myrtle could grate on a person in the best of times, and these weren't the best of times.

Then he stilled. *What was Myrtle wearing?* A gunbelt.

She was so skinny that she had the thing tied up to keep it on her non-existent hips. Both feet were braced, and both hands were wrapped around a pistol.

Even as Nathaniel watched, a man backed out of the general store, arms full of merchandise.

Myrtle drew back the hammer. "What do you think you're doing?"

The man turned, launching into an explanation before he was fully facing her. When he saw the gun, he dropped everything. Nathaniel didn't recognize him. Apparently, neither did Myrtle Dunlop.

"Who are you?" she snapped.

"Someone down on their luck. Just taking things my family needs."

The stuff at his feet included several watches, ladies' jewelry, and some fancy music boxes. All things that Silas had kept behind the counter. No food. No clothing. No medications of any kind.

"If you need something for your family to eat, there's a tent set up between here and the depot," Myrtle said. "If you need medicine, go to the saloon." Without taking her gaze from the thief or lowering the gun she tilted her head to indicate where each was located.

"If you need help with anything else go by the bakery down the road and talk to my husband. We'll help you all we can. But I'd better not see you picking up a single thing that doesn't belong to you. The people who own these businesses have families, too."

"Yes, ma'am," the man said as he scrambled away. Nathaniel was so relieved that Mrs. Dunlop could help handle the thieves—and that she was capable of compassion and discernment—that he smiled at her.

She scowled. "Don't you have something better to do than stand around grinning at people."

Nathaniel grinned even bigger. "Yes, I believe I do."

The grin faded just around the next corner, when he spotted a man beside a wagon, a woman on the seat, they were both looking right then left. Looking for someone or something. *Or for something to steal?*

He stepped over to them. "Can I help you?"

Several kids popped up from the back of the wagon, shoeless, wearing ragged, patched clothing. Startled, Nathaniel stepped back, and then smiled at them.

"We came to help," the man said. "We brought some food, too. Figured there might be folks what could use a good meal."

The woman held the reins with work-worn hands. "We had to finish the plowing and couldn't get here any sooner."

They were looking at the damage. "Never seen anything like it," the man said.

"Lord knows," the woman mumbled, eyes wide.

Nathaniel was overwhelmed, not only by their generosity, but by his own cynicism. They probably didn't have much, yet they'd brought food to share, and had come prepared to work.

After thanking them, and answering a few questions, Nathaniel spotted Henry Barnett and his wife, Jenna, nearby. As always, Jenna Barnett—a fussy, spoiled woman—was dressed as if ready to attend a ball. But for once, her expression was somber, as she carried a box filled with cookware towards the food tent. Nathaniel called to them, and after introductions and a brief explanation about the visitors, he left the family in good hands.

Nathaniel headed on, ready to face the next funeral. No matter how bleak things seemed, there were good people out there. He need never to forget that.

At the cemetery, he joined the others gathered around Silas Martin's grave. For the time being, the repairs to the church had ceased, and would commence again as soon as the last service was finished. It was good to see it taking shape again.

A gentle breeze played through the leaves of the oak trees scattered among the tombstones as Pastor Wilkie Brown, seated in a chair, read from the fourth chapter of First Thessalonians: *For the Lord himself shall descend from heaven with a shout, with the voice of the archangel, and with the trump of God: and the dead in Christ shall rise first: Then we which are alive and remain shall be caught up together with them in the clouds, to meet the Lord in the air: and so shall we ever be with the Lord. Wherefore comfort one another with these words.*

There was absolute comfort in those words. But watching those around him, Nathaniel knew that it might be long on coming to some.

Wilkie Brown spoke about Silas Martin being among the first people to settle in Moccasin Rock, originally selling merchandise from a tent. In time, Silas purchased one of the biggest buildings in town and set up shop, carrying everything from beans to barbed wire.

Silas Martin's wife, Lydia, was a stout, no-nonsense type woman with a head of springy gray curls and a determined nature. Now, Nathaniel didn't recognize her at first glance. She seemed to have diminished—not only in personality, but in size and stature.

Nathaniel also noticed the strain on Pastor Wilkie's face. It wasn't only from his injuries. This had been a trying few days. Just like the doctors, nurses, and undertaker, the pastor had been busier than he'd probably been in his lifetime. And he was grieving. The dead were his friends, too.

Nathaniel looked at those around him. They'd all lost friends, family. Eli was mourning, and doubly upset that he couldn't attend the funerals. When he'd asked how the visit to Judge Stewart had gone, Nathaniel thought briefly to shield him from any more loss, but in the end, he'd opted for the truth.

Mina Kirk's service the day before had been attended by her class. She'd tried to prepare them for life and had died trying to protect them. Her loss would be felt for years to come.

Carmichael Cook's service had been held earlier in the morning. Nathaniel had written to his family and had Caleb post the letter from Fair Haven. Nathaniel hadn't known what to say to the Cooks, but he'd offered his condolences, and let them know that their son had died among friends. He told them that the drug store was still standing and asked them what they wanted to do. Carmichael mentioned once that his family didn't have much money, and that one of the reasons he was excited about having his own business, was because he wanted to help support them.

The young pharmacist had also said that his folks worried about him living in Texas, fearful that Indians or outlaws would be the death of him. The weather probably never crossed their minds.

Nathaniel was struck anew by how fast things could change, how drastically. It wasn't like he'd had time to become close friends with Carmichael or Mina, and he hadn't known Silas really well, or the others.

But the world had lost people that were kind and decent. And that hurt.

Wilkie Brown ended the brief graveside service by quoting Revelation 21:4, *And God shall wipe away all tears from their eyes; and there shall be no more death, neither sorrow, nor crying, neither shall there be any more pain: for the former things are passed away.*

With the service over, Nathaniel walked straight to Peg's house, marched inside, said hello to his mother, hugged her, then picked Jed up and held him close for a few minutes before heading back to work. And all the way, he tried to figure out what to tell Lenore.

He wanted to discuss their plans for the future, tell her where his office would be, tell her where they'd live.

But he couldn't do that until he knew himself.

CHAPTER TWENTY-TWO

LENORE SMILED AT Nathan's grumblings as they stepped up the porch at Eli and Maggie's house.

Nathan's aggravation with his brother was a marked contrast to the stark fear he'd exhibited just over a week ago, and the best indication yet—to Lenore's way of thinking—that Eli Calhoun was on his way to recovery.

"I have never had a patient who was more difficult than Eli," Nathan said. "Except for Bliss. And none who ever threatened to shoot people who were trying to care for them."

Lenore understood Nathan's concern. It probably would've been better for Eli to recuperate in town. But he'd said he was going home, even if he had to walk. Nathan had been afraid that he would try. He'd let him go home several days ago.

The saloon still housed a few patients, but Deputy Bliss had been moved to the Horton Boarding House, and Big John Finley had moved to his own room over the saloon. According to Nathan, neither was well, but both were doing better. The biggest boost to Nathan's spirits had been Jillie Wilson suddenly waking up, wanting something to eat, and then wondering why everyone around her was crying, including the doctor.

Yes, things were better. So why hadn't Nathan talked to her

about staying? Was he unsure yet that he wanted her here for good? *Stop thinking about it.*

Maggie opened the door with a fussy baby in her arms. "Come on in," she said. "Caleb's in with Eli, they're talking about fugitives."

"They find one?" Nathan asked.

"No, at least not that I've heard."

Lucinda let out a wail right then that ended with a shuddering, heaving cry.

Brow furrowed, Nathan placed a hand on her head. "Is she sick?"

"I don't know. Peg was here earlier. She told me that Lucinda was probably teething, said rubbing her gums with a wet rag might help, or some clove oil." Normally unflappable Maggie looked flustered.

"About the only advice I've heard, too," Nathan said. "Do you want me to check her over?"

"Sure, thank you."

Since Eli was in the bedroom, they moved to the kitchen. Maggie asked Lenore to grab a quilt from the back of the sofa, and then place it on the table.

As Nathan examined the baby—looking almost like he was hurting with her—Lenore wondered if this sort of thing was difficult for him. He'd lost his first child to sickness. She couldn't imagine how one went forward from that, especially when it involved being around sick children often.

Nathan's mood seemed to lift when he pronounced Lucinda fit as a fiddle. Placing the baby on his shoulder, he rubbed her back. "I agree with Peg. Teething. She might get fussier, and even run a fever before the tooth breaks through the gum."

Maggie appeared relieved and disheartened at the same time.

"Can I hold her for a while?" Lenore asked. "Let you rest."

"I appreciate it, but she only wants me." Maggie's expression softened. "I think I'll sit on the front porch where it's cooler and rock her. See if I can't get her to sleep. But thank you both. I'm glad you're here. My first time with a teething baby, and a husband recovering from surgery. They're both a little fussy. It will pass."

Nathan's gaze sharpened. "What's Eli fussing about?"

"The fact that he can't be out there helping Caleb and the other ranger. Maybe it'll do him good to see you two and talk about something else for a while."

Maggie stepped outside, while Lenore and Nathan headed for the bedroom.

They walked in to hear Caleb saying, "He has to have someone helping him in the area."

"That's what I was thinking," Eli said.

Caleb was sitting in a chair. Eli was propped up in the bed with his injured arm resting on a pillow.

They both nodded to Nathan and Lenore but didn't stop talking.

"With the confusion and disorder around here, it would be possible for anyone to blend in," Caleb said.

"You'd think people would notice a man with a mark like that."

Nathan placed his black bag on the dresser. "Mark like what? Who are we talking about?"

"Vincent Shields," Caleb said. "The murdering horse thief from San Antonio. Someone tried to slit his throat once, left a nasty scar. And he escaped the hangman's noose back in his younger days. The man's got nine lives."

Nathan asked a couple more questions, but Lenore could tell that his attention was already on his work. He carefully lifted Eli's arm, removed the outer bandage, then the splint, then another bandage before staring at the incision. She wasn't sure exactly what he was looking for, but there was relief in his expression.

"Wiggle your fingers," Nathan told Eli, nodding when his brother did as he asked. "Good. I believe you'll eventually recover full use."

Eli's eyes narrowed. "Eventually? Can't you be any more specific?"

Nathan continued with his exam, apparently unperturbed. "No, I can't. What you're wanting me to say is soon, and that's not happening."

Eli sighed. "That's all right. No matter what you say, it's not going to be soon enough to suit me."

"True. Try to be patient. Healing takes time. Now that I'm more at ease about possible infection, I need to put a plaster cast on. I'll do that tomorrow. I know you're anxious to be up and out hunting fugitives but try to think of something else to occupy your mind."

"Good idea," Eli said. "Why don't you tell me all about that Wild West show you were part of."

Nathan daubed medicine on Eli's arm. "I was hoping you'd forgotten about that."

"Nope. And since it was a deathbed promise, you have to tell me," Eli said.

"I didn't promise, and you weren't on your deathbed. But if you must know, I was part of the Turner Wild West Extravaganza. Performing under the name—"

"The Texas Kid."

"Yep."

Lenore smiled when Eli and Caleb promptly bombarded him with questions. Nathan wasn't answering until Eli said, "At least tell us how it happened?"

"It's one of those strange things," Nathan admitted. "I'd left medical school. Was trying to decide what to do with myself."

Eli seemed confused. "You decided that the best thing was to pretend to be a cowboy?"

"No. I'd gone to one of the shows, killing time. A man named Ambrose Turner was the producer. The whole thing was an imitation of the Buffalo Bill Show. Turner didn't even try to deny it. Still, it was interesting, and entertaining."

Nathan took a roll of gauze bandaging from his bag and began rewrapping Eli's arm. "Toward the end of the show, one of the performers got his hand caught in a rope. Without thinking about it, I jumped in to help. It wasn't a serious injury. I splinted two of his fingers. Gave him instructions on how to care for them, and then left. Turner had been watching me."

Finishing with the bandage, Nathan again asked Eli to move his fingers before continuing his story.

"The next thing I know Turner's offering me a job. I wouldn't agree to travel with the show as the official physician, because I wasn't one, and didn't figure I ever would be. I agreed to go along and help out where I could. Over the next few weeks, I wrapped a few sprains, stitched a few cuts, that sorta thing."

Eli's brows drew together. "They called you The Texas Kid because of that?"

Lenore could sense Nathan's reluctance to continue. He hemmed and hawed around for a few minutes before answering honestly. "No, it wasn't because of the medical care I provided."

Nathan took a deep breath. "One day, one of the riders came down with an intestinal illness right before show time. He was so sick he couldn't even stand up, let alone ride. I later determined it to be a foodborne illness, but right then, the fellow thought he was dying, and I wasn't sure what it was. I isolated him from everyone else, made him as comfortable as I could and went to tell Turner that he'd be one rider short that night."

Eli and Caleb both leaned forward a little, completely caught up in Nathan's story.

"Turner didn't say anything at first. Then he said, 'Where are you from, kid?' I told him Texas. The next thing I knew, he pitched me some chaps, a buckskin jacket, and a hat, and told me to get ready."

Lenore was every bit as interested in this story as Eli and Caleb were. She'd met Nathan later. She'd didn't know this part.

"I would've given a pretty penny to see you decked out like that," Eli said with a grin.

Ignoring him, Nathan continued. "When I objected, vehemently, Turner said, 'All you gotta do is stay on the horse and not get killed. I'll pay you, good.' What can I say? I needed money."

Nathan turned to the pitcher on the dresser, pouring water into the basin, then washing his hands. "You and I had both ridden, so I decided to go for it. The next thing I know, Turner's yelling out over a bullhorn announcing The Texas Kid, and I'm looking around to see who he's talking about, and he's staring right at me."

Eli's smile widened.

Lenore handed Nathan the towel from his bag. He thanked her, then resumed his story. "I stayed on the horse that night, and the next day I woke up to a complete training schedule, and the offer of steady pay. But it wasn't only trick riding I had to learn. He expected me to become proficient in all manner of things."

"Like the shooting," Caleb said.

"Yeah, I guess I have a natural affinity for it. Like you two."

Eli frowned. "Okay, so I understand, sorta, how you became the Texas Kid, but why you?"

Nathan turned away. "I told you, I was there. That's all there was to it."

Lenore bit back a smile as the brothers kept after him, worrying over his story like a dog with a bone.

"There had to be somebody available that was a better rider," Eli said.

"I got better at it. Lots of time in the saddle. I trained for hours every day."

Eli still looked confused. "A lot of trouble for the man to go through."

Caleb agreed. "I have to admit it seems odd to go to all that effort to create a persona."

Nathan shrugged again.

Lenore couldn't keep her silence any longer. "I know why Ambrose Turner kept him on."

All three Calhoun brothers turned to look at her. Nathan was the first to speak. "Never mind, Lenore. No one's interested."

"I sure am," Eli said.

Caleb motioned for her to continue. "Me too."

"It was because of the women," Lenore said.

"Len, stop talking," Nathan growled.

Eli picked up his gun from the bedside table. "You go right on talking, Lenore. I'll protect you."

Nathan snorted. "I took the bullets out of that thing the day I operated."

At Eli's murderous expression, Nathan grinned. "Calm down, I gave them to Maggie. I didn't want the gun to get into the wrong hands while you were under."

"Thought it felt different," Eli grumbled.

Caleb stepped between Lenore and Nathan. "You didn't take my bullets. If you don't mind, brother, I want to hear what the little lady has to say."

Lenore peeked around Caleb's back, stifling a laugh when she got a glimpse of Nathan's expression.

She stepped out to make sure Eli could see her better. "I think Turner wanted Nathan to do the act because of the women who attended. Even though several of the other men in the show were better riders than he was, they weren't as…well, handsome. Women loved Nathan. Sometimes they threw flowers at his feet."

Eli and Caleb were laughing now.

"He wasn't wearing the buckskin garb when I saw him," she said. "He was dressing all in white by then. White hat and all. Even a white horse."

"Lenny…" Nathaniel threatened, before looking at the ceiling and mumbling something.

"I think sometimes the women even threw money to him," Lenore said, lowering her voice for a dramatic flair that would've made Shipley proud.

"Wait until I tell Bliss about this," Eli said, wiping his eyes.

Nathaniel's expression softened when he saw Eli laughing.

Figuring it was a good time to make her getaway, Lenore headed for the door. She made it into the hall before Nathan caught up to her.

"Hold on there, blabbermouth."

She glanced over her shoulder to see him standing there with hands on his hips.

"No one ever threw money at me."

Lenore laughed. "Sorry. I got carried away. The rest of it was true, and you know it. They were going to find out someday."

"It's worth it to see them laughing like that. They needed it. We needed it."

Through the door they could still hear Eli and Caleb laughing, talking about their brother being so pretty.

Lenore leaned in closer. "They do realize that y'all look alike, don't they?"

"Oh, it'll probably occur to them eventually."

Nathan stared into her eyes, the humor suddenly gone. He moved her hair back and caressed her cheek with his thumb. Lenore's breath hitched as he bent his head.

He was going to kiss her.

Caleb called out, "Hey, Kid. Where'd you go?"

Nathan groaned. "Wonder how long they'll keep that up."

"I need an update on Bliss," Eli said. "How's the old man doing? Seriously, come on, Nathaniel."

"Guess I'd better go talk to him," Nathan said.

"Okay."

It took a moment for Lenore to gather her thoughts after he'd gone. Nathan wouldn't be acting this way if he didn't mean for her to stay. *Would he?*

So why hadn't he talked to her about it?

CHAPTER TWENTY-THREE

"Bliss you have to eat," Nathaniel said.

"Don't have to do nothing."

The old man wasn't bed-ridden, but he wasn't showing much sign of improvement. Nathaniel had wrapped his ribs, and Bliss swore he wasn't hurting anywhere, so there was no reason he shouldn't at least try to get around. But even here at the boarding house he was laying on top of the covers, staring up at the ceiling. Irene Horton said that he hadn't eaten more than a few bites in several days.

Who would've thought that Bliss and Eli would turn out to be the two most problematic patients he'd ever had? And they'd reacted so differently. Eli wanted to get up, Bliss wanted to give up.

Nathaniel thought about forcing some food into the old geezer, then reconsidered. Despite Bliss's weakened condition, he'd probably still put up a fight that would leave Nathaniel with permanent scars.

Nathaniel gestured with a spoon to the bowl of oatmeal in his other hand. "C'mon, Bliss. Make an effort. This will go a long way to helping you recover your strength."

The old man let out a sigh worthy of Shipley Bidwell. "Don't need strength to lay in a bed. That's all I'm fit for."

Nathaniel placed the bowl and spoon on a bedside table. "I hope I never have to work on a lawman again. You and Eli have both been big pains in my posterior."

The old man's eyes narrowed. "Is that a fancy way of saying I've been a pain in the—"

"Yes. That's exactly what it means. Now I need you to snap out of these doldrums you're wallowing in."

"I'm fine," Bliss said. "How's Eli getting along?"

At least he was interested in something. "Eli's healing. I think he'll come out of this with full use of his arm, but nothing's definite yet. In the meantime, he's worried about you."

Bliss dismissed that with a pitiful half shrug. "Tell him not to give me a second thought, ever again. When he needed me the most, I couldn't do a thing. I still cannot believe that this town was being watched over by a farmer, a carpenter, and a fifteen-year-old kid. Burns my biscuits."

"It wasn't like there was anything you could do about the situation," Nathaniel said. "You were injured. Caleb's got everything under control now. And his boss, Captain Joshua Parnell is here, too."

Bliss said nothing.

"You're going to have to move on from what happened." Nathaniel wasn't talking about the injury now. Lenore told him about Ship carrying Bliss when they'd found him under the tree.

"Shipley Bidwell still lurking around?"

Just what he thought. "I don't know that I would call it lurking," Nathaniel said, "but he's been here helping."

Bliss mumbled something.

"Everything's going to be okay," Nathaniel said. "All you need to do is eat."

"Don't wanna eat. You're wasting your breath. Go find somebody that will benefit from your care."

Nathaniel turned at the sound of footsteps. Peg Harmon was standing in the doorway.

"If you have someone else to tend to, go ahead," Peg said softly. "I will be glad to take care of Mr. Walker."

The old man's eyes widened. It wasn't what Peg said, it was how she said it. Instead of an offer of help, it sounded more like a threat.

Nathaniel sighed. These two had a complicated history. Peg's husband had been the ranger that was killed when the O'Brian baby was rescued. The best Nathaniel could figure, Bliss promised the dying ranger that he'd take care of his widow. Peg hadn't wanted his help. Bliss had secretly deposited money into an account for her, for years. She'd found out about it a few months ago.

It was obvious to everyone around that Bliss was sweet on her, and Peg appeared to be warming to the idea for a while, but they'd hit a snag somewhere along the way.

Nathaniel wasn't sure if Peg was upset because Bliss tried to provide for her, or because he'd kept it a secret. Or if there was something else going on. He didn't even care. Separately, they were two of the finest people he'd ever known. Together they were a mess.

Nathaniel headed for the door.

"If you think I'm going to stand by and watch you waste away you've got another think coming," Peg said.

"And what business is it of yours?" Bliss bellowed.

Looking back, Nathaniel saw that the old man was sitting up now, a thunderous expression on his face. His color was better, and he seemed more alive and purposeful than he had in days. *Good.*

Nathaniel slipped away, leaving them to their argument, grateful for Peg's help. Bliss would probably recover now, even if it was only to torment Peg.

Taking a shortcut through the alley, he returned to the main street, encouraged by the signs of improvement everywhere, the sound of hammers ringing out nearly non-stop.

The general store had reopened, even though there were still repairs to be made, as had several other businesses, including the café and the newspaper, and plans were being made to dismantle the hotel.

With every passing day there were signs of normalcy, something needed almost as much as food and shelter.

At the saloon, Nathaniel stepped up on the boardwalk, stretched, took a deep breath, and then stopped breathing altogether when he spotted Jed walking up the street.

Alone. Crying.

Nathaniel flew off the boardwalk so fast his feet didn't touch ground until he was halfway down the street. The kid hadn't cried once, through all the upheaval he'd experienced. *Something was seriously wrong.*

Grabbing the boy up, Nathaniel comforted him, even as he checked him for injuries. None that he could see.

"Easy there, son. What's the matter?"

As Jed began tearfully babbling away, Nathaniel was only able to make out one clear word. Mama.

Something happened to Lenore.

"Where is she?"

Nathaniel couldn't make sense of what Jed was saying. Looking wildly around, he searched for Lenore, for Nickel. There were people everywhere, but no sign of her or the dog.

Setting Jed down, he put a hand on the boy's shoulder. "Show me, son. Take me to Mama."

With a little hiccup, Jed rubbed his eyes, turned and started back the way he came. When they got to the alley behind the hotel, Nathaniel was relieved to see Nickel.

Until he noticed that even though her tail wagged once, the dog stayed low to the ground, a whimpering sound coming from her throat.

Nathaniel called to her, but she didn't move, her attention riveted on something underneath the hotel.

Drawing nearer, Nathaniel stooped down, then turned his head to follow her gaze.

The sight that met his eyes would've brought him to his knees if he'd still been standing.

Lenore was laying beneath the damaged building with a pool of blood under her head.

Dropping down to his belly, Nathaniel scooted as far under as he could get. Which wasn't far enough. "Len! Grab my hand. I can't get in there, but I can pull you free."

"I can't move. I'm trapped." Her words were calm enough, except for the tremor in her voice.

"How did you get under there?"

"The kitten crawled under. Jed followed before I could stop him. When I got under here, the whole thing creaked and shifted, and then this part fell." Her voice broke. "Thankfully, Jed wasn't hurt. Neither was the kitten. I told Jed to go get his Daddy. He did it, didn't he?"

"Yes. He's a smart boy. Lenore, listen to me. I'm coming in to get you."

Now that Nathaniel was there, Nickel crawled under the building and curled up beside Lenore. "Please, get Nickel out of here," she said.

Nathaniel called to the dog, but she ignored him. "Don't worry, I'll make sure she's out when I get under there to get you."

Scooting forward on his stomach, Nathaniel had only gotten a few inches closer when someone grabbed his legs and pulled him back out.

Kicking to free himself, fists clenched, Nathaniel flipped over to see the grim face of his younger brother.

"You can't go under there," Caleb said.

"I can't until I do a little digging. Help me."

Caleb shook his head. "No, I mean you can't go in there. The whole thing is going to collapse."

Nathaniel pulled away. "Then I need to get under there faster. I'll go in from the street side."

Caleb grabbed onto his arm and yelled for Henry to grab the other one. They pulled him to his feet and away from the building. Then they were both talking, but all Nathaniel heard was a bunch of gibberish.

"Lenore is bleeding," he shouted. "She's pinned. I have to get her out of there."

Caleb grabbed him by the front of his shirt. "That's what I'm trying to tell you. If you go in there, from any side, it could come crashing down on both of you."

Nathaniel jerked away.

"Don't make me punch you," Caleb said.

He looked so much like Eli at that moment that it distracted Nathaniel. Thanks to that brief distraction, Caleb was able to subdue him, with the help of Henry Barnett, Walter Miller and Brody.

Nathaniel fought harder.

"Hold him," Caleb shouted, "even if you have to sit on him."

He was about to lay into all of them when he caught a glimpse of Brody's face. Despite his size, Brody was still a kid. And he was scared. Scared to disobey Caleb. Scared of Nathaniel. Scared for Lenore.

No kid should have to see this.

That's when he remembered. *Jed!*

Breath caught in his throat, Nathaniel looked around in time to see his son nearing the edge of the building. *He was heading back to his mama.*

Nathaniel tried to jerk loose, to run, but it was as if time was standing still.

Jed was on his knees now.

No! Nathaniel stopped struggling. The others did not loosen their grip. "Get Jed, stop him!" he managed to say.

Finally, the others realized he wasn't fighting.

They let go and turned toward the boy, all of them dashing forward but Jed kept moving away. Nathaniel called his name. Jed stopped and looked back at him. The tear-stained face nearly broke his heart.

Dropping to his knees, Nathaniel opened his arms. "It's okay, son. Come here."

When the boy reached him, Nathaniel picked him up and squeezed him.

Lenore's voice reached them, faint, tremulous. "Nathan, is Jed okay?"

Thrusting Jed into Caleb's arms, Nathaniel returned to the building and stretched out again to make sure she could hear what was going on. "He's fine. Everything's going to be okay."

Calling over his shoulder to Brody, Nathaniel waited until he reached him to explain everything. "Please, get Jed to my mother, make sure she understands how important it is not to bring him back here until…until we get Lenore out."

He then talked to Jed. "I'm going to take good care of Mama, but it might take a while. I want you to go with Brody. He's going to take you to Grandma."

As they left, Brody saw the kitten. He reached down, scooped it up and handed it to Jed.

As soon as they were gone, Nathaniel turned his attention to Caleb, Walter and Henry. He had to make them understand the urgency.

"I have to go under there and get Lenore," he pleaded. "She's pinned by something. She's injured. Even if I can't get her out yet, I have to stop the bleeding."

"And I'm telling you, that you can't," Caleb said. "You're too big. If you go under there and move anything, the whole place is going to come crashing down. On both of you. The damage to the building is not only from the tornado. After the fire, they didn't replace all the joists. They rebuilt on top of the damaged ones."

Nathaniel fought back panic. They were going around in circles. "I'm not going to stand here and watch my wife die." *Not again.*

"You won't," Caleb said. "We're not going to let that happen. But we have to think of some way to get to her that won't make the whole place cave in. Talk to her. See if you can find out exactly what she's trapped under. I'll see what we can do about getting some help. See if we can find some jacks."

On his belly again, Nathaniel called out to Lenore, "Caleb is getting some help. Where are you hurting?"

"My head. My leg, it's twisted under me."

"Can you pull free?"

"No. I would try again but the building won't quit moving."

Nathaniel's heart almost stopped. *Was the whole place coming down now?* Lenore could see and hear things from that angle that they couldn't.

"Tell me what you're seeing," he said.

"It's spinning round and round when I open my eyes."

Vertigo, not the building collapsing. "Sweetheart, we're going to get you out of there. Just stay as still as you can."

"You never called me that before."

"What?"

"You never called me sweetheart before."

He hadn't. He would call her that every day of her life after this. Before he could promise her that, Lenore started talking about things that Nathaniel should do for Jed, about caring for him. As if she wasn't going to be around. "Lenore, stop it! Everything will be fine. We're getting you out from under there."

Caleb and the others were discussing jacks, and leverage, cables and winches. Captain Parnell was shouting out orders to several other men.

All of Nathaniel's attention was focused on Lenore. He could see, but not well enough to watch her expression. He talked, asking her questions. Not only to gauge mental acuity, but because she was sounding drowsy now. "You mustn't go to sleep, Lenore. Stay awake, talk to me."

Some people with head injuries went to sleep and never woke.

CHAPTER TWENTY-FOUR

SOMEBODY TUGGED ON Nathaniel's sleeve. Gordon.

"Let me go under there, Kid. I'm smaller than you. I can get to her without touching anything."

Nathaniel's first reaction was one of profound relief, then regret. He pushed to his feet to explain why. "I know you want to help Lenore, but it's not safe, for either of you."

"Let me do this," Gordon said. "I've always wanted to be the hero. Just once in my life."

Nathaniel shook his head. He didn't have time for this. *Gordon must've heard all the same stories Lenore had.*

Gordon's jaw tightened. "Lenore is the one person I could always count on. Please let me help her."

Nathaniel wanted to say yes, but Caleb's warning ran through his mind. "The whole thing could come crashing down," he explained.

"You're not going to leave her under there!"

"Of course not." Nathaniel started to walk away, but Gordon grabbed his arm.

The young man's eyes were filled with tears. "I know she belongs to you, Kid. But I've known her since she was born. She's mine, too. And I'm sure I can help her."

Nathaniel stopped. This wasn't just about being a hero, Gordon was sick with worry over Lenore.

"Come with me. I'll get Caleb to explain to you what's happening."

Could this work? Gordon was smaller than any of the men there. Leading him around to the other side of the building, Nathaniel told Caleb that Gordon wanted to go in after Lenore. Everyone began talking at once, trying to figure out if it was possible.

Nathaniel looked around to see if Gordon was following the discussion. *But Gordon was gone.*

Sick at the thought of what he suspected was happening, Nathaniel scrambled back to the alley and hit the ground. Sure enough, he could make out a shadowy shape easing his way in from the street side.

Gordon had figured out his own way in, without waiting for the jacks.

Nathaniel held his breath as Gordon eased past piers and under the damaged beams heading toward Lenore. The building creaked and groaned. Caleb shouted at everyone else to step back.

Nathaniel could hear the others talking, but he was watching Lenore. He let out a breath when Gordon reached her.

"Can you see where the blood is coming from?" Nathaniel called out.

"From her head. Yes, there's a cut behind her ear. It's too dark to see if she's hurt anywhere else."

"Lenore couldn't pull herself free," Nathaniel said, "can you see what she's caught on?"

He heard the murmur of their voices, then Gordon shouted, "Her hair is under a rock. It was part of the foundation, I think. If I could cut her hair, I could get her loose."

Nathaniel rolled over and reached down into the boot where his knife was sheathed. He kept it razor sharp—sharp enough to do surgery if needed. He tossed it under the building in their direction, but not too close, handle first, then held his breath until Gordon had it in his hand.

For the next few moments Nathaniel alternated between prayer and panic as Gordon sawed away with the knife. One wrong move could send the blade into Lenore's neck...or send the building crashing down onto both of them.

"She's free," Gordon shouted.

Weak with relief, Nathaniel said, "That's great. But you're not done yet. Lenore's leg is twisted up under her."

As he cautioned Lenore to remain still, and Gordon to move carefully, Nathaniel was also hoping that moving her wouldn't result in more serious injury. In ideal conditions, he would've checked her neck and spinal column first. But these conditions were far from ideal.

"She must've rolled over at some point as the building started collapsing," Gordon said. "But she can't turn back over or around."

What? Finally, he understood what Gordon was trying to say. "Lenore, your leg is twisted up in a way that Gordon can't pull you toward him. You're going to have to scoot out backwards, using your elbows. But stay as low to the ground as you can. Follow my direction, my voice. When you're out, then Gordon should be able to crawl out right behind you."

The moment Lenore began inching backward, Nickel moved out of the way. Nathaniel called to her, and the dog obeyed this time, but even when clear of the building she stayed right beside him.

Sweat popped up on Nathaniel's brow as he watched Lenore's slow, laborious efforts. As soon as he could reach her, he put his hands under her arms and pulled. He wanted to keep pulling until she was pressed against him, not let her go, but without knowing the extent of her injuries, he couldn't risk further damage. He got her far enough to clear space for Gordon to exit, then placed her on the ground. Caleb and Captain Parnell were now guiding Gordon out.

The alley was crowded. Some people were helping, others gawking. Henry and Walter were trying to keep the gawkers out of the way.

Peg appeared, kneeling beside him. "I heard all the commotion. What can I do?"

"Can you bring me my bag? It should be in Big John's office at the saloon."

"I'll be right back."

As he examined Lenore, checking her pupils, and the wound to her head, Nathaniel could hear Caleb and Captain Parnell working with Gordon as he crawled out. "It's not far now," Caleb said.

Suddenly the building let out a groan, then a splintering, shattering sound that echoed up all three floors and into the alley. Everyone scrambled away, except for Gordon. Lenore's rescuer was now trapped.

When it seemed that the building had stopped shifting, Caleb and the others returned. Down on the ground again, they were trying to help Gordon. The path he'd been on, the one Lenore had used, was now blocked. They'd have to find another.

Peg returned with the bag and Nathaniel finished examining Lenore, relieved that her injuries weren't as bad as he'd first feared. She had a head wound, which accounted for most of the blood, and a sprained ankle. He asked her about other pain. She insisted there was none. But she was worried about Gordon.

So was Nathaniel. "They're working hard to get him out," he assured her.

In the midst of the commotion a woman yelled Gordon's name.

Lenore's eyes popped open at the same moment Nathaniel recognized the voice.

Ophelia. Nathaniel wrapped his arms around Lenore, daring the woman to touch her, but Ophelia rushed past them and knelt beside the building.

What was she doing?

"Gordon, get out from under there right now."

"I'm trying."

"Try harder."

"I'm trapped," Gordon called out. "It's okay...Mama. Don't worry."

Nathaniel's startled gaze flew to Lenore's, but his stunned reaction was mirrored in her eyes.

Then Gordon yelled, "Kid, is Lenore okay?"

Nathaniel shouted, "She's fine. You did it, Gordon, thank you." Then watched in horror as the rest of the building collapsed, folding in on itself—dust and debris billowing out in waves. There were people running, shouting and screaming.

But the scream that brought tears to Nathaniel's eyes, was Lenore's.

He lifted her in his arms, then got Caleb's attention. "I'm getting her outta here."

"Go," Caleb said, "we'll take care of this. If we need you, we'll come get you."

The look they exchanged said more than words. Nathaniel wouldn't be needed.

He headed for Peg's house, holding Lenore close. She'd stopped screaming, but she was crying into his shirt as if she'd never stop, telling him to go back and help Gordon. "They're all trying, Len. They're doing their best."

Peg was running along beside him now, carrying the bag he'd forgotten. When they got to the house, she pushed the door open.

His mother hurried into the front room, her eyes widening at the blood on Lenore.

"She's going to be okay," Nathaniel assured her.

"Oh, thank God."

"Where's Jed?"

"In the kitchen."

"Good. Please keep him in there until I can get Lenore cleaned up. I have to stitch her up. Jed doesn't need to see her yet."

"You're right," she said.

"Do you need my help?" Peg asked as Cordelia returned to the kitchen.

"Could you heat some water? I'll also need a rag and a couple of towels."

Peg opened the door to the room that Lenore and Jed were using, and Nathaniel carried her inside, Nickel right behind him.

Peg grabbed some towels.

"Will you spread one out on the bed," he said, before placing Lenore on top. She wasn't asleep, but she was unresponsive. It took some effort to get her to swallow the pain relief he readied, but once she had, he gave it time to work, then tended to her wounds, talking to her the whole time, explaining each step.

Afterwards, Peg gathered up the soiled rags and towels. "I think I'll go back to the boarding house and check on Bliss."

"Thank you for doing that," Nathaniel said.

Peg gave a brisk nod as she left. "That man is not going to die on my watch."

Nathaniel believed her.

After she was gone, his mother came in with a cup of coffee. "I'll make some tea for Lenore when she wakes, she likes it."

Nathaniel hadn't known that. He watched Lenore, trying to decide what to say, how to help her when she woke. She'd lost a friend today. From the sound of it, the one who'd been her closest confidant most of her life.

His mother returned later to tell him that there was a visitor at the door. Nathaniel halfway expected to see Ophelia or Shipley Bidwell, but it was Henry Barnett standing on the porch.

Nathaniel stepped outside to speak to him. Henry handed him his knife.

"Caleb wanted me to tell you they found Gordon's body. He said to let you know that he died instantly."

Nathaniel's throat tightened. "Thanks. And thanks for all your help earlier."

Henry nodded. "Is your wife okay?"

"Yes, she's fine." *At least physically.*

When he went back inside, Jed was walking down the hall peering into doorways, looking for Lenore. Nathaniel picked him up. "Mama's sleeping." Easing the door open, he pointed to Lenore. "It's nap time." The boy seemed satisfied with that.

Lenore woke shortly afterwards. "Where's Jed?"

"With Mama. He's okay."

He could see her trying to put the pieces together, and the moment she remembered what happened. "Is Gordon..." She couldn't finish.

"Yes. I'm sorry, Len. He's dead. They recovered his body a little while ago."

She cleared her throat. "Did he call Ophelia *mother?* Did I dream that?"

"It wasn't a dream. You didn't know?"

"No." This time she cried silently.

"It's okay to cry," Nathaniel said.

"I don't want to scare Jed. He was worried about me."

"I made sure he knows that you're fine."

Seeing Lenore try to suppress her sobs was almost as heart-wrenching as hearing her screams. Slipping off his boots, Nathaniel crawled into the bed and held her.

Nickel hopped up in the chair Nathaniel vacated and closed her own eyes.

After a while, Lenore relaxed, her body losing all tension as she drifted into sleep. But Nathaniel didn't let her go.

It felt good to hold her again. *It felt right.*

CHAPTER TWENTY-FIVE

LENORE WOKE TO the sound of voices in the hall, even though there was only the faintest suggestion of light in the room. She relaxed when she realized that one of them was Jed, and the other was Nathan.

She'd had nightmares, dreaming that Ophelia had tried to take Jed again. Thankfully, that wasn't real. But everything else was.

Tears clogged her throat. *Sweet Gordon.* He'd done what he'd done so many times before, put himself in harm's way in order to see her go free. But this time she wouldn't be able to thank him for it.

She drifted back to sleep, waking to full morning light. The clock on the chest of drawers said it was nine o'clock. She needed to see Jed. And Nathan.

Hobbling to the mirror, Lenore stared at her reflection—eyes swollen from crying, a bruise along one side of her face, and several scratches. There was also a bandage behind her ear, and her ankle was wrapped tightly.

Her hair was a mess. She'd worn it down the day before, pulled back by a ribbon. Now it was several inches shorter on the left side, than the right.

She pulled it back to reveal a bandage behind her left ear.

Lenore remembered, almost as if it were a dream, Nathaniel saying he was shaving a spot on her head, and that he'd have to stitch up the jagged cut. It would leave a scar, but no one would see it. She was grateful he hadn't shaved more of her hair. And grateful to be alive. But she was so tired.

Lenore remembered waking, confused and scared. Nathan had held her and told her that everything would be okay. *And murmured endearments.* He'd even called her sweetheart and darlin' several times.

She needed to talk to him. Lenore hurried through her morning routine as best she could, then made her way to the kitchen.

There was no sign of Nathan, but his mother was there. And Jed. Lenore's heart warmed at the look on her son's face when he saw her. Jumping down from his chair, he grabbed on to her skirt.

Off balance, Lenore sat down, then picked him up, comforted by the feel of his arms around her neck. Nickel waited patiently. Lenore snapped her fingers, inviting her faithful friend to share the space in her lap with Jed.

Mrs. Calhoun smiled. "I do believe those two are glad to see you. I am, too."

"Thank you. I am so glad to be here." She didn't ask about Nathan, but his mother seemed to understand what she wanted to know. "Nathaniel's gone to check on some of his patients. He said for you to rest. Left some medicine for you on the dresser. He'll be back this evening."

Lenore tried to rest. But she couldn't. Her ankle was throbbing, and she had a headache.

She found the powder Nathan left, folded inside a piece of paper, and sprinkled it into a glass of water, drinking it all. It didn't take long for her to drift off to sleep once the pain subsided. When she woke it was dark. Limping to the door, Lenore eased it open, not wanting to wake Mrs. Calhoun.

But the door across the hall opened anyway. "Do you need anything? Water? Something to eat?"

"No, but thank you."

Cordelia smiled. "Worried about your son?"

"A little." *And a little about yours.* "Is Nathan back?"

"No, but he sent word that he'd be sitting with someone tonight. One of the patients developed a fever. Jed is sound asleep. Go on and get some rest."

Cordelia's words were softly spoken and filled with maternal concern. It brought Lenore's thoughts back to Gordon and Ophelia.

She and Gordon had talked about their mothers when they were young, but as she thought back on it now, she realized that Gordon hadn't seemed curious or concerned. *Now she knew why.*

Lenore's head ached as she closed her eyes and tried to sleep, but it was nothing compared to the ache in her heart.

❧

Nathaniel sat up all night with Big John Finley. The man had some internal injuries that had gone undetected until fever set in. Nathaniel had operated, assisted by Montgomery Helms, with the fever finally breaking around daybreak. Since Helms was staying at the saloon, he'd offered to sit with the patient while Nathaniel went on home for a while.

Just as Nathaniel headed down the stairs, Caleb walked in.

"I was coming to look for you," Nathaniel said. "I wanted to tell you how much I appreciate everything you did at the hotel."

"I sure am glad that Lenore's okay, but I'm sorry about Gordon."

"Yes. Me too." Nathaniel told Caleb what Gordon said right before he'd crawled under the hotel. "In my opinion, that was a very heroic thing to do," Nathaniel said.

"Absolutely," Caleb agreed.

"What happened to Ophelia?"

Caleb shook his head. "No idea. She disappeared during all the commotion. Shipley Bidwell came up right toward the end. He seemed as devastated as Lenore. Asked if it would be okay to bury Gordon here in the Moccasin Rock Cemetery."

"I don't see why anyone would object to that," Nathaniel said.

"Me either. That's what I told him. I checked with Pastor Wilkie and he said he thought it would be fine."

"Thank you for doing that. By the way, I've been meaning to ask you about your plans. Will you rebuild a house here in town?"

"Been giving that a lot of thought," Caleb said. "Think I'll go ahead and get started on a house out on the ranch land."

The youngest Calhoun had been dreaming of a ranch for a while. Wanted his brothers, and their families, to be a part of it. Just one more thing that Nathaniel didn't know how to proceed with at the moment. But he wasn't about to say that.

Apparently, Caleb had figured it out anyway. "I don't know how to put this. But if you need money to rebuild your clinic, and your home, I can help. I'm sorry I didn't think to say something sooner."

"I appreciate that," Nathaniel said, "but I wouldn't have taken it anyway." Caleb had inherited money from his mother, Amos Calhoun's second wife, and Caleb had established a charitable foundation with the money. He and Abby had a way of quietly helping people. No one ever knew where the money came from. Nathaniel wanted them to keep it up. He told him that now. "I would love to be able to help others in the same way, someday."

Caleb stared at him, brows lifted. "You're literally saving lives. I thought you'd probably refuse the money, though. Let me know if you change your mind. Guess I'd better shove off. Someone else thought they saw Vincent Shields."

With everything that had happened, it took a moment for

Nathaniel to remember the fugitive. "I'm surprised he'd still be hanging around. Pushing his luck, isn't he?"

"My thoughts exactly. There's something about the whole thing that doesn't seem right," Caleb said as he left.

Back at Peg's house, Nathaniel eased the front door open in case Lenore was resting, but noise from the kitchen drew him in that direction.

He leaned against the doorway a moment, enjoying the sight of his wife and son. Lenore's hair was a little shorter, and her face was bruised, but she'd never seemed lovelier, or more dear.

Nathaniel straightened and she saw him.

"Your mother and Peg are gone to help a woman who birthed twins recently," she said. "It's only me and Jed."

"How's your head? Your ankle?"

"Much better." She acted almost shy, touching her hair, smoothing it and then pushing it back. And there was the sorrow still lingering in her eyes. Both made her appear especially vulnerable.

"I like your hair."

Color rose in her face. "Thank you. Your mother trimmed it."

"She did a good job. It suits you."

Lenore smiled. "You hungry?"

"Starving."

She dished up a bowl of stew, full of chunks of beef, potatoes, turnips and onions, and placed it in front of him.

"Hey, one of my favorites." Nathaniel took a bite, chewed and swallowed. "It's even better than the last time I had it."

He could tell his remark pleased her, but he was unprepared for the kiss she dropped on his cheek as she passed by.

Nathaniel wanted to pull her back and return the favor, and then some, but she hurried away and began moving things around in the cupboard—as if that one small act had taken all her courage.

He was still marveling in the moment when Jed said, "Mama" and then pointed to his own cheek. Lenore obligingly dropped a kiss on his upturned face, and then hurried from the room. Nathaniel winked at his son.

And Jed grinned at him.

Lenore called to the boy from the bedroom to come and get his shoes on. Jed clambered down and took off.

Nathaniel was glad they were gone. He was so happy he felt as if he might burst, but the tears in his eyes would've worried them both.

That night, he found Lenore curled up in a corner of the sofa, eyes swollen, a handkerchief balled up in her hand. Everyone else was asleep. He sat beside her, pulling her close.

At his prompting, she told him stories about her and Gordon, some making her cry, others bringing laughter. Nathaniel was glad that she'd had a friend during her growing up years, but what a strange childhood, for her and Gordon both.

She swiped at her eyes with the handkerchief. "I often wondered why he didn't leave. Now, I know."

"I have to admit that I've been curious about that myself," Nathaniel said. "Why do you think Shipley Bidwell stayed?"

Lenore straightened with a sigh. "I guess because he loves Ophelia. And even though he's highly educated, in some ways Ship doesn't have the sense God gave a ninny goat."

Startled, Nathaniel looked at her. "What?"

She repeated it. "That's a saying, right?"

Trying not to laugh, Nathaniel cleared his throat. "I've heard of a nanny goat, but not a ninny goat."

"Really?"

"Yep."

"Well, don't that beat all."

Nathaniel held it together until Lenore left the room and then laughed, finding it harder and harder to remember how it felt to live without her in his life.

He'd liked her from the first day they met, but he'd never figured on feelings that could run this deep. How different would life have been for them if Ophelia hadn't interfered?

He sighed and pushed to his feet. "What if?" could drive a person insane. "What now?" was the only thing he could concentrate on.

The next day, Lenore told him she planned to talk to Shipley at Gordon's funeral that afternoon. "I have so many questions," she said. "And only two people will be able to answer them."

He didn't need to be told that she'd rather talk to Shipley than Ophelia.

For a while, Nathaniel and Lenore were the only people at Gordon's gravesite besides Wilkie Brown. Nathaniel was beginning to wonder if anyone else would show.

Then, one by one, the folks who'd been working at the hotel trying to rescue Lenore, including Caleb and Captain Parnell, arrived to pay their respects. And finally, Shipley.

Nathaniel wondered if Ophelia would show and was glad that she didn't, but only because of what it might do to Lenore.

Wilkie Brown did a good job with the service, especially considering he hadn't known Gordon. It occurred to Nathaniel that preachers often had the same problem as doctors—knowing some people well, and others in passing, and never laying eyes on some until there was a need.

In Nathaniel's case it was examining and treating; in Wilkie's case it was praying over them as they lay in their sick bed...or were lowered into the ground.

When the service was over, Lenore hurried toward Shipley. Nathaniel figured he knew some of the questions she would ask. *Had Ship known all along that Gordon was Ophelia's son? Did they conspire to keep it a secret from the others? Why?*

But after a quick hug, Ship begged their apologies and left. Lenore frowned, obviously confused by her friend's dismissal.

"He probably had somewhere to be," Nathaniel said. "I'm sure he'll be in touch with you soon."

"Maybe so. But he sure was acting strange."

Yes, he was.

CHAPTER TWENTY-SIX

A WEEK LATER, the church and school had both been repaired. Another step closer to normalcy.

The board of education had decided to suspend school for the remainder of the term, but church services would commence immediately.

On that first Sunday, there was sorrow at the thought of those that were gone and the empty places in the pews, but there was comfort in being together again to worship.

The door, and several windows, were propped open to stir the air. The odor of fresh paint overpowered the smell of flowers someone placed at the front of the church, but it wasn't unpleasant, especially considering it represented a new beginning.

Some of the pews had been damaged by rain, as had the piano bench, but the piano itself was fine, as was the pulpit.

Miss Hattie took her place at the piano and began playing *Blessed Assurance*.

For no reason that he could name, Nathaniel was moved by the song as if hearing it for the first time. *"Angels descending, bring from above, echoes of mercy, whispers of love."*

Apparently, he wasn't the only one.

Pastor Wilkie mentioned the song when he stood behind the

pulpit and preached later, preaching as if he'd been saving up words and thoughts for weeks and had to get them from his head to their hearts all at once.

First he read from the third chapter of Ecclesiastes, reminding the congregation—tearfully at times—that, "*To every thing there is a season, and a time to every purpose under the heaven: A time to be born, and a time to die...*" and moving on into James 4:14. "*Whereas ye know not what shall be on the morrow. For what is your life? It is even a vapour, that appeareth for a little time, and then vanisheth away.*"

Wilkie also spoke of happy reunions someday, of seeing their loved ones again. It was a message of hope and encouragement, but also a challenge.

"As long as there's a breath of life left in you, God's not done with you yet," he said. "I love the song we sang earlier. Just the image that it brings to mind is enough to give you chills. But the power can be found in the title. Two words. Blessed Assurance. Accepting Jesus as your Savior can bring you that assurance. The world will still be full of trouble, and even soul-shaking sorrow and woe at times—we've all experienced that recently. Anybody that tells you that being a child of God will protect you from that is either gravely mistaken, or a liar."

Wilkie, who was still healing, leaned on the pulpit. "While there are no guarantees of a carefree life in Christ, you can be assured that he is with you, through whatever happens. And if you accepted him as your Savior, when you step out to meet eternity, you step from this world into the presence of God."

Pastor Wilkie's gaze passed over the congregation, lingering on no one, touching on all. "No matter how numerous the sins, or how big, the blood of Jesus covered it. If you want to know more, if you'd like that blessed assurance, I would love to talk to you about it. Anytime, anyplace. Starting now."

Wilkie motioned for Miss Hattie to return to the piano and

for all to rise. Nathaniel joined in as everyone else began singing *Amazing Grace*. Everyone but Lenore. She was silent and shaking like a leaf. Nathaniel studied her in concern. He'd been so caught up in the message that he hadn't noticed the tears in her eyes. She glanced toward the front of the church, and then up at him. He squeezed her hand, then stepped into the aisle to let her out.

He remembered well his own such moment last fall. After years of hearing the story of the Gospel—the birth, death and resurrection of Jesus Christ—he had finally listened. And understood what it meant for sinners. For him.

Nathaniel held Jed now and prayed. He'd prayed for Lenore before, and those prayers had been heartfelt. But they'd been more focused on her life and relationship with him, not her relationship with God.

Afterwards, he could tell by Lenore's smile that she'd made a momentous, life-changing decision, even before Pastor Wilkie announced it to the congregation. Nathaniel held back until everyone else was done with the hugging and handshakes.

He put his arm around her. "How do you feel?"

She smiled. "Relieved. Secure. Joyous. Pastor Wilkie said that the angels in heaven rejoice over even one sinner's repentance. Can you believe that? Isn't that an incredible thought?"

He pulled her closer. "Yes. It is."

Lenore and several other people were baptized the very next Sunday. Despite the hot weather they'd had on several occasions, the Brazos was still chilly, but Pastor Wilkie had said he was willing if they were.

First in line was Lenore. Nathaniel watched her wade out into the water, heard her gasp, then heard Wilkie's voice, "Upon thy profession of faith, I baptize thee, Lenore Calhoun, now my sister, in the name of the Father, the Son and the Holy Ghost."

Lowering her backwards into the river, Pastor Wilkie said,

"Buried in the likeness of His death," then pulled Lenore up as he solemnly intoned, "Raised in the likeness of His resurrection."

When it was done, Maggie led Lenore away to change into dry clothing, while Wilkie baptized the others.

Afterwards, there was a meal, with people in attendance that Nathaniel had never seen before. It wasn't necessarily a reason for concern. A baptism drew a crowd, as did a potluck gathering.

He was glad to see Eli up and moving through the throng, wearing his gun and badge again. Caleb had bought him another Colt .45 Peacemaker to match the one he'd always carried, and Maggie got him a gunbelt with double holsters.

Eli's arm was still healing, but Nathaniel knew as soon as that cast came off, he would be practicing his draw. Hopefully he'd be satisfied to learn to shoot left-handed if need be.

Bliss was there, too. He seemed to have mellowed a great deal in recent days. He was smiling, his gray hair had been cropped close, he'd shaved, and he had on a new shirt. He was also humming.

He smiled when Nathaniel walked up. "Well, if it isn't my favorite doctor."

Nathaniel crossed his arms. "You're certainly in a better mood these days."

"What are you talking about?"

"You're kidding, right?" Nathaniel started to explain, but he'd lost the old man's attention. Bliss Walker's gaze was trained on the serving tables that were groaning under the load of ham, chicken, vegetables, pies and cakes. But it wasn't the food that held him spellbound. Peg Harmon had filled a plate and was headed their way.

"She said she was making that for me," Bliss murmured. "Make yourself scarce."

Oh, good grief.

Nathaniel sought out Lenore and Jed, feeling a contentment

that, at one time, he'd never thought to experience again as they sat on the grass and balanced plates on their laps.

"I'm happy for you, Len. I'm sorry that I didn't talk to you about God earlier."

"I'm not sure I would've listened." Lenore lifted a roll, and then placed it back on her plate. "I didn't tell you everything about my grandfather reading to me. It wasn't only the book about gracious living. He also read me Bible stories. I loved them when I was little. So I knew about God. Then I heard a preacher at a tent revival talking about sin. Ophelia had sent me in to pick pockets. Most of what we were doing was included in what that man was describing. Some of it I didn't understand, but I knew what stealing and lying were. And I was guilty. After that, I didn't want to hear Grandpa read the Bible anymore. I figured that was for other people. Good people. Gordon listened, but I learned to block it out completely. I knew I needed to be different, but I didn't know how. Ophelia decided what I did, and when."

No wonder she'd been scared to go to church. "And now you understand that God's forgiven you."

"Yes. Most assuredly." She paused, looking him in the eyes. "But I want to make sure you do."

Nathaniel was so taken aback by her statement that he couldn't speak for a moment. "Of course, I do," he said. "Why would you say that?"

"Because you haven't said what you want to do now...now that you know we're for certain married."

Before Nathaniel could tell her the things he was worried about and working on, there was a commotion near the dessert table. An elderly woman dishing up peach cobbler had been stung on the hand by a bee.

Nathaniel was tending the sting—applying tobacco supplied by her husband—when he noticed Caleb and Captain Parnell take off toward town. Had someone spotted the fugitive? Or trouble of another kind?

Eli and Bliss started out after the other two. Leaving the woman in her husband's care, Nathaniel hurried to stop them.

"Don't even think about it," he growled.

They both stared at him, doing a slow burn—unable to help, and unable to conceal their disgust.

As everyone else resumed eating and visiting, Nathaniel watched them both carefully, scared they'd tried to sneak away. Hopefully the fugitive would be captured soon, for everyone's sake.

~§~

"Will you hand me that paint brush?"

Nathaniel did as Lenore asked, hiding his smile and resisting the urge to ask if she planned on giving herself a second coat.

They were painting Peg's back porch, after repairing it. They made a good team. Lenore was used to hard work and it showed, but she hadn't done much painting in the past.

He'd been wanting to talk to her, about what she'd said after her baptism the day before. But it was embarrassing to admit that he didn't have a way to provide for her. They needed their own home. And Peg needed her company gone. Not that she'd said that.

Nathaniel didn't know much these days, but he did know that Peg Harmon would never pay for medical care, at least from him, for as long as she lived, and if she ever needed a place to live, she'd have one. If he ever figured out where *he* was going to live, that was. It rankled not being able to move forward.

He was so wrapped up in his thoughts that it took him a moment to realize that Lenore had just mentioned she'd always wanted a porch.

A porch? "Why?"

She shrugged. "Never had one."

"You never lived in a house?"

"We stayed in them a handful of times," she said. "When the weather turned bad, we'd park the wagons. Sometimes in someone's pasture, or barn, if they'd let us. And sometimes, they'd allow me and Ophelia to stay in the house for a while. If the people were reluctant to grant us inside privileges, I would be called on to illicit sympathy. Ophelia would tell our hosts that I was a poor little orphan she'd taken in, and then go into some tragic tale of how it happened."

Lenore dipped the brush into the bucket, then resumed painting. "Grandpa was so angry when she did that. Looking back on it now, I think she must've had some hold over him. Because he never took me and left. Anyway, after we'd made it into the house, she'd usually let me be. Those were the only times that I can remember getting to be a child."

She grew thoughtful. "Gordon was a few years older than me, and the winter I'm recalling he was interested in the war stories of the man who lived there, so I spent a lot of time alone, wandering around. It was a big old house with lots of nooks and crannies. Since we normally lived in such cramped quarters, I was fascinated by it all, even the front porch. The old man and woman used to sit there together in the morning, all bundled up, watching the sun rise over the hills. I thought that was the most wonderful thing. To wake up each day, with the same view. To have something, some place, that was always yours, always the same, only changing with the seasons."

Perspective was a funny thing. Nathaniel had also longed for home and roots, but he'd never stopped to think that a porch could represent all that. He would make sure Lenore got one. Such a simple desire. He could make that happen. He *would* make that happen.

CHAPTER TWENTY-SEVEN

THE NEXT MORNING, Nathaniel wasn't feeling quite so optimistic. Standing across from his office, or the spot where his office used to be, he watched a bird hop across the empty lot.

The debris had been hauled away after everything that could be salvaged had been.

Well, not everything, he noted as the bird tugged a worm from the ground, gulped it down, and flew away. If only his own problems were that easy to fix.

Should he try to take out a loan and rebuild? Or should he look for another building? There were a couple of vacant ones, and they were fairly cheap. But they weren't free. And not all were the right size for a clinic. The drug store was. He'd gotten a telegram from Carmichael Cook's family thanking them for the notification regarding the death of their son. They said they were arranging to sell the drug store. Nathaniel wanted to buy it. It was the right size, the right location, and the bottom floor had been completely renovated.

He sighed. No matter what he decided, it would take funding he didn't have. He'd had no insurance, and now no money. Should he have taken the offer of help from Caleb?

No. That just didn't feel right. There had to be another way.

Should he relocate to Fair Haven, or even farther afield, as some were talking of doing?

No. Moccasin Rock was where he wanted to practice medicine, where he wanted to live. This town meant something to him.

Some people might believe it was coincidence that drew all three Calhoun brothers here—where Abby Horton lived, where Maggie Radford ran for help, where Lenore had been caught. But Nathaniel wasn't much of a believer in coincidence.

He'd prayed for God's guidance, to show him a way to stay, and where to rebuild his practice, if it was meant to be. The answer that came to him was another loan. Was that even possible? He had absolutely nothing to put up for collateral.

He wouldn't know until he tried. Drawing in a deep breath, Nathaniel whispered another prayer, then crossed over to the bank. He greeted the clerk, then asked to see Mr. Jackson.

Once he was seated across from the banker, Nathaniel explained his dilemma.

"I want to buy the drug store," he told Jackson. "That way I can practice medicine here, and Carmichael Cook's family can get the money they need. But I'll need to take out another loan."

The banker leaned back in his chair, an odd look on his face, and Nathaniel's hope plummeted.

"Strangely enough, I just left a meeting where we tried to figure out how we could talk you into staying," Jackson said.

Stunned, Nathaniel blinked at him.

Jackson smiled. "The people of Moccasin Rock need a doctor. You're a good one. You're vested in the community. We're prepared to help in several ways. Including a loan, and a grant. The drug store was mentioned as a possible location."

Nathaniel managed to close his mouth and stop blinking. *Thank you, God.*

"Where are you going to live?"

Pulling himself together, Nathaniel said, "If I'm opening a

clinic in the drug store, I might as well use the rooms on the second floor to house my family." Lenore's porch would have to wait a little longer, but he didn't think she'd mind.

Jackson stood and shook Nathaniel's hand. "I'll get started on the paperwork. Are you sure you want to stay?"

"As long as there's a breath of life in Moccasin Rock, I hope to be here practicing medicine. God willing, that is. Thank you, Mr. Jackson."

Nathaniel couldn't wait to tell Lenore what had happened and to show her the building that would house the clinic and their future home, but he wanted to clean it out first. He needed to gather all of Carmichael's personal belongings and get them off to his family. He should've done it already. Same with the things from Sister's house. He'd get all that taken care of first, then show Lenore the new building. Hopefully, she'd be as thrilled as he was. They'd be together soon, in their own home, as a family.

Nathaniel stopped by the boarding house, hoping that Caleb might be free to give him a hand at Sister's place. Abby and baby Joseph were in the kitchen, but there was no sign of his younger brother.

"He and Captain Parnell are tracking that fugitive," Abby said. "They spoke with a witness who positively identified him. Something about the way he spoke."

The way he spoke? If the man had a distinctive accent Nathaniel hadn't heard anyone mention it.

"I'll sure be glad when that man is in custody and things get back to normal," Abby said, then paused as a look of sadness passed over her face. "You know what I mean."

Nathaniel did. Life was moving on. They were all adapting, scurrying to keep up. Yet they were still hurting. There would be a time when these were distant memories, but it was difficult to imagine now.

"It'll be okay, Abby. How are you feeling, physically?"

"I'm fine. Peg came and checked as soon as we got back from the cave. She was so glad that Lenore had been with me."

"Me too."

Nathaniel fussed over the baby a while, cheering Abby up when he declared Joseph perfectly healthy, and one of the prettiest infants he'd ever seen. Both statements were true.

After leaving, Nathaniel sought out Lenore, asking if she thought the two of them could load everything by themselves.

"Sure. It wasn't much."

"Good." Nathaniel knew he'd be hard pressed not to blurt out the news about their new home while they were together, but he'd wait. "Since we'll be loading and hauling furniture, I'll see if Henry will loan us a team of mules with the wagon and see if we can't get closer this time."

They didn't make it all the way to the cabin door, but it was closer than they'd gotten before. "This will have to do," Nathaniel said.

Inside, he took a tin of matches from his pocket and lit a lantern that was hanging on a nail near the door, then opened the shutters.

Something was different from the last time they were there, but he couldn't quite put his finger on what it was.

"Does something seem out of place?"

Sadness flickered across Lenore's face. "Maybe it's because Sister isn't here."

"Maybe." *But there's something else.*

"We were busy with the kitten that day, I can't remember anything in particular," Lenore said.

Nathaniel looked around again. There was more to move than he'd thought.

"This may take a while," he said. "I'll go ahead and put the biggest pieces in the wagon first. The rest we can place in the yard for now."

"Where do you want me to start?"

"Anywhere's fine. All of its gotta go."

Nodding, she pulled an old spinning wheel from the corner and cleaned the cobwebs from it before placing it in the yard.

He took the iron bedstead apart and loaded it, then the table and chairs, while Lenore packed the dishes, pots and pans away in a crate, using faded dish towels and aprons for padding.

In no time at all, there was quite a pile of stuff outside. Nathaniel began putting some of the smaller things into the wagon. "This might take two trips," he admitted when he stepped back inside.

"Was thinking the same thing, myself."

Lenore opened the cupboard door. "What about the food in jars? And the herbs and dried weeds."

"I'm not sure how old any of it is. Or even what it is." Nathaniel picked up several small jars, tins and wooden boxes, opening and sniffing each one. "Sister had her own way of labeling things. Best toss it all, to be on the safe side. We can wash the containers. Someone should have some use for them."

After doing so, Lenore moved to a trunk, pulling it away from the wall to open it. "When we get back to town, I'll wash these clothes before we pass them on."

"Good idea."

Nathaniel picked up the rocking chair from beside the fireplace. The arms were worn, especially where Sister's fingers had rested. *She'd whiled away many an hour in this thing.*

"I think I'll keep this," he told Lenore.

"Good. Do you suppose it would be okay if I kept the cauldron that Sister cooked in?"

"Of course." He paused. "As long as you don't plan on cooking opossum in it."

Lenore smiled, but didn't make any promises.

Backing out the door with the rocker, the sound of footsteps behind him was Nathaniel's only warning before a blow to the head brought him to his knees.

Lenore screaming his name was the last sound he heard as pain exploded in his head.

✍

When Nathaniel came to, his hands were bound together in front of him, but he didn't realize that until he grabbed for his head. Blood was dripping down his forehead and into his left eye. He blinked several times trying to clear his vision.

With a groan, he looked around, trying to recall what happened. Then he remembered.

Lenore! He spotted her, similarly trussed up, sitting on the ground beside Sister's cabin. She'd been gagged but he hadn't.

He pulled his wrists up again. *He could use his teeth to untie the ropes.* No. It was a mass of knots. More than necessary.

Nathaniel tried to get to his feet, discovering they were bound as well.

Falling over, he made another attempt, but ended up in the same position. He rose up on one elbow to give it another go when he noticed a third person nearby.

A big man with a bushy black beard and eyebrows was sitting on one of Sister's chairs near the edge of the clearing, cleaning his fingernails with a knife, and watching Nathaniel with an expression of amused hostility. That's what had seemed different. One of the chairs was missing from inside. One that he'd pulled over to Sister's bedside.

It took a moment to place the face. *This was one of the gamblers at the Boone Springs saloon.* The one who'd first objected to Lenore leaving.

Nathaniel had pegged the man for a mean one the first time

he'd seen him, but he didn't understand why a poker game should incur this kind of wrath and revenge.

"What do you want?" Nathaniel asked.

The man stood, folded the knife and placed it in his pocket, and moved to Lenore. He removed the gag.

Lenore drew in several deep breaths.

"You gonna scream anymore?" the man asked, voice low and raspy.

She shook her head. "What do you want from us?"

The man ignored her and turned to Nathaniel. "You robbed me. I didn't take kindly to it."

Nathaniel wasn't sure his confusion was entirely from a blow to the head. "We left the money she cheated you out of, it was right there on the table when we walked away."

Lenore and the gambler both glared at him.

"I didn't cheat for that money," Lenore said. "And I didn't steal. That ace was up my sleeve when you got there, Nathan. I sure as shootin' wasn't happy about leaving that money on the table. It was mine. I earned it fair and square."

Nathaniel's mouth dropped open. *She was serious.* But now wasn't the time to talk about it. If the man was angry about the money, then he'd give him money.

"I'll find you some cash," Nathaniel said. "Just let us go back to town."

The man tilted his head to one side. "You must think I'm stupider than I look. Besides, I wasn't talking about the money. I'd planned on leaving there that day with this pretty little thing."

A chill slid down Nathaniel's spine.

"But now that you mention it," the man said, "I am low on cash." He spat on the ground. "That old lady didn't have anything worth taking, but at least this was a place to stay for a while. I had planned to keep on living here after she was gone, then she ruined everything."

"I think she tried to warn us about you," Nathaniel said, as understanding dawned.

"Yeah, I was here both times." He laughed. "Right back there in the woods. Can't believe you two went to all the trouble of burying her. It's good to know you can dig your own graves, though. Too much effort for me."

The man was enjoying this, toying with them. That's why there were so many knots in the rope, and why Nathaniel's hands were bound in front of him. Their captor wanted him to try and get away.

"Who are you?"

"That's none of your business." He scratched at his beard, turning his head in such a way that Nathaniel could see a scar across his neck. He recalled Caleb's words, *"Someone tried to slit his throat once."*

This was Vincent Shields. The man that the Texas Rangers were searching for. And escaping the hangman's noose had probably resulted in the laryngeal trauma, hence the strained speech and raspy voice.

Nathaniel didn't say any of that out loud. "Why did you want to stay here?" he asked, trying to keep his voice as calm and even as possible.

"Got an injury that's taking longer to heal than it should. I was on the run from the law when I stumbled across this place. It was the perfect hiding spot."

Nathaniel remembered then that the man had seemed unsteady when he'd stood from the poker table. And he was favoring his right leg even now.

"The old lady might still be alive," Shields said, "if only she hadn't threatened to tell you about me. All I wanted her to do was tell people I was her kin so I could go on living here until I healed, and maybe even after that. But she wouldn't. She died faster than I thought would happen."

What?

Shields scratched at his beard again. "She was always going on and on about those remedies of hers. Offering to doctor me up. So, I turned things around, doctored her up. I was rummaging through her remedies and saw a big X that she'd drawn on one. Can't recall which one it was. There was all sorts of dried weeds, leaves and berries. She told me the one with the X could be used for headaches, really, really bad ones, but it was only to be used as a last resort, and only a small dose. It could kill a person."

He snapped his fingers. "Water hemlock. She told me all about it. Unfortunately for her. Thought it would take longer for her to die. Going to miss her cooking."

Nathaniel's stomach lurched at the man's casual dismissal of what he'd done. *Sister was at least the third person he'd murdered. So far.*

Shields shoved Nathaniel back down and took the money from his pockets. "Is this all you got?"

"Yes."

"You'd better not be holding out on me."

"I'm not."

The man pulled Lenore to her feet. "What about you?"

"I don't have anything."

He looked at Lenore's hands, bound together in front of her, then grunted when he found no rings. He pulled her hair back, looking at her ears. Lenore winced.

Nathaniel wasn't sure if it was because Shields was touching her, or if he'd touched the tender spot where she'd been stitched up. Either way, Nathaniel's blood was boiling.

Shields moved on to her neck, searching for a necklace, then lingered there a minute. Grinning. The sight of his filthy hand against Lenore's skin made Nathaniel's stomach pitch. And judging by the look on her face, Lenore's too.

The man glanced back at Nathaniel. "No jewels for the little woman, huh?"

Mind racing, Nathaniel didn't answer. He was trying to figure a way out.

Lenore jerked away from him, Vincent grabbed at her, catching part of her skirt. His expression changed. "Here now, what's this? You holding out on me?"

He was trying to get something out of Lenore's pocket, and she was fighting. Her dress tore, and she fought harder. Nathaniel, struggling to get to his feet, made it to his knees before Vincent Shields kicked him back down again.

Returning to Lenore, the man finally wrestled the item from her pocket. "Well, looky here. You *were* holding out on me."

In the midst of his furious reaction, it dawned on Nathaniel that it was his watch the fugitive was holding, and that Lenore was still trying to grab it back.

"Let him have it, Lenore!"

"I was going to give it to you," she said. "I promise."

"I can get another one. Let him have it."

"No." She kicked at Vincent, her boot landing right in the knee he'd been favoring.

The man went down on his other knee, howling in pain. The wound must've become infected. *Maybe Sister tried treating it with potato scrapins.*

While he was down, Lenore made it to Nathaniel and was trying to untie his hands, even though her own were still bound. Shields staggered to his feet, pulled her from Nathaniel and backhanded her across the face.

Since her hands were bound, Lenore couldn't catch her balance. She fell to the ground with a cry that echoed in Nathaniel's head.

Straining against the rope he lunged for her. "Lenore!"

It was a moment before she sat up. There was a swollen place on her cheek, but the narrow-eyed gaze she had trained on Shields let Nathaniel know that she was starting to get her senses back.

Grasping at any reason for the man to untie him, Nathaniel offered to examine the leg.

Shields grunted. "I seriously can't figure out whether you think I'm stupid, or if you are. All I need is my jug from the barn. I'll be back in a minute and we'll all have some fun."

Nathaniel knew in that moment that there was no reasoning with Shields. He and Lenore could both die, and Lenore would suffer before she did.

As a normally peaceable person Nathaniel was shocked at the rage building inside of him. He'd never been much on shooting people, especially after he'd worked to repair a few bullet wounds, but part of that was because there'd always been men like Eli and Caleb to step in when needed.

Nathaniel wished he'd told them more often how grateful he was for that. He knew they didn't enjoy shooting people, but they were willing. As soon as he got an opportunity, he would tell them how much he appreciated it. And there would be an opportunity. *Please God.*

For now, Eli and Caleb weren't here. And sometimes it fell to a man to protect himself and his family. Right now, he'd give anything for a gun. *At least he still had his knife.*

"Lenore." He repeated her name several times before she responded. "Are you okay?"

"Yes."

"Listen to me. That man is the fugitive, the murderer that the Texas Rangers have been hunting."

She blinked a few times, then her mouth dropped open. She seemed more alert than she had a moment ago.

"We've got to get out of here," Nathaniel said. "Do you remember the closing number from Turner's show?"

"Yes. Still gives me chills."

Really? "No one was hurt. The Indians were well-compensated for their part in the massacre and usually made it to the evening chow line before the rest of us."

"I know that. I wasn't worried about them, I was worried about you."

"Oh. Don't worry, I became an expert at throwing a knife with my hands tied, and this time the rope won't be on fire."

"Well that's a comfort."

Good, she was getting riled up.

"Why can't you use the knife to cut the rope?"

"That would take too long. If he catches me…" Nathaniel didn't finish the sentence, it didn't bear thinking about. "Throwing the knife will be faster, but I'm going to need you to keep him distracted long enough for me to get my hands close to my boots. Put up a good fight."

Fight like your life depends on it. "I'm so sorry that you have to do this."

"It's okay. I'll do what needs doing."

And he knew she would.

They heard Vincent returning before they saw him.

"Try not to get between him and me," Nathaniel whispered.

She nodded.

Over the next few minutes, as Lenore struggled with the man, it was all Nathaniel could do not to scream. He lowered his head, letting the other man think him defeated, until he got the knife in his fingers. They were numb, and it took him several tries. Vincent looked at him once, smiling in triumph, then returned his attention to Lenore.

Nathaniel grabbed the knife, eased it up to the right position, then raised his bound hands and threw it with all his might, sinking it into the man's left arm.

Shields let go of Lenore, screaming as he hit the ground.

Lenore scrambled forward, stepping on the man's other hand before he could remove the knife.

"Get the knife and cut me loose," Nathaniel said. "Hurry."

She did. Nathaniel made quick work of restraining Vincent.

The man was sitting up, still moaning in pain, when Lenore drew back her fist and punched him right in the nose.

Nathaniel grinned. *Seemed fair.*

"That's for Sister," Lenore hissed.

Fairer still. "Your hand okay?"

Lenore flexed her fingers. "It probably hurt me more than it did him, but it was worth it."

After making sure she was okay, Nathaniel turned to Shields. "I can patch your arm up if you'll let me. Of course, I'm not untying you to do it. I'm not stupid either."

"I'd rather have it rot off, you sorry son—"

The man's last words were muffled by the gag that Nathaniel shoved in his mouth. "Now, now. Can't have you talking that way around my wife."

It took him and Lenore both to get the man to the wagon. Even bound and gagged he was fighting. "I think he'll fit into that space in front of the bed," Nathaniel said. "I don't want to leave him here."

They were still struggling to get him into the wagon when a familiar voice drawled, "Need some help?"

Nathaniel looked up to see Caleb and Captain Parnell on horseback.

"How did y'all know he was here?" Nathaniel panted. "And why didn't you get here sooner?"

Both men dismounted. "We didn't know he was here, not for sure anyway," Caleb said. "Someone mentioned seeing a lantern up here last night, and I remembered you saying that the woman who lived here had died."

"Figured it might be Shields," Captain Parnell said. His eagle-eyed gaze took in Lenore's disheveled hair, swollen face, and torn dress. "What are y'all doing here? What happened?"

Nathaniel explained why they were there, and what Vincent Shields did. Nathaniel could easily read the anger in Caleb as the story unfolded, yet Captain Parnell remained impassive. His gaze was trained on the fugitive now.

"I'm sorry," Caleb said. "We checked here before. The woman assured us that she hadn't seen anyone."

"That's because he threatened her," Nathaniel said. "She made a point of telling us she was alone on a previous visit, too. Then when she was dying, she made some cryptic remarks that I didn't understand."

"She was afraid of him."

"Yep. For good reason. Shields admitted to us that he murdered her. Poison."

Again, Caleb's anger was easy to read, but Nathaniel wasn't sure what Parnell was thinking. Then the lawman reached down and grabbed the ropes securing Vincent Shields' wrists behind his back and yanked. The man howled.

"On your feet, big fellow," Parnell said. "Can't wait to get you to jail so you can brag about how you managed to kill a defenseless old lady."

After they'd loaded Shields into the wagon, stuffed down between the bedframe and the trunk, Nathaniel checked the ropes one more time.

"Don't worry," Captain Parnell said softly. "If he gets loose, he won't get far."

After loading the rest of Sister's belongings, which only took a few minutes with the extra help, Nathaniel and Lenore climbed up on the wagon seat.

Before they headed out, he leaned in to kiss her—mindful of the swollen spot on her face, and the others somewhere nearby. "You okay?" he whispered.

She blinked a few times, then her lips curved into a smile. "Yes. How's your head?"

"A little sore. But it could've been so much worse."

Lenore sobered. "Yes. I'm glad you still carry that knife."

"Me too. And I'm getting a gun for the other boot."

CHAPTER TWENTY-EIGHT

BY THE TIME they got back to Moccasin Rock, and Captain Parnell had taken Shields to the jail, and Caleb had helped Nathan and Lenore unload Sister's belongings at the saloon, to give to others later, Lenore was ready to drop.

She wanted to see her child, a tub of hot water, and a bed, in that order. *But that probably wouldn't happen.*

"You go on to Peg's house," Nathan said. "I'll get the wagon back to Henry and then be right there."

"Okay." She'd expected him to bring up the subject of the watch on the way home. *Had he forgotten?*

In a way, she wanted to go on and get the discussion over with, but first she was going to spend some time with her son.

Lenore stepped through the front door to find Ophelia sitting on the sofa.

Holding Jed.

Her first instinct was to grab him and run, but he was asleep, and Ophelia—who had her arms around him—had a strange expression on her face. What if she hurt Jed when Lenore moved closer?

Cordelia Calhoun, confusion and anger obvious, stood between Ophelia and the door. "Jed was sleeping on the sofa," she whispered.

"This woman walked in, glanced around, then picked him up and sat down with him in her lap."

"What did she say?"

"Not a thing." Cordelia held up a cast iron skillet. "If she'd tried to leave with him, or hurt him, I was fixing to let her have it. I'm glad you're here. Do you know who she is?"

"Yes."

Nickel growled. "Shh, girl. It's okay," Lenore said. *But it wasn't.*

What should she do? She would attack Ophelia without a second thought if it would ensure her son's safety. But she was afraid it would make things worse.

What was keeping Nathan?

"Ophelia?" Lenore wasn't sure what to say to her, but the woman didn't respond anyway. It occurred to Lenore that Ophelia seemed older. *No, she seemed old.* Her hair had turned gray several years earlier, but it had enhanced her beauty. The woman had once been vibrant, eyes shining. Lenore had such clear memories of her sitting with the others around the fire at night.

But occasionally, there was a look in her eyes, as if she were remembering another time or place. She looked like that now.

But this time she was holding Jed. *Like he belonged to her.*

Even though Cordelia was there to help, terror was building in Lenore. Her worst days started with Ophelia taking Jed. *It couldn't happen again.*

Praying was still new to Lenore, but she did it now, knowing that God didn't always answer prayers the way a person wanted. No matter what happened, she couldn't handle this on her own.

Ophelia started humming, then looked down at Jed with a smile.

Lenore was trying to figure out if that was better or worse, when Nathan walked into the house. He looked at her and his mother, puzzled, until he turned and saw Ophelia.

He lunged for Jed, and the older woman tightened her grip. "You won't take my baby."

Her words, low and fierce, swirled around in Lenore's head.

Then Ophelia looked at her, making another bizarre statement. "I found you a good husband. He had money. He was loathsome and lecherous, but he would've died sooner or later. Why did you have to ruin it? I never have been able to figure that out. You ruined it for both of us." There was genuine confusion in her tone.

Bile rose in Lenore's throat. She grasped Nathan's hand, needing his strength.

Footsteps on the porch signaled another visitor. Nathan stepped over to open the door, but Lenore was frozen in place.

"Come on in," Nathan said softly. "I'm glad you're here. We have a problem."

Thinking he was talking to Eli or Caleb, Lenore was surprised to see Shipley Bidwell walk in.

He looked at Ophelia, but the older woman was still staring at Lenore.

Ship's expression was bleak as he turned his attention to Nathan. "If you'll leave, I'll handle this."

"Not a chance," Nathan snapped.

"He's right," Lenore said. "We're not leaving without our son."

"I promise, no harm will come to the boy. I'd rather die myself. I only want to talk to Ophelia alone. Try to figure out what's happening. She's had some…problems lately."

Lenore and Nathan exchanged glances. "If this is some kind of trick," Nathan told Ship, "I promise you will regret it."

"It's not."

After a few moments of whispered discussion, Lenore and Nathan stepped outside, trailed by Cordelia.

They didn't go far, barely beyond the porch, and Nathan kept his gaze trained on the door.

Lenore paced back and forth, twisting her hands and praying.

A few minutes later, Ship stepped out with Jed—awake now and rubbing his eyes. All three of the adults reached out to him.

Ship handed the boy to Nathan, but he addressed his remarks to Lenore. "Ophelia's convinced herself that this is her son. She's lost touch with reality. I'm not sure what will happen when she remembers that Gordon is dead. I'll get her out of here. Can you take Jed somewhere else for a while?"

Nathan nodded, then turned toward the center of town with Jed.

Lenore followed for a few steps, then stopped and looked back at Ship. "Where will you take her?"

"To Fair Haven, at least for the night. Then we'll probably head east. I have some old friends there I'd like to see." His smile was wistful. "Tell truth, I'm tired. I wouldn't mind finding a place to land for a while."

Impulsively, Lenore hugged him. "I hope you find it."

Ship patted her back. "Thank you, lass."

For all the man's strange ways, she would miss him.

Ship went back inside to Ophelia, and Lenore joined the others headed toward the main street. The neighbor's door opened, and a young man stepped out on the porch. A little dark-haired girl stood beside him.

"Hey, Doc. Is everything okay? Why don't you come in and sit a spell?"

"Thanks, Walter," Nathan said, then told Lenore, "This way we can keep an eye on things at Peg's. Kinda hated to leave with Ophelia still there."

"Me too," Cordelia said.

"You'll like the Millers," Nathan told Lenore as they stepped up on the porch, then followed Walter inside and to the kitchen.

He introduced her to everyone, sat Jed down, then moved to the window to watch Peg's house. Cordelia seemed to be well-acquainted with the Millers, and began talking to Little Dove, Walter's wife.

"Saw you standing outside," the man said, his gaze flickering over Lenore. "You need help with anything?"

Lenore had tried to smooth her hair on the way home, but there wasn't much she could do about her dress or her swollen face. Once again, she hardly resembled what most would consider a proper wife.

"It's complicated," Nathan told the man after a quick glance her way. "But everything should be okay soon. We appreciate the hospitality."

"Yes, thank you," Lenore said. She appreciated their kindness, and Nathan's discretion.

Walter's wife was a beautiful woman with black hair that hung down to her waist, and a shy smile. She placed a coffee pot and a plate of some sort of sweet bread on the table, and invited them to partake.

Lenore was glad that Little Dove and Cordelia had plenty to talk about, because she was caught up watching Jed. He was staring at the girl, Ruthie, with a look of awe. *He'd never been around other children.*

Ruthie brought a basket to the table. There were toys and other treasures inside, including a small metal chicken. She turned a key on the side, winding it up, then placed it on the table and let it go. Jed's eyes widened, then he laughed as the chicken awkwardly hopped forward.

At the sound of his laughter, Nathan turned from the window to watch, then shared a smile with Lenore as the children sent the toy marching across the table several more times.

Hopping down from Lenore's lap, Jed went to sit beside Ruthie on the rug as she showed him the other treasures, including several rocks, a pencil, and a penny.

"Ship and Ophelia are leaving," Nathan said after a while. "I think we can go on back to Peg's house."

After thanking the Millers again, they left, Nathan holding Jed close.

"When's Peg supposed to be home?" he asked his mother.

"She's up at the Holcomb's place again. Spending the night."

At the house, Lenore locked the backdoor, while he locked the front, barring any trouble from the outside.

But there was still potential for trouble within, and she needed to face it.

⁓

Nathaniel sat at Peg's kitchen table later, thinking about all that had happened in the past few days. He'd nearly lost Lenore, twice, and then walked in to find Ophelia holding Jed.

He felt as if he'd aged ten years in the past few weeks. The blow to his head wasn't helping.

Everyone else had eaten supper and gone on to bed, but he couldn't sleep. Elbows on the table, he went back over the events again, thanking God with all his heart that things turned out okay—at the hotel, then with the fugitive, and with Ophelia.

Soft footsteps announced Lenore's arrival. There was a vulnerable, almost frightened look in her eyes. *Or was it dread?* "What's wrong?"

She handed him the watch. "I'm sorry I didn't tell you I had it. I thought I'd lost it in the tornado, then found it when I was gathering the last of the salvageable items from the house."

Nathaniel leaned back with a sigh, relieved that it wasn't something serious. He'd forgotten all about the watch.

Cupping it in the palm of his hand, he ran his thumb over the lid. He could've drawn the design with his eyes closed. This, and memories, were once all he had.

Tessa's picture would be gone, of course.

He pressed the lever to open it, surprised to see Tessa's face staring back at him.

And even more surprised that all he felt was a sweet sadness, not the gut-punch of grief he'd expected.

He understood why Lenore kept the watch. It was worth something. "Why did you keep the picture?"

"I don't know," Lenore admitted. "I took the watch to give to Ophelia that night, to appease her, but then when I saw what was inside, I hid it. Later, I looked at the back of the picture, seen where she'd written, 'To Nathaniel, all my love, Tessa' and I knew she must've died, or you wouldn't have married me. I was jealous at first. She looked so sweet and innocent, something I wasn't. I had to pry that watch from your hand the night I left Birmingham, so I knew you still loved her."

Nathaniel swallowed around the lump in his throat. *What a miserable memory for a wedding night.*

Lenore took a deep breath. "Then at some point, Tessa also became important to me. I started talking to her. I know it sounds tetched…crazy, but it was a way to keep my mind off everything. Ophelia was awful mad when she found out Jed was on the way. I've told you about that."

Nathaniel pushed to his feet and drew her close. "I'm so sorry you had to go through that alone. I wish I could've been there to protect you."

Lenore wrapped her arms around his waist, then placed her head on his chest. "Since I couldn't go into town, it got lonesome. I figured if you loved Tessa, she had to be someone worth knowing. We'd both married you, but you'd only truly picked her. I know I wouldn't have been your choice. But, like I said, I couldn't be jealous of her. Neither of us got to keep you for long."

Nathaniel pressed his face to hers, unsure if it was her tears or his that he felt.

Pulling back, he slid his hands up to cradle her face, careful to avoid the area that was swollen. "I did choose you, Len. If I hadn't felt something for you, I would've never let myself get pulled in to that sorta scheme. I might've helped you get away, but I wouldn't have married you. I like to think I'm a nice man, but I'm not that nice."

Wide-eyed she stared at him. "Really?"

"Yes, really. And I do love you. I'm going to be honest, that happened pretty recent, and is still happening. I can't say that was the truth of it when I married you. I've already told you that I wanted to help you get away from that life, and that I was lonesome. But I also liked you, and I was attracted to you. A lot. I think that's why I felt so guilty. I felt like I shouldn't have been."

"But Tessa was gone," Lenore said, bewilderment in her voice.

"She was gone, but I'd never let her go." Drawing Lenore close he kissed her. "Do you know where I went when I left the day before the tornado?"

She shook her head.

"I went to Galveston to talk to Tessa's parents. I wanted them to know about you and Jed. I wanted to tell them all about you."

"What did they say?"

"They've passed away."

"I'm sorry."

"They were good people, Len, and they would be thrilled to know about you and Jed. They would like you, and they'd be happy for us. While I was there, I said my goodbyes to Tessa and Becky, made peace with what happened." He kissed her again. "I'm sorry it's taken so long to do that, and so long to tell you."

Before they could talk more, or kiss more, his mother's footsteps sounded from the hall. "Oh, I'm sorry," she said. "I thought everyone was asleep. Just came to make sure I covered up the cornbr..." Her words trailed off. "Is everything okay?"

"Yes," Lenore murmured, squeezing his hand and then hurrying from the room.

"Everything's going to be fine, Mama." And for the first time in a long time, Nathaniel believed it.

The next evening, he sat on the sofa, watching his son pull a string along the floor over and over again. The kitten pounced on it every time. Jed laughed every time. And Nathaniel couldn't help but do the same.

Nickel yawned, the only one not amused by such shenanigans.

Nathaniel was still eager to be in his own home, and relieved that it would be happening sooner rather than later. He'd worked on the second floor of the drug store most of the day and couldn't wait to show it to Lenore. He was glad that he'd told her about the trip to Galveston. She understood. Maybe better than he did.

Things had been busy in town, but it was blessedly routine—tonsillitis, bursitis and a croupy cough today. He hadn't seen a tornado related injury in days. And he'd been home to have a regular supper with his family tonight.

Afterwards, he'd pulled the big tub inside for Lenore to take a bath while he watched Jed. Which he was. But he was also watching the hall, hoping to get a glimpse of his wife in a towel as she hurried to the bedroom to dress.

A knock sounded at the door. It was Shipley.

"Can we talk," Ship said, voice low.

Nathaniel hesitated. *He didn't want Ophelia anywhere near his family, ever again.* "Are you alone?"

"Yes."

"You want to come in?"

"No. I'd rather talk to you outside."

A sense of foreboding caused Nathaniel to leave Jed inside, door cracked enough to see him from the porch. "What can I do for you?"

Shipley took a deep breath. "Ophelia was arrested in Fair Haven last night. She tried to steal from a merchant there. It didn't go well."

The sense of unease intensified. "What happened?"

Ship's hands were shaking. He wasn't acting. "She stabbed a deputy. He shot her. The deputy's going to be okay, but Ophelia didn't make it."

"I'm sorry, Ship."

"I don't blame the man. I'm not sure he had time to think of another way to stop her."

Nathaniel couldn't disagree, but he still felt badly for Ship.

"She was buried in Fair Haven this morning."

"What do you plan on doing now?"

Shipley pressed a hand to his forehead, seeming disoriented for a moment.

"Come on in and rest awhile, Ship."

Shaking his head, the man reached into a bag near his feet and withdrew a book. "I can't remember if I told you or not, but the rest of the wagons have disappeared. Ophelia hired the wrong people, one time too many. This morning, I sold the one that she and I lived in."

Ship handed the book to him. "While clearing it out, I found something that I thought Lenore should have."

A Bible.

"That belonged to Jedidiah Adams, Lenore's grandfather. There's some family history in there that I thought she might be interested in."

"Do you want to give it to her yourself?"

"No." Ship wouldn't look him in the eye.

The man wasn't only grief-stricken, he was nervous about something.

"I'll make sure she gets it."

Ship cleared his throat. "There's something in there, some family history, that I'm not sure Lenore wants to know. Or needs to know. I'll leave it up to you whether to tell her or not. I should've told her at Gordon's funeral, but I didn't have the nerve."

CHAPTER TWENTY-NINE

Intrigued, Nathaniel opened the Bible while Ship waited, thumbing through to the page where someone had listed a number of births and deaths. He skipped over most of them, stopping when he got to Lenore's name.

Lenore Millicent Adams, born in Gatlinburg, Tennessee, January 15, 1871. *Lenore was younger than he'd thought.*

Before he could wrap his mind around that, Nathaniel's gaze dropped to the next line: Father, Graham Adams. Mother...

A cold chill swept through him. "Ophelia was Lenore's mother?"

Ship nodded. "Lenore's father traveled with the show. He died right after Lenore was born. Gordon's father was Ophelia's first husband. Lenore's father was her second husband. The children were born about five years apart. Gordon's father had taken off with someone else several years earlier."

"Were they Ophelia's only children?"

"As far as I know. I never heard of any others. Ophelia never quite got over her first husband leaving her. She resented her son. He looked like his father, and Lenore looked like her father. Gordon wasn't allowed to call her mother, but at least he knew the truth. She never even told Lenore."

Nathaniel choked back a response to that.

"Don't judge her too harshly," Ship said. "Ophelia had a rough life."

Shipley might have some sympathy for the woman, but Nathaniel didn't.

"As far as I know, Lenore never suspected the truth," Ship added. "Her grandfather came to take her when he found out that his son died. He didn't want to leave the baby with Ophelia."

"But Ophelia wouldn't let Lenore go?"

"Right. This was all before I met them. I don't know exactly what transpired. I joined the show when Lenore and Gordon were still children, but I didn't know the truth until a few years ago. I do know that Jedidiah gave up his life to stay with Lenore. Ophelia let him be part of the show. At least she gave Lenore that much."

Nathaniel couldn't hold his tongue. "Ophelia abused her own daughter and threatened to leave Jedidiah by the side of the road if Lenore didn't do what she wanted. She took Lenore's child away. And threatened to keep him if Lenore didn't jump every time she snapped. Ophelia kept her in bondage. I'm saving my sympathy for Lenore."

Head down, Shipley stared at the ground. "I wasn't aware that Ophelia made those threats. I stopped the physical abuse. If she had actually kept Lenore chained up, any of us would've set her free. But Ophelia was using bonds of a far more insidious nature."

Curiosity got the better of Nathaniel. "Why did you marry her, Ship? Why did you stay?"

"That's two very different questions, lad. I married her because I loved her. But in some ways, I stayed for Gordon and Lenore." Ship sighed. "There are no easy explanations. Ophelia had an exotic beauty that captured my attention from the moment I saw her. But she never figured out how to be more. When her looks started to fade, she grew desperate."

Shipley picked the bag up and closed it. "That's the reason she was obsessed with money. Ophelia was too old to attract attention the way she once had, and the constant travel was wearing on her physically. She knew it was only going to get worse with time. She'd decided to go to the coast and eventually take a ship overseas. She had this elaborate ruse planned. She would be this American actress who'd fled from scandal. She used my background and knowledge of theatre to prepare for the role. I didn't really understand, but I didn't see any harm in it. But her plan started to unravel when Lenore got arrested and we couldn't keep pushing southward."

Thank God!

"Ophelia was so furious that she became unhinged. When she showed back up here with the wagon, I was so relieved. I wanted to help, wasn't going to leave her on her own." He closed his eyes. "Ophelia picked the wrong men to marry in the past. I like to think that I was different."

Watching Shipley walk away, Nathaniel struggled with what to do. He flat-out didn't want to tell Lenore. *She was happy now.*

But it was wrong to keep that sort of information from her. *Lord, please help me do the right thing. Say the right thing.*

Nathaniel stepped back into the house and found himself face-to-face with Lenore. Her eyes were huge, and she was even more pale than she had been right after the accident.

"You heard?"

"Yes." There were no tears, but not because she wasn't hurting. There were times in life when the grief was so muddled with confusion and anger that you couldn't cry, couldn't make sense of it until later. Nathaniel believed this was one of those times.

He opened his arms, offering what little comfort he could. When she was ready to talk, he'd be ready to listen.

As Nathaniel suspected, it was the next evening before Lenore mentioned Ship's visit. And even then, she spoke mostly of Gordon.

They were sitting on the porch, listening to the night sounds around them, and enjoying the cool breeze. "I can't believe I had a brother," she said, voice wobbly. But there were still no tears. "I keep wondering what I would've done differently had I known."

"He never let on?"

She shook her head. "He always watched over me, though, like giving me that elixir in case I got in trouble."

"Did you have to use that often?"

"No. Only with you. The other times I was in trouble there was no time to wait for them to take a drink of something. But Gordon hit more than one man over the back of the head after they'd pulled me into an alley or the back room of a gaming hall."

How had Lenore even survived?

"I keep wondering if Gordon knew how much I appreciated him and cared for him," she said. "Did I ever even say those words?"

"He knew, Len." Nathaniel told her what Gordon said right before he crawled under the building to rescue her, about how she'd always been there for him. "He insisted on going under there to get you. And when we wouldn't let him, he snuck in. He also told me that you were his, said he'd known you since you were born. I think he was trying to tell me that you were his sister."

"I've been going over everything in my head," Lenore said quietly. "Trying to sort through years of conversations and memories, but I'm having trouble. Thank you for telling me that."

She swallowed several times. "Is it okay if I go to Fair Haven, to the cemetery?"

"Of course. Do you want me to go with you?"

She grabbed his hand. "Yes. Because I don't really know why I'm going. I mean, I'm not really mourning her. But I feel I need to go."

Nathaniel didn't know what to say to that.

The cemetery at Fair Haven was huge, but it didn't take long to find Ophelia's grave the next day. Shipley Bidwell was standing in front of it, head down, suitcase at his feet. He'd come to say his goodbyes, too.

Lenore walked toward Ship, but Nathaniel hung back, letting them have their time to talk. He was watching, though, ready if Lenore needed him.

After they talked for a while, Ship and Lenore embraced. Lenore finally started crying. Her heart was broken. And it was breaking Nathaniel's.

He recalled what Ship said, about Ophelia having a hard life. Nathaniel didn't doubt it, but he didn't believe it was an excuse to make other people your victims. He'd known people who'd lived through unimaginable tragedies. They hadn't turned on others. It had made them more compassionate.

During the next few days, Lenore pored over her grandfather's Bible. Studying scripture he'd marked, and reading the names of her relatives, even saying how glad she was to know her birthdate and age. But she still seemed to struggle with what Ophelia had done, or more importantly, hadn't done.

Eventually Lenore arrived at a version of events she could live with, seizing on the fact that Ophelia hadn't let Jedidiah take her away.

"She never acted like a mother to me at all," Lenore told Nathaniel. "She ignored me a lot, and later turned on me, but in the beginning, she had to care a little since she wanted me to stay, don't you think?"

Lenore was desperate for any shred of evidence that Ophelia cared for her. Nathaniel nodded, and offered what she needed to hear, what she needed to believe, but he wasn't sure he believed it.

"When I was young, I felt so alone at times," Lenore said, "wishing for my mother. Since talking to Ship, I've tried hard to make sense of everything. But I just can't. I've prayed, a lot. I know there are some things I'm not going to understand until I get to heaven. This may be one of them. I'm going to have to quit worrying over it, or it will ruin my life."

Nathaniel couldn't agree more.

Lenore seemed to be struggling with something else. "The thing that hurts the most, is hearing Shipley say my grandfather gave up his life for me. That makes me so sad that I feel like someone's squeezing my heart."

"That's how Ship phrased it," Nathaniel said. "I'm willing to bet that your grandfather *found* a life with you."

"You think so?"

The hope in her eyes was almost painful to see. Nathaniel was glad he could answer honestly. "Yes. I really do."

Then he told her about their new home, glad he did when her face lit up. "I wanted to wait until I could get it cleaned up and painted before I showed you," he said. "You never have to feel alone again, Lenore. You have Jed, and me, and my family. They're your family now, too. We'll get married again. Invite everyone to the wedding, all our friends. You can plan it however you want, make a big party of it."

Instead of smiling as he'd hoped, Lenore frowned and looked away, then left the room, saying she thought she heard Jed calling. But Nathaniel hadn't heard a thing.

CHAPTER THIRTY

Maggie opened the door as soon as Nathaniel stepped up on the porch the next day.

Good. He'd come to see Eli, but he wanted to talk to his sister-in-law, too. "How's our patient?"

Maggie waved a hand. "Frustrated. And not here."

"Where is he?" Nathaniel held the door open, and then followed her inside and straight to the kitchen.

"When I heard you, I thought it might be him," Maggie said. "I suspect that he's off somewhere practicing that draw of his. So help me, if he reinjures himself…"

She didn't finish her sentence. "Never mind, I'm praying for patience."

"I'll find him before I leave and make sure he's okay. How's Lucinda?"

Maggie smiled. "Better, and she has a brand-new tooth. The cutest thing you've ever seen. I would show you but she's sleeping. Have a seat, tell me how things are with you."

Nathaniel told her about Ophelia's death, and Ship's departure. But he did not tell her about Lenore's parentage. That was Lenore's story to tell when, or if, she decided to.

He did want Maggie's opinion on something else, however.

"I was hoping to have a wedding where all our friends and family could be there, but Lenore didn't act all that excited about it."

Maggie removed a towel covering a large bowl, tipped the bowl over and pulled a mound of dough out onto the breadboard. "Tell me what you said. You Calhoun men may make the best husbands, but your proposals lack something."

"What are you talking about?"

"Are you aware that Abby had to propose to Caleb?"

He nodded. "I knew that."

"Did you know that Eli declared his love to me by saying he wanted to be buried next to me in the cemetery?"

Nathaniel grinned. "I did *not* know that."

Maggie stopped kneading the dough and wiped her hands on the towel, a dreamy, lovesick look on her face. "It was really rather sweet. He stumbled over his words. Hemmed and hawed. Seeing such a strong man completely discombobulated over you is something that every woman should experience at least once in her life."

As fascinating as this glimpse into the female mind was, Nathaniel needed Maggie to stick to the problem at hand. *His.*

"What did I do wrong?"

Maggie's expression turned thoughtful. "Did you tell her that you wanted a big wedding?"

"Yes. Told her to plan a big party."

"Hmm. I think maybe Lenore's reluctance isn't so much about marrying you, as it is about planning a wedding."

"Why?"

"Have you ever noticed how she's always willing to help, but most of the time, she waits for someone to tell her exactly what to do?"

Nathaniel straightened in his chair. "No."

"And that she hesitates, like when we're gathered for a meal. She waits to see what everyone else is doing or saying, then mimics their behavior. I think she feels unsure of herself."

Did she?

"When you were out of town," Maggie said, "Lenore and Jed were here. We went down to the creek, and Lenore was in her element. She was chattering away, talking about plants and animals. Totally different than she acts most of the time. But as soon as we came back in, she was shy, hesitant. She'd offered to make dinner, but then she asked several questions about the cookstove. It occurred to me that she'd probably never used one before she moved into your house. Then she asked me several other questions about running a household that I thought was unusual. You told her you wanted a fancy party. I'm willing to bet she's never even been to one, let alone planned one."

"Why didn't she say so?"

Maggie shrugged. "Does she ever? Say what she really feels, I mean. And does she ever make decisions? Or does she defer to you about everything?"

He didn't know.

For the next few days Nathaniel watched Lenore. It didn't take him long to realize that Maggie was right. Lenore did lack confidence. Part of that was her upbringing. To call her childhood unconventional was putting it mildly. But it was more than that. He remembered her saying that when she couldn't pick pockets for a while, Ophelia decided she should trap animals for their meals, cook, and so on, then Lenore had said, "I didn't even do that well enough to suit her."

And her grandfather had her memorizing a book on how to be a better female. He'd done it for all the right reasons, no doubt, but it still might have made Lenore wonder what was wrong with her the way she was.

Nathaniel had been part of the problem, too.

He hadn't been cruel to Lenore, but he'd picked up right where Ophelia had left off, as far as telling her what to do and when to do it. He'd been more guard than husband.

But he wanted a wife, not a prisoner.

How did one go about building self-confidence in someone else? Nathaniel had sometimes felt out of place in medical school, and often teased about his "backwoods" ways. In the end though, no one could argue with his grades. Most of the things Lenore excelled at—including playing cards in gambling houses and picking pockets—were dangerous or against the law.

Helping her grow confident could take some work.

Nathaniel tried drawing Lenore out, and asking for her opinion. She still left every decision up to him. Even the clothing they picked out for Jed, and furnishings for the new home. She'd open her mouth and then close it again, deferring to him. No matter what he said she was agreeable.

It was driving him crazy.

The whole thing had him looking back on their time together since Lenore got to Moccasin Rock. She'd tried to disagree with him at Sister's that first time. And when he'd objected, she'd stopped talking. And she'd shown a flash of temper when he'd asked if Nickel needed a bath. But now that he was remembering, he'd seen her swallowing back her first reaction even then. That wasn't healthy.

And it needed to stop.

Being able to tell people what was on your mind was important. If you were never able to express your true feelings, it could eventually destroy a person.

Now that he recognized what was going on, Nathaniel was determined to get Lenore to tell him how she really felt about things. Once she was comfortable saying what was on her mind, then they'd work on the other things.

She'd have her own kitchen. Her own home. She would do things her way. He didn't want her to be a copy of Abby or Maggie, or any other woman in town. He recalled how she'd kissed him the day he'd complimented her on the stew. That might have been the first compliment he'd ever voiced. Had he ever told her she was beautiful?

First things first. Nathaniel wanted Lenore to start giving him her opinion. And he knew where to start. There was one thing he hadn't mentioned to her yet, and he not only wanted her opinion, he needed it.

Sitting on the banks of the Brazos later—an area he'd come to think of as their spot—he and Lenore watched Jed and Nickel playing nearby.

"Did I tell you that Eli and I are going into the cattle business with Caleb?"

She turned to look at him. "No."

"I think he's calling it the Calhoun Cattle Company. It's something Caleb dreamed up, and he has the money to get it going. But he doesn't want to do it without me and Eli. And our families. Is that something you'd be interested in?"

She shrugged. "I don't know anything about cows."

"Me either. Caleb said that won't matter. Said it will take years to get the company built up, and we'll all get to do our part. He's bought some land around Eli's place. So, I'll eventually buy some out there, too. What do you think?"

"I think it's fine. I'll help however you need me."

Nathaniel was glad to hear that she supported the idea. He wanted her by his side. And he had the feeling she was telling the truth about being fine with it. "I'll build us a house out there."

"Out near Eli and Maggie?"

"Yes, and Caleb and Abby. We'll still have the place in town."

Lenore smiled. "That sounds wonderful."

She probably meant that, too. She would enjoy living near Maggie and Abby.

They were getting nowhere. So, Nathaniel pushed her. "I was thinking about maybe building a house shaped like a circle."

Her brows drew together. "A circle?"

"Yep, a round house. What do you think?"

"I'm having a hard time imagining it."

He picked up a stick and sketched a design in the dirt. "We could put the kitchen in the center, it would have six doors. Each door would lead off to a hallway."

"But wouldn't it be hot in the kitchen? How would air get in?"

Good grief. Wasn't she going to tell him how ridiculous that was? Wasn't she going to try to talk him out of it?

Nathaniel would keep on until she did. "Do you think that's a bad idea? Do you think it would be better to put the kitchen somewhere else?"

"Well…no."

Okay. "When we have more kids, we'll put each one on a different hall. As long as we don't have more than six, they can each have their own room. If we have a dozen, they'll have to double up."

She turned a troubled green-eyed gaze his way. "But if they were spread out like that, wouldn't it take forever to get them all to bed at night."

"Not more than thirty minutes or so. Are you saying it would be better if the bedrooms were closer togeth…"

Nathaniel's words trailed off. Lenore was nibbling on her bottom lip. *He wanted to help her with that.*

With a little shake of his head, he got back to the task at hand. "See, here's the brilliant part. I could put our bedroom over the kitchen."

"Over?"

"Yes, didn't I tell you about the second story?" He continued, throwing in more and more outlandish details.

She looked so horrified, so worried, that Nathaniel almost told her none of it was true. But when she didn't object, he plowed on.

"I've even toyed with the idea of maybe putting a slide on the second floor for easier access to the bottom. What do you think?"

Her jaw tightened. She opened her mouth, and Nathaniel waited. No matter what she said, he was going to meet it with thoughtful consideration.

"I think you don't have the sense that God gave a ninny goat," she snapped.

Anything except that. Nathaniel tried not to laugh, but it was no use. Covering his face with his hands, he fell on his back and howled.

She pulled on his arm. "What is so dad-blamed funny?"

He lowered his hands. "You are. All I wanted was for you to tell me what you really thought. I'm not going to build a circle-shaped house."

Lenore's shoulders drooped in relief. "Good. Why did you tell me that?"

"Because I don't want you to live in fear."

She blinked. "I'm not afraid of you."

"I don't mean fear for your life, I mean fear of expressing an opinion. We're not going to agree on everything, but I still want to know what you really think."

"And you'll listen to what I'm saying?"

"Always. We have to communicate. It takes two people to make a marriage work, Len."

"Okay. The first thing I want to do is help you design that house."

He laughed. "It's a deal. Then what?"

"I want to talk about those twelve kids."

"Too many? How about half a dozen?"

Lenore shrugged, a smile playing around her lips as she considered the question. At that moment, he wasn't nearly as interested in her answer as he was her lips.

CHAPTER THIRTY-ONE

LENORE CLEANED THE mirror in the bedroom, determined to eliminate every streak.

They were moving into this place tomorrow, and she wanted everything to be perfect. Nathan had worked so hard getting it ready for them. Now he was working on the office downstairs.

Earlier in the day he'd shown her the front door to the clinic. There was now gold lettering that read, "Moccasin Rock Clinic, Dr. Nathaniel Calhoun." He'd left Carmichael Cook's name on the door, too, and added the words, "In Memory" above it.

Lenore had never gotten to meet the druggist, but she knew that Nathan thought highly of him. It was a perfect way to honor the man.

She'd been here every day this week, cleaning and planning, and loving each minute of it. The place was huge, at least to her.

She could hear Jed in the next room, playing with a couple of small wooden horses. Bliss had carved them and brought them by, and Eli brought him some wooden building blocks. Those ponies had been jumping over those blocks all day.

Eli had stayed and talked to Nathan, thanking him for working so hard to save his arm, and he wasn't just talking about the surgery. Eli had only recently discovered that someone had wanted to amputate, and that Nathan had threatened to shoot whoever it was.

Apparently, threatening to shoot people was a normal reaction for Eli and he was beyond proud of his brother for watching over him that way. Eli had gotten all choked up, while Nathan just grinned and shook his head.

Earlier in the week, she and Nathan had gone to Fair Haven and picked up a few furnishings, and they'd each kept something special from Sister, but the place was still so empty it echoed. Then when Nathan's patients heard that he was trying to rebuild, to start again from scratch, the town folk began bringing things by.

One by one, they'd dropped off everything from doilies and linens, to a washboard and furniture, and lots of food. Their admiration and appreciation of their doctor had brought tears to Nathan's eyes.

The Millers brought a cupboard that Walter had built and Dovie had painted. It was truly lovely. Ruthie had talked nonstop about helping her mother paint. Then she'd followed Jed around. The two of them were now fast friends.

Mr. Finley from the saloon had given them a table and several chairs. Mr. and Mrs. Dunlop brought by a lace-trimmed tablecloth that was one of the fanciest things Lenore had ever seen. But then Myrtle started giving directions on how to properly care for it, which sorta took the fun out of it.

"She doesn't think I have the sense God gave a nin…" Lenore murmured, then paused to correct herself. "A nanny goat."

Lenore would miss Cordelia and Peg, but she was looking forward to sharing a home with her husband and son. Besides, there might be a change in living arrangements at Peg's soon anyway. The old deputy was sweet on her, and one of the doctors from Fair Haven seemed smitten with Cordelia Calhoun. Lenore didn't think that Nathan had caught on to that, yet.

Once she was satisfied that the mirror was spotless, Lenore

glanced at her reflection before moving on, but she no longer studied her face, wondering if she resembled her mother.

There was no resemblance. Thankfully, they weren't alike in any way she could figure.

She'd done a lot of praying in the past few weeks, and the peace it brought her was hard to figure, and harder to describe. *But it was real.*

She still didn't feel like her old self, but maybe she never would. She hadn't ever really known who she was.

Her grandfather had told her so many stories about her father. But he'd never told her anything about her mother. He'd either change the subject or deny knowing anything. Now she understood why.

All those years, she'd tried to imagine what her mother looked like. In Lenore's young mind she'd resembled the princesses that Ship described. Lenore had never once considered that her mother was sitting on the other side of the fire.

Pushing those thoughts away, she checked on Jed and Nickel, then grabbed a broom and moved on to the kitchen. Maggie and Abby had been here the day before, helping her sew curtains. She'd ironed them earlier and was waiting for Nathan to help her hang them.

Lenore glanced at the clock. He should be here soon. For the past couple of weeks, he'd been especially secretive. Not in a bad way. She knew the difference. When she questioned him about it, he kept putting her off. For some reason he was up to something he didn't want her to know about. She would have to trust him.

The door opened a few minutes later, and Nathan, all gussied up in his new church clothes, greeted her with a smile, and then a question. "Where's Jed?"

"In his room. Why?"

"Because we're going on a picnic."

"A picnic? Where?"

"You'll see. Put on your prettiest dress."

Prettiest? Were you supposed to get gussied up for a picnic? Lenore had no idea, but she did as he asked. Fortunately, she had a pretty dress. Out of the clear blue sky, Maggie and Abby had dropped one off recently. Abby said it was a gift for delivering Joseph.

Lenore had assured her that it wasn't necessary, and then hoped Abby didn't take the dress back once she'd opened the box. It was about the prettiest thing Lenore had ever seen—a soft green color, trimmed in a dark green nearly the exact shade of her eyes.

Once she tried it on, Maggie and Abby had been delighted at the fit, discussing the garment's scooped neckline, gathers and graceful folds, while Lenore scarcely recognized herself in the mirror.

Now she donned it again, needing Nathan's help with the buttons. He stared at her wordlessly for a charged moment, not even blinking, before turning her around and getting to work on the buttons. "You look incredible," he whispered as he fastened the last one. He dropped a lingering kiss on her neck. Lenore was a little wobbly as they went down the stairs.

On the street, he led her and Jed to a buggy with fancy leather seats, and fringe around the top. Lenore had never ridden in anything like it. Jed was fascinated. Seated between her and Nathan, he clutched the toy ponies, and watched with wide-eyed wonder as they passed through town.

Despite Lenore's repeated attempts to get information from Nathan, he refused to say anything more about where they were headed. He turned on the road to Eli's house, but passed right by the driveway without slowing down.

Nathan gave her a secretive smile before leaving the road and crossing a field. Within a few minutes, Lenore wasn't sure where they were—the middle of nowhere, the best she could determine—but it was a beautiful, peaceful place, dotted with wildflowers and surrounded by thick clusters of live oak trees in several directions. Nathan stopped and helped her down.

"We'll walk from here." He picked up Jed, and then offered his arm to her. About the time it dawned on Lenore that they hadn't brought any food to this picnic, they topped a hill.

There, sitting in the middle of a large grassy area was a...porch.

All by itself. Gray paint on the wooden plank floor, a tin roof and cedar post rails.

Confused, Lenore looked at him.

"Since it'll take months to build the new house, I started with the porch. I know how badly you wanted one."

"This is for me?"

Nathan sat Jed down. "Yes. And I'll get us some rocking chairs. I thought you might like that." He was starting to sound embarrassed. He tugged on his collar. "Pretty idiotic, huh?"

Lenore threw her arms around his neck. "No, it's not. I love it."

He gave her a sheepish grin. "Did I mention that I'm going to build a house to stick on it?"

"Yes. What shape?"

"House shaped?" He laughed, but a moment later, his expression had sobered. "Life is hard sometimes, Len. It won't be like those fairy tales that Shipley told you."

"I know that."

"But I'll try my best to give you a happily ever after." Nathan stuck his left hand in his pocket. A little frown flickered across his face. He searched his right pocket. Then he patted at the pockets on his trousers, shirt, vest.

When she saw anxiety building, Lenore couldn't do it anymore. She held out her hand, a gold band shining from her palm. "Were you looking for this?"

His shoulders drooped. "Yes, you little thief. Do you routinely check my pockets, or did you realize what I was up to?"

"I figured something was up. And since you gave me such fits about the house you were going to build, I decided you deserved to sweat."

He grinned at her. "I won't argue with you. Will you wear it? Will you marry me, again?"

"I will be thrilled to wear it. But we don't have to have a ceremony. We're already married."

Nathan stared into her eyes. "I really would like to say our vows again, Len. With family there. I'll tell you what, I'll even plan the whole thing."

"You mean it?"

"Yep. Any thoughts on when?"

"Any time at all is fine by me."

"Anytime?"

"Yes."

"How about now?" Hands on her shoulders, he turned her around.

Walking out of the cluster of trees were Eli and Maggie, Caleb and Abby, Cordelia, Bliss, Peg, Pastor Wilkie Brown and several other people. Carrying picnic baskets, blankets, even chairs.

What in the world?

CHAPTER THIRTY-TWO

Nathaniel watched the expression on Lenore's face, hoping he'd done the right thing. Before everyone reached them, he hurried with an explanation. "I thought maybe you'd enjoy this more. Just a simple ceremony here outside."

"It's perfect," Lenore said, to his relief. But Nathan was still a little worried about something else.

"Len, I've been honest about how I felt when we first married, and how I feel now. But I don't think I've heard you say how you feel about me."

"I thought I loved you when I married you," she said, "but now, I believe it was more infatuation."

Normally, Nathaniel would've smiled at how she drew that last word out. But he was too worried that she'd stopped there. *Hopefully there was more.*

"Now, I'm sure it's love," she said softly. "But it's more than that, more than I can put into words. It's admiration, excitement. You're more than a good husband, you're a wonderful father, son and brother. You're the finest man I know. And you make my heart beat faster, and my stomach do flip flops with only a smile or a wink."

She stopped talking, a stricken look on her face when she saw the tears in his eyes. "I knew I wouldn't do a good job of explaining."

"You did a perfect job," he whispered.

The ceremony itself was a blur of solemn promises, good wishes and smiling faces that Nathaniel would remember in bits and pieces for the rest of his life.

Both Eli and Caleb stood up with him as best man. His mother cried off and on, mumbling to herself that her babies were grown now. Nathaniel smiled every time she said that. They'd been grown for a long while. Since she'd missed most of it, he didn't care if she fussed over them the rest of her life.

Wilkie Brown conducted a ceremony that was by turns solemn and lighthearted. Lenore's hands were shaking, but her voice was steady as she said her vows, as was his.

Jed didn't really understand what was happening. He understood the joy and love, though. Which was exactly what Nathaniel wanted.

Afterwards, when everyone was gathered in groups talking or eating, Nathaniel was surprised to see his mother with Dr. Montgomery Helms. "I was in the area," Monty said, "and, with your mother's blessing, thought I'd tag along and wish you well."

Smiling, Nathaniel shook his hand. "I'm glad to see you." A few minutes later he noticed the way his mother was looking at Helms, and the way the man was looking at her.

Eli noticed about the same time, and politely asked Dr. Helms if they could have a word in private. They stepped over behind the porch, where Montgomery good-naturedly endured an interrogation from Eli, and surprisingly enough, from Caleb.

Nathaniel nodded encouragement to Monty as the other two questioned him, glad that the man was taking it all in stride, and that Eli hadn't started all this in front of their mother.

Mama might be getting another chance at happiness. Once Eli was satisfied of Monty's character and intentions, he seemed to realize that, too, and gave his mother a tearful, one-armed hug when they returned Monty unscathed.

Bliss ambled over. "Now that you and Lenore are hitched, Peg and I are catching the next train to San Antone. We're getting married, too."

When all three of the Calhoun brothers hollered and slapped him on the back at the same time, the old man nearly fell over.

"Don't break me," he croaked.

Later, Nathaniel and Lenore were touched to discover that everyone had pitched in for a photographer. The man came in on the train, and Eagan Smith hauled him and his equipment out to the wedding site in one of his new wagons.

Using the porch as a backdrop, images were captured of Nathaniel and Lenore, then them with Jed, them with Mama, and then one of the three brothers and their wives.

Nathaniel recalled standing with them in a similar pose after Eli's wedding a few months earlier, the only one without a wife. He'd been happy for Eli and Caleb, but he'd felt so alone.

He'd had no idea that Lenore and Jed were just over the horizon. *But God had known.*

EPILOGUE

Five Years Later
April 1897
Calhoun Cattle Company, Triple C Ranch
Moccasin Rock, Texas

A BABY IN his arms, Nathaniel leaned against one of the cedar porch posts and watched the Calhoun cousins playing in the yard, his thoughts turning to other Aprils, of other spring days.

Moccasin Rock had never recaptured the pace and excitement of pre-tornado times, but the folks who'd stuck around had stayed because it meant more to them than a windfall or a potential opportunity.

With its quiet streets, and unhurried pace, it was almost as if Moccasin Rock had gone back in time, while Fair Haven had thrived and grown, just as everyone predicted. The smaller town suited Nathaniel fine.

Most people around the area referred to time as simply "before" and "after." The word tornado was rarely used. It didn't need to be. Everyone understood. It was the moment life changed for all of them.

Ten months after he and Lenore were married, he'd finished the house to go with the porch. In his opinion, it wasn't much to look at, but Lenore acted like it was a mansion. She loved the pretty kitchen, and the cookstove, but sometimes she prepared a meal in the fireplace, or on a campfire outside—her preferred method of cooking—using the old cast iron pot that had belonged to Sister. So far, she hadn't served up any opossum. That he knew of, anyway.

Placing the baby on his shoulder, Nathaniel moved to one of the rocking chairs. The sun was slipping into the horizon. One of his favorite times of day.

The Calhoun Cattle Company was up and running. The Triple C Ranch was the site of several homes, including Eli and Maggie's, Caleb and Abby's, his and Lenore's, and Bliss and Peg's. There were also three bunkhouses. It was the largest employer in the area.

Moccasin Rock was still the Yates County seat, although everyone knew that eventually it would be part of Claiborne County. The new courthouse had never been built, there was never an opening ceremony for the bridge, and the hotel had not been replaced.

Eli was still the sheriff, even though he spent as much time as possible at the ranch. He still wore the matching Colts and was once again lightning fast—maybe a little faster left-handed. It didn't impress the cows as much as it did most people.

But Eli's guns made them all feel safer, as did Caleb's. For that matter, all the women, and one of the kids carried guns, and knew how to use them.

Nathaniel carried one, too. Being prepared for trouble wasn't the same as looking for it, or even the same as worrying about it. Nathaniel was living every day to its fullest, grateful for every breath. Enjoying every sunrise. But he wasn't going to be caught unarmed again. So far, except for the occasional rattlesnake, he hadn't had an occasion to use it.

He was still the town physician, while getting in plenty of

doctoring on the ranch. Half of it on animals, a good chunk of it on the kids.

Caleb was still a Texas Ranger, but more and more of his attention was focused on the cattle company. Captain Joshua Parnell had retired from the rangers and now headed up the security at the ranch.

Big John Finley moved, regretfully, to Boone Springs and opened a saloon there, where there was more business, and Silas Martin's widow had relocated the mercantile to Fair Haven for the same reason.

The Dunlops had stayed, and Myrtle was now the mayor. She'd taken to carrying some of the basic provisions—coffee, flour, sugar, sewing notions, and so on—in her bakery. She still rubbed people the wrong way, yet most folks admitted that she did a good job running things.

Wilkie Brown had also stayed. Not long ago a woman named Amanda showed up in town, and within a month she and Wilkie were married. No one knew anything about the new Mrs. Brown— a quiet, pretty woman with dark hair and a scar above her left eyebrow.

Myrtle Dunlop had insisted on a full investigation into the woman's background, then backtracked in a hurry when Wilkie simply packed his bags and headed for the train station with his new wife. Nathaniel didn't know any more about the woman than the others, but he did know that Wilkie wouldn't have married her without talking to God about it first. That was good enough for him.

Walter Miller and Little Dove had opened a furniture store in the old saloon. The pieces were crafted with such skill and attention to detail that the Miller's had customers coming from many of the bigger cities to do business with them.

Bony Joe's Café and Eagan Smith's livery stable were doing

okay. The train still stopped, but there wasn't always anyone arriving or departing these days.

The Hortons rented the occasional room, but Bob Horton made more money from a steady stream of dime novels. Notably, and most embarrassing to Nathaniel, was the one about The Texas Kid. Eli and Caleb had given him fits when it was published, until they'd discovered that they were both featured in it, too. Lenore, Maggie, Abby and all the kids had gotten a kick out of it.

Lenore got the occasional postcard from Shipley Bidwell. He'd made it back to the east coast and was running a theater there. He hoped to come and visit someday. They were all looking forward to seeing him. Even Bliss. Or so he said.

Henry and Jenna Barnett had two children now, both girls. They were beautiful, and every bit as fussy and spoiled as their Mama. Henry was still farming, still raising horses and mules. He had a silly grin on his face any time the girls in his life were near, or even mentioned.

The Wilsons were still farming, still raising kids. They'd had two more children to round their brood out to eleven, and didn't even know how many animals they had. Jillie Wilson, now thirteen, was one of the brightest kids Nathaniel had ever known. She'd recently asked if she could visit the clinic the next time a surgery was scheduled. He was considering it.

Bliss and Peg were finally starting to show their age, moving slower, mentioning a few aches and pains, but they were happy together. All the Calhouns thought of them as family and wanted them to take it easy. Bliss wanted no part in that, neither did Peg. No matter what medical advice Nathaniel offered up, Bliss would say it was nothing that a little hard work couldn't fix, while Peg nodded along in agreement.

Maggie had lost her father three years ago, and Caleb's aunt Victoria was also gone. Abby's grandmother was still doing well.

His own mother was thriving. She'd married Dr. Montgomery Helms and they'd purchased Peg's house when she and Bliss moved to the ranch. When needed, Monty assisted him at the clinic. Nathaniel was grateful for the help, and especially grateful for the happiness Monty brought his mother. All the children, even Caleb's, called them Grandma and Grandpa.

His mother spent a lot of time telling her grandkids stories that had been handed down through the years, just as she had with him and Eli. They'd been too young to really appreciate what she told them of the heroes who'd died at the Alamo, and their ancestors who'd fallen at Goliad, and fought and won, at San Jacinto. Even if it wasn't their stories, she reminded the kids, it was their history. Nathaniel appreciated the opportunity to hear it all again.

But he was most grateful for the Bible stories she told the kids. Not just to hear her reading them again, but that God had given them all other chances to hear of His saving grace.

The baby in his arms stirred, and Nathaniel set the rocker in motion, thankful for these small moments.

In the past few years, a number of strangers, even some drifters, people without a purpose or plan, had passed through Moccasin Rock.

Nathaniel had a chance to treat a few, Eli and Caleb put the fear of the law into some, Pastor Wilkie had a chance to preach to them, and they'd found work for some at the ranch. The women had provided more meals than they could count, and sometimes a story of hope. They had no way of knowing if any of it amounted to anything, but people left Moccasin Rock with a full belly, a lessening of their load, and something to think about.

Brody had taken to ranching like a duck to water. Robby Horton and Jamie Wilson, both sixteen now, had also found work at the ranch. All three of the boys were eager to go on a real cattle drive like in the "old days." So far, the extent of that had been going with the herd to catch the train, and then riding with them to Fort Worth.

The ranch was Caleb's dream, and they were all being pulled along. Occasionally, Nathaniel and Eli had to rein their younger brother in, and every now and then, Caleb had to light a new fire under the others. For whatever reason it worked.

It had not surprised any of them that the women had made their mark on the Calhoun Cattle Company in more ways than one. In addition to the children and homelife, they all had a hand in running the ranch.

Abby had a head for numbers and after some training, was now the bookkeeper for the operation. Maggie hired and oversaw the bunkhouse cooks and helped Abby with the charitable foundation established by Caleb. Lenore helped with that, too. But Lenore also possessed an unusual ability that had proven beneficial on more than one occasion. She could spot a fraud a mile away. It had saved them thousands of dollars on everything from stock to equipment.

But the most important thing to the Calhouns, husbands and wives alike, were the children running, laughing, and screaming, right in front of him.

Jedidiah Nathaniel was a happy, healthy, perfectly normal eight-year-old, who took his position as eldest child seriously. Nathaniel tried to keep him from bossing the others around, but it was usually a losing battle, especially when Jed did it for all the right reasons.

Nathaniel hid a smile now as the boy picked up his tearful little sister and headed his way.

"She stepped on a rock, Daddy. And she won't let me look at her foot."

Nathaniel shifted the baby again, then examined his daughter's foot, all while sharing a wink and a look with Jed. *Girls.*

Then Cordie smiled at him, and his heart turned over. Four-year-old Cordelia Rebecca had wrapped him around her finger the moment she drew her first breath. A sweet, angelic, fair-haired child, named for her grandmother and, at Lenore's urging, a sister she would never know. Someday, when she was older, Nathaniel would tell her about the other Rebecca.

The baby in his arms was Edward Gordon Shipley Calhoun. Such a big name for such a tiny boy. He was four months old now and they hadn't agreed on what to call him yet, with everyone suggesting, and using, something different. If they didn't figure it out before the kid started talking, Nathaniel planned to ask him what he wanted to be called.

Eli and Maggie had added a little boy to round out their children to three, although it was hard to think of Brody—now twenty, and six-foot something—as a child. Thankfully, he was one of the gentlest souls a person could ever hope to meet. Lucinda, almost six, was a tomboy who climbed trees, rode horses, and dove into creeks with equal abandon.

Eli and Maggie's youngest was four-year-old Amos Rueben, named after his grandfather Amos Calhoun, and Rueben "Bliss" Walker.

Little Amos had been born with a stubborn streak a mile wide. Maggie said the boy got it from Eli, and Eli said he got it from her. Nathaniel suspected that it was a bit of both. And with that particular combination of blood and backbone, the kid wouldn't be afraid to take on the world. Although Nathaniel had wondered for a while if he would even learn to walk. When Eli wasn't carrying him around, Bliss was. And Brody did too, if he got a chance. Lucinda tried. Maggie was expecting another child around Christmas, and, if a girl, there was talk of her being named for Peg Harmon. Since Peg had delivered most of the kids, it seemed more than fitting.

Caleb and Abby's oldest child, Joseph Hamilton, was now five. Already the kid had an easy grin and a ready laugh. A charmer like his old man. And there was a second child now, a sweet, dark-haired girl named Julia Irene. Caleb had said all along that his second child would be a girl, and he was right.

It wasn't just the Calhouns who were watching a new generation growing up on the ranch.

There'd also been a surprise litter of puppies born to Nickel. Well, Nickel probably wasn't surprised to find out she was expecting, but the rest of them were.

Two of the puppies—fully grown now—looked like their mother and were running around the yard playing with the kids.

Nickel was probably dozing in the kitchen. The old girl wouldn't be with them forever. When she was gone, Lenore would take it hard. For that matter, so would Nathaniel. That dog had come to their aid over and over again.

Lenore was of the opinion that sometimes God's helpers came in the furry, four-footed variety. Nathaniel wasn't going to argue with her.

The door opened, and Lenore stepped out to join him. *The thief who'd stolen his heart.* He loved her with an intensity that scared him sometimes but was secure in the knowledge that his love was returned in equal measure.

Nathaniel couldn't imagine a time when he'd be immune to the tremble of her lip, or the way she pronounced some words. One would always make his heart catch a little, the other would always make him smile.

Lenore was one of the strongest people he'd ever known. A wonderful wife, mother, and friend. She didn't look scared, or unsure, or ready to run now. There was a confidence in knowing where she came from and what she'd overcome, but more importantly, where she belonged.

"When's someone coming to claim these extra Calhoun kids?" he asked.

She settled into the other rocker. "Should be soon. They're running a little late. Why? Do you have plans?"

His only response was a wink, which brought a smile in return.

The sun was gone, and the full moon was now hanging so low it seemed as if one could reach up and touch it. On second thought, this was his favorite time of day.

He reached out to take Lenore's hand.

Their life together wasn't exactly the stuff of fairy tales, but there was love enough for a dozen happily-ever-afters.

AUTHOR BIO

A seventh-generation Texan, Laura Conner Kestner spent 25 years in community journalism before pursuing a career in fiction. Her first novel, Remember Texas, was published in 2018, followed by A Texas Promise in 2019, and A Texas Moon in 2020.

Laura's won several writing awards, including a Genesis Award from the American Christian Fiction Writers, a Daphne du Maurier award for excellence in mystery/suspense from the RWA Kiss of Death chapter, and an Emma Merritt award from RWA SARA. She's a three-time GOLDEN HEART® finalist, a 2019 HOLT Medallion finalist, and a WILL ROGERS MEDALLION AWARD finalist for 2019 and 2020.

For more information, or to contact Laura, please visit
http://lauraconnerkestner.com
or email her at texasplaces@gmail.com

Made in the USA
Coppell, TX
04 November 2020